KU-731-965

Only Make Believe

Marilyn Beck

S T A R

published by
the Paperback Division of
W. H. Allen & Co. Plc

A Star Book
Published in 1989
by the Paperback Division of
W. H. Allen & Co. Plc
Sekforde House, 175/9 St. John Street,
London, EC1V 4LL

First published in the United States of America
by Jove Publications, Inc., 1988
Reprinted 1989 (twice)

Copyright © Marilyn Beck, 1988

Printed in Great Britain by
Cox & Wyman Ltd, Reading

ISBN 0 352 32437 6

Marilyn Beck is Hollywood's top columnist on the stars with an estimated daily readership of 38 million people. *Only Make Believe* is her first novel. She lives in Beverly Hills with her husband.

To Stacy Jenel Smith for her unfailing friendship over the years. And for the invaluable assistance, research, collaboration, cooperation, professionalism, and care she devoted to *Only Make Believe*. Without her efforts, this book would not have been born.

To Arthur
With all my love

PROLOGUE

$\sim\!\!\!\sim\!\!\!\sim$

TO ALL APPEARANCES, Ann Peters was the embodiment of the woman who had it all.

President of production for a major motion picture studio, she was that rarity in a male-dominated industry: a woman who had risen to a peak of power. She was considered a superwoman, hailed as a trailblazer. Her achievements had been chronicled in feature stories in the national news magazines, as well as in the *Wall Street Journal* and the *New York Times*. When *Life* magazine ran a photo spread of the powers behind the scenes in Hollywood, a photograph of Ann split a page with a picture of Sherry Lansing, who, as chief of production at Twentieth Century–Fox, was the only other woman to have attained such a rank in the industry.

Ann was a rarity in another less visible respect. She was a survivor among those women whose destinies are determined by their looks and by the men who manage and manipulate their careers and their lives—women who are used, often abused, and invariably discarded.

By the early eighties, Ann had long since saved herself from that fate.

She made no attempt to camouflage the onset of middle age or her size-twelve body—or to hide the fine etchings of a scar that ran along her left cheek. The last vestige of an injury she had once believed would be permanently disfiguring, it now served to accentuate her looks rather than detract from them.

With azure eyes and a mane of raven hair pulled back sim-

1

ply in a barrette, she was magnetically attractive. She radiated happiness, enthusiasm, and warmth. Hidden from the world were the inner scars formed by the sorrows that had marked her life.

Ann was wrapping up her first important meeting of the day when the call came that was to rock her world.

During the preceding hour and a half, she and producer Marty Ransohoff had mowed down what seemed to be the last roadblocks to making *Red Diamonds* with Paul Newman and Meryl Streep. Now, in the casual sitting area of Ann's spacious, alder-paneled office, she and Ransohoff discussed the Bali location over a catered lunch.

Ann shunned such power luncheon palaces as Ma Maison, where Orson Welles, still living on his 1940 *Citizen Kane* glory, would hold court and dine on gourmet fare and vintage wines supplied gratis by management—and where the current show business names would vie for "A" tables to reinforce their status in the industry. Ann had no patience for such games. She never had.

In the outer office, Ann's secretary, Estelle, waited, ready to pounce with a list of calls her employer should return before looking at dailies on the new Whoopi Goldberg picture.

Memos, readers' reports, correspondence, and a stack of computer printout budget analyses had been put to one side of Estelle's desk, awaiting Ann's attention later in the day.

Rob Lowe and his agent were expected at four. There was a dinner meeting with Steven Spielberg set for six, followed by a screening of a John Cassavetes feature that Cassavetes was trying to get Sentinel to distribute. It was a typically tight schedule for Ann, and it was about to be derailed.

As she and Ransohoff emerged from the inner suite, Ann heard Estelle handling an incoming call with an odd tone of hesitancy.

"Who's that?" asked Ann, as Ransohoff mouthed a "goodbye" and made his departure.

"Cindy Mantussi," Estelle said sourly.

Ann raced back into her office, her breezy demeanor abruptly vanishing along with the color in her face.

The small, white frame house was the second from the corner in a run-down neighborhood in Bloomfield, New Jersey. Beds of bright flowers struggled valiantly, vainly, to counteract the ugliness of the cracked asphalt driveway and the rusting 1972 Oldsmobile mounted on blocks on the lawn.

Lyla Mantussi, a plain-faced, square-jawed woman with an excess thirty pounds distributed over a stocky frame, was vacuuming the raveled, brown shag living room rug when Ann Peters called.

"Why didn't I listen to you?" Lyla cried a few moments later, as Ann's message sank in. "What are we going to do?"

"Can you and Joe make it to La Guardia by six your time?" Ann asked. "I'll have a plane waiting for you."

There was a long pause as Lyla raised her heavy glasses and wiped the tears away.

"I don't know if Joe will come," she said at last.

"To hell with him, then," Ann answered angrily.

"Please, don't say that."

"How do you expect me to feel? His daughter's about to destroy her life and you're telling me he's still nursing his goddamn grudge!"

"I don't know. Oh, I don't know," Lyla wailed.

"I'm sorry. I shouldn't have yelled at you."

Lyla pulled a handkerchief from the pocket of her plaid housedress and fought to control her sobs.

"Try to stay calm," Ann said. "And get to the airport as soon as you can."

By the time Ann stepped through the roof access door of Sentinel Studios' twelve-story office building, the Bell Long Ranger was awaiting her at full rev. She shouted thanks to the transportation manager as she clutched her trench coat together and pushed against the wind to climb into the helicopter.

In minutes the lot below had shrunk to toy size. The stark glass skyscraper from which they had taken off lay behind them, and they were zipping over the tan, hangar-shaped soundstages, past the London and Charleston streets, the terra-cotta tile roof of the sprawling Spanish-style building that housed the executive suites of such top studio brass as Ann.

The chopper headed northeast, flying over the smog-gray, gritty glare of Hollywood proper, over Sunset Boulevard, the old Palladium, the freeway, out toward the San Fernando Valley and the Van Nuys Airport, where Sentinel's eight-passenger Lear jet was being prepared for Ann's departure.

She stared ahead, repeating a silent prayer like a mantra: *Stop them from committing this tragedy. Please God, don't let them do this.*

"It'll be fifty for the chapel fee, plus a donation for the minister," the clerk said briskly, raising her voice over the clang and whir of slot machines from the casino just outside the chapel entrance. "Usually people give him around thirty dollars. And if you want a bouquet, it's thirty for a small spring flower mix or forty for a large. The large is much better. They put in some of those big tulips from Europe."

The groom-to-be gave the woman a grin. He was awash in good will. Even as he was making these arrangements, his fiancée was in their room freshening up after several hours of enthusiastic rehearsal for the honeymoon.

"That won't be necessary; I'm getting flowers elsewhere," he said. "But we will definitely be wanting pictures. Do you have a photographer?"

"We've got the full line, sir. Audiotaping, videotaping, whatever you please."

The old lady softened as she took in the cut of the young man's unruly, sun-bleached hair and his stylishly casual Bill Blass suit. The aura of wealth cloaked him subtly.

She didn't know that standing before her was one of Hollywood's most notorious former juvenile hell-raisers—a reformed playboy now.

"Thank you for the help," he told her. "We'll see you later."

"You bet," she said sweetly. "Eric and Cindy Evans. It has a real nice ring."

He stopped short and turned back. "By the way," he said, "if anyone should happen to call and ask you whether we're getting married here, I'd appreciate it if you'd say no."

"Why?" The clerk gave him a closer inspection. "Should I know who you are?" she asked, unsuccessfully trying to make the question sound like a joke. "Are you somebody famous?"

"No."

"I have a lot to keep track of. I hope I don't forget."

Eric deftly pulled a hundred-dollar bill from his wallet and handed it to her with irritation. *"Don't* forget," he said.

The guests were just beginning to arrive at the stately Chevy Chase home of Senator Evans of Texas. Small groups en route to the entrance filed past the row of mullioned windows that ran along the brick façade of the Maryland residence.

Officially described as a small cocktail party, the gathering was really an informal meeting at which the main topic was to be the relaxation of handgun sale restrictions, one of the senator's chief interests. A maid and butler in traditional black and white uniforms were already serving canapés, while the hired bartender was filling his first orders of the evening.

Much to Evans's annoyance, his wife steered him away from the arriving guests and drew him into the study.

"Well?" he asked irritably. He stood impatiently before her, arms crossed, jaw tilted upward.

She took a deep breath. "You're not going to like this. I just talked to our son." Then the words came out in a rush. "He's marrying that little Italian girl. They're in Las Vegas right now."

"Marrying her?!" Evans looked as though he had been kicked in the crotch.

"I know Eric could do better, and I know how you feel about her. But he really loves the girl," she said plaintively.

"Where is he staying?" The senator's voice was icy.

"Hank, it's too late. There is nothing you can do."

"You just watch me. I'll fly to Vegas tonight. The marriage will be annulled by tomorrow."

He headed briskly out of the study, then paused at the door and, without turning, told his wife, "I will never forgive you for this, Mary."

"I know," she replied in a lifeless monotone.

Cindy Mantussi relaxed on the simulated zebra-skin hotel bedspread, while steam from the shower was, she hoped, taking the wrinkles out of her white wool wedding dress. She giggled at the wonderfully trashy mirrored ceiling, then studied her reflection—a pretty young woman with long hair the color of wheat and honey and a tanned body encased in a clinging pale pink satin slip.

As she rose from the bed and began to dress, she smiled slightly, remembering Eric's thunderous pronouncement: *We're going to be happy, goddamn it!*

Laughter was one ingredient Cindy was determined to keep alive in their marriage. Yes, she thought—with so much against them, she and Eric needed to be able to laugh.

Ann reached her destination after what seemed an eternity.

She hurried through the entrance of the hotel, then rushed to a bank of house phones near the registration desk, where she asked for Cindy and Eric's room. There was no answer.

Ann checked her watch and a tremor of anxiety surged through her. It would be hours before Lyla and Joe Mantussi arrived from the East Coast. She could not wait. She would have to confront Cindy and Eric alone.

"The wedding chapel . . . where is it?" she asked a security guard breathlessly. He motioned across the football field—size casino.

You're the only one I asked to come . . . I thought you'd be happy for me. Cindy's angry-sad accusing words resounded in Ann's mind as she pressed past the green felt islands where throngs gathered at craps and blackjack. Her panic increased with every step across a seemingly endless sea of red carpet.

Finally she found the blue neon CHAPEL OF THE DOVES sign and descended the four steps leading to its double doors.

She slowed momentarily in the tiny antechamber, then took a deep breath and went inside. She was wrenched by the sight of the couple at the altar.

As she made her way up the aisle, memories crashed in on Ann like waves, one atop the other, bringing an undertow of horrifying images. She felt dizzy and dazed. This was the worst nightmare she had ever had, and it was real.

The minister looked up from his Bible, and Cindy turned around. Her expression changed rapidly from pleased surprise to angry disbelief as she saw Ann move toward her instead of slipping quietly into one of the pews.

Then Ann heard herself choke out the words. "I'm so sorry. You can't get married. You should have been told . . ."

The wedding couple, the minister, the photographer, the

witness stared at her. "I need to talk to you outside," Ann said in a whisper.

"Are you crazy?" Eric hissed.

"Get out of here," Cindy snapped angrily.

"You can't marry," Ann repeated. Her words, escaping through a veil of pain, were racked with sobs.

"You can't marry," she repeated. "You're brother and sister."

PART 1
The Girl

ONE

ANN PETERS WAS a product of one of the most romantic unions in history. At least, that was the way her mother had viewed it.

She was born Ann Beaudry, the second daughter of Major Peter G. Beaudry and his Turkish wife, Ezel.

Her sister, Lyla, was two years her senior. Lyla felt her place usurped by the tiny baby her mother brought home from the hospital, and the years did nothing to lessen her jealousy, for Ann possessed a quality that made people respond to her more readily than to her sibling. Lyla dealt with the inequity by going into quiet, sullen withdrawals that made her even less appealing.

That Ann was prettier, livelier, and brighter was undeniable. From the first, she was her father's favorite, an enchanting little doll with dark hair and olive skin and blue eyes so piercing and so anxious to please they could break the heart of a far sterner man than Major Beaudry.

Ann's father was handsome, lean, and broad shouldered, with close-cropped brown hair, cold blue eyes, and lips that seemed to be perennially frozen in a grim line. An emotionally distant man, he often lapsed into states of brooding contemplation. His wife would watch him as he sat lost in thought, worshipping him from a discreet distance with an expression that suggested she felt privileged to be in his presence.

With her trim dresses and suits, her dark lipstick, and her neatly rolled hairstyle, Ann's mother looked the essence of a

11

modern, secular, westernized woman. But Ezel Beaudry was in fact only one generation removed from the mandatory veil, and that veil, though invisible, was a very real element in her emotional makeup.

Ezel filled all of Pete Beaudry's requirements in a wife: she was quiet, undemanding, attentive, subservient, and grateful. She kept things neat and did as she was told. It didn't matter to Pete Beaudry that his spouse, a former shop girl ten years his junior, remained so unsure of her English—and herself— that she bashfully retreated from exchanging more than a few words with his friends and associates. Some of them wondered how so brilliant a man could possibly be happy with such an uneducated woman, but he had deliberately sought out his wife and did not want her to change. "Loudmouthed females who think they know everything" made him nervous. To his way of thinking, America was full of them. It was his often-voiced opinion that it was impossible to find a woman like his wife anywhere in the United States.

Major Beaudry—as Ann's mother always referred to him, and thought of him—did very important work that Ezel understood only on the simplest level: the Americans gave their foreign friends the most modern and sophisticated weapons and sent experts to help them learn the most up-to-date military systems. Pete Beaudry, who spoke French, Turkish, Russian, and some Arabic, was one of the officers who coordinated this aid, working with diplomats on one side, the army on the other. He was often away from home, whether home was in Silver Spring, Augsburg, Izmir, or Ankara.

During Ann's seventh and eighth years the family lived in Ankara. It was the happiest period of her childhood. There were visits to the city's model farm, where delicious yogurt and ice cream were sold by colorfully costumed vendors. There were visits to the children's zoo. And, best of all, there were occasional family holidays at the Youth Park, with its fair booths, musical performances, rides, and picturesque lake.

Inside the family's apartment, however, any suggestion of local flavor was banned. By the major's edict, their living quarters were always to reflect America. And so they did, when he was there.

Ezel cooked the dishes her husband wanted when he was in

residence. But when he was away, she prepared Turkish delicacies with virtuoso skill.

Pete Beaudry always kept the radio tuned to the Voice of America or Armed Forces Radio. Together he and Ann listened to broadcasts of baseball and football games, and she learned to share his love of American jazz. Ezel and Lyla preferred Turkish music, which they listened to only when the major was not present.

Both girls were given an all-American education. They attended class with the offspring of Embassy diplomats and bureaucrats. The history and customs of the United States were stressed by their Chicago-born teacher, who also occasionally arranged for screenings of Hollywood-made family movies. Walt Disney's *Snow White* and *Cinderella* enthralled Ann.

Unlike her sister, who was an average student, Ann excelled in her studies. She did so well in class that her teacher was prompted on one occasion to write her parents a note of praise. Her father's reaction was one Ann never forgot. He read the note, then patted her cheek. "That's fine," he said warmly, but without much enthusiasm. "I'm glad your teacher likes you. But learning isn't that important for a girl. Just stay as sweet as you are. That's what will make me happiest."

"The teacher likes Lyla, too," Ann pointed out quickly, noticing her sister standing nearby.

"Uh huh." The major nodded absently. He picked up his newspaper and went into the bedroom without so much as a glance at his older daughter, who was painfully aware she could never hope to elicit the affection from her father that Ann seemed to receive without trying.

By then Lyla's jealousy had bloomed into sharp, fearful resentment. She secretly hated Ann's constant effect on her life. If Ann walked into a room when adults were talking to Lyla, their attention would immediately shift to her younger sister. Ann was almost sure to learn any new game faster and better than she. It seemed to Lyla that, deliberately or not, her sister took people and things away from her—and that her only protection was to guard what she could zealously, to keep her playmates away from Ann, to refuse to teach Ann such schoolgirl tricks as making fortune-telling boxes out of paper. If Lyla felt any guilt over her selfish behavior, it was erased by her desperate desire to be first *somehow*.

Ann was sensitive to her sister's feelings. She coaxed

friends into including Lyla in birthday party invitations and such. She also tried hard to make sure Lyla was never forgotten by their father, but she was still too much a child not to enjoy his attention.

Despite his authoritarian ways, Ann could see love in his smile when she brought him a cup of tea, his slippers, a present of flowers or crayon drawings or pretty stones. His smile was her greatest reward, and she worked hard to gain it. They shared a special bond, an understanding from which everyone else was excluded.

And then, suddenly, it ended.

A life of stress, the residue from bitter experiences, a self-imposed emotional isolation, all came to a final, tragic conclusion for Peter Beaudry.

At the time, the Beaudrys were living in Virginia, in a shady residential corner of Alexandria. Ann was eleven years old, Lyla thirteen.

After their insulated existence in Ankara, it had been difficult for the girls to adjust to the crowded American public schools, and they had drawn closer while learning to cope with their new surroundings. They had also had to learn to live with Major Beaudry's continuing presence at home, for he had been put on an extended, enforced leave. His moods were by turn morose or irritable. Even Ann could no longer make him smile.

One terrible heat-wave day, the sisters returned from school to find the entrance to their home cordoned off by police. An ambulance was blocking the driveway. Strangers gathered nearby, staring and whispering, as two ambulance attendants appeared in the doorway, rolling out a gurney.

And then, all at once, the girls' mother was there, running to them, sweeping them into her arms, pressing their faces tightly against her body and crying out, "Don't look!"

The words cut through Ann, slicing their way into her soul and leaving an irreparable wound. The echo of those words filled Ann's head even as the days that followed melted into a blur.

Don't look! resounded through the sympathy calls of neighbors and military personnel.

Don't look! was like a low roar, the ocean heard in a seashell, as Ann and Lyla stood beside their mother, surrounded by lush green grass and row upon precise row of pristine white headstones.

People were kind but ill at ease. What does one say to the family of a man who has committed suicide?

Like sudden stop-motion pictures from a bad dream, Ann took in impressions: the white gloves of the men in dress uniforms who handed her mother a carefully folded American flag; her grandmother, who looked so startlingly old; her grandfather, pink and white and unaware in his wheelchair; her Uncle Wayne, a fuller-faced, thickly upholstered version of Ann's father.

Although he lived several hundred miles away, Wayne Beaudry was soon to become an integral part of her life.

"Don't worry. I'll take care of things; I'll see that you and the girls are cared for," he assured Ann's mother at the graveside. And, indeed, his presence became the sole light in those dark days when Ezel was so immobilized by grief that even the simplest decision was beyond her. He handled everything, from filling out the forms for her widow's benefits to selling Major Beaudry's Chevrolet Impala, which Ezel had never learned to drive.

As the months passed, Wayne frequently drove up from his home in Baton Rouge to make sure Ezel's banking and bill-paying were under control.

He emphasized the importance of putting the tragedy behind them. He promised them that the pain would ease. But the sound of music or the sight of some forgotten belonging of her husband's continued to cause Ezel to burst into tears.

Nothing seemed to matter to her as it had before the fatal incident. She tried to pay attention to details, but they eluded her. Housecleaning and personal hygiene were ignored; the cupboards were left unstocked. With her husband's death the life went out of Ezel.

As Wayne promised, things did change—but not for the better.

It became increasingly difficult for Ezel and the girls to get by on their benefits; Ezel never questioned why and was never aware that Wayne was siphoning off a portion of her money each month as "salary" for managing her affairs.

Ezel was aware only of how much brighter things seemed during Wayne's visits; he transformed her lonely life of struggle into a party with lots of laughter.

Ann was the first to notice that her mother increasingly looked forward to Wayne's visits — and that the visits began to last longer and longer.

Lyla shrugged when Ann mentioned it. "What are you worried about? Uncle Wayne is helping us."

Although Ann hated herself for her suspicions and tried to ignore them, in the darkest part of her soul, she felt that Lyla enjoyed the fact that with Wayne it was she who was the favorite.

Ann could not ignore Wayne's abrupt, almost hostile attitude toward her. It seemed to Ann that her uncle secretly hated her. Her feelings toward him were a mixture of resentment and fear.

School offered a welcome escape from the gloom and stress at home. Her teacher singled her out as a group helper to tutor the slower children in math. She was sought out as a friend by the other girls. To her joy, she was chosen to play the Ghost of Christmas Past in the school production of Dickens's *A Christmas Carol*.

She loved the hours she spent on the school's tiny stage, costumed in sheets and a tinfoil headdress, thoroughly lost in rehearsing her role as guide into the young Ebenezer Scrooge's life. It was a pleasure so great that Ann could not believe anything could ever surpass it.

But it was surpassed by far on the afternoon of the play. As she performed, she was aware that everyone in the auditorium, grownups and children alike, silently watched her, liked her, and *believed* her. When the play was over and she and the other children in the cast were taking bows, the audience rose as one to applaud.

It was magic so powerful that Ann used the memory as an escape, replaying every second until the faces, the applause, the compliments became as threadbare as the cherished memories of her father.

It was magic that, for a time, even overcame Ann's dread of Wayne.

TWO

EARLY ONE MORNING Ann padded out of the bedroom she shared with Lyla and went down the hall to her mother's room. There in a flood of sunshine she found Wayne, standing by the window, stretching. He was naked. Her mother was still asleep.

Wayne's eyes bore into Ann's, and she froze like a frightened doe. He neither spoke nor smiled, simply walked a few steps toward her and pushed the door shut in her face.

Ann retreated into her room, choking with outrage and embarrassment, and flung herself on her bed. She pretended to be asleep when Lyla stirred, arose, dressed, and left the room.

Finally, Ann steeled herself to go down to breakfast. Lyla was busy wiping off the blue linoleum table where Wayne sat smoking and glancing idly through the sports section. Ann's mother was at the stove, cooking. Ann walked in, head down, and quietly took a chair.

"Aren't you going to help your mother?" Wayne asked.

"Yes," she replied in a small voice. When she glanced at Wayne, his eyes were like walls of stone. He knew she was upset, and he didn't give a damn. Ann proceeded to set the table, angrily clattering dishes and clanking silver until Wayne shouted, "Watch it! You're going to break something!"

"What's the matter with you?" Lyla asked sharply.

Ann frowned and shook her head.

Wayne lit another cigarette and studied the box scores in the paper.

When Ezel brought breakfast to the table and sat down,

17

Wayne tossed the newspaper under his chair and scooted forward, all at once re-energized.

"I have a surprise for you," he announced grandly. "How would you like to go home?"

Ann looked up in time to catch Lyla's baffled expression and her mother's uncomprehending gaze and accepting Mona Lisa smile. "I've wanted to go to Istanbul ever since I was a kid," he informed them. "I used to imagine it: living in Constantinople, the most exotic city in the world. I was fit to be tied when Pete beat me to it. Those postcards he used to send..." Wayne chuckled, shaking his head. "I was going to visit you all about four years ago. Did you know that?"

"Really?" Ann's mother asked nervously.

"We didn't live in Istanbul," Ann interjected. She didn't want to go across town with Wayne, let alone to the other side of the globe.

He continued, directing his comments solely to Ezel. "So I figure, let's go now! We'll have a hell of a great time. Sail the Black Sea, see ancient Troy. I could even buy a little nightclub. I've been doing a lot of thinking about it."

Buy a nightclub? Ann's stomach knotted. He didn't mean a trip—he was talking about moving there, to live! She looked around frantically. Neither her sister's nor her mother's expressions had changed: Lyla still looked baffled; Ezel still wore her placid, pasted-on smile.

Wayne's grin grew wider. "We can live like kings over there instead of scrimping and scraping here. We've got you as our built-in interpreter," he said to Ezel. "I'm sure your folks will let us camp with them until we get set up."

"We can't live there without Papa!" Ann blurted out, looking at her mother. "It would be different. We—"

"Where are your manners?" Wayne cut her off. "When we want your opinion, we'll ask for it."

"I don't want to leave!" Ann cried.

"That's enough!" Wayne shouted. "Go to your room."

As she rose to leave the breakfast table, Ann looked imploringly at her mother, but Ezel was not about to defy Wayne. Ann walked out, gasping with repressed sobs.

In truth, Ezel was also horrified at the thought of returning to her native land—but for reasons different than her daughter's. She couldn't bear to think of the shame her family would feel if they discovered she was living with a man to whom she was not married. As it was, her father and mother had never gotten over her marriage to Pete, a Christian and a foreigner.

Although Wayne had told Ezel repeatedly that if they were to marry, it would put an end to her widow's benefits, she knew her family would never understand or forgive her for living in sin.

"It'll be paradise! I don't know why I didn't think of it sooner," Wayne went on excitedly.

Ezel rushed from the table, a napkin clutched to her mouth. A few seconds later, the sound of running water came from the bathroom. She didn't want Wayne to know she was getting sick.

Ann couldn't sleep that night. Wayne's voice rose up the stairs and through the door of the bedroom she shared with Lyla.

He was quite drunk, she realized.

". . . Oh, for chrissakes—they'll be fine! Kids are very resilient."

His words grew louder, more angry.

"If they want to live here so bad, they can come back when they grow up."

Another fragment came a few minutes later. ". . . Your problem is, you have no sense of gratitude."

And then, after a pause, "If he was so goddamn perfect, why'd he kill himself? Maybe he was too good for all of us. . . . So he left you with shit. Isn't that right? Shit!"

By morning, Ann's mother was making plans to leave but now with a certain sense of relief, for Wayne had agreed not to ask her relatives for help.

She and Wayne and the girls would stay in Istanbul; Ezel's family, who lived hundreds of miles away, need not know of her domestic situation. Wayne's solution to their financial problems was simple: they would have plenty of money to set up if they sold the house.

"Why do we have to go with him?" Ann asked tearfully. "It'll be terrible! I don't want us to go."

Her mother sat down on the living room sofa and drew Ann to her. She looked into her daughter's eyes with the expression of one about to impart a profound truth.

"What is this whimpering? This is not my sweet little Ann. Listen to me, darling. Someday you'll understand; I need

Wayne, and so do you and Lyla." She smoothed back Ann's dark bangs and said, "We would be helpless without him."

The weeks and then the days and then the hours flew past. Ann's school, the shady block where they lived, the faces of her friends were all suddenly like a landscape viewed from a train hurtling through the countryside. And Ann, sealed behind glass, was unable to get out, unable to touch, unable to stop.

Their date of departure held a terrible irony in itself. Coincidentally or not, Wayne had booked passage for the family on the second anniversary of his brother's death.

The third anniversary of Pete Beaudry's suicide found Ann in a second-floor classroom of the Besiktas High School for Girls. She sat among four rows of students in black pinafores with white Peter Pan collars.

Her teacher, an intense woman with somber, darting eyes, talked about President Johnson's impending visit and about Americans and their presence in Turkey. She seemed to be directing her comments at Ann. Her tone was challenging, as if she were daring Ann to disagree with any of her statements, which Ann sometimes did.

Ann's command of the Turkish language was faulty, and she spoke with an American accent she didn't attempt to improve—one of her many unconscious ways of trying to hold on to her past, her father's memory. Although half-Turkish, Ann often found herself singled out as a representative of *Amerika*, and a few of the girls were very unpleasant to her because of that. Others were nice to her, but Ann had no real friends and felt isolated.

On this particular day, she refrained from picking up the verbal gauntlet thrown down by the teacher. She was preoccupied by her memories of that terrible day three years before and by the worsening situation at home.

When classes were over for the day, Ann left the school amid a throng of chattering, giggling young girls and walked down the wide, plane-tree–shaded avenue. At the corner, she waited for the bus. No longer did the family-of-sorts live nearby in an airy, sun-washed suburban residence that had a courtyard bursting with flowers. Now every morning Ann boarded a crowded city bus to make the trip over the Galata Bridge to the suburb of Besiktas, and each afternoon she returned to the center of town and the dingy apartment into which they had recently moved.

At fourteen, Ann had begun to show promise of becoming a pretty young woman, despite an aquiline nose and some leftover childhood chubbiness. Over the last year she had developed a nervous laugh.

Lyla, who at sixteen was two years too old to be admitted into the high school, had grown into a gawky, slow-moving girl with a perpetually sad expression.

Wayne was wrong; kids were not so resilient after all.

Ann sat in silence on the bus. She did not look at—and certainly did not talk to—any of the males on board.

This was one of the last times she would be making the trip. It had become too expensive to keep her in school. Everything had become too expensive. The money from the house in Virginia was gone, and now Wayne was grabbing all of the family's other income—Ezel's widow's benefits, the money the girls earned as English tutors—to funnel into his latest enterprise.

With a Turk serving as front man, thus circumventing the laws restricting foreign ownership of businesses, Wayne had bought a nightclub.

Huriyah—*black-eyed woman* in Arabic—was situated in the bustling center of the Sirkeci district, and it was into that crowded area that the Beaudrys had relocated.

A weathered hall frequented by workmen and hoodlums, Huriyah was nothing like the "plush little nightclub" Wayne had envisioned. But its clientele suited him handsomely, and he flourished in the atmosphere. Ezel, on whom Wayne had bestowed the responsibilities of cook, assistant, and janitor, had faded considerably. She was only thirty-six, but she now looked far older.

Ann stared silently through the smeared glass of the window as the bus jittered through noisy, fuming traffic that moved at breakneck pace.

"There are only two speeds in Istanbul: fast and stop," she had once noted, earning a laugh from her uncle. But this day, Ann didn't even notice the roar of the cars and trucks. Lost in thought, she barely saw the incongruous mix of elegant, ancient domes and minarets, vacant lots of dirt and weeds, and modern high-rises and tenements as the bus wound its way toward the Sirkeci area and finally screeched and shuddered to a stop.

She rose, alighted, and started on the seven-block walk through narrow, crowded streets to her latest home—a two-room apartment in a building with a stained and chipped plaster façade.

The interior walls were so thin one was never free of the sounds of radios and angry conversations emanating from adjoining apartments, the strident chorus of engines, screeching brakes, and honking horns from the streets outside. The hallway was dimly lit and always heavy with the aromas of spices and Turkish tobacco blending with the ever-present traces of exhaust fumes.

Ezel had just risen from bed when Ann returned from school. She was not feeling well but was determined to spend the evening helping Wayne at his club. If she didn't, he would certainly want Lyla or Ann, or both, to take her place. Ezel didn't want the girls anywhere near Huriyah.

The back portion of the club was a brothel.

THREE

THE CLATTER OF his boots mingled with the sound of his labored breath resounded in Hank Evans's ears as he made his desperate run.

Surrounding him were the graying flat façades of Istanbul's Great Bazaar, its maze of endless stalls displaying a cornucopia of goods: leather, carpets, sheepskins, brass, gold, silver, junk. Ahead rose a line of purple-gray domes etched against an azure sky.

Evans sprinted down a rickety gangway between weathered red-tile rooftops. Mounted on high wooden stilts like a trestle, inclining and declining according to the manmade topography, the narrow gangway stretched half a block before sharply zigzagging over the aisles that snaked beneath it. Hank slowed for a split second, glanced back, aligned himself—and then sprang across a five-foot gap to the side of a peaked rooftop, where he scrambled to keep his footing.

"Cut!" blared a hoarse voice through a bullhorn.

"Crap," Hank muttered.

"Hank," called the director, "we have to try it again. . . . Will somebody please get those kids away from the window?"

Evans edged slowly down the roof to a hidden ramp that took him back to the gangway without his having to make another leap. Beads of perspiration slid under his red western shirt as he trudged up the wooden plank. Catching his breath, he wiped his forehead and glanced to his left. Three grinning boys were squeezed into an arched portal, waving wildly and

23

excitedly calling out the Turkish version of his name: "Honk! Honk!"

He responded with an angry glare, and the boys instantly disappeared from the window, crushed. Then Hank stormed back toward the camera's rooftop position where director Vincenzo Domenici and several members of his crew were clustered.

"What kind of horseshit is this? Why the hell didn't anyone see those kids *before* I risked my ass?" Evans bellowed.

The crew members froze, and Domenici heaved a heavy, strained sigh as he sought to control his temper. He knew from experience that to argue with his star when Hank was in one of his rages would only mean the loss of more time.

Evans's stunt man, Roy Carter, tall and muscular though neither quite so tall nor so muscular as Hank, came forward quickly as the actor angrily closed in on the director. He clapped the star on his shoulder with an amused smile and a nod of approval. "Hell of a jump, Hank ol' boy. Keep this up and I'll be out of a job."

The compliment had the intended mollifying effect.

"I wish ol' Vincenzo would learn to look before I leap," Hank complained, pushing back a limp shock of his wavy brown hair.

Although he was hot, tired, and frustrated, although perspiration traced his boldly hewn cheekbones and wove lines in the makeup masking the shadow of his beard, Evans remained strikingly attractive. His were the kind of square-jawed, purely masculine good looks that, like fine leather, would only be improved by weathering and years. The exertion of running the hot gangway deepened the glow in his tanned complexion, and his anger served to put an invigorated spark in his blue-gray eyes.

A crowd was gathered on the cobbled street below, waiting to get a good look at Hank Evans and, if they were lucky, perhaps an autograph, too.

Evans had captured the heart of Istanbul long before production on the movie had started.

The *Milliyet* and the English-language *Daily News* had carried stories heralding his arrival in the exotic city. Hank Evans had come to make an action-packed thriller with a glamorous international cast. Evans was quoted as complimenting everything, from Turkish hospitality to *ic pilav,* the traditional dish of fried rice with raisins and pine nuts. He grinned his famous squinty-eyed grin for dozens of photographers—professionals and snapshot-happy tourists alike.

The United States Consulate was giving a reception for Hank Evans, his castmates, the movie production team, and its Turkish liaisons; invitations were fervently sought and jealously guarded. In the meantime, the papers reported that Evans was spending much of his free time with local socialites and dignitaries.

To many, Hank Evans seemed less like a foreigner than an old friend whose movies had, in recent years, provided a welcome-if-brief escape from the worries of their country's political turmoil. Dubbed or subtitled Hollywood films were part of the standard fare in the cinemas of İstiklal Avenue. Hank Evans, Gary Cooper, John Wayne, Jimmy Stewart, Charlton Heston, and other major Hollywood stars could often be found on screens there, rounding up dogies and heading up posses in Turkish.

The fact was, Evans had gotten his start working as a wrangler in several John Wayne movies. The Duke, who prided himself on having a retinue of cronies who went with him from film to film, had finally handed Hank a small part in the 1952 *The Quiet Man*.

It had turned out to be a jumping-off spot for Evans. From it had come his role as the noble cavalry officer in *Montana Train*—the movie that had given Hank Evans his image and his fame. The role had made him a star and brought him worldwide attention. Indeed, a faded *Montana Train* poster currently adorned a theater near Taksim Square.

In the eight years following the film's release, he had played cowboys, a soldier, a sailor, and a cop, but in every character the essence of the cavalry captain was clearly present.

Small wonder that by 1963, people had come to believe Hank Evans *was* that lionhearted, two-fisted hero.

Hank was back in position and ready to make the run again when the director called lunch.

"What? What about the shot?" Hank demanded.

Domenici shrugged. "Sorry. We have a camera problem. We'll have to get it after lunch."

Before Hank had a chance to get upset, Roy Carter gave him a friendly poke on the shoulder.

"How would you feel about going out for a little unwinding tonight? I've been doing some reconnaissance." The stunt man winked.

Hank nodded, brightening visibly as they started down the wooden steps to the street.

When it came to blowing off steam after a grueling day's work, Carter was without peer. He was also particularly talented at finding the ideal spots: a pink whorehouse in Acapulco, a floor show with an unbelievable snake act in Rio, a backstreet club in Paris that featured imaginative sex acts involving a mix of men, women, and animals.

Istanbul presented special challenges. Although Turkey had a national alcoholic beverage—raki—and a government distillery, Hank and his pals had discovered that the effect of the Muslim belief against consuming liquor was also present. One just didn't find good drinking spots on every street.

Arching his brows and grinning, Carter informed Evans, "Your driver told me about a place over by the railroad station that sounds real interesting. One of the owners is an American . . ."

Ann would never have mentioned reading about Hank Evans's visit had she had the faintest notion of the havoc the information would wreak in her already unsteady household.

Wayne had snatched the paper out of her hands with the eagerness of a miner unfurling a map pinpointing a mother lode of gold.

Wayne was hardly the man to forget Hank Evans's reputation for generosity. In the States, tales about Evans had been repeated and repeated until they had become legend. One had it that he had given a green Rolls-Royce to a Chicago bartender named Pat Flynn, just because Flynn had introduced a concoction he had dubbed Captain Hank's Mint Daiquiri.

Wayne had managed to locate Evans's driver and had paid him 250 lira—about $25—to bring Evans to Huriyah. He had no idea the driver was enjoying sudden prosperity as a result of other cash offers for delivery of the star—or that the going rate was only 200 lira.

"I want you at the club every night as long as those movie people are in town," Wayne instructed Ezel. "If they come in, it'll be a very special occasion." He paused. "Do you understand?"

Ann saw the look that passed over her mother's face, and although she couldn't fathom why, she felt ashamed and repelled.

"It's not good," Ezel said, shaking her head pathetically. "Not good."

"Not good?" Wayne snorted. "It's a compliment, for chrissakes!"

"What are you talking about?" Ann asked, disturbed by their conversation.

"Go outside, Ann," was her mother's reply.

Hank Evans was staying in the Royal Suite of the Pera Palas, a collection of rooms with high ceilings and mosaic-inlaid archways, a view of the Golden Horn, opulent nineteenth-century furnishings, bathrooms larger than the average hotel room, and a roster of past residents that included King Boris of Bulgaria.

At nine o'clock that evening, Hank's buddies were waiting for him in the cavernous lobby. A ragtag crew, still wearing their work clothes, they looked out of place in the rococo setting as they stood talking and laughing loudly only a few feet from the small nook reserved for the Muslim faithful to pray.

The ornate bird-cage elevator descended at a serene speed well suited to royalty. In it were Hank Evans and Howie Hewitt, the unit publicist for the movie *Fortress of the Seven Towers*. Hewitt, a portly man with a graying mustache and thinning hair combed from one side of his shiny pate to the other, appeared an especially poor physical specimen next to Evans's well-chiseled features and lean body.

Seeing them, Roy Carter cried, "Is that himself?" and the group moved as one to watch Hank and Howie step out of the elevator.

"What's the story on the *Look* layout?" Evans asked the publicist irritatedly. "Are they sending someone or not?"

"I don't know yet," answered Hewitt. In truth, the magazine had decided to wait on its Istanbul movie adventure story.

Filmmaker Jules Dassin and his wife Melina Mercouri would soon be arriving in the city to lens a jewel heist story called *Topkapi* with Maximilian Schell and Peter Ustinov. Hewitt was having nightmares about *Topkapi*. If *Look* covered that film and not *Fortress of the Seven Towers*—indeed, if the

Topkapi troupe upstaged Hank in any way—Hank's ego would be bruised, and that meant it would be hell to be anywhere near him.

To get Hank in more of a fun mood, Carter lapsed into his Amos 'n' Andy voice.

"Well, if it isn't ol' Howie boy," he said, clapping Hewitt on the shoulder. "Do you think you'll be joinin' us for a little relaxation tonight?"

Hewitt smiled faintly and shook his head, edging away.

He was one of several members of the *Fortress* team who had been instructed by the studio and by Evans's agent, also executive producer of the film, to try to keep Evans from getting tanked. It was a suicidal mission and one Howie had already decided to forget.

When Evans was sober, his personality could range from the charismatic, likable character the public knew so well to an arrogant, impossible-to-please, bloody pain. Hewitt could cope with that. It wasn't unusual to come across mercurial temperaments in his line of work. However, when Hank was drunk, his mood swings could be frightening.

No one around him was about to remind him of that fact as he set out in search of the underbelly of Turkish nightlife. Besides, Hewitt told himself, it wouldn't do a damn bit of good to say anything to Evans. It was Hank's tendency to do the opposite of whatever Hewitt recommended.

"Sorry. I've got other plans," Hewitt said as he turned to go.

"Don't forget the proofs," Hank called after him.

The men walked expectantly out of the Pera Palas, visions of undulating odalisques in their heads. They piled into Evans's limousine and were soon exhanging loud jokes and complaints about the day's shooting, about Domenici, about the fool production coordinator responsible for hiring extras who felt compelled to walk out of shots at prayer call.

The limo moved across the bridge and into the old city, shooting through streets clogged with traffic as it headed in the direction of the railroad station. It finally stopped at a dark alleyway jammed with parked cars.

The group got out and took in the surroundings. The street was alive with boisterous workmen, a stunning contrast to the reserve of the locals with whom they worked on the set. An incredible din blasted out of the building to their left, a noise so loud it forced its way through thick wooden doors. Evans's driver indicated the entrance with his outstretched hand.

"Huriyah," he said with a smile. Two hundred and fifty lira earned—and so easily!

Hank and his entourage were filled with happy anticipation. Evans was the first to reach the entrance. He gave the cast-iron loop a heavy bang. "Open sesame," he said with a laugh.

A balding, mustachioed attendant opened the door, a spark of recognition instantly evident in his eyes at the sight of Hank Evans's smiling face. He ushered the Captain and his buddies through a small, dark entryway with a threadbare red-velvet curtain fringed with heavy gold cord. He spoke rapidly, animatedly in Turkish. There would have been no way to understand anything he said in any language; the blood-pounding racket from within the room drowned out his voice.

He pulled back the curtain, revealing a cavernous amber-lit hall thick with pipe and cigarette smoke and packed with wooden tables. There were many single women eating and drinking beside the men, a radically different scene from the one the Americans had observed in most cafés and clubs in Istanbul. Muslim tradition dictated that women took no part in public gatherings.

The faces of these women were garishly painted, and the tight, tawdry dresses they wore brazenly outlined their bodies and signaled they were practitioners of the world's oldest profession.

At the front of the hall, furious drumbeats and crashing tambourines provided accompaniment for a singer, while violins played at a nerve-exploding high pitch against the quick rhythmic plucking of a *saz*. Loudspeakers amplified the sounds to an earth-shattering volume.

Next to the musicians was a makeshift stage—wooden boards nailed together atop three tables—on which a belly dancer with a worn costume and an equally worn body performed. Her dance wasn't really a dance at all, but an ungainly striptease punctuated by lewd shakes.

To the right, a narrow stairway led up to a corridor lined with twelve closet-size enclosures. Men stood awaiting their turns with the women inside.

Hank Evans turned to Roy and shook his head, laughing. "This is one hellhole!"

"I know!" Carter shouted back over the din.

Hank's response was cut short as Huriyah's co-owner hurried over and introduced himself. Hank Evans took one look at Wayne Beaudry, smiling an unnaturally wide smile as he pumped the actor's hand, and had him figured out: *Another idiot trying to brown-nose something from me.*

"You're an American!" Roy shouted. Wayne nodded. "What the hell are you doing here?!"

"Just lucky!" The exploding noise in the hall made further explanation impossible.

Then Wayne shouted to Hank Evans, "I'm your biggest fan! Anything you want, it's on the house!"

"That's a mighty nice offer," said Evans. His voice, though low, was resonant enough so that he did not have to scream to be heard. The warmth in his eyes was now replaced by a glacial coolness. "Does that go for my friends, too?" he asked.

Wayne nearly choked. But how could he possibly say no? "For friends from home? Anything!"

Roy Carter clapped Wayne's shoulder and cried out, "Good deal!" and the rest of Evans's entourage expressed thanks as they moved to a table as far away from the loudspeakers as possible. Hank Evans sat down first, then his flushed and laughing troops filled up the long bench. Evans motioned Wayne over. His eyes darted meaningfully from woman to woman, sizing them up.

"Got anything fresh?"

"Why sure!"

A minute later, Wayne marched into the kitchen with a red-brocade dressing gown in his hand. It was an item he reserved for special guests, and Ezel winced at the sight of it.

"He's here!" Noting her expression, he added, "There are millions of women who'd pay to fuck Hank Evans. See that you make him happy."

Wayne threw the robe at Ezel, who picked it up off the floor as if it were contaminated. The dishwasher and the two cooks glanced over disinterestedly and then went back to their work.

The cubicle had all the appeal of a neglected roadside service station bathroom. It was dimly lit to mask the flaws in its dirty yellow walls and in the hard-faced, sagging whores it housed. When Hank Evans entered, Ezel was standing against the far wall.

He glanced at her and smiled. She looked better than he had expected. He sat down heavily on the carpeted cot, his back to her, and began to pull off his boots. He groaned slightly, flexing his toes.

"I hope you're up to raising Lazarus from the dead, honey. I am one tired sonofabitch."

"Would you like me to massage your feet?" came the low voice from the corner of the cubicle.

Evans turned and inspected her more closely. That she spoke English came as a surprise. Her question struck him as more suited to a Tokyo geisha house than this Istanbul dive.

He drew in his chin with a slight shrug. "That's a happy idea," he replied.

And so, with the sounds of reckless whamming and bamming, groaning and laughing emanating from the adjoining cubicles, Ezel knelt at Evans's feet and began to give him a well-practiced massage.

"I guess you learned English from the owner," he said.

"No. I learned from my husband."

"Your husband, huh?" he questioned.

"Yes." She smiled faintly. "He was a major in the United States Army."

With that comment, Ezel captured Hank Evans's interest. Before long, he coaxed her into telling him her life story.

When Ezel released his feet, Evans stretched them out, making slow circles; he leaned back, feeling the tingling warmth from the massage, and groaned with contentment. Then, as he looked down at Ezel's downcast, careworn face, he caught a hint of its former beauty. He noted her slight shoulders and marveled that such a diminutive woman had such iron strength in her hands.

"Here," he said, gesturing for her to sit next to him on the cot. "So what happened after he died?"

Ezel sat down next to Evans and resumed her story, describing the changes in her life. Evans listened attentively. He didn't really believe her, but he was tired and her storytelling intrigued him. He could tell his friends that he had stumbled onto his very own Scheherazade.

Starved for attention, Ezel poured out her heart. When she eventually spoke of Wayne's violent binges, Evans's expression was somber. Ezel would never have guessed that she was speaking to a man whose own violent binges were, in fact, worse than those of her lover.

"My children are very scared—and so unhappy." She paused, sighing. Her voice was filled with misery and a sense of hopeless finality. What was done was done.

The thought flickered through Hank's mind that she might be telling the truth, but he dismissed it. He had worked with too many good actresses to get suckered by an artful Turkish whore. He waited for her to reach the point he was sure she was working toward so skillfully: what she wanted out of him.

"My children dream of going back to America. I pray every day to find a way to send them."

Bingo!

"Why don't you bring them by the set tomorrow?" Hank suggested casually. "We'll be at Hagia Sophia all day. We can talk some more then. Maybe I can help you."

"I would be so grateful!"

He studied her expression, but she gave no clue that he had just called her bluff, and that impressed him. Of course she would never show up. The whole story about the children had obviously been dreamed up in hopes he would give her a generous handout.

Ezel rose and stood in front of Evans, reaching for the sash that held the red robe together. He clasped his hands around hers. He suddenly realized how urgently his body needed sleep. Another six A.M. call and twelve-hour day loomed ahead, and, much as he hated to admit it, Hank Evans's astonishing stamina was becoming a trifle less astonishing as he approached forty.

He stood, still holding her hands, and winked mischievously. "See you tomorrow," he said. And then he was gone.

Despite Wayne's fantasies, there was no mint-green Rolls-Royce from Evans, no lavish gift of any kind. Evans handed him a twenty-dollar bill as he left, not even waiting to sample the special meatball and rice dish called *kadin budu*, or *woman's thigh*, that Wayne had directed the cooks to make especially for Evans. Considering the drinks and the food consumed by Hank's party, the time five of the men had taken up with the whores, plus the 2500 lira paid to the driver, Wayne's loss was substantial. Worse was the reality that nothing more was forthcoming. He vented his rage on Ezel, screaming curses as they walked back to their apartment through the foggy night.

FOUR

THE FORTRESS PRODUCTION team had received permission to transform parts of Hagia Sophia, the massive Church of Divine Wisdom, back to its pre-1935 identity as a mosque. Because the sixteen-hundred-year-old architectural marvel with its enormous dome had been a museum for some time, it had been easier to gain access to it as a filming site than it would have been to use any holy landmark.

Hank and his entourage were stationed a few yards away from the director and crew, who were busy setting up the lights and camera for a shot in the nave of the building. Echoes of their voices bounced back from the vast archways and floated up to the intricate acanthus leaf designs that decorated the inside of the dome.

The building seemed to demand quiet. Certainly it had that effect on a group of extras who stood silently on the sidelines, waiting for the director's order to assemble on the gold and wine-red carpets that had been laid out over the marble floor.

On the sidewalk outside, Ezel took a last appraising look at her daughters. She hesitated a moment, pulled a comb from her handbag, and handed it to Ann with instructions to tidy her undisciplined bangs. All three were wearing their best clothes. As they went into the building through the entrance where the film equipment trucks were parked, Ezel's voice quavered with nervousness.

"Ann, you talk to them," she instructed.

"Yes, Mama." Ann nodded, aware that Lyla resented being bypassed as spokesperson.

Hank Evans and his friends would have had no way of knowing the trio was present had it not been for the loud voice of the assistant director.

"I'm sorry," he called out, "this section is closed today. We're shooting a movie here."

There was a pause and then his voice rose again. "A lot of people want to see Mr. Evans. If we let everyone who wants to meet him come in, we'd never get our work done."

That was followed by a final outburst. "Look, if he was expecting visitors, he'd have told us."

Just then Claude Dupart, a young French actor, noticed the trio being held at bay on the other side of the nave. He pointed them out to Hank Evans, who yelled, "It's okay, Don!" The AD shrugged and stepped aside to let Ezel and the girls pass.

"Well, well," Hank greeted them with a grin. "So these are your daughters."

"Yes," Ezel answered softly. "Lyla and Ann."

"How pretty!" Hank said, struck at once by the brilliant blue of Ann's eyes.

Lyla gazed at the floor, sure the compliment had been intended for her sister alone, as Ann bashfully said, "Thank you."

Hank took note of Ann's voice. It was sweet, her accent undiluted American. He glanced at Roy Carter, who raised his eyebrows slightly and gave Hank a smile.

Ezel pulled a dogeared wedding picture from her purse and handed it to Evans, who studied the tinted faces of the young officer and his bride. The expression on his face changed from playful politeness to a look of sober wonder.

"This was taken in 1948," Ezel said. "He was attached to the Embassy. He helped at talks, one year later."

"What talks?"

Ann's mother sighed and looked at her daughter—it was Ann's cue to take over.

"The talks President Truman set up to make sure Turkey's border was secure against the Soviet Union," she dutifully replied.

"Oh, *those* talks." Evans chuckled.

Ann reddened. Out of the corner of her eye, she saw Lyla suppressing a smile.

"Go on, honey," Evans urged. "Explain it to us."

Ezel nodded encouragement, and Ann complied. In short

order, she covered the Truman Doctrine, Turkey's role in NATO, and Major Beaudry's progression from General Russell's staff through his years as military attaché to the embassy in Ankara.

Suddenly everyone on the set seemed interested in Hank's new friends. The group around Evans's chair grew larger. Questions flew, and Ann answered them as best she could.

When it was time for Hank to face the cameras, he asked the Beaudrys to stay. The trio watched patiently as the camera rolled and again and again Hank took off his shoes and carefully picked his way through the crowd of praying extras. At the next break, the company once more congregated around Hank and his visitors. This time Ann's stories were about Korea, about Major Beaudry's term as a liaison between the Turkish officers and General MacArthur.

Hank Evans's skepticism totally evaporated and was replaced by fascination with Ann and her intelligence. He asked where the girls went to school, and Ezel replied with a sigh, "There is no more school for them; there is no money. Now Wayne is saying they must work in the club."

Ann stared at her mother. It was the first she had heard of the idea.

Evans also looked up sharply. He found himself harboring the notion of playing the hero—this time in earnest. Still, he wasn't sure what help he could provide—or cared to provide—so he simply suggested that Ezel "come out and see us again."

The next day, Ezel took some money from a small wooden box she had secreted under her daughters' bed and took the girls on a bus trip to the ancient walls on the southern approach to the city, on the Sea of Marmara. The movie company was shooting at the site from which the film's name was taken, the Seven Towers Castle, Yedikule. Ezel and the girls walked along the crumbling stone walls of the fortress, once a notorious prison, until they located the motion picture team's bivouac.

They found Evans and his compatriots complaining about the nauseating smell from the nearby tanneries. What audiences would ultimately see—the jagged walls against a vivid blue sky, the shimmering sea—would give no clue to the one aspect of the location site the crew was to find most memorable.

"Just keep smiling, Cap'n," snickered Roy Carter as he clapped his hand on Evans's shoulder, "and think of all those tourists who'll see the picture and come out here expecting paradise."

"Oh Lord," Hank begged facetiously, his face to the sky, "give us this day a shift in wind!"

Hank's visitors provided a welcome distraction. He greeted them warmly and spent much of his time between camera calls with them. He decided upon a course of action.

The girls were about to be the recipients of one of Hank Evans's famous bursts of generosity, the generosity that Wayne had eagerly anticipated and failed to receive.

"I know all about her," the secretary told Howie Hewitt as he stood at the counter in one of the rear offices of the United States Consulate. "Mrs. Beaudry has been here many times. The fellow she lives with is a bad character. In fact, he got himself in a jam last year, suspected of black-marketing dollars. None of us would be surprised if she came in here one of these days crying that he'd been thrown into prison. We've tried to help *her,* but she's a little bit, er . . ." The secretary tapped a finger to his temple.

"I understand," said Hewitt.

"Those girls are awfully lucky to have run into Hank Evans. What a great man. Wait till I tell people what he's doing. You know, everybody was so impressed with him at the reception. He seemed just as nice in person as he does in the movies. We're certainly going to miss the excitement of having him here."

Hewitt's smile was tight. Making all these arrangements for Hank was really cutting into his work time, and Howie felt some justifiable resentment that this particular chore had fallen to him.

He had production notes and press releases to finish, photos to go over—the list of his wrap-up activities was endless. Worse yet, he had a ridiculous twelve-day sea journey to endure because the studio insisted he shepherd Hank Evans back to New York, and Hank Evans refused to fly.

It would take a week just to get across the Mediterranean —a veritable milk run with stops at several ports Hank insisted on seeing. *Then* they would board the *France* for the Atlantic crossing. Howie hated bobbing up and down on the water. He was prone to seasickness. All in all, he had a lot to feel miffed about. And now he was confronted with a bush-league bureaucrat who wanted to prattle on about Hank Evans's virtues. Well, Hank Evans wasn't always so virtuous, not that Howie was going to go into *that*.

"Aren't they lucky girls, going to live with Hank Evans," exclaimed the secretary.

Howie laughed and said quickly, "They're not going to live with him. Hank has a friend, a minister, who has a boarding school called the Christmas Star Ranch. He takes in a lot of homeless kids."

"Isn't that beautiful?"

Howie produced a wan smile. Sensing that the conversation was at an end, the secretary became businesslike.

"You'll want the passports. I'll see if they're ready."

Updating passports, attending to tickets, arranging for luggage to be transported. *Oh, well*, thought Howie, *if I'm going to be Hank's flunky, at least for once it's for a good cause*.

The passengers crowded against the railing of the *Timor* as the ship moved away from shore and cut through the Bosporus. Lyla and Ann were in the midst of a jostling crush of foreigners. A young British couple eyed the raucous Russian tourist group with clear-cut disapproval. A huddle of Syrian men in flowing robes talked loudly in Arabic, while an Italian mother yelled commands at her two sons as they tried to squeeze through the crowd. At the rail an elegant Eurasian woman with a perfect chignon and a veiled blue pillbox hat bestowed a smile on her traveling companion.

One of the Russians noticed Lyla and Ann and muscled his friends aside with a grin, clearing the way for the two sisters to observe the view.

The *Timor* was passing the Golden Horn; in the distance, the Galata Bridge linked the old city to the new. Istanbul was enveloped in dusk, the bulbous domes of its mosques, the hundreds of towering minarets receding in the pink gray sunset. The unearthly sound of the muezzins calling the faithful to prayer was faintly discernible over the chill breeze rising off the water.

How many times, Ann wondered, had she seen this view from the ferry? More times than she could count. And yet, strangely, it was as if, in seeing it all for the last time, she was seeing it all anew.

A painful ache rose inside her. She saw her mother's face in her mind's eye . . . then her father's. Ann felt Lyla take her hand. She glanced over and saw tears sliding down her sister's cheek.

As the air grew cooler, the other passengers moved below. Alone on deck, the sisters held hands and wept as the walls of Topkapi disappeared into the blue haze.

Hank Evans checked the view once or twice through the portholes in his cabin, but he had other things on his mind. He was brooding over the press schedule that Howie had received by wire from Sentinel Studios. The full-scale press junket planned to coincide with the release of Hank's movie *Last of the 49ers* was scheduled to begin the day after the *France* docked in New York. Howie didn't tell Hank about the final personal note from his boss: "Make sure you get Evans on his stinking boat and don't let him out of your sight until you're in New York."

Now, as Hank paced his stateroom suite in stocking feet, he read through the schedule and tossed it down page by page on the plush red carpet—an act that made Howie extremely uncomfortable.

Roy Carter sat at the cherry wood desk, nonchalantly leafing through a magazine. Hank's bodyguard and Didi Lewis, the *Fortress* makeup woman—who had enjoyed her role as one of Hank's special friends so much she had traded in her plane ticket for passage on the ship to remain close to the star—sat on the cut-velvet sofa going through some of the new stills from the movie.

"You want a week of interviews *and* the press conference?" Hank complained. "That's too much. Not when I'm all dragged out like this."

Howie longed to point out that for most human beings this needlessly complicated voyage would constitute a dream of rest and relaxation, but he held his tongue. Instead, he smiled broadly as he tried to cajole Hank. "You know how it is. Hey, I know you understand."

"Yeah, I know how it is, Howie," Hank replied. "And I'm always real good about helping you people out. But this I'm not going for."

"Ooh, Hank!" cried Didi. "These shots of you in the cape are fabulous!"

"Let me see." He moved behind her and leaned over her shoulder to view the glossies. "Um *hmm*. Not bad."

"Somebody planned the junket without realizing, uh, you don't like to fly," Howie lamely persevered, adding a slight chuckle to keep it light.

"Then somebody made a mistake," Hank said quickly. He went to the suite's wide brass daybed and stretched out. "When we get to Piraeus, I want you to wire Sentinel and say they've got to push the junket back."

"Stanley Weiss isn't going to like it," Hewitt noted. Invoking the name of the flamboyant, almighty chief of Sentinel Studios was Hewitt's most potent weapon. He knew that Weiss, the man who had given Evans his start, who had once been his mentor and friend, was someone of whom Hank was in awe.

"Fuck Stanley Weiss!" Hank exploded, sitting bolt upright as Hewitt shrank back and the others suddenly jolted to attention.

"But Hank, Stan said—"

" 'But Ha-aank, Stan said,' " Evans mimicked Hewitt with a biting laugh. "Jesus. You sound just like my wife. I get enough limp-wristed advice from her—I don't need it from you."

Hank's blowup had a sobering effect on the entire party. Howie stooped to scoop up the pages littering the floor.

Hank lay down again with a sigh. "So push it back at least two weeks, or I won't do a damn thing."

"Jeez . . ." Hewitt complained lamely.

"I don't think you appreciate all Hank went through on this picture," Didi told him patronizingly. "Not to mention all he's doing for those two girls."

A loud groan rose from the daybed as Hank Evans pulled a pillow over his face. "Where are they?" he asked.

Not an hour out of Istanbul, he had totally forgotten about Ann and Lyla.

"Down in their cabin, I suppose," Howie replied.

Hank sat up with a laugh. "You brought them with *us?*"

Didi giggled, and Hank's bodyguard joined in the laughter. Roy looked up from his magazine to share in their amusement.

"That's what I thought you wanted, Hank. Was I wrong?" Howie asked. "I mean, weren't you taking them to meet your friends at the boarding school?"

"Well, yes, but I figured you'd put them on a plane with Lois or somebody." Hank caught Howie's look and the edge in his voice and shrugged. "Oh, well," he said, humoring Howie. "It doesn't matter."

"It's so heartwarming what you're doing," Didi announced. "It ought to be written up in all the papers so people all over America will know what a generous man you are." She cast a meaningful glance Hewitt's way.

"Have a couple pictures taken with that younger one, Hank," Roy suggested. "She's a doll."

"Boy, you're not kidding." Hank nodded, half smiling.

"I think they said she's fourteen and the older one is sixteen," Hewitt noted, a little too deliberately. The statement thudded through the stateroom.

There was a pause, just a beat, then Evans chuckled.

"Any other information you'd like to pass along, Howie?" he asked caustically.

Lying on the bunks in their tiny cabin, Lyla and Ann were trying to come to terms with the sudden change in their lives.

"Do you think Mama wanted to send us away all along?" Lyla asked.

"What difference does it make?" Ann said heatedly, her eyes fixed on the low ceiling just over her head. "She did it."

"For us. She did it for us. Don't say you don't think so."

"I don't know what to think."

"Don't you realize people would cut off their arms to be where we are? Ann! We're going back home and we're going to a nice school and it's all because of *Hank Evans!* He *likes* us! Especially you," Lyla added, masking her jealousy with a light, teasing tone.

Aware of Ann's silence, Lyla went on. "You must have noticed how he looks at you. He really likes you. . . . Ann?"

"I heard you."

"Doesn't that make you happy? Maybe he'll send you to college. Maybe he'll *marry* you." Lyla giggled. There was a long silence. Lyla got up and saw that Ann was curled up on her bunk, her eyes shut tight. She put a soothing hand on her sister's forehead.

"I was only trying to make you laugh," she said, suddenly contrite.

"I feel so strange, leaving Mama like this."

"I know. So do I. But she'll be all right. And in a few years, we'll both marry wonderful, rich husbands, because all the men will say, 'If Hank Evans thinks these Beaudry girls are so special, they must really be something.' Then we'll come back and see her and bring her every present you can think of. Or we'll send her tickets to come see us. It will be wonderful."

Ann nodded, falling in with Lyla's dreams. "I'd like to have a great big house," she said, "with lots of room for my family—a big family—and the biggest and most beautiful room of all will be for Mama. You and your husband will live just down the street, and we'll see each other every day."

"We'll live in Hollywood," Lyla said grandly. "Hank Evans will find out you're a great actress and he'll make you into a big movie star."

She muffled her laughter and ducked as Ann threw a pillow at her.

Ezel sat at the kitchen table in the Sirkeci flat, watching the clock on the wall. She felt sad but peaceful. She had made one of the most painful decisions of her life—she had sent her daughters away, and she knew it was for the best. Hank Evans was taking them back to the States, to a fine school, away from Wayne and the life of degradation that awaited them at the club.

She sighed deeply. The sigh was interrupted by a sudden sharp cough.

Ezel looked at the red-streaked handkerchief in her hand and frowned.

Yes, she thought, it was for the best. She would not have been able to protect Lyla and Ann had they remained here. But now they were safe. Now she had made everything all right.

She glanced down again at the blood-spattered handkerchief. She was glad she had never let them know. They never would have left if they had known.

FIVE

SEGREGATED FROM THE first-class passengers on the upper decks, Ann and Lyla were quick to realize they would not have the companionship of their benefactor during the trip.

While Evans and his entourage dined on lobster medallions with caviar at the captain's table in the formal dining room, Ann and Lyla lined up to take thier meals in the cabin-class buffet hall, which was essentially a floating cafeteria. While the star danced with the loveliest women in first class, Lyla and Ann walked the lower-deck promenade or remained in their cabin, reading books lent to them by Howie Hewitt.

Evans disembarked for a few hours of amusement at Piraeus, but Ann and Lyla remained on board, tensely waiting for the *Timor* to get underway once more. He left the ship again at Cagliari, anxious to take in the beauties of Sardinia —the female variety particularly—and to find Tony Quinn, whom he had heard was staying at a villa in the area with his Italian lady love and their infant son. The thought of including Ann and Lyla in one of his jaunts never entered his mind. They got little more than a glimpse of the port of call during their overnight stay. Hewitt took them along to the small hotel where he spent a frustrating two hours trying to make phone calls, bought them lunch, then returned them to the ship with instructions not to venture out alone.

And so it went.

Hewitt's seasickness governed his days, so his visits to the sisters were infrequent. Nonetheless, he remained their sole link to Hank Evans and his group—until their final day aboard the ship that was taking them to England, where they would begin their Atlantic crossing.

They were sitting on a bench in the crowded, smoky lounge, observing a game of checkers between a Frenchwoman and her granddaughter, when they heard a high-pitched voice announce, "I found them!"

They turned to see Hank Evans's friend Didi, trailed by Howie, snap-snapping her way through the room in high-heeled sandals garnished with artificial grapes. A lemon-yellow bikini and a white terrycloth robe slung over her shoulders completed her costume.

She plopped down on the bench beside Ann and declared loudly, "Have I got a surprise! Mr. Evans has arranged for you to have dinner in first class tonight. How do you like that?"

"If you feel up to it," Hewitt added mournfully. Clearly he did not.

"That would be wonderful," Lyla exclaimed.

Ann's forced smile did not escape Hewitt's notice. Both felt a sense of unease—Ann without knowing exactly why, Howie because he recalled, and understood only too well, the expression that came over Evans's face every time Ann's name was mentioned.

"Listen" Didi proceeded blithely, "you kids will need something decent to wear. We dress for dinner, and Hank doesn't want to be embarrassed. Come with me and I'll see if I can't rig up something for you."

The sisters accompanied Didi to her stateroom and watched entranced as she extracted a rainbow of cocktail gowns from the closet. Didi's quarters were less than half the size of Hank's, but they seemed the height of luxury to Lyla and Ann. The girls were awed by the array of clothing—and would have been astonished to learn that she had culled these bare essentials from her five trunks of clothing now stored in the *Timor*'s hold.

"You don't mind us wearing your beautiful clothes?" Lyla asked.

"Not if nothing happens to them," Didi retorted sharply. "I just don't know what we'll do about your shoes," she added, grimacing as she looked at Ann's scuffed black flats with their worn heels.

"Oh, well. First things first. This one's a little long-waisted for me, maybe it will work on you." Didi held a full-skirted beige taffeta and champagne lace dress up to Lyla. "No. Too fitted."

Lyla touched the lace reverently. Good fit or not, she was obviously enthralled at the idea of wearing the dress. Didi was quick to see the unflattering contrast between Lyla's plain face and limp hair and the sophisticated gown.

"May I try it on, just to see?" Lyla asked eagerly.

"You don't have the tits. The darts will cave in." There was a moment's pause as Didi studied Lyla's still-hopeful face, and then she relented. "Okay. Try away."

"Oh, thank you!"

As Lyla slid into the dress, Didi turned her attention to Ann.

In the end, Didi's efforts at "rigging up" semiformal attire for the girls fooled no one.

Lyla wore the champagne lace dress and, as Didi predicted, it only accentuated her flat chest. Ann wore a knee-length white brocade cape that reached midcalf on her. She kept the heavy garment on throughout dinner to camouflage her own inexpensive cotton skirt and blouse.

The dining room was sparsely populated. The *Timor* was encountering heavy seas, and anyone with a tendency to *mal de mer* now had a full-blown case.

There were vacant seats at Hank Evans's table. His bodyguard was up on deck taking deep breaths; Howie Hewitt was indisposed in his stateroom.

Evans was obviously bored with his dinner companions. He found them as stuffy as a locked attic—with the exception of an Italian Grand Prix driver and his luscious wife. But Hank's hopes for a titillating private encounter with the woman were hampered, at least during the dinner hour, by the fact that her husband was seated squarely between them.

"Here we are!" Didi announced as a waiter slid back her chair. The girls hung back shyly, feeling uncomfortable under the stares of the chic, sophisticated people surrounding Evans.

"Lillian and Ann," Evans said, introducing them. Lyla reddened, but no one corrected him.

"Ah, your young charges we have heard so much about." The race driver nodded appreciatively. *"Che bella."*

Once seated, the girls were promptly forgotten; they were free to observe without being noticed. Evans delivered some rambling political pronouncements and answered questions put to him by his guests, but his eyes seldom left the Italian woman, who reveled in his obvious attraction to her. Didi, who tried to pretend she didn't notice, babbled shrilly and only succeeded in annoying Hank. The Grand Prix driver was oblivious to Hank's behavior, engaged in conversation with an English lawyer across the table. Roy Carter seemed all but out of it, drowsy from the seasickness medication he had taken before dinner.

Lyla carefully studied the people around her to determine the proper fork to use, as one course followed another and yet another. Ann tried to keep her sense of unease at bay by thinking about the many people who had passed through this faded dining room in its days of glory.

Sometime after the entrée and before the sherbet, the ceaseless rolling of the ship began to have an effect on Lyla, Didi, and the race car driver. Conversation dwindled to a near halt, and the hardy could scarcely help noticing the greenish tinge seeping into the complexions of the stricken.

"It is a bit nasty tonight," the British lawyer allowed, finally opening the topic for discussion.

"Ummmm," groaned the driver.

"I can't take it," Didi declared. She stood up, looking suddenly haggard.

"If you will excuse us," the driver echoed, rising, "I can't take it, either." His wife folded her napkin daintily and rose to follow him, casting a glance at Hank Evans, who responded with a frustrated frown.

Lyla staggered after them, her pleasure in the lace dress forgotten. She paused just long enough to thank Evans and to push Ann gently back into her seat.

"Stay," she told her. "I'll see you later."

The lawyer's wife called across the table to Hank, "I hope you're still feeling fit, Mr. Evans."

"I've never had any trouble with seasickness. It must be my English blood." He chuckled affably.

"Ooh. Quite right," she said, raising her glass to him, enormously pleased.

Evans finally turned his attention to Ann. "By the way," he said, as if they had been conversing for hours, "I'm sorry about the mistake in your booking."

Although he appeared a study in warmth and kindness, he was making Ann feel increasingly uncomfortable.

"It's such a shame you girls had to stay cooped up in cabin class. You should have been up here all along."

"Oh, we don't mind," she answered, flustered. "It's been very nice."

"It wasn't what I wanted. And I want you to know I'm going to see that we make it up to you aboard the *France*."

"How lucky you are," the lawyer said with more enthusiasm than he had shown all evening. "We were aboard the *France* on her maiden voyage three years ago. She's a marvelous ship!"

Evans hailed the waiter. "Let me have another Scotch. And make it a double."

It was nearly eleven o'clock when what had shrunk to a small group finally left the dining room.

By then, Evans's eyes were heavy-lidded and bleary from alcohol. As he said his goodbyes to the Britons outside the dining room, he looked like a man about to collapse from fatigue.

"You can make it back to your cabin by yourself, can't you, honey?" Roy Carter asked Ann. She was about to answer, but Evans spoke first.

"She's not going back to her cabin. I'm going to give her a tour of the upper decks."

"In that case," Carter said, starting to back away, "enjoy yourselves." Carter thought better of leaving Ann alone with Hank, who was obviously getting into one of his drunken states, but he was too tired to try and tangle with the star.

Evans took Ann's arm. Ann felt her heart begin to pound against her chest.

"It's so nice of you, but—"

"No buts." Evans said with alcoholic cheerfulness, his speech slurred. "This is the final night aboard ship. Come on."

He led her to the promenade. A chilling wet wind blasted through the door as Evans opened it.

"It's too cold out there!" he shouted. He took Ann's hand and led her back inside.

His hand grasping hers set off a sensation of discomfort in Ann. She didn't know how to act, what to say to this man who said nothing as he led her along the passageway.

He stopped suddenly before a door, unlocked it, and, never releasing his grip on her hand, led Ann inside his stateroom.

In the sitting area, a brass lamp with a dark red shade cast a harsh light that gave the entire suite an unfriendly look.

When Hank Evans turned away from the door, it seemed to Ann as if he were wearing a mask—or perhaps for the first time he was without one. The calmness and the kindness were gone.

"I think I should go," she stammered.

"We just got here. Let me have that cape." He slipped the wrap off her shoulders and tossed it over the back of a desk chair. "Come on," he said. He stretched out his hand and led her to the couch. Ann sat down nervously.

She watched in anxious silence as Evans kicked off his shoes and strode to the bar cabinet. She wanted to leave. She wanted to leave very badly. Evans took out a crystal tumbler and filled it with Scotch. He tossed down half the drink in a gulp and returned to her side.

Ann fought back her fear. She tried to reassure herself that there was nothing to be frightened of. But then all at once Evans was on top of her, his mouth engulfing hers, his tongue forcing its way between her lips.

She pushed free of him, tears welling in her eyes, and stumbled from the couch, pleading, "Please, I have to go . . ."

He pulled her back down beside him and laughed. "Hey, honey, relax. We're just gonna sit here and talk for a little while. Okay?"

Ann said nothing.

"Okay?" Evans asked again, this time pressing roughly on her arm.

"Okay," she whispered.

"You want to know about the school you're going to go to?" he said, stroking her arm. "You want to know what Uncle Hank has planned for you?"

She managed another whispered "Okay."

He drew back, took another swig of his drink. And then suddenly he was kissing her again, his teeth pressing painfully into her lips.

She attempted to pull away; he reached for her blouse and pulled at its buttons. She put a hand up to stop him; he pushed it aside and yanked her shirt open.

"Please don't," she begged.

"Don't?" he questioned with a loud chortle, his left hand

becoming a vise that clamped her face as he tugged at his belt with his free hand.

And then his body was over hers, holding her prisoner. His hand jammed its way between her legs. She gasped in fright. His fingers went farther, still farther, until she cried out in pain.

"Please don't!" she sobbed, caught in a sweeping rush of panic and tears.

Evans's only response was to raise his body up long enough to undo his pants, while he held her pinned down with his legs. His mouth found her breasts. He bit at her nipples as Ann screamed, "Don't!"

"Don't *what?*" Evans hissed, his eyes glazed, his lips twisted into a sneer.

"Don't what?" he repeated in a harsh whisper, his teeth now drawing blood as he bit harder and harder. Ann could not speak. She felt smothered by her tears, by his hot stale breath.

"Don't do what to you? Fuck you? Is that it?" He jerked her arm. "Say it!" There as a sharp jolt of pain as he swung the palm of his hand against her cheek.

"Stop!" she sobbed. In mounting panic, she thought of Lyla in the cabin far away, of her mother farther still. There was no escape, no one to save her.

"Say it. You don't want me to what?" His hand gripped her arm, squeezing it harder and harder. "Say it."

"Don't . . . f-fuck me," she choked out the word she had never used before.

"Yes. I'm going to fuck you."

"No!"

"You don't want me to fuck you?"

Ann shook her head violently.

"But you do! I know you do," Evans whispered. "Tell me the truth. You want me to fuck you, don't you? Say it. Say, 'I want to be fucked.'"

She shrieked, giving way to her terror.

Evans sat back on her stomach, and she felt the sharp sting of a slap, much harder than the first had been. His turquoise ring hit her cheekbone, cutting a track near her eye. He stifled her cry with a hand cupped roughly over her mouth.

He forced her legs apart. Now a sensation of jamming and tearing, and with it, a hot searing pain.

It would have to be over soon, a strong inner voice told

her. *It would have to be over soon. It would have to be over soon. It would have to be over soon.*

"Your mother's a whore," Evans spat as he plunged into her again and again. "Your mother's a whore and you're a whore, too, aren't you?"

"No."

"Tell the truth."

"No . . . Yes?" she ventured—anything to stop him. But it did no good.

"Whore!" he screamed, as he violated her again with one final, violent plunge. Then he pulled himself free and half-pushed, half-threw her onto the floor.

Ann caught a flash of his face again and heard the reverberation of her mother's voice commanding: *Don't look!*

The world surged away in a burst of pain as the back of her head hit the sharp edge of the brass-framed table.

SIX

THE SHIP'S DOCTOR cleaned and dressed the gash in Ann's head, put her sprained arm into a sling, and confirmed that she probably had a slight concussion. The pain and horror of the rape were underscored by his numbing contempt. "Your sister should be more careful," he told Lyla reprovingly.

It was Roy Carter who paid the doctor handsomely for his services and his silence—especially for his silence. Neither Ann nor Lyla saw Hank Evans again.

The girls stayed close to their cabin throughout the Atlantic crossing. Ann was thoroughly traumatized, not only by the attack but by Evans's threats against her, against Lyla, even against their mother.

She begged Lyla not to tell anyone about the attack, not to send a message to Ezel, not to think of altering their travel plans.

Evans, Ann told her sister, had threatened to call his friends in Istanbul and have Ezel thrown into prison if there was the slightest hint that the girls were trying to make trouble for him. He had warned that fates equally bad or worse would be in store for herself and Lyla. There was no need for him to be more specific. As far as the sisters were concerned, Evans was capable of anything.

It was Howie Hewitt who helped Lyla get Ann aboard the *France*. He never knew exactly what had happended; he knew not to ask.

It was Hewitt who helped the girls through customs in New York. He had been instructed to deliver them to La Guardia airport where they were to catch a plane to Corpus Christi, Texas, and the Christmas Star Ranch.

But once back in the country, Ann had only one desire—to get as far away from the influence of Hank Evans as possible. She wanted no part of him, or his friend and his school.

Hewitt told the girls to wait while he phoned to confirm their flight. The instant he was gone, Ann put her arm around Lyla's shoulder and said urgently, "Let's get out of here. Hurry, let's just get away."

Before there was time for second thoughts, Lyla scooped up the pair of scuffed fabric suitcases that held their possessions and quickly followed her sister out of the terminal.

"Where are we going?" Lyla demanded.

"I don't know, but we've got to keep going."

"Where are we going to stay; who's going to take care of us?"

"We'll take care of ourselves," said Ann with a certainty she did not feel. "We'll find jobs, some kind of jobs."

Fear and the need to be far away from Evans and his aides drove her, thrusting her into the role of her older sister's leader. She started to trudge on, but Lyla hung back stubbornly.

"We don't know where to go!" she whined, panicking. "Where are we going to live?"

"We have the money Mama gave us," Ann reminded her. "We'll find a place to stay, and then we can figure out what to do."

She hailed a passing cab and, with Lyla trailing close behind, approached the driver's window.

"How much to take us to a nice, inexpensive rooming house?" Ann asked.

"How do I know?" he asked impatiently. "Look, girls, I got no time for games."

Ann stepped closer. "We're new here. We were hoping you could tell us where we could rent a room."

The swarthy young man glanced at Ann, at the suitcases, at Lyla with her lost expression and faded, frumpy cotton dress, then back at Ann, her arm in a sling, her face still bearing bruises.

"What happened to you?"

"It was an accident," said Ann.

"Yeah? Aren't you two a little young to be by yourselves?"

The only response was a pleading look from Ann. He studied her again and drummed his fingers on the steering wheel a moment, considering.

"Okay. Hop in. I'll take you over to where a friend of mine used to live."

They sank into the rear seat of the cab, which was soon inching through traffic-clogged streets flanked by buildings so tall they seemed to pierce the sky. Ann noticed a tiny figurine of a saint mounted on the dashboard of the taxi and silently gestured toward it. Lyla nodded. They exchanged a look of relief. It was a sign, they thought, that the driver was a good man.

"May we ask you some questions?" Ann said hesitantly.

As it turned out, he was a fount of information. By the time the cab pulled up in front of a row of dingy brownstones, he had given the sisters more advice about the city than they would ever be able to remember.

"Go in, ask for Hannah Markowitz," he instructed, pointing toward a doorstep with a wrought-iron rail. "If she don't have no empty rooms, she probably knows where you can get one.

"And you take care of yourself, honey," he called out to Ann as he pulled away.

It was Hannah Markowitz who answered the door. She was an older woman with gray hair and a full, unlined face distinguished by a pair of penetrating dark brown eyes. Her rounded body was packed like a sausage into a lavender floral print housedress.

While Lyla explained that they were looking for a room, Hannah Markowitz dried her hands on her apron and eyed the two sisters with the look of a schoolteacher listening to a feeble excuse for tardiness.

"I don't rent rooms to minors. How old are you?" she asked Lyla.

"Eighteen."

"Sure you are." Hannah glanced at Ann.

"My sister had an accident. She's not feeling well. She needs to lie down," Lyla said quickly.

Hannah hesitated a moment, then with a sigh said, "Okay. Come in."

She led them into a parlor with weary but well-kept furniture; tatted doilies covered the worn armrests of the couch and chairs.

"I'll make some tea," she announced. "Then we'll talk."

Ann and Lyla quickly discovered that Hannah Markowitz could not be lied to. She was as relentless in her probing inquiries as she was about keeping her tables dust-free. She soon learned the girls' actual ages and the real nature of Ann's accident. One thing they did not tell her was the name of Ann's assailant.

"Have you reported this man?" Hannah asked soberly.

"We can't," Ann replied, head bowed. Then she raised her eyes, looked squarely at Hannah, and repeated, "We can't. We won't. Help us. Or tell us to go, but promise you won't tell anyone about us."

After a moment of strained silence, Hannah rose and instructed the girls to follow her up the stairs.

She led them to a small room with a dresser, a mirror, a chair, and a double bed covered with a white chenille spread. Off to one side, a door led to a bathroom. On the other was an alcove with a refrigerator, a sink, and a small counter, atop which rested a hot plate left by the previous tenant.

"I can't let you stay more than a day or so. This is the only room in the place besides mine with a private bath, and it's supposed to go for fifteen more than the others. I want someone in here who can pay. Understand?"

Ann and Lyla nodded silently. Hannah took in their doleful expressions and sighed. "Look, get some rest. Come back down later and we'll talk some more."

Ann and Lyla quickly came to appreciate their great fortune in finding Hannah Markowitz. Her warning that the room was theirs for a day or so was forgotten as she took more and more interest in the sisters. In part, she felt personal gratification in seeing that her assessment of their characters proved accurate: they were both hard-working and managed to pay their rent—including the extra fifteen dollars—on time.

Lyla answered a newspaper ad and got a job scrubbing newly vacated apartments for a small cleaning concern. It was hard menial labor, and the filthy condition in which many of the apartments were left often made Lyla feel nauseated, but the work had one advantage: payment, cash under the table, was made according to the number of rooms Lyla finished.

She worked with such speedy relentlessness, she was soon paid better than the other women on the cleanup team. Her heavy, broad-shouldered frame and the muscles she had built cleaning the Istanbul apartment stood her in good stead.

Ann soon found piecework that she could do in the apartment while her injuries healed. She stuffed and addressed envelopes for a nearby secretarial company, and she beaded sweaters and scarves for a friend of Hannah's who had a small garment-manufacturing firm.

The days sped past. Anxious to let their mother know their whereabouts without alarming her, they wrote to say that Evans had decided to place them in school in New York instead of Texas. The letter was returned unopened with a scrawled notation: "Moved, no forwarding address."

"I thought she would be anxious to hear from us," Lyla said with bitter disbelief. "She didn't even leave word where she was going."

Ann sprang to her mother's defense. "She wouldn't have done that."

"But she did," said Lyla, waving the unopened envelope. "Where could she have gone?"

They were not to learn the answer to that question for several years. In the meantime, their distress over losing contact with their mother was superseded by a much more pressing problem.

Hannah Markowitz cornered Lyla one evening.

"I want you to take Ann to see my doctor," Hannah instructed, pressing some money into Lyla's rough, calloused hand.

"Thank you, but Ann's better now."

"Take her to the doctor, Lyla. Every time I knock on the door up there, she's either crying or sleeping. I've also heard her vomiting in the morning, after you've left for work."

Lyla found Ann sitting cross-legged on the bed, surrounded by bolts of material and containers of glass beads.

"Mrs. Markowitz thinks you should see a doctor."

"I'm all right. I'm just tired. So are you. You work harder than I do."

"Look," Lyla said, displaying the money. "She gave me this and her doctor's address. Why would she do that if she didn't think something was wrong?"

"I don't know."

Lyla took off her sweater and hung it over the back of the chair. She sat down, frowning, and watched Ann's face begin to take on a reddish glow. "What is it?"

"There is one thing I've been worried about," Ann admitted at last. "I think maybe I got hurt worse than we thought when . . . you know."

She never referred to the rape directly, only with a conspicuous pause, the habit she and Lyla had formed to communicate about the unspeakable.

"Why?" Lyla asked gently.

Ann swallowed hard. "Right after . . . I was bleeding a lot, but since then, I haven't."

Lyla leaned forward and stared at her, alarmed. "Are you saying you haven't had your period since then?"

Ann nodded.

"Why didn't you tell me? My God, are you pregnant?! Why didn't you say something?"

"That can't be what it is," Ann protested, her voice choked with horror. "It can't be that!"

"Of course it can!" Lyla reached over and tugged at the back of Ann's blouse, pulling it tightly across Ann's breasts as she looked for telltale changes in her sister's body.

"What are you doing?" Ann cried, moving off the bed quickly, out of her sister's reach.

For a moment, the girls froze, eyes ablaze with fear as they stared at one another from opposite sides of the bed. Then Lyla's hand moved to her mouth.

"Oh, Ann, I'm so sorry."

"But," Ann panted in confusion and despair, "but, Lyla, it can't be. . . . I stopped having my period because I was sick, because of . . ."

"No. You got sick because you're . . . because of . . ."

Ann's hands covered her face as she cried, "No! Oh, no!" She burst into tears, and Lyla enveloped her in a hug, for once feeling comfortable taking on her rightful role as the older, more knowledgeable of the pair. Indeed, Lyla had picked up details about sex and reproduction that no one had ever explained to Ann.

"Don't worry," Lyla said soothingly as she felt Ann's hot tears on her shoulder. "We won't go to Hannah's doctor. I'll tell her you're fine. Then we'll find you a doctor who'll stop it for you."

Armed with a name, an address, and directions to a clinic recommended by one of her workmates, Lyla led Ann down to the subway for the ride to the Bronx. If the decrepit building hadn't been enough to strike fear in their hearts, the waiting room was. It was crowded with women wearing vacant expressions. Four of them sat jammed side by side on a legless, torn, red Naugahyde couch. Several others stood or sat cross-legged on the brown vinyl floor. A dirty, unattended toddler, wearing only a soiled diaper, padded barefoot about the room, screaming. Ann and Lyla had plenty of time to absorb every detail of the smoke-filled room. Their wait lasted five hours.

Finally Ann's name was called. Lyla was turned away at the inner office door by the nurse, who was dressed in street clothes. "She's my sister," Ann entreated.

"Sorry. Patients only."

Ann endured the humiliation she felt during the gynecological examination and steeled herself to answer the doctor's questions. Then he made a terse announcement.

"Sorry. I'm afraid your pregnancy is too far along to terminate."

The journey back to Forty-eighth Street, in the ugly, anemic, fluorescent light of the subway, seemed an eternity.

SEVEN

〜〜〜〜

THE DISCUSSIONS BETWEEN Ann and Lyla were endless, their worries innumerable. In the days that followed, they made a series of decisions, all the while feeling they bore a crushing weight from which there was no escape.

First and most important, they promised one another they would never abandon Ann's baby. The fact that the child was fathered by Hank Evans was deliberately and forcefully put aside.

They decided Lyla would hold down two jobs, starting as soon as possible. She and Ann would step up their efforts to find Ann work she could do at home.

They shared a constant fear that the juvenile authorities would separate them if their situation became known and place Ann in a facility for unwed mothers.

"We'll tell the neighbors the baby is mine," Lyla suggested. "Nobody would report me; they all think I'm eighteen anyway."

Ann had to smile. "But, Lyla—how would you explain having a baby without ever getting . . . you know . . . big? What would you tell people?"

Lyla bit her lip and stared off into space for a minute. Then she said slowly, "What if I did get big?"

"What?"

"What if I went to the thrift store and found a maternity dress and put a pillow under it or something?"

Ann was doubtful. "Would anyone believe it?"

x

58

"I'll do it," Lyla insisted, as Ann listened in amazement. "We'll make sure it looks right. We can do it."

"You'd have to wear padding every single day. And what would you say when people asked about your husband?"

"What else can we do? Besides . . ." Lyla paused a moment, studying her interlocked fingers. Then she looked up at Ann, tenderness shining in her eyes. "You know, it would make me feel closer to your baby, and that would be nice."

"Our baby," Ann answered softly, and Lyla smiled.

Ann arose and went to the closet; she looked through its contents and pulled out an old plaid jumper of her sister's. "I want to try something," she said, returning to Lyla. "Put this on."

"Why?"

"If you're really serious about this, I have an idea."

"What?" Lyla asked.

"I heard a story once about a lady who was expecting but didn't want anyone to know," Ann said as Lyla slipped the heavy woolen jumper over her clothes. "She hid it by wearing loose clothes and pretending she was gaining weight."

"So?"

"If you wear maternity clothes and padding, people will look at you and . . . maybe they'll see that something doesn't look right. But if you *don't* wear maternity clothes, they'll believe you're pregnant and you're trying to hide it. They'll think they're smart to have noticed."

"Really?" Lyla asked, sounding unconvinced. Ann led Lyla back to the closet where a full-length mirror, smoky with age, was mounted on the back of the door.

"Stick out your stomach," she directed.

Lyla did, and Ann turned her sideways. "Now, put your hand up here on your back."

Lyla gaped at herself in the mirror. The combination of her heavy, large-boned frame, her swaybacked posture, and the loose, bulky jumper over her clothes created an effect that was inconclusive but highly suspicious. Lyla's cheeks burned as she viewed her "pregnant" form.

"But I can't stand like this all the time," she pointed out.

"You won't have to. Just often enough to give people the idea. Then, later, we'll add *some* padding, a little at a time."

They tested the look with a pillow carefully tucked beneath Lyla's jumper.

"I'm enormous!" Lyla cried.

"It looks funny, but there'll be time to work out something better," said Ann. "You won't need that until the last few weeks."

Ann had other suggestions, based in part on her own feelings over the last few weeks. "If you pass someone in the hallway, act as though you're so tired you're about to fall in a heap. Stop on the stairs and take a few breaths, then *drag* yourself up the steps. If someone asks if you're all right, go like this—" Ann sighed and gave Lyla a quick, pained smile, momentarily caught up in the theatrics of the exercise. "Then say, 'Yes, I'm fine. Just a little tired, that's all.'"

Agreed on their plan of action, they made a trek to a nearby thrift store, which yielded another jumper and a loose, empire-style dress.

Meanwhile, Ann got through her fourth month of pregnancy camouflaged in Lyla's clothes, which were three sizes larger than her own. Thereafter, both sisters were limited to wearing the ersatz maternity clothes.

One evening during Ann's fifth month of pregnancy, Hannah cornered Lyla as she came in from work.

"I'm not even going to ask you, because I don't want to hear any more denials. I just want to know what you two figure on doing. I can't have a baby living here."

"Don't worry," Lyla lied. "Everything is taken care of."

"I see. Whatever that means." Hannah moved off, throwing up her hands in frustration.

"You're . . . you're not going to say anything, are you?" Lyla called after her.

Hannah neither turned back nor broke stride. "About what?"

Something started to change in Ann's psyche when she felt the first light butterfly movements of the new life within her, when the baby took on an identity for her, when she could place her hand upon her belly and feel a kicking foot or a tiny flailing hand, when she could hold silent, reverent communion with the baby lying within her, talk to it, or sing soft lullabies. In spite of the horror in which it had been conceived, she loved this living soul with a deeper love than she had ever experienced.

As that love grew, she began to see that the vague vow she

and Lyla had made to one another—that they would find a way to care for the child—was sadly lacking. And she sought to give the vow form and definition. She became far more aware of money matters. She pored over the newspapers Lyla brought home, not only seeking work opportunities, but examining rental and even real estate ads and seeking food bargains.

Ann had become adept at preparing meals on the hot plate, but she knew that once the baby came their minuscule food budget and meager facilities would be painfully inadequate. They would need larger quarters—but how could they possibly afford them?

Confined to a single room with no telephone, Ann became increasingly frustrated as the weeks passed. Lyla was becoming more and more irritable and less and less willing to listen to her ideas.

Indeed, Lyla's work—in a delicatessen by day and out on cleaning jobs several nights a week—made it unnecessary for her to pretend exhaustion.

As Ann had predicted, Lyla was being closely observed by those around her—particularly by Joe Mantussi, the delicatessen owner. As time went by and Mantussi's suspicions appeared to be confirmed, he came to marvel at the courage and strength of the young woman with the perpetually aching back whom he watched hustling to serve his customers. His initial contemptuous feelings about Lyla's condition faded as his admiration for her increased.

Lyla had no idea of Mantussi's interest in her until one evening when he quietly drew her aside. He took her hands in his, and, lowering his jaw into the deep folds of his chin, his heavy eyebrows knit, he said somberly, "Just tell me this: is the guy still around?"

"Guy? No!" Lyla shook her head, pulling back from his grip. "There isn't any guy!"

Mantussi smiled slightly, nodding, before he continued.

"All right. I'll put it this way. Suppose there is this very nice young girl who gets into trouble. Suppose she thinks if she tells her boss the truth, she'll lose her job."

"That's not how it is."

"Suppose the boss wants to help this girl. She's a good girl. She'd make a fine wife. She made a mistake, but this man is forgiving—in the right circumstances." Mantussi studied

Lyla's face and her widening eyes as he slowly proceeded. "Suppose we say this man has always liked children and wanted some of his own. We could even say he had a wife once, and they tried, but it just never happened. It would make a man like this happy to marry this girl and give her child a name." He raised Lyla's chin with his stubby fingers. "He would be proud to do it."

"I don't know what to say," Lyla answered breathlessly, confused. "You don't—"

"Shhh. Just think it over. It's a nice story. It should end nice."

Lyla trudged home slowly and mounted the stairs of the boarding house with a heavy tread that evening. A proud and smiling Ann was waiting at the door to their room.

"I got paid today," she called out as she waved six five-dollar bills aloft. But one quick look at Lyla's face halted her. "What's the matter?" she asked.

The pressure and worry that had become Lyla's constant companions fused with the echoes of Mantussi's words and boiled over into an unexpected diatribe.

"You might think it's all right to live like this, but I don't," Lyla cried as she tossed her handbag onto the table. "I hate everything about our lives—and it can only get worse."

Ann recoiled as if she had been slapped, while Lyla continued in a fury. "I'm the one walking my feet off, having people shout at me all day long. Now I'm the one who'll have to worry about how we're going to care of a baby. You say *we* will find a way to feed the baby. *We* will bring it up somehow. How? *How?*" Lyla's hands curled into fists, and she shook with emotion as she shouted, "I can't do it!"

Stunned, Ann could only murmur, "But, Lyla, you're the one who's been saying 'we.' I thought that was what you wanted."

"What did you expect me to do? What kind of a person do you think I am? Could I leave you? What could I do?"

"Do you want to leave?"

There was no reply.

"Lyla . . ." Ann whispered.

Lyla's eyes were suddenly brimming with tears.

"What is it?"

"I can't tell you!"

She could not even bring herself to look at Ann. She started away, looking for an avenue of escape.

There could be no happy ending to Mantussi's story, she thought despondently, because it was Ann who was pregnant. Lyla was angry and resentful, but most of all she was torn with guilt over the thoughts that had filled her mind during her walk home.

"Something is really wrong!" cried Ann, giving in to her own frazzled feelings. "You've got to tell me! Is it serious?"

She took a step forward.

At that moment, her water broke.

She gave a small cry as Lyla, aghast at the sight of the puddle collecting at Ann's feet, rushed to her.

At four-thirty the next morning Hannah Markowitz was awakened by an urgent pounding at her door.

To Lyla, it seemed an eternity before Hannah answered, the picture of cosmetic consumerism with eye cream and face cream slathered over her skin and yellow and green plastic curlers fitted snugly beneath a pink hair net.

"Ann needs help!"

"Oh, God."

"There was a lady who was supposed to come," Lyla babbled almost incoherently as she led Hannah down the hallway, "but she's still not here, and it must be almost time!"

Hannah raced up the stairs behind Lyla, her untied bathrobe belling out behind her. She stepped into the sisters' room, took one look at the terrified girl lying on the bed, and became instantly furious.

"I don't know what the hell you two were thinking of! Go use my phone and call an ambulance, Lyla!"

"No!" Ann cried out.

"They'll take our baby away," Lyla protested.

The argument was interrupted by Ann's sharp gasp of pain. Hannah moved swiftly to her bedside.

"Oh, my. We're close," she said.

The anger vanished from her voice. Hannah went into a new mode, issuing commands and asking questions. How long had Ann been in labor? How far apart were the contractions?

"Should I try to call the midwife again?" Lyla asked.

"No time," Hannah replied, rolling up her sleeves. "Go

downstairs to the linen closet. Bring me the plastic sheet and all the clean towels you can carry as fast as you can."

Ann gritted her teeth and forced back a shriek of pain; the sound came out as an aching, gasping moan. Beads of perspiration coursed down her cheeks and onto her throat.

"You're doing so well," Hannah remarked soothingly. "Don't hold your breath like that. Do like this: puff-puff-puff. It'll be easier on the baby. Do you understand?"

Ashen, Ann managed a nod, tears of pain blinding her.

Lyla rushed back into the room to hear Hannah instructing Ann: "When I say push, I want you to push, but not before I tell you. . . . wait . . . good . . . wait . . . wait . . . push!"

"I brought the sheet," Lyla murmured.

Hannah commanded again: "Push. Good. Now breathe . . . good."

"It's coming!" Lyla gasped, staring wide-eyed.

"Bear down . . . bear down . . . keep pushing . . ."

This time there was no forcing back the primordial wail that came rolling from the depths of Ann's throat. And suddenly Hannah Markowitz was holding a seven-pound human being by its feet—tiny eyes tightly shut and rosebud mouth pinched with indignation at its rude introduction to life. The baby's color deepened to bright pink as, with a mighty breath, out came its first, angry cry.

"It's a girl!" announced Lyla, and Ann cried and laughed in relief and joy as Hannah handed her her newborn daughter.

It was the evening of the first fall rain. The clouds had broken, parting like a curtain to reveal the black starless inner-city sky. The air was heavy with the fumes of wet garbage and oil-slicked asphalt.

Ann barely noticed her surroundings as she followed Lyla through the narrow, soaked streets toward Mantussi's delicatessen.

In her arms was Cindy, her miracle, the five-day-old bit of squirming, yawning life who had changed everything for Ann —herself, the entire world. Somehow, now, all the grief, the wounds, the terror of Hank Evans's attack seemed distant.

Ann felt imbued with a strength and clarity she had never before known. All her fragmented worries and nebulous plans had suddenly been forged together into a single, all-important goal: ensuring Cindy's well-being.

She had felt strangely unconcerned about the future in the five days since Cindy's birth. Despite very little uninterrupted sleep, a sense of euphoria had engulfed her, a deep contentment and peace. Lyla had never been sweeter or more attentive. It had been as if, for five days, the gods, along with Hannah Markowitz, had looked the other way.

This first venture out was unplanned.

In the afternoon, Lyla had gone to Mantussi's to tell him she was ready to return to work. She had returned home a short time later in an agitated state, saying that Mantussi insisted she take more time off—with pay—and that he wanted to see "Lyla's baby."

Ann's eyes sparkled in the faded, flickering neon of a beer sign as she nuzzled Cindy's face outside Mantussi's window.

"Do you think I should carry her in?" Lyla asked.

Ann nodded reluctantly. "Go to Auntie Lyla," she cooed to Cindy.

Lyla smiled as she stepped forward and opened her arms to the blanketed bundle.

Those few seconds were to become indelibly etched in Ann's mind, for that simple, seemingly inconsequential act was a prelude to a moment that would profoundly change their lives.

Inside, Mantussi had already shut off the overhead lights. In the dimness, they could barely make out the counter and stools, the crowded rows of groceries, the tables and chairs.

"Joe?" Lyla called. Ann noticed that she said "Joe," not "Mr. Mantussi."

A stocky, balding man appeared at the kitchen door, wiping his hands on the soiled apron covering his belly. At the sight of Lyla, his chubby face took on a glow.

"Ohhh," he breathed, moving closer, "you brought the little one. Let me see."

He touched the blanket tenderly as Lyla shifted the baby toward him. "Isn't she a doll? What a little doll," he exclaimed.

Ann would long remember the inexplicable discomfort and sense of foreboding that rose in her at that instant.

"I'll take her," she said, stepping forward and reaching for Cindy.

Mantussi gave Ann a quizzical look.

"This is my sister, Ann," Lyla explained.

Mantussi nodded and said, "Hiya," without an overabundance of warmth.

Then, turning his attention back to Lyla, who was still holding Cindy while Ann stood by anxiously, he added, "Wait out here. I got somethin' for ya."

A moment later Mantussi reappeared from the back room, carrying a baby seat.

"My sister let me have this," he said, placing the padded, molded plastic seat on the counter. "Her kids have outgrown it. Thought you could use it."

"How nice!" Lyla exclaimed excitedly. She promptly set the baby in the seat and began fiddling with the straps. "Look what you've got, Cindy!"

Her mouth fixed in a thin smile, Ann watched the baby wriggle and flex.

"Lyla, I want to talk to you," Mantussi said.

Although his nervousness was obvious, Ann didn't notice it. She was too interested in getting to Cindy, adjusting the blankets around her, making sure she was comfortable.

"Okay," said Lyla. She seemed ill at ease, almost gawky.

"Alone," Mantussi added. He nodded toward the kitchen.

"Watch Cindy?" Lyla asked Ann. She sounded giddy.

Ann gave Lyla a sharp, questioning glance and nodded. Feeling a sudden burst of resentment at the "Lyla's baby" charade, she took Cindy out of the seat and cradled her in her arms.

Lyla and Mantussi disappeared through the kitchen's swinging double doors. Ann immediately went to stand next to the grill, near the opening through which the cook took orders and passed plates to the waitresses. There, she could hear everything.

Lyla's words drifted back.

"I—I want you to know, Joe, there isn't anything I'd rather do right now than say yes. I do want you to marry me, but I just can't. I've got to think of Ann. I can't explain, I . . ."

Ann closed her eyes. She brushed her lips against Cindy's cheek and took a deep, ragged breath. From the kitchen came the sound of Mantussi's worn shoes shuffling toward Lyla.

"You got more than your share of responsibilities with yourself and your little doll," he said. "The baby's gotta come first."

There was a long pause.

"Look," said Mantussi, "I'll give you a home. I'll give Cindy a father. What kind of a girl is your sister that she'd want to stand in the way of that? If . . . if you do want to marry me."

"I do! Maybe . . . Well, let me talk to Ann."

There was a long silence before Mantussi said, "Lyla, two new mouths to feed, one of them a baby who's going to need so much—that's goin' a long, long way. I can't afford to take care of your sister, too. I don't have room for her. All I've got's my one room upstairs. Don't you have other relatives she could live with?"

"No . . . there's no one but me." Lyla burst into tears. "I'm sorry, Joe!" As she turned and made her way out of the kitchen, Joe close at her heels, Cindy loosed a shrill wail.

The baby, tucked into her new hand-me-down seat atop the counter, was all alone.

Ann was gone.

Ann ran blindly, splashing through puddles, oblivious to the water that soaked her feet and crept up her pants legs. Despite her agony, she moved with conviction.

Cindy would have a real home with Lyla and Mantussi. She would have security. She would have the things a child needed—things a fifteen-year-old unwed mother could not give her.

She remembered Mantussi's tender voice. *Ohhh, what a doll.*

Yes, thought Ann as she raced up the stairs of Hannah Markowitz's brownstone, *Cindy will have a father.*

Getting out of their way was the only solution, Ann told herself again as she raced into her room and began to toss a few belongings into her suitcase.

She groped under the mattress for the cigar box that contained emergency money, grabbed a few bills, closed the box, and replaced it.

There was no time for reflection, not a moment to hesitate; there was no need to. She had never felt so sure of herself and what she was doing.

As she pulled on her heavy coat, Ann looked briefly at the baby's makeshift crib—a bureau drawer.

Now she'll have a real crib, she told herself.

Real clothes. Real dolls. Real books.

Real chances.

Numbed by the pain of her decision, Ann closed the door behind her and rushed down the stairs, through the parlor, and out into the chill of the night.

Two days later, Hannah Markowitz answered her telephone to hear Ann's weary, frightened voice.

She listened to Ann's breathless explanation for a moment, then said, "Surely you didn't have to leave, darling. There must be some other way. . . ."

"Please, just tell me—is Cindy all right, and is Lyla going through with the wedding?"

"Your sister has been very worried. You should talk to her. She's at Mantussi's."

"Please, Hannah, just tell me. You must know," Ann urged, her hand tightening over her ear to shut out the sounds of traffic outside the phone booth. "I know you understand."

There was a long pause, and then Hannah said, "Cindy's fine. She's here, in fact. And Lyla and Joe are going to Maryland to get married this weekend."

"Oh, good! Do you know if Joe . . . knows the truth about me?"

"Where are you, honey?"

"I'm still in New York, but I'm going to leave if everything's working out all right."

"I don't know what you mean by *all right*."

"Does Joe know?" asked Ann impatiently.

"Yes."

"Thank you, Hannah. You've been so wonderful. I'll never forget you."

"Wait!" cried the landlady.

But the only response was a dial tone.

EIGHT

LONG BEFORE ANN made her traumatic departure from New York, Hank Evans had dismissed her from his memory.

Indeed, within days of his return to the United States, he had put the entire episode behind him and was totally absorbed by the demands of his business and social life in Hollywood—particularly his social life, much to the dismay of his wife, Mary.

In any case, Hank Evans made it a rule never to look back.

Since his youth, he had been quick to dispense with the past, or to alter any troublesome details of his life history, as he saw fit.

If his frequent references to his father's courtroom decisions and his days on the bench gave the impression that Evans Senior had been a judge—instead of a boozing, womanizing, ambulance-chasing publicity hound of a lawyer—Hank was not about to correct the assumption. His descriptions of his mother as a pious Sunday school teacher gave no clue to the bitter and puritanical woman whom Hank had despised and feared throughout his childhood.

Hank had pulled up his small-town Texas roots and begun reinventing himself piece by piece more than twenty years before his encounter with Ann. She had hardly been the first person he had hurt and then dismissed from his mind, and she certainly would not be the last.

Things were more complicated for those actually inside Hank's world, starting with his wife.

Marrying up into the moneyed and prominent Carstairs

69

family had been Hank's goal, and within a few years after he had achieved it, he had very quietly put an end to his role as Mary's dutiful spouse and gone back to playing the roué.

Several months after the birth of the daughter he had unknowingly sired, Evans was in a fit of rage. In a stunning bit of role reversal, his wife had left him.

For all its obvious signs of wealth, the house had an air of austerity. Antebellum in style, with a pillared white façade and massive oak doors, it appeared stark and forbidding among the other homes on its fashionable residential street in Houston.

In the doorway stood a woman who seemed ideally suited to such surroundings: a wrinkled dowager in a slate-gray satin dressing gown. Her name was Mildred Carstairs, but she was best known to her friends and the public alike as Hank Evans's mother-in-law.

She peered out through the darkness at the taxi in the driveway, watching as the driver carefully took a pair of two-thousand-dollar suitcases trimmed in black crocodile from the trunk. He waited deferentially for his passenger to lead him up the walkway and into the entry hall.

Now that she was out of range of the Hollywood gossips, Mary Carstairs Evans dispensed with the dark glasses she had worn on her trip—the longest emotional journey she had ever taken. She raised her teary eyes, reddened and devoid of makeup, to meet those of the frowning woman at the door.

With a few wispy strands of blond hair escaping from the silk scarf covering her head and her shoulders sagging wearily under a sheared mink jacket, Mary looked the part of a refugee—a wealthy refugee.

"Hello, Mother," she said exhaustedly as the two women exchanged a stiff hug.

"Where is Eric?" the older woman asked.

"He's taken a trip with a little friend of his," Mary replied as she paid the driver and shut the door behind him. "Eric's gotten to be good friends with Sheilah Smith's son."

"Oh, really?" Mildred questioned, suddenly smiling as Mary nodded. The vibrant, red-haired actress-singer was one of her favorite personalities.

"Yes. The boys have gone to Hawaii with Sheilah and her husband."

She pulled off her scarf and began unbuttoning her jacket as her mother shook her head.

"What a disappointment. I thought the one good thing to come out of this would be a chance to see my grandson."

Mary stared at her angrily. "Obviously I don't want him exposed to any more of this than he has to be."

After a moment of silence, her mother nodded, compressing her lips.

"Mary, Mary." She sighed. "What are you planning to do? Surely you're not thinking of divorcing Hank."

Mary hung her head at the sound of her mother's slightly softer tone. "I don't know what I'm planning," she admitted. "I just want out. Staying married to him is killing me."

"I don't want to hear that."

"Then I'd better go to bed." Mary shrugged, reaching for her suitcases. "I don't have the energy to lie to you."

"Leave those. Come and sit with me for a few minutes. I want to talk to you." The woman in gray gestured toward the drawing room.

"It's almost three A.M.," Mary protested.

Mildred glanced at her daughter, the high arch of her thin unpenciled brows briefly rearranging the deep wrinkles of her forehead. "Were you really planning to sleep?"

The drawing room was oppressively close. Once it had been a hub of social activity, but now, with her husband dead, her health declining, her daughter and sons all grown and married—*well* married—Mildred had withdrawn into a quieter life.

Mary followed her mother into the room, which was dimly lit by low table lamps and a small blaze in the fireplace. She looked around distractedly for a moment. The sight of her old surroundings conjured up ghosts.

In her mind's eye, a vision of herself glided gracefully into the room.

The young Mary, fresh from finishing school and ready to make her debut . . . a happy, carefree time . . . She feels she is destined to become a great belle, and she is primed to become a daring flirt. She knows how appealing she looks in her full-skirted white taffeta dress—her first strapless dress—white gloves, high heels . . .

Her color rises at the sight of the handsome young actor, a friend of a friend, smiling at her from among a group of visitors at the far end of the room . . .

Her heart pounds as she looks away, and pounds all the harder as she waits to catch his eye a second time . . .

She finds her moment when nobody but he is looking and coyly mouths, "Help me." . . .

Suddenly, the tapestry love seat and chairs were faded and empty again, Mary's apparitions gone as her mother's voice dragged her back to the present.

"Mary, you know I always love to see you, and God knows it's been over a year—but not like this. I think you're making a terrible mistake. You should go back to Los Angeles as soon as possible and patch things up with Hank."

Mary moved toward the fireplace, preferring to watch the flames flicker and dance than to face her mother's all-knowing look.

"You wouldn't ask me to return to Hank if you knew what my life has been like," she murmured.

"Is Hank having an affair?"

Mary laughed a little wildly. *"An* affair?" She turned back with an angry sweep of her arm. "You say that as if it's something new."

Her mother stared at her, momentarily squelched.

"It's so many things I couldn't begin to name them all," Mary went on. "It's Eric. It's that Hank is bent on turning him into a miniature duplicate of himself."

"What's the matter with that?" her mother said challengingly. "All fathers want their sons to be extensions of themselves."

Mary went to the love seat and sat down, rubbing her forehead. "Hank took Eric hunting last week. I didn't like it at all—a six-year-old out in the woods, using a rifle. The kick practically knocks him over. Hank actually 'helped' Eric shoot a deer."

Mildred took a seat opposite her daughter, listening intently.

"Eric was overexcited, wanting to prove himself to the men. He didn't get a good enough look before he shot," Mary continued despairingly. "It turned out to be a fawn, and not even a yearling. Eric was completely devastated. I just thank God Hank didn't 'help' him shoot some poor ranger."

To Mary's vexation, her mother responded with a chuckle.

"I'm sure Hank thought he was going to do something that would build the boy's character. And he's probably right," Mildred stated, returning to her usual stern, authoritarian manner. "If you always had your way Eric could grow up to be too soft."

Mary glared at her.

"If you were really thinking about Eric, you would never have left Hank," her mother went on. "And what if you did get a divorce? Oh, you might find another man of some stature—if you were very, very lucky. But to find a man of Hank's stature would be a miracle. You're still attractive, but realistically, you're already thirty-two years old; the bloom is off the rose. You know that, don't you?"

Mary emitted an angry sigh as she stood. "Get to the point, Mother."

"What if you weren't lucky? You'd probably be comfortable enough—but your position would be gone. I don't think there's a sorrier creature than the ex-wife of an important man. Now you keep company with all the best people. You're invited to the White House. Wherever you go, you're accorded first-class treatment. Do you think any of that would last?"

"I've had plenty of time to think about all that," Mary replied. "I've thought about it for years."

"You would be out in the cold, while Hank would remarry"—Mildred snapped her fingers—"like that. He's a man who needs a wife. Then, of course, there would be children . . ."

Mary stared at her, her face darkening.

Her mother shook her head with the smug look Mary detested. "Do I have to make it any clearer? You've seen what usually happens to children from first marriages when there are children from new marriages. The father starts to distance himself from the older ones. With babies at home, he feels young again.

"Soon all the attention, all the gifts, all the introductions to people who can be important to Eric later on—everything would be channeled into the new family."

"That wouldn't happen with Eric!" Mary cried.

"And of course," her mother continued dryly, as if Mary had said nothing, "there is an inheritance to think about."

Mary angrily resumed her stance in front of the fireplace,

her arms crossed. "There are more important things than money and social standing."

Her mother wafted up behind her, her watery, faded eyes glittering over Mary's shoulder as she said, "Name one."

A pause. A beat.

"Love."

"Whose love? Hank dotes on Eric. And I know Eric worships Hank." Mary didn't answer. A closer look, and her mother saw a tear sliding down her cheek.

"*Your* love? You're not in love with someone else?"

Mary nodded.

"Oh, don't be a fool!" exhorted her mother.

"I'm the soul of discretion," Mary answered. "If I weren't, I wouldn't be here. Frankly, I came because it's the one place I felt I could go without raising anyone's suspicions." She shook her head, eyes trained on the flames. "Not that I wouldn't leave Hank for . . . this man . . . if I could."

Mildred Carstairs moved stiffly to the coffee table and extracted a cigarette from a large silver box. She shut the lid with a firm snap and stood, fuming.

"This is so unlike you, Mary. I can't believe you'd consider throwing away all you have because of some naïve romantic notion. You know as well as I do how quickly men's passions fade."

Mary suppressed a small smile.

"Does Hank know?" her mother asked.

"No, and he's not going to. I'm leaving him because our marriage is dead. No other reason. It's dead and gone to dust."

"It's not," her mother persisted. "You have a partnership."

Mary looked back at her with curiosity.

"As I said, Hank is the kind of man who has to have a wife. You've trained him to rely on you. You're part of his social life, part of his image. You've invested thirteen years in this marriage, in Hank, from the time he was far less important a man than he is now. You helped build him. How can you even dream of throwing it all away?"

"There is no love," Mary repeated hoarsely. "There hasn't been in so long."

"Then you must adjust. You can, you know. I did."

Mary made a helpless gesture. She had no answer for that.

"It will be far worse if you disrupt Hank's life," her mother told her. "He'd never forgive you. He's a vengeful man. Think about how that could affect you—and Eric."

Finally, Mildred had managed to strike a chord.

After a long silence, Mary shook her head. "Funny," she said softly, "when I packed those bags and walked out that door, I felt as though a thousand-pound weight had been lifted from my shoulders. I was a free and independent woman. It took me years to be ready to do that."

"You'll never be ready to do that," her mother retorted. "I raised you to be a lady."

Even as Mary's mother was feverishly trying to talk her into returning to Los Angeles, Hank was mapping out retribution.

He was royalty in the Hollywood kingdom, and, as he was about to make drastically clear, he could shut the gates of his castle to Mary with a resounding clang if he chose to do so.

When she did return, a mere four days later, she found that Hank, too, had left their Beverly Hills home, but not before he had had all the locks changed and put the estate up for sale.

Mary went across the street to the home owned by Sheilah Smith, where the actress's personal secretary was working in her absence.

"I need to use a telephone," Mary tensely said—and that was all she had to say before Sheilah's bright, close-mouthed employee led her to a study where she could make calls in private.

There, Mary soon discovered that her and Hank's unlisted phone numbers had been disconnected with no referral. Hank's office number yielded not the familiar voice of Hank's longtime secretary, but that of a stranger at a new answering service.

"They're on vacation," Mary was told. "Would you care to leave a message?"

Mary then phoned the Kahala Hilton and asked for Sheilah Smith herself.

"What a surprise," Sheilah said at the sound of Mary's voice. Then she added chillingly, "Did Eric forget something?"

"What do you mean?"

"Hank called two days ago and wanted us to put him on the first plane back. . . . Didn't you know?"

Mary's next call was to their attorney, who was also an old buddy of her husband's.

"Sorry to hear about you and Hank," he said uncomfortably.

"Where is he?" Mary asked.

Silence.

"I'm his wife, goddamnit!" she screamed. "You're going to be sorry later on if you don't give me the number now!"

"Wait a mintue, Mary. Settle down. You're understandably upset, but it won't do you any good to get angry at me."

"Just give me the number!"

"I don't have a number. Hank is traveling."

"Where?"

"I'm not exactly sure."

"Does he have Eric with him?"

Silence.

"Does he have Eric with him? . . . *Where is Eric?*"

"The Greensborough Academy. Didn't you know . . . uh . . . isn't that where you had decided on enrolling him?"

Far from deciding, she had actively resisted the idea. The last Mary had heard, they had all agreed to think about it for the following year. Greensborough had been Hank's idea. Eric had pretended to be delighted about the prospect of boarding school, but then, he would do anything to please Hank.

At the thought of her little boy left confused, alarmed, and all alone in a strange place, Mary at last broke down. "How could he?" she whispered into the receiver.

The attorney listened in deep distress; he hated the situation in which he had been placed. Evans was the one who paid the bills, but, he reasoned, it might be wise to gamble on the side of history—that the Evanses would get back together—and be helpful to Mary.

"Please," she begged in tears. "Tell me everything."

The attorney finally told her that Hank's secretary had been dispatched to the military school with Eric that very morning to get him admitted and to pay a year's tuition in advance.

Then, reluctantly, he told Mary that Hank had accepted a friend's invitation to spend a few days in Palm Springs. Hank was planning to attend a Boys' Club benefit gala at the Racquet Club without her—an act, Mary instantly realized, that would be tantamount to making a public announcement of their separation.

The fund-raiser was certain to have a large turnout of celebrities, in addition to the political heavyweights in whom Hank was increasingly interested—and in addition to the press. And no one would fail to notice the absence of Hank Evans's wife by his side.

Even as she hung up the phone, Mary knew exactly what she would have to do, and she knew she would have to do it immediately. If news of their split got out, it would be that much harder. And Hank would be that much meaner.

It was late afternoon, and the fact that there was still a gaping hole in his column was taking the edge off of Lorne Wagner's anticipation of the evening's party. There was really little for him to do in preparation for the sit-down dinner for forty. He noted smugly that there was not even any need to recheck the seating arrangements. Every person on the impressive list of industry leaders he had invited would be there —a testament to his clout as the star columnist of the *Los Angeles Journal*.

Ezra White was not only catering the food, he had also arranged for the lavish floral centerpieces, the musicians, butlers, maids, and bartenders, and the festive candy-striped tent that was being hoisted beside the pool.

It was all gratis, of course—in exchange for a paragraph or two of praise for White, "Hollywood's premiere party planner."

Other plugs in the column—for Beverly Hills jewelry stores and haberdashers, five-star foreign hotels and local gourmet restaurants—made it possible for Wagner to live in the luxurious style of the luminaries about whom he wrote, while paying taxes on a newspaperman's salary. He was even provided with a new Mercedes "on loan" each year by a motion picture producer who was a partner in an auto-leasing firm specializing in imported luxury cars.

The *Journal* had strict rules against employees accepting even token gifts, but the paper looked the other way when it came to Lorne Wagner's payoffs and deals.

Wagner settled into the leather chair behind the desk at his home in the Flatlands of Beverly Hills. He still needed a couple hundred words before he could put the column to bed. He leafed through his Rolodex, flipped past the unlisted phone numbers of the Newmans and the McQueens, paused at the card that had the name and telephone number of a top agent who was among his key sources of information. For three weeks, ever since she had given a story to Joyce Haber, his competition at the *L.A. Times,* Wagner had been punishing the agent—refusing to accept her phone calls. It seemed a good time to exhibit forgiveness.

"When was the last time Vicki phoned?" Wagner called out to his secretary.

"Yesterday," came the voice from the next room.

"Get her for me and say I'm returning her call."

"You're giving in?"

"Maybe."

Within a minute, the agent was on the line.

"What timing!" she cried. "Lorne, have I got a hot one for you. Hank and Mary Evans are *pffft.*"

"No!" He beamed. "Where did you get it?"

"You won't tell anyone?"

"Need you ask?"

"Joy Knight, the realtor. But be careful. Nothing is official yet. I just heard that Mary's left and he's putting the house on the market."

"Vicki, I love you!"

Nervous about the consequences of running the material without checking it out—and lacking the time to secure confirmation—Wagner decided to write it as a blind, or at least myopic, item.

What tall-in-the-saddle Texas-born movie hero is about to become a lone star? It's marriage on the rocks for him and Mrs. E. . . .

The sun had just slipped behind the summit of San Jacinto Mountain, which now held the desert city below in the palm of its shadow-glove.

Photographers had assembled near the canopied brick entrance of the Racquet Club of Palm Springs, through which dozens of socialites and luminaries were soon to pass.

For decades, the posh club, presided over by Janet Gaynor's one-time leading man Charlie Farrell, had attracted presidents, royalty, social register names on the order of Ford, Lodge, and du Pont—and most of all, the brightest lights of Hollywood. Mike Todd and Elizabeth Taylor had honeymooned there, as had Robert Wagner and Natalie Wood,

Ginger Rogers and Jacques Bergerac, Rock Hudson and Phyllis Gates.

The hot-blooded Latin siren Lupe Velez had once emptied the club's bar and dining room of men, drawing them poolside like a magnet by shedding her sarong and taking a moonlit swim unencumbered. Prince Philip of Britain and his polo team had been introduced to the twist at the legendary place. And Howard Hughes was remembered for his unusual luggage—a paper sack.

Now, if anything went wrong with Mary's plan, the club might add to its claims to fame by becoming the place where Hank Evans's wife made a pathetic spectacle of herself.

Few noticed the limousine that remained motionless, its motor purring, at the far end of the drive fronting the hotel. In the corner of the back seat, wearing a newly purchased black and white Dior gown, sat Mary—feeling her nerves grow more taut with each passing moment.

"There," she called to the driver. "Pull up behind that Rolls."

The limo nosed behind the Silver Cloud. She waited a second, then another, anxious that her timing be exact. Then, as a valet opened the door of the Rolls, she lightly stepped out onto the drive, a smile snapped brightly in place.

Hank didn't notice her until she swept in beside him. He shot her a quick, dumbfounded look before he regained his composure and she gained control of his elbow. Together they walked along the sidewalk and into the hotel, smiling for the photographers and Hank's fans.

If there was one thing Mary could count on, it was Hank's aversion to public scenes.

"What the hell are you doing here?" he whispered through his smile, as the cameras surrounding them flashed and clicked.

"Did you expect me to lie down and play dead?" she beamed. "What did you tell Eric?"

A middle-aged man in a plaid jacket approached with his autograph book open to an empty page. "*Montana Train* is my favorite movie. If you could just . . . if you could just . . ."

Hank made his mark—and it was indeed a mark, for his signature had no recognizable letters in it—and returned the album with a lukewarm I'm-a-nice-guy-but-don't-push-it smile.

He and Mary walked through the hotel complex, toward the grand ballroom.

"How the hell did I know what you were going to do?" Hank muttered.

"I told you I would be back before Eric came home. How dare you try to punish me like this."

"What I heard was, 'We're finished.' And as far as I'm concerned, we are."

"Don't push me any further, Hank . . ." Mary broke off as she noticed a silver-haired couple from Rancho Mirage who carried tremendous weight in their political party. "Hello, there!" she said brightly as she and Hank went into their act. And so it went, couple after couple, group after group— Dinah Shore with author Tommy Thompson, the John Waynes, the Bob Hopes, the James Stewarts, the Gregory Pecks, the Kirk Douglases, the Bing Crosbys.

For the next hour and a half, the argument was put on hold as the Evanses conversed with powerful friends about Hollywood, about Washington, about the disgraceful new permissiveness in films, President Johnson's Far East tour, the Malaysian-style village being constructed near Malibu for Hank's upcoming movie project, civil rights, and the miniskirt.

Seated together at a prime table for ten—causing a certain degree of distress among the banquet room staff, which had expected Evans to be a party of one—they ate roast beef and apricot mousse and listened to speeches.

All the while, neither gave the slightest hint of the anger raging between them.

Mary was fearful that Hank would keep his vow, that once they left the club his "we're finished" fiat would again go into effect. She had to settle things—now.

As the first notes of a fox trot sounded from the orchestra, she found her chance.

"Darling, we haven't danced together in ages," she crooned.

Hank sighed slightly, then put on his I'm-just-an-ol'-softie smile for the benefit of their table companions.

On the dance floor, she immediately began stating her case. "Let's be adult about this, Hank. There are things you want and things I want . . ."

* * *

The next morning, Lorne Wagner's item was a hot topic of gossip in studio commissaries, executive suites, Nate 'n Al's deli, the Polo Lounge. The next afternoon, Hank's lawyer was drafting an angry retraction demand. Hank was threatening to sue Wagner and the *Journal,* loudly decrying Wagner's "scurrilous lies."

By the following week, a reporter and a photographer from a prestigious weekly magazine were trekking out from New York to Beverly Hills to do a major at-home layout on the devoted Evanses.

"That item?" Mary responded to the interviewer's question. "It's a mystery to me. We're as happy as we've ever been."

PART 2

The Young Woman

NINE

THE GARDEN ROYALE was a third-rate nightclub on the edge of New Orleans' famed French Quarter—a club that appeared dingy and tawdry even from the outside.

Still, when Ann spotted a WAITRESS WANTED sign in the dusty display window of the lounge, her attention was captivated. She had had her fill of trying to eke out a living on kitchen and cleaning jobs. Cocktail waitresses made more money than she had ever earned. Seedy as it might be, Ann rationalized, the Garden Royale looked upscale compared to the Istanbul club she remembered with so much grief.

She squared her shoulders and went inside.

The long, narrow shotgun barroom was only half full. It was midafternoon. The blades of the ceiling fans made ineffectual swipes at the cigarette smoke that rose through the gloom. Ann followed the sound of Dixieland into an adjoining courtyard, where members of the club's six-piece house band were rehearsing a number with a female impersonator who was featured in the Royale's late-night revue.

Ann stood awkwardly on the sidelines until the music faded, then approached the piano player, a middle-aged man with a sleepy, weather-beaten, hound dog face, and asked shyly where she could find the manager.

"What do you want him for?" snapped the musician.

"I came to ask about the waitress job."

He laughed and shook his head, then took a slug from the tumbler sitting atop the upright piano and wiped his mouth on the sleeve of his faded pinstripe shirt. The rest of the band rose to take a break, walking by Ann as if she were invisible.

"Is the job taken?" she persisted.

The piano player stood and stretched. "Run along home, darlin'."

Ann stayed put.

"Oh, hell, you wanna talk to the boss?" The piano player motioned to the top of an iron stairway. "Up there."

Ann found the small office at the end of the second-floor hallway, and from there it was easy. The manager didn't even question her identification.

The next day she joined the ranks of the Garden Royale waitresses, outfitted in too short black dirndl skirts, too skimpy white off-the-shoulder tops, and too high heels.

It was a long, long way from her life in New York.

The journey Ann had taken to New Orleans had been hard and frightening. She had traveled to Louisiana looking for some sense of connection, hoping to find it in the city in which her father had been born and raised. Instead, she had found profound loneliness—with no solace from the men who had been attracted too her quiet beauty and vulnerability.

By the age of seventeen, Ann had trusted the affection briefly lavished on her by several men—a college boy, an Army private, a businessman. Not knowing that her aura of unguarded, haunted loneliness shone like a beacon to those who would save her and those who would exploit her alike, Ann had been hurt again and again. Her mother's oft-repeated message—*A woman is nothing without a man*—was deeply etched into her soul.

She went by Ann Peters now; one of her first acts in New Orleans had been to change her name. She had been terrified that Hank Evans might find her and punish her in some way, as if that dreadful night aboard the *Timor* had been *her* fault.

She had since outgrown her unreasoning fear, becoming mature enough to realize that, realistically, bringing her back into his life would be the last thing Evans would choose to do.

Nonetheless, Ann Peters she had become, borrowing her father's first name, and Ann Peters she remained.

Ann had called "home" many times since her arrival in town. Lyla had wept with relief the first time Ann had reached her, but then, all at once, she had turned on Ann in a rage: "I don't care where you are. Don't come back. You made your decision, now you have to live with it."

As time passed, from conversation to conversation, Lyla's response to Ann's voice varied from loving concern to icy hostility to panicky evasiveness.

"Call only when Joe isn't home," Lyla had instructed.

"No, you can't say hello to Cindy," she'd curtly refused.

The news of their mother's death had brought a momentary return to closeness. Ann had written to the American consul in Turkey hoping to get help in contacting Ezel. She had then learned of her mother's lost battle against cancer.

Ann could hear Lyla crying on the phone when she told her about the correspondence. Her own tears fell silently.

Suddenly, she heard Lyla catch her breath: "It's Joe . . . he's home." And she hung up—but not before Ann got her to reluctantly agree to send her a picture of Cindy, the one tangible reminder of her daughter she would have to carry with her over the years.

It had not occurred to Ann that leaving New York would mean total separation from her daughter and her sister. She had made a snap decision, desperate for Cindy to have a real father and a real home—so much more than Ann could have given her at the age of fifteen, unmarried and poor. In the beginning, yes, she had expected that Lyla might have a hard time reconciling Joe Mantussi to the truth. But Ann had also expected that later, once the family was secure, she could somehow reestablish her ties, even if it had to be from a distance.

After nearly three years, however, Ann had realized that although Joe knew all about her, he would not accept the presence of Cindy's natural mother in his—or the child's—life.

As for Lyla, she was clearly afraid of her husband. Ann was certain that her sister was unable to challenge Mantussi on her behalf.

Ann's happiness over landing her new job was quickly punctured by the Garden Royale piano player, whose name, she learned, was Jim Henley.

Her first night at the club, he blocked her path and grumbled, "How do they feel at home about you working here?"

"Nobody's there to feel anything," Ann answered, and edged around him. "Excuse me."

He looked after her, shaking his head.

Waitresses were expected to put up with the pinching fingers and grabbing hands of "friendly" customers and to maintain a good-sport smile. An open threat of violence had to be evidenced before the bouncers would go into action . . . if then.

Sure enough, Ann had an encounter with such a patron less than two hours into her first shift. Henley's back arched as a drunk yanked at Ann's arm, pulling her roughly atop his lap. Grinning vapidly through stained yellow teeth, he beseeched, "Honey, ya just gotta go out with me. I got money." He looked around at his companions. "And I'm clean," he added.

"How about another round?" said Ann as she tried to pull free.

"Let her get us another round," one of his friends called out.

The drunk released her, but not before putting her hand to his lips. "I'll be waiting, sweet baby. Now that I've found you, I'm not going to let you go."

Henley saw Ann move back toward the bar. He sighed and closed his eyes for a moment, then slowly, grudgingly, got up from the piano and casually sauntered over to the table.

"You know whose girl she is, don't you?" Henley asked the drunk. "Leland Lester's. I'm just warning you because things got pretty ugly for the last fella who made a pass at her. He had his knees broken by some of Lester's friends."

Before the night was through, Henley had imparted similar stories to two more of Ann's overzealous admirers and convinced yet a third that she was engaged to a Green Beret known as The Scalper who was on leave and due at the club at any moment.

Against his will, Jim Henley had taken Ann under his wing. She was so obviously vulnerable, so damned young.

After a few weeks, he discovered Ann was interested in singing. He led her to the upright and suggested she give it a try.

Ann tentatively launched into "Bye, Bye Blackbird." As she went along, she gained volume and momentum, catching the attention of the few customers who sipped drinks nearby.

The girl's appearance was far more impressive than her

voice. Her scanty uniform accentuated her full, firm bust, her narrow waist, and her magnificent long legs. Her mass of dark hair was caught up atop her head in thick rolls, with only wisps of bangs escaping onto her forehead. Heavy eyeliner and dangling white cube earrings completed the pseudosophisticated look Ann had affected as camouflage for her youth.

As she finished the song, a customer called out, "Hey, gorgeous! If you're done screeching, how about getting me a drink?" Mortified, she went to take his order.

"Don't feel too bad. You can carry a tune," Henley asured her when she returned to his side. "You're just going to have to do a lot of work if you want to be a singer."

Ann worked hard, finding practice a good way to fill her lonely hours. The promise of a singing debut with the band became her primary focus, her overriding preoccupation.

Eventually, Henley was impressed enough with her progress to convince the bandleader to let Ann try singing a song onstage at about four A.M., just before the band packed up for the night. It turned out to be a good idea gone awry. The noise of the cleanup crew drowned out Ann's soft voice. The few drunks left in the place were too preoccupied with their whiskies to even look in her direction.

Henley was determined not to let Ann give up after such an unfortunate start. Although shaken, she agreed to try again. The next night was better. Her rendition of "Muddy Water" won the attention of several tables of customers. Even the busboys interrupted their work to applaud.

"Feel better?" Henley asked.

"Yes," she answered happily.

He smiled slightly. The expression looked foreign on a face whose muscles had long ago atrophied into a frown.

"Now you can quit if you want to," he kidded, knowing full well that she wouldn't.

Ann made her inauspicious singing debut in November. By January, everyone at the Garden Royale was aware that she regularly stayed long after her shift to sing two or three tunes.

In February, Henley persuaded the bandleader to let Ann sing a few numbers earlier in the night—a practice the manager of the club soon stopped.

"You know better than that," he ridiculed the bandleader. "We can't have a novice out there singing during Mardi gras."

During carnival season, the scene at the Garden Royale became a near rendition of a riot. Ann left work each night with fresh bruises from being crushed against tables, chairs, and bodies. She was worn to a frazzle by the time it was nearly over, but the biggest challenge was yet to come.

When Ann reported for work on Monday evening, Henley took her aside.

"I've got news for you," he said, looking pleased with himself. "One of the 'girls' has a friend who's an important guy in Hollywood. He'll be here tomorrow, and he's all primed to hear you. Be ready to go on at nine o'clock; we've got it all fixed. You'll do 'Baby Doll' the real sexy way. Lots of growl. You've been practicing, haven't you?"

She didn't understand. The "girls," as Henley referred to the Garden Royale's cast of female impersonators, did indeed have a large following within the high-powered homosexual substructure of show business, and the Garden Royale was a magnet when these men visited New Orleans. They invariably arrived for the late show, the one that featured the impersonators, and then took off into the night to make the rounds of the gay clubs.

"But why would he . . ." Ann's voice trailed off, and she shook her head.

"His name is Carl Adams. He's supposed to have helped turn Kim Novak into a star," Henley went on. "Maybe he can give you some advice, help you a little."

"Thank you," Ann faltered, still confused. "You don't know . . . I'm really grateful." Then she asked, "How did you get the okay for me to sing?"

She couldn't help but be suspicious. If the manager hadn't wanted her to perform during Mardi gras, why would he agree to let her go on stage at the climax of all the celebration?

Henley gazed downward for a second or two, then he reached into his pocket.

"I forgot to give you your costume," he said, opening his hand.

Ann gaped at the two red-sequined, tasseled pasties and the g-string that rested in his palm.

She grimaced. "Oh."

"I just said," Henley cut her off, *"I forgot to give you your costume."*

He stuck the articles back into his pocket. "Bring a nice dress."

"Jim," Ann said, "you could get into trouble."

"It wouldn't be the first time. They'll get over it."

"I don't want to cause you any problems."

"Well, then, Sunshine," Henley drawled, "you'd better do a good job."

The next night, as prearranged with Henley, Ann disappeared into the ladies room at a quarter to nine and slipped into a straight-line, shocking-pink crêpe minidress. She edged unnoticed into the lounge and watched as the Pearl Bailey impersonator finished his routine. Then, her heart racing wildly, she hurried toward the stage, barely hearing "Pearl" exhort the audience to welcome a singer "who looks an awful lot like one of our little waitresses."

He winked as he passed Ann on the steps at stage left.

"Get nasty," he advised.

The spotlight blinded her, but she could feel the presence of the crowd. Too soon, she heard her lead-in. She felt unprepared, in a daze, as she began to sing. The audience listened to her first few bars with increasing restlessness. Ann was on the verge of losing them completely when Henley's instructions popped into her mind: "The real sexy way . . . lots of growl."

Suddenly, her body surged with the music. Dipping her shoulder down and tilting her head back, she breathily crooned, "I want to be somebody's baby doll, so I can get my lovin' *all* the time . . ."

The crowd began to whoop and holler.

Magically, the rhythm and the notes felt right, as if she were on some sort of overdrive, functioning outside herself. And they liked her, they were with her. Or, at the very least, they were humoring her.

Then it was over, and she was walking off the stage to the accompaniment of emphatic applause.

"Mel-low!" called Henley. The drummer signaled his agreement with a loud rap on his cymbal, then began the slow beat-comma-beat-comma-beat that heralded the Seven Veils act.

Ann quickly moved toward the front of the club, where "Pearl Bailey" was waiting. "They love you," he exclaimed in a loud stage whisper as he slid from his stool at the bar. In his wake came a tall, slim figure in a blue-velvet Edwardian jacket and ruffled shirt—the important friend.

"Ann, I want you to meet Carl Adams—*the* Carl Adams."

Ann turned and looked up into a puckish face sprinkled with freckles. A black velvet tam was perched atop his bald head. Prepared, from his appearance, for a high, wheezy voice, she was surprised when Carl Adams's words came out in an imperious rat-a-tat blast.

"That was nice, but I think you'd be doing yourself and everyone else a favor by leaving 'Baby Doll' to the Bessie Smith records and getting into something contemporary.

"Outside of that, I liked what I saw—very much. Very much. I want to talk to you before I leave town," he said, pointing at her to emphasize his intent. "Come to the Roosevelt tomorrow at four-thirty."

Ann nodded, and Adams nodded back. With that, he was off, with quick, gliding strides.

Ann moved back toward the bandstand and managed to catch Henley's eye. She nodded and grinned excitedly, giving him an okay sign. He didn't smile back. He shook his head warningly. The manager was standing right behind her.

"I guess you think you're pretty smart, putting one over on me like that. Where's the costume you were supposed to wear?"

Ann pivoted, gasping. She knew she was supposed to act perplexed and innocent; Henley was to take full blame. But her hangdog look gave her away.

"Are you going to put it on for the next show?" he demanded.

She shook her head mutely.

"Then you're out of a job, sister," the manager said in a fury. "Not so funny now, is it?"

Later Henley insisted, "It's nothing to worry about. He just had to blow off steam. I'll get him to change his mind."

But he didn't sound entirely confident.

"Mr. Adams is in the middle of a long-distance call with Bob Evans at Paramount Studios. He's very, *very* important in the movie business," said the blond young man as he led Ann into the hotel suite. He spoke softly and flashed a conspiratorial smile. "It will be a few minutes. May I offer you some tea?"

"No, thank you," Ann replied as she settled into a brocade wing chair.

"Fine," said the man, blinking. Then he left Ann alone to marvel at the plush surroundings.

Ten minutes later, Adams came barreling in and plopped down on the sofa. He wore a quilted green-satin smoking jacket that failed to cover the hem of his silk boxer shorts and his spindly, knobby-kneed legs.

Making reference to the phone call that had occupied him, he sighed dramatically and said, "It's been like this all day. Absolutely mad." Then, as if noticing her for the first time, he added, "Hi."

"Hi," Ann replied.

"We're going to talk about your career, right?" Adams asked with a surprisingly charming smile.

Ann smiled and nodded.

"Okay, before we get started, let me fill you in a bit on what I do. Or did your friends already tell you?"

"They said you're a manager. That you helped Kim Novak with her career."

Adams nodded. "I was at Columbia when the studio decided to groom her to replace Rita Hayworth." He chuckled and shook his head. "Hard to believe, isn't it? That was over ten years ago."

Left unsaid was any mention of his role—if indeed he had had one—in the molding of Novak.

Instead, he went blithely on as if speaking to a child. "You see, Ann, there used to be something in Hollywood called the studio system. That's when all the young actors and actresses were groomed for stardom by the major studios. The studios not only assigned them roles but taught them how to pose for photographs, what to wear, how to behave—all those things. There isn't any studio system today. But for a few lucky people, there's me. I help them develop themselves and their talent. And, if I do say so myself, I've been successful.

"Of course you probably know that Jane Broderick is one of my people," he said. "And Sam Dallas. And I signed Erica Steele before anyone knew who she was."

He hesitated a moment, almost as if anticipating applause.

Ann didn't quite know how to respond. "That's wonderful," she said.

"You have no idea how many times I'm asked to look at new talent, and it almost never amounts to more than my having to tell some kid he'd be better off in accounting. But I must say, you interest me."

"I do?"

"Do you know who I thought of when I saw you out there singing on that stage?"

Ann shook her head.

"Monroe." Adams nodded reverently. "Yes. I thought of Marilyn singing 'Happy Birthday' to Jack Kennedy."

Ann could feel her cheeks burning. *He was joking . . . wasn't he?* But Adams seemed to be serious.

"Ann, if you really want a career you should move to Hollywood. I can help you there," he emphasized, as Ann's eyes widened. "I think you might even have a future in films."

After all the time she had lived in dread of Hank Evans, Ann was suddenly being advised to move to Hollywood, to try to get into his world. She couldn't keep from smiling at the irony, a smile that Adams misread.

"I know. It sounds like a fantasy. But it doesn't have to be," he insisted. "You think about it." He found a business card amid the piles of paper on the coffee table, scrawled on it with a silver fountain pen, then added, "I'm giving you my private phone number. When you come to California—and I know you will—call me and we'll get you started. My house has three guest rooms, so you're welcome to stay with me until you get situated.

"Strictly business," he assured her, glancing up.

Ann smiled slightly.

Adams led her to the door and dismissed her with one final statement: "You do understand, don't you, that there are hundreds of people who would positively kill for the opportunity I've just handed you?"

Ann walked out of the Roosevelt shaking. Was Adams for real? There was certainly no arguing with the fact that he had money—no arguing with Kim Novak and Jane Broderick, either.

How intoxicating to imagine herself a part of the scene Adams had sketched. She tried to envision becoming so rich she would never again have to worry about money; Cindy would never have to worry about money.

It just can't be as simple as he makes it sound, Ann thought, and decided she would probably be wise not to take the whole business too seriously.

It was shortly after six o'clock when Ann reached the Garden Royale. She found Jim Henley sitting at a table in the deserted courtyard, alone with his customary tumbler of bourbon. To Ann's dismay, he was leaning, almost lying, against the back of his chair, his chin on his chest, looking extremely disheveled. He glanced up and mumbled, "What did Adams have to say?"

Ann stopped a few feet from the table and shrugged. "He said a lot of things. He wants me to go to Hollywood. It was all kind of silly."

Henley trained his eyes on her, a strange look of expectation on his face.

"So, when are you leaving?"

Ann waved her hand dismissively. "I'm not going anywhere."

"Why not?"

She looked hard at Henley. "What about my job?"

"I've told you a hundred times, you've got no business here. This place is nothing but a dead end. Please, get the hell out of here. You'll never get a better chance."

She settled into the chair opposite him, gazing at him curiously. Several seconds passed before he spoke. Then, like a man giving a deathbed confession, he muttered, "I've got a son who's never going to see life outside an institution. I've got a wife who doesn't give a damn about anything since we had to put the boy away. And I feel things for you no man in my position has any right to feel. If you don't get out of here, sooner or later I'm gonna do something that'll turn it all sour between you and me."

Henley looked up and made an awkward attempt at a smile. Then he reached across the table, taking Ann's chin in his hand. "Look around you. What do you see?"

She studied her surroundings. Measured against Carl Adams's promises, everything at the Garden Royale seemed particularly dreary and bleak.

"For me, this is the end of the line," Henley said. "For you, Adams could mean a beginning."

"But . . . Jim . . ."

All at once Henley jerked himself upright and violently swept his arm across the table, sending the full ashtray and the empty glass flying. A well of frustration suddenly overflowed.

"Get out! Get out!" His voice broke and he half sobbed, "Get your little ass out that door!"

TEN

THE PORTER GROANED with effort as he heaved the black metal trunk out of the baggage compartment of the bus and shoved it onto the curb.

Rubbing his gloved hands on his coveralls, he glanced up at Ann, standing on the sidewalk with a pasteboard suitcase at her side. It seemed doubtful that this slim young girl in the wilted blue seersucker minidress could deal with such an oversized, overweight piece of luggage. "Are you sure you can handle the trunk by yourself?" he asked skeptically.

"I think so," she replied, upending the twenty-dollar flea market special onto its two tiny wheels and pulling its heavy leather strap over her shoulder. She started off slowly under the strain of the precariously balanced trunk, having learned the hard way, after a seemingly interminable trip, that any excessive speed would send the unwieldy case crashing. After a moment, however, she felt its weight being lifted off her shoulder.

"Where do you want it?" the porter asked.

"Over there, I guess," she answered, pointing toward a bank of pay phones.

The depot was gray and dirty, crowded and noisy, filled with hippies, vagrants, and weary women with fussy, over-tired children.

Somehow, Ann had expected things to look different in Hollywood.

She walked beside the porter through the crowds, uncomfortably aware of the glares from fellow passengers still waiting for their bags to be taken from the bus.

"I hope you don't have a body stashed in here," the porter joked.

"No—just all my worldly possessions."

"I almost believe you."

The porter waved off her attempt to give him a tip.

"If you have some free time," he began, then stopped himself as Ann shook her head, smiling gently. "You have someone coming to meet you, I hope."

"Yes. Thank you."

Despite her exhaustion, Ann was charged with nervous energy.

She rifled through her shoulder bag for Carl Adams's business card and inserted a coin into the slot of the pay phone. She had seen enough of this insanely sprawling city on the long ride into town to realize she could use some advice in locating an inexpensive hotel room.

"Mr. Adams's office." The female voice on the other end of the line was briskly efficient.

"Hello? Yes, this is Ann Peters. Is Mr. Adams there?"

There was a slight pause, then, "He's in a meeting. May I say what this is regarding?"

"I'm the singer from the Garden Royale in New Orleans," Ann explained, just slightly daunted. "He told me to phone when I got into town, and . . . well, I'm here." To her immense distress, Ann found she was punctuating her words with a juvenile, nervous giggle.

"He'll have to get back to you. What's your number?"

"I don't have a number yet."

"Then you'll have to try later."

"Wait!" Ann exclaimed. "I was hoping someone there could give me some advice on a good, inexpensive hotel. Is there any—"

"Hold, please." The voice cut her off. The next sound was the beep of the operator asking for another dime.

Out of the corner of her eye, Ann noticed a shirtless, unshaven young man with a cascade of bushy hair and a flower painted on his cheek. He was waiting to use the phone.

"I'm going to be a while," she told him.

"Peace." He smiled mildly, holding two fingers aloft in a

"V" sign. Ann took this as his way of saying he didn't mind waiting.

Finally, another voice came on the line: "Have you been helped?"

"I wanted to talk to Mr. Adams."

"He's left for the day. What is this regarding?"

After another explanation, another abrupt statement that she would have to call back later, another long wait on hold, Ann's attempt at reaching Adams was finally terminated by the sound of a dial tone.

So it went for four days. The "personal number" Adams had written on the back of his card turned out to be no more than his direct office line. Each of her calls was answered by the same haughty secretary. Adams remained so inaccessible and his aide so cold that Ann not only believed the manager had forgotten her, she came close to wondering whether their New Orleans meeting had been a figment of her imagination.

Frustrated and angry, battling desperation, Ann tried to tell herself it might be for the best. The questions that had plagued her throughout the long cross-country trip were still unanswered. Was Adams a friend of Hank Evans? If so, would Evans recognize her, would he remember her—and take steps to make sure she could not tell the tale of their past?

You're being irrational, she had told herself again and again, whenever her fears of Evans resurfaced. But rational or not, it had been much easier not to worry about him in New Orleans.

Ensconced at the YWCA, trying to get from place to place by bus, constantly surrounded by seedy-looking people, Ann wondered how the city could have such a glamorous reputation. She didn't realize that there was an invisible boundary between the Hollywood in which she was staying and the glittering world whose legend she knew so well. She never would have guessed that certain smartass children of stars laughed about going into "Baja Beverly Hills" on the rare occasions when necessity forced them to leave the confines of their geographically desirable stomping grounds.

She was almost down to her last dollar when she found a job waitressing at a twenty-four-hour drive-in.

But Ann was determined not to give up on Adams until she

had at least spoken to him. Since phone calls had proved ineffective, she had no choice but to try to contact him in person.

The minutes stretched into an hour, then an hour and a half, as Ann sat in the small waiting room furnished with antiques and adorned with vintage movie posters.

The receptionist who had informed her that Adams was out and would be out for most of the day glanced in Ann's direction, raised her eyebrows, and sighed.

Ann barely looked up from her magazine when the door opened again and a tall, trim masculine figure in tight white and black pinstripe slacks and a fringed leather jacket strode past.

"Is Carl back yet?"

"No. I'm so sorry. But it's great to seé you!"

Ann couldn't help but notice that the receptionist was suddenly sparkling with congeniality.

"Well, you too." The man chuckled. "I saw Carl at the El Padrino with Hugh Hefner and Peter Lawford over two hours ago. I'll bet he hasn't even left yet."

"Probably not," the receptionist said laughingly. "Would you like to wait in his office? I can fix you a drink."

"No. I just stopped by to—" He stalled midsentence as he glanced in Ann's direction. A wide smile broke across his face, and Ann smiled back automatically, caught by the sudden intensity of his respnose. ". . . to pick up the contract."

He had the kind of patent-leather good looks television loves: gleaming toothpaste-commercial teeth, a firm chin with a small cleft, doe eyes with heavy lashes, wavy sun-bleached brown hair combed back from a widow's peak.

He turned back to the receptionist. "Could you get the contract for me?"

"Sure," she replied, standing. She hesitated just long enough to shoot a glare in Ann's direction, then disappeared into Adams's private office suite.

The stranger seated himself close to Ann.

"I haven't seen you here before," he said. The way he leaned toward her, the spark in his eyes, his easy, confident grin all spoke of a man who was used to striking up conversations with beautiful women and used to finding himself welcomed.

He had an instant, wildly unsettling effect on her.

"I guess that's because I haven't been here before," she answered with a nervous laugh.

"Is Carl going to represent you?"

"I don't know yet."

"You don't know yet?" he repeated in a gently mocking tone. It was obvious that he was aware he was making her flustered and that he enjoyed the game, which made Ann feel all the more flustered. His eyes delivered a provocative, intimate, silent communication, even as his voice remained light and teasing. "Why don't you know yet?"

"I, um . . . I haven't talked to him since I got here."

"Here to this office or here in town?"

"Town," she said, suddenly feeling like an eight-year-old.

"Where are you from?"

"New Orleans."

"No kidding? That's one place I've never been."

"Oh?"

"But I've always wanted to go there," he added, nodding with mock gravity. He cocked his head. "Maybe you can show it to me sometime."

Somehow, without Ann's even being aware of it, he had taken her hand.

Once again she was reduced to "oh."

"What's your name?"

"Ann . . . Ann Peters."

"So tell me, Ann Peters, did Carl tell you he was going to make you a big star?"

She laughed, nodding. Suddenly it sounded so ridiculous.

He shook his head. "Carl told me the same thing," he huffed in an exaggerated complaining tone. "You know the hardest part about dealing with Carl? Getting him to finish lunch before four o'clock! You're laughing! I'm serious."

At that point, the receptionist returned. The man let go of Ann's hand and coughed, casting her a deliberately overacted conspiratorial look, his eyebrows raised. Ann couldn't stop the laughter that rose in her.

The receptionist, clearly not pleased by the display, produced a manila envelope and handed it to Ann's coconspirator.

"Great." He gave her a broad smile. "You know, on second thought, I could use a glass of ice water. You mind?"

When the receptionist was gone, he turned back to Ann, his shoulders shaking with repressed laughter.

"Now, tell me, Ann Peters, what exactly did Carl say to you?"

"He, uh, said he thought I would have some good opportunities if I came here."

"Uh huh. Opportunities for what? He didn't make a pass at you or anything, did he?"

Ann stared at him. "No," she replied, all at once ill at ease. "He . . . he likes men. . . . At least, that's what I was told."

He feigned a shocked expression, clucking his tongue.

"He doesn't?" she asked breathlessly.

The man grinned, and Ann realized he had been teasing her.

"Well, not *all* the time." He shrugged. He lifted his hand and made a rocking gesture. "Carl likes to think of himself as an equal opportunity kind of guy."

"Oh."

"You'll discover he's always got a nice-looking lady on his arm in public. Sometimes it's his ex-wife."

"But you don't have to worry about Carl," he added dismissively. "He's a pussycat. How did you meet him . . . ?"

Ann began telling him of the Garden Royale meeting, a subject that naturally led to her current plight. After a few minutes, the door flew open and Adams shot into the room.

"Hey, Sam!" Adams said.

Sam. Ann noted the name carefully. Sam what? She watched the two in a blur of anxiety.

"Let me guess," Sam said in greeting. "Four martinis?"

"I had one. Just one."

"I know. You just can't tear yourself away from gossiping with Lawford," Sam said.

Adams shrugged, then his eyes moved to Ann and he flashed her his Mr. Charm smile. "Well, look who's here. So you made it out, did you?"

Ann was so relieved that Carl Adams remembered her, she was ready to forget the unanswered calls. Sam, however, was not.

"She's been trying to reach you for two weeks," Sam told him accusingly. "She's been holed up at the *YWCA* ever since her *bus* got in. She's working at that *drive-in* down on Fountain."

"Oh, God," Adams exclaimed, chortling.

Ann didn't understand the humor of the situation, but it was obvious Sam and Carl found it quite droll. They exchanged a look of merry astonishment; Ann had the uncomfortable sensation she was being made fun of.

"I'm so sorry," Adams told her. "My secretary gets a little overprotective at times." He looked back at Sam. "You know it's been utter madness around here this week."

"So what are you going to do for her?" Sam demanded.

"Do? Why, we're going to do everything. I expect very big things for this girl."

"My. Sounds serious," Sam commented.

Adams turned to Ann. "How soon can you get your things together? I want you to stay at my place until we can find you a nice apartment. Do you have a car?"

"Does she have a car," Sam repeated. "She took the bus to get here and she's staying at the Y. Does she have a car."

Adams cast him a withering look before asking Ann, "Why don't you go right now, and I'll send someone over to pick you up?"

"I'm supposed to be at work by five."

Adams made a face. "Forget about that job."

"Really?"

"Of course, really. I don't want it said that my new star is out pushing the blue-plate special at Rosarita's Drive-in, now do I?"

She looked from Adams to Sam as she backed toward the door. "I hardly know what to say. Thank you so much!"

They watched as she backed into an end table, grabbed the lamp she almost knocked over, and righted it just in time.

"Can we see that again?" Adams added. "You did it so well."

Sam smiled slightly, his arresting gaze focused on Ann's face, his eyes glimmering with mirth.

It was too much all at once, Ann felt. And now she had made the world's biggest fool out of herself.

"Ann," Sam called as she turned toward the door. She looked back and he nodded, his brows arched meaningfully. "I'll catch up with you at Carl's."

"Okay!" she replied, aware that she sounded too eager, but too elated to care.

She stopped in the hallway, taking a deep breath to release

the tension that had built up in her. Then, feeling as if her legs were about to give way, she hurried toward the elevator.

Back in Adams's spacious office, the two men traded views on Carl's new find.

"What do you think?" Adams asked.

"Cute. Appealing, sure," Sam shrugged. "But I don't know why you had her come all the way out from Louisiana. Is she that hot a singer?"

"Are you blind? That girl has something special. She has the vulnerable sensuality of another Marilyn Monroe."

Sam rolled his eyes. "Another Marilyn Monroe!" he repeated with a derisive laugh.

"I'm not kidding."

"She's not even blond!" Sam exclaimed.

"I'm talking about *presence*. I'm talking about *vibes*."

Sam grinned and shrugged. "Whatever you say, Carl. Your instincts have been right so far. I just don't see it."

"I could have sworn you did," Adams said pointedly. "Or wasn't I seeing your famous heavy-on-the-make routine?"

"That doesn't mean she's another Monroe, for chrissakes. Do you realize how frustrating life would be for me if I had to wait for another Monroe to come along before I got turned on?"

"Yes," Adams said snidely, "but fortunately we know you get turned on by anything that walks."

"Fuck you," Sam answered, laughing.

"Seriously," said Carl, smiling complacently as he leaned back in his leather chair, his fingertips touching, "there will be a lot of press at my party for Janie Broderick tomorrow night. I'm going to have my 'new Monroe' at the house; she'll be at the party and, ah, I was just thinking it would be nice if you could pay some attention to her while the press is around. You know, make a little fuss. . . ." His voice trailed off.

"What a tacky idea," said Sam.

Adams leaned forward and spread his stubby fingers out over the green paper blotter on his mahogany desk. "Where would you be without my tacky ideas?"

"What do I get if I do this?"

"I would consider it a favor," Adams said smoothly.

His tone was mild, but his message was clear. Sam needed Carl Adams's professional help—help he could no longer afford.

As Sam pondered the word *favor* Adams added, "Just think about it. Watch this girl tomorrow night. You'll see what I'm saying about her is right."

Palm trees cast fingers of late afternoon shadow across the pavement as Ann sat aboard her trunk in front of the Y, waiting for Carl Adams's driver. She was not prepared for the car that pulled up at the curb. Lacquered red and shimmering with chrome, with an elongated hood and a Lalique radiator ornament in the form of a maiden in a flowing gown, it had the appearance of a stretched-out luxury version of a classic MG. Seated behind the wheel of the Excalibur was the wispy blond youth she had seen in Adams's room at the Roosevelt Hotel; beside him on the ivory doeskin seat was a brunette woman.

"There she is," the driver said to his companion. Pushing back her long hair with an air of boredom, she took Ann in from behind lavender granny glasses.

The blond jumped out. "So," he said with a smile, "we meet again. Ready to go to Carl's house?"

Ann noticed—it would have been hard not to notice—the woman's see-through blouse worn with hip-hugging bell-bottom pants. Both she and the blond were models and aspiring actors who were being helped by Adams, Ann learned as the car made a halting trek through the congested streets of Hollywood.

"Does Mr. Adams know a lot of stars?" she asked, trying to sound casual.

The blond nodded. "Naturally. He's met everyone at one point or another."

"Does he know Hank Evans?"

The woman next to Ann lit a cigarette and leaned back with an amused smile. "Why? Are you a fan?"

"Just curious."

"How about it," she asked the blond driver. "Does Carl know 'The Captain'?"

"No, thank God. Not as far as I know."

Ann laughed aloud with relief. "Why 'thank God'?"

"He's a goddamned redneck warmonger, that's why," said the blond. "And a terrible actor. He *grimaces*. Did you see *Malay Moon*? Ugh! I cringe."

The knowledge that Evans was not among Adams's close acquaintances made Ann feel instantly more at ease. Now, as the gleaming automobile turned onto Sunset Boulevard, Ann found she could enjoy the sights and sounds without a filter of anxiety to darken her view. She watched the parade of colorful characters—fashionable people in designer clothes of stripes and paisleys and psychedelic prints, a sizable flower-child contingent in tattered gear. They passed Sunset Strip clubs with familiar names such as Gazzarri's and the Whisky A Go Go. Billboards screamed the glory of *Bonnie and Clyde* and *Casino Royale*, while radios in passing vehicles blasted out the newly released "Sgt. Pepper's Lonely Hearts Club Band."

Ann looked around in surprise as Sunset changed abruptly from a crowded urban thoroughfare to a sedate boulevard lined by rolling green landscapes and elegant estates. It was her first glimpse of Beverly Hills.

They whisked past the flamingo-pink buildings of the legendary Beverly Hills Hotel and several miles later finally turned right and moved through the white arch that marked the entrance to Bel Air. After cruising through a series of labyrinthian turns, the Excalibur entered the wrought-iron gates of a classic Mediterranean estate.

Moments later, feeling like a peasant invited into the palace of a king, Ann was being escorted through an oval entryway with an indigo-tiled floor and a neoclassical marble nude of Prometheus rising majestically from a crystal pedestal.

Adams greeted Ann over the noise of hammering coming from behind the house.

"I have to leave for a screening in a few minutes," he said, glancing at his watch, "but let me give you a quick look around."

He led Ann through the reception hall, stepping over a rolled carpet and around a crew polishing the patterned marble floor. There were other signs of activity in the formal dining room, where an aluminum scaffold had been set up so that the fourteen-foot-high sky blue ceiling could be cleaned.

"I'm having a party tomorrow night," Adams explained. "That's one of the reasons things have been so chaotic. Now here," he went on without pause, motioning toward a delicate candelabra in the center of the long mahogany table, "is one of my treasures. It was used in *Gone with the Wind*. One of my great passions is collecting objects that have a connection with Hollywood history.

"I have a cherry wood desk that once belonged to Irving

Thalberg." He looked at Ann expectantly, then added, "You know, the great wunderkind studio chief of the Golden Era. You've read *The Last Tycoon* haven't you—F. Scott Fitzgerald's *Last Tycoon*?"

Ann shook her head.

"Well, when you do, keep in mind that Thalberg was the inspiration for Monroe Stahr and think of my desk," Adams instructed. He seemed perfectly serious that she should read the novel in order to appreciate his furniture.

He trotted out of the room at a quick clip, and Ann hurried to follow.

In the bar area, Adams pointed out another of his treasures, an upright piano lacquered blue and covered with white stars. It had been used, he said, in the Judy Garland–Mickey Rooney movie, *Love Finds Andy Hardy*. Atop it were framed, autographed pictures of both stars and another of a young Natalie Wood and Robert Wagner taken shortly after their 1957 wedding, beaming from the bow of a luxury cabin cruiser.

Noticing that Ann's gaze rested on the photo of the couple, Adams remarked, "Aren't they charming? How I'd love to see them get back together."

At the rear of the house, an arched and columned loggia faced Adams's indigo-tiled pool; the manicured garden was partly obscured by a huge red-and-white-striped tent.

"That's for the party," said Adams. "There are a million other things to take care of tomorrow, so I had it set up today."

"I've come at a very inconvenient time, haven't I?" Ann asked apologetically. "You're so busy."

He shrugged. "It's always like this."

Adams's secretary and his houseman were waiting for him at the front door.

"Glenda, this is Ann," said Adams. Then, to Ann's surprise, he added, "She needs a dress for tomorrow night. Call Gianni and take care of it. Try for something in a nice blue to bring out her eyes."

"Mr. Adams, I really can't thank you enough," Ann breathed.

He smiled. "You'll make it up to me someday."

ELEVEN

CARL ADAMS HAD begun describing himself as "terminally star-struck" even before his freshman year at Cleveland's exclusive Oxton Academy, and he had continued to proudly proclaim his fatal attraction for Hollywood headliners after he had become a neighbor and confidant of the town's most influential names.

By his early teens he could answer the most obscure movie-star trivia questions; he could recite endless setside anecdotes, though he had no closer contact to a soundstage than the entertainment industry research books and the gossip columns whose contents he eagerly devoured.

He wanted to be a person of power and influence in Hollywood, a man who created stars and movies, and, most of all, he wanted to be an intimate of show business luminaries. He was well on his way toward achieving those goals before he ever set foot in California. For when Adams arrived in Los Angeles in 1954, he came equipped with the one tool guaranteed to bring him instant popularity and an entrée into the movie business—

Money.

Once word spread through town that Carl's family was the Fortune 500 Adams clan whose name was stamped on paper products ranging from grocery bags to toilet tissue, he found plenty of eager would-be friends and business partners.

But Adams turned out to be hardheaded about just where and how he would invest his considerable portion of the family fortune. He didn't care to be considered a dilettante. He wanted to be a celebrity. And he wanted to be admired and feared.

His first act in Hollywood was to land a job in the press department of Columbia Pictures.

Later, he made much of his employment there—when his former coworkers were out of earshot—crowing about the stars and the films that had been hyped by the studio at the time of his employment, as if he had had a major role in planning and executing all the important campaigns. In truth, it had been less than three months before Adams had grown impatient with his underling status and had left Columbia for greener pastures.

That is, he had bought his way into a position at a theatrical agency.

Years afterward, he talked of his "lean days as a fledgling agent," his struggles on the way up.

"I lived on my salary during the entire time," he would report proudly, attempting to prove that he had made it on his own, without relying on family funds.

He never realized that behind his back, he was snickered at for making living on a salary sound like a remarkable achievement.

After less than a year of that harsh existence, Adams had rented plush Beverly Hills office quarters and announced, with lavish fanfare, the opening of Carl Adams Management.

Now—twelve years, dozens of clients, three movie deals, and one marriage later—the manager/sometime-producer/full-time wheeler-dealer felt secure about his place in Hollywood. He was satisfied the industry crowd no longer thought of him as "Carl Adams, the Adams Paper heir."

It was true. By the time he invited Ann to become one of *his* people, Adams was known primarily as one of Hollywood's premier party givers.

Drastically dwindling box office receipts were making austerity programs the order of the day as studios teetered on the brink of bankruptcy. The broadly ballyhooed first night Hollywood functions were neither as lavish nor as well-populated by celebrities as they had been just a few years earlier.

Time-honored filmland social gatherings drew those who didn't count much in the business any longer—Cesar Romero, Zsa Zsa Gabor, Jack Oakie—while the rising crop of turned-on Tinseltown elite scorned klieg-light openings and other traditional affairs. The likes of Roman Polanski and Sharon Tate, Jim Brown, Candy Bergen, and Doris Day's rebel son, Terry Melcher, kept themselves separate as privileged members of private counterculture sets.

The situation made Adams's parties all the more attractive.

Next door to Adams's Bel Air Road manse, John and Michelle Phillips had recently moved into the English Tudor mansion that was Jeanette MacDonald's former home—and the married Mama and Papa's headquarters had quickly turned into a prime late-night gathering spot of the switched-on set.

A steady parade of their friends, with their long hair and hippie clothes, raised the eyebrows of many of their establishment neighbors. But Adams adored being so close to the happening crowd. And Adams, with his whatever-turns-you-on attitude and his ever-plentiful supply of great gossip and the finest drugs money could buy, was also a welcome neighbor.

He was unestablishment enough to be acceptable to the Now clique, yet he was such an unabashed lover of old-style filmland flair that he also had popularity with the veteran guard of industry powers. To the gay fraternity, Adams was one of its own. In short, he had a suitable face for any occasion—and the best of several worlds.

As times grew worse in the industry, Adams's parties stood out by becoming ever more opulent. His affairs drew the key media people who could be instrumental in promoting Carl's clients, his projects, and Carl himself. They became such a prime ticket to seeing and being seen by those who counted that uniformed guards were on duty to check invitations and screen guests.

There were other parties that Adams gave to which no media was invited—intimate gatherings most often held at his beach estate tucked in the foothills near Point Dume, gatherings that became legendary for their debauchery.

Adams had four walls knocked out of his seaside hideaway, transforming the study and several adjoining rooms into one grand salon. He held court there, surrounded by young male and female beauties, slipping off from time to time to one of the upstairs rooms that were equipped with erotic art, mirrored walls and ceilings, king-sized beds, and a phantasmagoria of sexual devices. There was a fifteen-foot marble Roman plunge bath in the huge upstairs bathroom, an indoor swimming pool off the ground-floor salon that was kept at a constant eighty degrees, and a sauna that could hold a platoon.

Some of Hollywood's hottest, brightest lights popped up at his Malibu bashes—to look, to mingle, to make contact with someone else's husband or wife, or both. Adams knew he was often the topic of delicious gossip at the chic spots, that the chic people would giggle and gasp and whisper, "Have you heard about Carl Adams's parties in Malibu? Have you ever been to one? You'll never guess who was there the other night . . ."

"You're lucky Carl sent me instead of going with you himself," the secretary, Glenda, told Ann as they drove toward the Beverly Hills flats the morning after Ann's arrival.

"He adores shopping but he has no taste. None. And what makes it worse is that he wants so badly to have it. He'll ask, 'How about that for style?' or 'Do I have class or do I have class?'"

Ann said quickly, "His house is beautiful."

"Credit a decorator for that."

"It's so nice of him to let me stay there; I hate to impose."

"You don't need to worry about imposing on Carl," the secretary snapped. "He wouldn't have you there if he didn't think he could get something out of you. Besides, he likes being surrounded by pretty people. I'm sure he's looking forward to showing you off."

By the time they reached the flatlands of Beverly Hills, Adams's secretary had made it evident that she considered herself the indispensable ingredient in Adams's success. She also made it clear that she was not adequately appreciated.

Ann could barely wait to get out of the car.

The entrance to Salerno's made her marvel. The shop was fronted by two-story walls of glass flanked by green marble and gold filigree. The interior, and all its contents, screamed elegance. As Ann padded behind Glenda into the hushed quiet of the huge boutique, it crossed her mind that Salerno's was like a shrine.

Glenda, however, was in no mood for reverence. She was in a tearing hurry.

"We don't have time to wander," she warned in a sharp schoolmarm tone when Ann hesitated by a counter with a display of lavish silk scarves.

Nevertheless, Ann couldn't help stopping short at the sight of Ann-Margret emerging from a fitting room in a stunning pink Rudi Gernreich minidress and tights.

A Salerno clerk approached and asked, "Would you care for some tea, espresso, perhaps a glass of Chardonnay?"

"How nice," Ann smiled. "I'd—"

"We have no time." Glenda cut her off. Then she clamped a cold hand on Ann's arm and tugged her along toward the rear of the shop. In less than two minutes, she had selected an abbreviated ice-blue tea dress with a cloud of organza ruffles and ripples and sent Ann to the dressing room where she was to try it on.

Irritating as she was, she didn't dampen Ann's excitement one bit. And that excitement was renewed when Ann heard a tantalizingly familiar English voice just outside the dressing room door.

"I can't decide."

"It would go wonderfully with those silk harem pants," answered a second woman.

Ann peered out just in time to see Julie Christie slipping out of a magnificent, long, midnight blue Damascus brocade coat.

She couldn't help giggling as she recalled her first impression of the seedy side of Hollywood.

Glenda took one look at Ann in the tea dress and quickly decided, "That will be fine."

"Fine" was hardly an adequate word, thought Ann as she reluctantly took off the Donald Brooks creation.

Had she known the price, she would have been shocked into disbelief—it was more than a half year's rent on the apartment she had shared in New Orleans. Not that Carl would have to concern himself with payment for the dress; he had an arrangement with Gianni Salerno that provided for the loan of gowns to Carl's clients in exchange for Adams's endorsement of the shop.

It was just one of Adams's endless deals.

Ann felt as if she had been caught up in the vortex of a whirlwind. If the mood at Adams's home had been chaotic on Thursday, by Friday it was frenzied, with armies of workmen and caterers and delivery men swarming about the house and grounds.

By evening, blankets of ivory roses—the first cutting of the season—covered the stone wall fronting the mansion. Lavender tulips, air-freighted from Holland, entwined with baby's breath and white orchids, cascaded in wild profusion down the banisters of the reception area. The floral theme was repeated on the fences of the tennis court, where a dance floor and a twelve-piece orchestra had been installed, as well as in the Barnum and Bailey—sized tent where seating and a feast for two hundred were being set up.

As Ann dressed for the party, she studied herself in the mirror, reverently touching the silky ruffles of the designer dress that draped her slender body.

Would that nerve-rattling man named Sam be there to appreciate it? She wondered and shivered in anticipation.

For a moment, the dream that had sustained her on the cross-country bus ride, through the nights of barren moonlit landscapes and the days of shimmering desert sun, sprang to life again.

She was walking up the steps of Lyla's home; her sister was standing at the door, arms outstretched, smiling. She felt the warmth of Lyla's tight, enveloping hug. From the backyard, her child came romping in, laughing, her eyes bright with happiness. Ann caught Cindy in her arms. "She's going to have it better than we did," she told Lyla. "We never have to worry about money again."

She started at the knock on the door.

"Are you all right?" called the houseman. "Mr. Adams asked me to tell you, most of the guests have arrived."

A few minutes later, nervous and insecure, Ann walked out of the house, feeling as if she had gone through Alice's looking glass.

In the garden conversation wafted around her.

"I was in Puerto Vallarta during *Night of the Iguana*, and, darling, let me tell you," said an MGM VP, "it was really chaos.

"There was Ava Gardner carrying on with a Mexican beach boy. Elizabeth Taylor was scared to death that Ava was carrying on with Richard Burton, and she was *so* insecure, acting like a shrieking hausfrau instead of a woman carrying on the most notorious affair in the world. I mean, darling, the press from all over the world was there camping out on the beach to get a shot of Richard and Elizabeth. And Richard, well, let me tell you, he loved it. He acted terribly proper when Elizabeth was with him, but when she was out of sight . . ." There was a pause, a chuckle, then the executive resumed. "Do you know what he told one reporter? He said Elizabeth's ass was so big, if she weren't careful she'd have to carry it around in a sling. Does that man know how to throw out a quotable quote."

Ann drifted through the crowd almost in a trance. Familiar faces were everywhere. "Excuse me, dear," said a man who brushed past her—and Ann caught a glimpse of Elliott Gould. At the sound of boisterous laughter, she looked toward a group near the outdoor bar. There she saw champion drinker Lee Marvin.

At last, Ann spotted Carl Adams. He stood in the center of a small group near the pool. Even from a distance, Ann could tell from the high-energy sound of his voice, the sweeping movements of his hands, that he was *on*, in his Mr. Charm party mode.

"Well, hel-lo!" he sang as she approached. He kissed her on the cheek, recited the names of those around him, and announced, "I want you all to meet Ann Peters—one of the most exciting young performers I've seen in years."

The buildup didn't end with that. Ann stood by in disbelief as Carl blithely informed his companions that she was the talk of New Orleans. "I had to go see this girl I kept hearing so much about. As soon as I did, I understood all the excitement . . .

"Ann's here to see about a couple of films . . .

"Of course, we want to be sure she starts off with the *right* project. We're in no hurry. She has her singing to fall back on. . . . She was the top draw in the New Orleans supper clubs . . ."

Soon Adams was the center of an impromptu, unofficial reception line as he made introductions and greeted guests, continually inserting glowing comments about Ann into his repartee.

She maintained a frozen smile as her hand was pressed by guest after guest. She made feeble attempts to respond to polite questions posed by people who really had no interest in her or in her answers, who were eager to return to the industry gossip and chitchat that was their lifeblood.

"Isn't that Sam Dallas?" she overheard someone remark.

The speaker nodded toward a group on the far side of the patio.

Ann looked and saw the man she had met at Adams's office.

Sam Dallas? *He* was Sam Dallas? There was no question that the people near her were looking his way.

"I heard he's up for one of the new parts on 'Peyton Place,' " said a woman standing near Ann. "They're expanding to another night, you know."

"Sam Dallas on 'Peyton Place'?" her friend asked caustically.

"Anything's possible."

"I can guess where you heard that. Wouldn't by any chance be from Carl, would it?"

The group drifted away, leaving Ann wracking her brain to place Sam Dallas, the actor. She vaguely recalled his name in connection with reruns of a television show called "Runabout," about two drifters in the Old West; it had been popular when she had lived out of the country.

"Did Carl tell you he was going to make you a big star? . . . he told me the same thing."

Ann recalled Sam's comment and realized it had been meant as a joke. She also realized he must have been aware that she did not recognize him.

How awful.

Across the patio, Sam Dallas was as busy thinking about Ann as she was about him.

He studied her from a distance, trying to determine what it was about her that Carl found so special.

He had seen Adams introducing her to his most favored guests—and noticed that most of them had lighted up as if three-hundred-watt bulbs had suddenly been turned on.

He watched as Ann was joined by a director and his socialite wife—the very director, Sam noted sourly, who had an eleventh-hour change of heart about using Sam for a part in a feature film two months before.

Losing the role had been a blow. The truth was, Dallas was now deeply in debt, living off residuals from his old series, plus the generosity of some free-spending friends. His last show had been "Coast Guard Cutter," a short-lived series that had died two years before. And then his career had cooled like a corpse.

He still drove the Jaguar that had been a negotiation perk when he had re-signed for "Runabout." The car was so old now it qualified as a classic and thus helped him keep up a front in a town where status symbols were all-important. He told intimates he couldn't bear to part with it, but it was Dallas's financial state—not sentimentality—that accounted for his decision to hold onto the car.

As Dallas fixed his attention on Ann, he caught bits of her animated conversation. Encouraged by the director's interest, she relaxed and regaled the filmmaker and his wife with tales of life in the Vieux Carré. Dallas's blood pressure rose and his curiosity flamed as he heard them laughing uproariously.

A short time later, he saw Ann wander away to a poolside table, where she was quickly cornered by the *Los Angeles Journal* fashion editor.

Sam left the group he was with and moved closer to Ann.

"I love the look," he heard the fashion editor gush as she flipped a tiny notebook in a silver case out of her purse, "and you wear it spectacularly! Tell me where it's from."

"It's a Donald Brooks design from the special collection at Salerno's," Ann recited per instructions. The editor jotted the information down, glancing up with another appreciative smile.

Sam had to agree, the girl wore that designer number as though she had been born for it. She was a standout, he thought as he studied her from behind—her long shapely legs, the graceful incline of her neck. And there *was* an unconscious sensuality in that dusty Indian summer voice. All right, he decided, there was more to her than he had thought at first. Still, he was by no means convinced she was as special as Carl believed her to be.

By the time the fashion editor started her retreat, Sam was at Ann's elbow. She turned and bumped into him, then caught her breath and stared.

"You're going to have to watch that," he said smoothly, with a slightly mocking smile.

"I'm sorry!"

"Don't be sorry. You can run into me anytime."

Ann reddened.

"It looks like you're having a good time," he observed. His smile turned seductive, the light in his eyes tender. "I keep seeing you flitting around in that pretty dress, getting everyone's attention. It's a nice party, isn't it?"

"It's wonderful! I've never seen anything like it," answered Ann, in a voice that was, to her embarrassment, too loud and too animated.

Invisible sparks charged the air, bringing down her guard, canceling her judgment.

Sam placed his hands gently upon her upper arms. The gesture sent a shock wave through Ann's body.

"That's good," he said in a low voice. "You know what this party is all about, don't you?"

Ann struggled to answer, finding the question difficult to digest in the face of Dallas's closeness. What was the party about? It was about Jane Broderick's new movie, which Carl Adams had coproduced. Ann knew that. But she sounded more than a little uncertain when she mentioned the title.

"No. That's not what it's about." He glanced furtively over Ann's shoulder. "It's about meeting important people who can help a career. It's about making an impression on them. It's about getting your name in the press. Now, I've seen Carl showing you around—and forget this 'Mr. Adams' jazz, okay baby?".

"Okay." She smiled softly.

Anything was okay. Anything Sam said. She was mesmerized.

"But I haven't seen you talking to any press except that hag from the *Journal*. You don't care about making your dress famous. You care about making Ann Peters famous. Right?"

She nodded. Once again, Sam's eyes darted quickly away and then came back to rest on her. Ann barely noticed that odd bit of business, so caught up was she in her bubble of emotions.

She forgot she was standing on a crowded patio as Sam's hands moved up to cup her cheeks. His eyes searched hers, his face moving closer. She closed her eyes and felt his light kiss on her lips.

At that moment, a flash of light exploded over them. A grinning member of Hollywood's paparazzi stood in front of them, boasting, "That picture will get pickup everywhere."

"Jesus!" Sam stormed. "Who the fuck let you in here?"

He grabbed Ann's hand and led her into the house, while stunned members of the crowd stared after them. By the time they reached the lounge, his shoulders were shaking with silent laughter.

"So goddamn easy," he mumbled gleefully as he led her through the crowded room.

"You mean . . . you mean . . ." Ann sputtered.

Sam didn't answer until they reached the entryway, where only Prometheus could hear.

"By next week, he'll have sold that shot to the tabloids. By the week after that, I'll have given an exclusive interview to *Star World* all about you. Good, huh?"

"How could you?" Ann cried, engulfed in humiliation and disappointment. Without thinking, she ran out of Adams's house and down the walkway. Seconds later, Dallas followed after her.

"Ann! Ann! . . . Hey!"

He could barely believe what he was doing as he raced to catch up with the figure moving quickly ahead of him on the dark strreet. She had just done the impossible. The unforgivable. She had turned away from him, rejected him outright. So why was he chasing her when there were dozens of broads back at Adams's who'd love his attention?

Goddamn, she's fast, he thought as he increased his pace.

It took every ounce of his energy to slowly close the gap.

"Ann! Come on!" he shouted pleadingly as he strained to catch her arm. "Hey! What's the big deal? I was only trying to help you!"

In a sudden burst, fueled by her humiliation, Ann shot down the street, far, far out of his grasp.

Sam stopped, furious.

He felt mortified as he stood sweating and panting, his usual cool obliterated.

To hell with her, Sam thought, and concentrated on regaining his composure. He turned his face away from the glare of passing headlights—he certainly had no desire to be recognized at the moment—as he started the trek back to Adams's home and the army of valets waiting to retrieve the automobiles of departing guests.

Once he reached the house, he glumly retreated to the study with a double Scotch.

Adams found him there hours later.

"What's the matter with you?" he asked.

"Your new find is a flake," Sam said in a huff.

"Why?"

"Haven't you noticed she's not here? She got pissed off and left about ten—just ran off into the night. God knows where she is."

Adams grinned at him, highly amused. "What did you do to her?"

"Nothing! I did nothing," Sam insisted, standing.

"What about the incident on the patio that the photographer shot? You look worried," Adams goaded him.

"What's the matter with you? What if she flipped out? What if the cops picked her up? I'm going to go look for her." Sam picked up his leather jacket as Adams watched, shaking his head.

"Hold on a minute, Dorothy," Adams said with a smile, stopping him. "Everything you want is right here in Kansas."

"What?" Sam snapped.

"Now, tap those ruby slippers of yours together three times and repeat, 'There's no place like home,' and I'll tell you all about it." Adams's smirk grew bolder as Sam turned away angrily.

"Ann isn't the flip-out type. No, I can already tell, she's a responsible young lady. I saw her saying goodbye to people more than an hour ago. You must have missed her."

"Swell."

"And now she's all tucked up in her room, safe and sound, probably falling asleep thinking about the meeting I set up for her with Robin Rubin at Fox next week."

Dallas marched out to the sound of Adams's laughter.

"She got to you! She got to you! Now I've seen everything!"

TWELVE

~~~~~

IT BEGAN WITH a phone call the next morning.

Ann was sitting alone in the breakfast room, sipping coffee and wondering what the day would bring, when Adams's houseman George appeared to tell her she had a call. Adams strolled into the room just as Ann was rising from her chair.

"Who is it?" he asked George.

"Mr. Dallas."

Adams turned to Ann.

"Don't take it," he instructed.

Forcing herself to ignore the thrill she felt at hearing the caller's name, Ann nodded. "I don't want to."

"Good." Adams turned to George. "Tell him Miss Peters never wants to speak to him again and that she finds him despicable. Does that about cover it?" he asked Ann.

"Well, I—"

"Believe me, he deserves it."

Within the hour, a deliveryman from Harry Finley's Florist arrived with three dozen long-stemmed red roses for Ann.

Her new manager headed her off at the doorway. "Who are they from?" he asked the deliveryman, and nearly doubled over with glee at the answer: Sam Dallas.

"Sorry, she doesn't want them," Carl said, as Ann stared longingly at the gorgeous flowers.

"Oh, I . . ." she started to say before she was cut off by Adams.

"Don't weaken now, sweetie. He can do better than this.

120

You're insulted, aren't you? The least he could do is something original."

Ann forced a shrug and a smile despite the pang she felt. "But," she stalled, "but I don't need—"

"Need? Forget that word." Carl grinned at the deliveryman. "Tell Harry I said hello. No offense, you understand, but Ann has her personal reasons."

Over the next three days, more calls came from Sam Dallas. Several times Ann stood by listening to George explain that she was busy, that she was not interested, that she asked Mr. Dallas not to call again. Each time, Ann felt dismayed. Each time, she was convinced Sam would become angry and never ever want to speak to her again.

She was wrong.

On Tuesday, she hovered just out of sight of the foyer as George turned Sam Dallas away at the door.

"Miss Peters has gone to a luncheon meeting in Beverly Hills," he lied, per Adams's instructions.

"Where?" she heard Sam ask, and felt her heart start at the desperation she heard in his voice.

"I'm sorry, sir. I've been asked not to give you that information."

By that time, Ann was ready to rebel. She felt sorry for Dallas, sorry for herself, sorry to have started such a fuss, but Adams convinced her she must hold out a little while longer.

On Wednesday, as she was basking in the sun by the pool with three of Adams's actor-model protégés (Adams was a firm believer in the deeply bronzed look and insisted she "get some color"), she heard the determined honking of a car in the driveway.

"It's got to be Dallas again," said one of the sun worshippers with a smirk. Ann bolted inside, just in time to see Adams closing the front door.

He was laughing. Seeing her, he said, "If you can do to a few other key gentlemen what you've done to Sam Dallas, darling, you'll have it made. He's practically rabid over you."

"What did he say?"

"He had some half-baked idea about wanting to give you driving lessons."

She answered darkly, "I thought you were at a meeting."

"I just got back." Carl passed his palm under her chin. "I know. You're sorry for him, aren't you? Don't be. Believe me, I know Sam better than you do. He's a big boy. He can take it."

Ann looked longingly at the door, then at Adams.

"Oh, really?" he asked.

Smiling, he reached for the doorknob, opened the door, and gave it a slight shove. "In that case, don't let me stand in your way. Just please don't make it too easy for him."

She crossed the threshold just in time to see Sam Dallas's green Jaguar roar away.

"Don't worry," said Adams. "He'll be back."

On Thursday, dressed in the dusty rose Saint Laurent suit Adams had ordered for her, Ann went with him to meet Robin Rubin, a veteran producer headquartered at Twentieth Century–Fox Studios.

Adams's Excalibur purred onto the lot, past façades of turn-of-the-century row houses. Lights and reflectors were being set up, a camera adjusted. Women in bonnets and bustles, men with top hats, canes, and spats stood waiting for a call to action. "They're doing *Goodbye, Jenny,*" Adams explained.

Ann felt—and sounded—like a child on Christmas morning. "It's wonderful!" she cried, clapping her hands together.

Adams couldn't resist the pleasure of looking at the lot through the eyes of an excited newcomer. Rather than heading directly to the administration building, he drove past the commissary and toward the north end of the bustling studio, moving slowly in order to negotiate through arteries clogged with equipment trucks, trailers, pedestrians.

"That opened last year," he said, pointing toward the massive Century Plaza Hotel that rose in the distance above the Fox buildings. "Of course, the back lot used to stretch all the way out there."

"Really?" Ann marveled.

Adams grinned. "It was only a couple years ago that Frank Sinatra was here filming *Von Ryan's Express.* Mia Farrow was twenty at the time, costarring in 'Peyton Place.' She'd dress up in one of the negligees from the wardrobe department and saunter over to the *Von Ryan* set. I'll never forget seeing her one day: five hundred male extras doing a World War II picture out in the dirt and dust and heat, and then this vision in filmy nylon appeared."

"In . . . a nightgown?" Ann asked disbelievingly.

"Why not?" Adams asked cheerfully. "She thought she looked good in it. Obviously Frank agreed. At least, she certainly managed to get his attention."

Ann's meeting lasted all of twelve minutes. Robin Rubin was pleasant, full of optimism, encouragement, and ideas, but when Adams got down to mentioning *Secret Request*, the feature Rubin was about to start casting, the man deftly diverted them. He thought Ann would be ideal for several other people's properties.

Adams seemed unsurprised by the way the meeting had gone and far from defeated.

He had accomplished his purpose: he had gotten Ann a meeting with Rubin.

Later, Ann would hear him tell others, "You know, Robin Rubin has been talking to Ann about *Secret Request*"—making it sound as if she were being seriously considered for the film, as though Ann Peters were suddenly generating interest in important places. Or so Carl hoped. It was a typical Adams maneuver.

"As long as we're here, there are a couple people I'd like to see," he told Ann as they came out of Rubin's office. "Want to come along?"

"If it doesn't matter, I'd rather explore a little," she replied.

Adams shrugged. "Just stay out of everyone's way."

A few minutes later, she was walking past the executive parking lot, back toward the *Goodbye, Jenny* set. She hesitated as she noticed a green Jaguar in one of the parking spaces.

"How was your meeting?"

Ann wheeled around, and there stood Sam Dallas.

"Are you going to give me a chance this time or are you going to run away again?" he asked.

She felt the blood leave her face. He looked sullen, angry, haggard—and nervous.

"I have never gone to such lengths to make up with anyone," he complained as Ann stared at him, tongue-tied. "Okay, it was tacky, crazy. But honest-to-Christ, Ann, I did not mean to upset you. And I still don't see why it's such a big deal you won't even hear me out."

Sam held up his hand as she fumbled for an answer. "You know I actually felt sorry for you that night? 'Poor kid,' I thought, 'here she is, dropped into the middle of all this insanity, and she doesn't know what's going on.' But you sure fooled me. Hell, you're not going to have any trouble getting by, are you? You're hard."

"That's not true!" Ann cried.

"Just tell me this: did we have something going or am I completely nuts?" Sam glanced up at the overcast sky, his mouth drawn into a taut line. "Tell me what I have to do. What do you want from me?" He looked down at her intently.

Ann shook her head. "Nothing."

"Oh, come on—can't you tell I've been going crazy? I'm supposed to be in Santa Barbara right now! But I had to try getting to you outside of that fortress of Carl's. Give me a break, baby. I'm lost out here."

"It's all right," Ann insisted. "It really is."

"Look, I can help you," Sam continued, by now so convinced of Ann's implacability that he continued battling to win her over, not registering her words. "Carl doesn't know anything except business. Just try to talk to him about discovering a character or figuring out why a line doesn't work—he goes completely blank! He doesn't know a thing about the creative process. Is he going to be able to help you when the breaks come? No way. But I can. Just give me a chance. How about it?"

Ann's answer was a shy, embarrassed smile. "When you kissed me, I didn't think you meant it," she murmured.

"What?" he nearly shouted.

There was a pause, a beat. And then he drew her to him and kissed her again—this time a long, slow, sensual kiss. She clung to him, burying her face in his chest, not daring to look at him.

"I was afraid you didn't mean it," she told him, smiling, breathless, elated, giving in completely.

"Mean it?" he whispered. "I'm in love with you."

When Carl Adams finally emerged from his base-touching mission in the Fox administration building, he found a note on his windshield.

GONE TO JUPITER WITH ANN. DON'T WAIT UP. WILL BE BACK AROUND 1990. CHEERS—SAM

He loves me, Ann joyously told herself that evening as Sam's Jaguar swiftly cut through Laurel Canyon to his house.

She hugged his arm and saw his sidelong glance, the slow smile, in the dim green light of the dashboard.

She knew she would never forget the smallest detail of the day—the mystic romance of the drive along Pacific Coast Highway toward Santa Barbara, the slate gray ocean emerging, then disappearing behind curtains of fog. She would never forget how proudly Sam had introduced her to his acquaintances at the small beach community theater or how she had loved hearing them talk about their upcoming production of *A Doll's House*. She would never forget the shared happiness of the drive back to L.A., the connected feeling as she walked into Scandia with Sam for a late supper, or her joy as Sam had begun plotting her career.

He seemed to know everything she should do. And he made it clear he intended to play a part—a large part—in getting her started, for his every sentence on the subject began with "we."

"We're going to start by getting you into Jon Salinger's class; he's the best coach in this city..."

"We're going to check out your wardrobe..."

"We're going to look into a dance class for you..."

He loves me, Ann thought ecstatically as they stood in the darkness just inside the door of his home. She kissed him passionately, welcoming his touch when he undid her soft pink blouse.

She was swept by desire as Sam carried her to his bedroom, leaving their clothes strewn behind them in careless disarray on the floor of the entryway.

He set her gently on the bed and hovered over her, a soft smile playing across his lips.

"I love you, Sam." She rejoiced in the sound of his name. "I love you so much!"

He kissed her mouth and then her breasts. "God, you're beautiful," he said, breathless with desire.

And with that, he was suddenly inside her.

Ann didn't care that it was over in a matter of minutes. She didn't miss having an orgasm. She didn't know she hadn't had one—or what one felt like.

It was enough to have Sam's arm around her as he fell asleep. It was enough to feel safe and happy for the first time in seven years.

PART 3
The Wife

THIRTEEN

"PAST?" SAM ASKED, smiling, as he wrestled Ann's trunk through his bedroom door—*their* bedroom door now.

It was three days after their encounter on the Fox lot, and Ann was taking up residence with the man she loved.

"You don't need to tell me anything, baby. The past is the past. We're into today and tomorrow."

Sam's plans for today and tomorrow consisted of collecting Ann's things, getting high, and making love.

She listened enraptured while Sam tapped some marijuana into the bowl of his water pipe and waxed poetic on the topic of their romance.

"You know what I think? We were cut from the same piece of soul cloth, you and I. That's why we knew so fast. You're the wind and I'm the sail. We belong together."

"I don't care what you did." Sam put Ann off again, as they walked along the Santa Monica beachfront. The sun was just setting on their fifth day together. "Just answer me one question: do you love me?"

"You know I do!" cried Ann. "But—"

Sam caught her up in his arms and carried her toward the gilded sea. "Hey, everybody! Look what I've got," he yelled as they crossed the nearly deserted stretch of sand. Her memories of dark times and heartache were swept away in their laughter.

Ann felt an increasing sense of urgency to tell Sam about her past life. She tried several more times during their first

129

week together, between nights on the town with Sam's friends, lovemaking by sun, stars, and firelight, and meetings with Carl Adams.

Adams was somewhat annoyed at Sam for "snatching Ann away." But he took it philosophically, quickly seeing advantages in the relationship between his two clients. He had never intended to have Ann as more than a temporary guest; now she was Sam's responsibility.

Sam's answer to Ann's halting attempts to bare the truth was a "no confessions" rule. He unilaterally "forgave" Ann for any and all past affairs, while Ann remained convinced that once he understood what she kept trying to say, he would want to know all about Cindy.

The right moment would come, she told herself.

One evening Sam arranged for her to perform at an after-hours club owned by a friend. Smiling at him through the darkness, Ann sang "Come Rain or Come Shine" just for him, her voice full of love.

It was their eleventh day together.

"That was so damn beautiful I can't believe it!" Sam exclaimed, when Ann returned to their table. "You sing like an angel. From now on, that's going to be our song."

Ann nodded. "Is it really possible to be this happy?" she asked him.

"Sure it is," said Sam. Then he added, "Let's make it official."

Ann beamed. "Official?"

"Yeah. You, me—man and wife and all that. What do you think?"

She leaned over the table and threw her arms around his neck, crying out, "Oh, yes!"

"I think you like the idea," gasped Sam.

"What's the guy's name?" Sam was taking hurried notes at his kitchen phone while Ann stood by, watching anxiously.

It was happening so fast.

Sam was wearing a three-piece slate-gray pinstripe suit.

Ann wore a white satin minidress with elaborately gathered Elizabethan sleeves, a crown of ribbons and daisies upon her head. The ensemble, another loan from Salerno's, was geared toward making her a model of the chic bride, 1967-style.

But she wasn't ready to be a bride. Not quite. Not yet. As she watched Sam jot down information from the press agent Carl Adams had arranged to publicize the wedding, she couldn't help thinking that her future happiness—her entire life—hinged on what would happen in the next ten minutes.

The right moment she had been waiting for just hadn't materialized. She had planned to have a long talk with Sam the night before, but then Sam had been "kidnapped" by two buddies for a stag party.

Now, less than two weeks after she had first entered Sam's house, they were preparing to meet a judge, a press agent, and a photographer—with shadows still between them, important truths still untold.

"So the photog will meet us on the courthouse steps at two. . . . Hey, thanks for everything. We'll see you later."

Sam hung up.

"Let's skip the whole thing and go straight to Acapulco," he joked, rubbing his palms together.

Ann smiled thinly. "Sam . . ."

"I've been through my share of opening nights, but I've got to tell you, this is worse," he said. "Well, what do you say we go do it?"

"Wait. I have to talk to you first."

"Oh, no." He grinned. "Here we go again. You're a mass murderess? You were Lucrezia Borgia in a past life?"

"Please, darling. It's serious."

At that, Sam nodded and took a seat at the kitchen table, watching her expectantly.

"A little less than four years ago," Ann began, holding out the snapshot of Cindy, "I had a baby."

She watched Sam's face darken as he reached for the picture of her daughter. He examined Cindy's laughing face under the oversized, floppy hair bow as Ann went on.

"I gave her up to my sister and her husband because . . . well, because I just couldn't give her the kind of home they could. It was the hardest thing I ever did."

Sam gravely pursed his lips. "What about the father?" he asked in a low voice.

"He was . . . an older man . . . someone my mother met at the club. I hate him. He . . . raped me."

For a long moment, Sam just sat nodding slowly, weighing the information, fitting it into his mental equation of Ann. She bit at her knuckle nervously, while a voice within her silently warned, *You've got to tell him!* But she couldn't force the name *Hank Evans* past her lips.

And as she once again tried, Sam interrupted her: "I don't want to know who it was. Baby, as far as I'm concerned, it's just what I said before—we're living for today and tomorrow. Four years ago? That's ancient history." He shrugged. "I'm not going to hold something against you that happened when you were just a kid. From this point on," he said, standing and carelessly pushing Cindy's photo aside on the table, "let's just forget it ever happened."

"Forget my daughter?" Ann sputtered.

Sam stiffened in surprise at her outburst.

"You just said you gave her up to your sister," he replied defensively. "What else can you do? You pick up, you go on."

For a terrible moment, Ann had the sensation she was looking into a stranger's eyes.

Then the rationalizations began.

Of course Sam hadn't really meant *forget* it; of course he was right about picking up and going on; of course he was wiser than she—he was a man. *Her* man.

She nodded slowly.

Sam kissed her cheek lightly, his happy mood restored. "Feel better now?"

A few minutes later, they left for City Hall.

By the time the press agent handed her a bouquet and the photographer posed her and Sam inside the license bureau, Ann was able to smile with all the requisite bridal radiance.

Hank Evans did not notice the young woman in the wire photo captioned ACTOR DALLAS WEDS that was picked up by the paper near his Texas ranch, but in New York, Lyla and Jo Mantussi certainly noticed the pair smiling from a page inside the *Daily News*.

Ann's long letter had already arrived. She had painstakingly and—she hoped—reassuringly explained that she had told Sam about Cindy and about them and that he understood everything. She had said that she hoped they could all meet soon.

She had tried hard to convey the message that she was happy and secure; she wanted them to know that she posed no threat.

No longer was she the unwed mother, the secret shame. She was established, married, with her own life three thousand miles away. She had a fresh start, and, carried away completely by her emotions, Ann made the happy assumption that the walls between herself and the Mantussis could now come tumbling down.

The day after she and Sam returned from their honeymoon, she dialed the Mantussis' number.

Joe answered. As soon as he heard her voice he asked sharply, "What are you calling for?"

"Joe, I was hoping we could—"

"Get one thing straight. Just 'cause you got money now, don't think anything's going to change. If you ever, *ever* show up around here with any funny ideas about breaking up this family, so help me, I'll kill you."

"I wouldn't!" Ann exclaimed.

"Just stay out there with those weirdos and 'do your own thing' and leave us alone. Got it?"

A few minutes later, Sam found Ann facedown on their bed, crying.

"Baby! What is it?" he asked. Then he passed her en route to the closet, where he began to select his clothes for the evening.

"My brother-in-law," Ann said tearily. "He was angry that I called."

Sam groaned in response but said nothing. Ann sat up and turned toward him.

"Sam?" she asked softly. "Did you hear me?"

"Yeah." He shrugged, glancing at her over his shoulder. "I guess that means we can't expect to get a new toaster from them, huh?" he said flippantly, then sighed at the sight of Ann's frown.

"Hey, I'm sorry. But maybe you shouldn't call them. Why give them a chance to get to you like this? Fuck 'em."

"But . . . my sister . . . my daughter—"

"*Their* daughter," he corrected, flipping through his shirts. "I'm your family now."

"I know that, darling, but . . ."

"Come on, forget about it. We've got to get going."

She nodded mutely and went into the bathroom to wash her face.

A congratulations card arrived from Lyla the next day. "To

My Sister on Her Wedding Day," it read, followed by a touching verse. Ann imagined Lyla spending a great deal of time carefully hunting through card racks to find the perfect sentiment—spending hours perhaps.

It was enough, just enough, to allow Ann to hang onto the belief that her sister still cared.

"You're beautiful. You're talented. You're wonderful. And you don't know shit about anything. You're lucky I'm here to help you."

So began Ann's education under the tutelage of her new husband.

He was not what one fancied as a Pygmalion. For every book on acting he gave her to read during their first few months together, for every trick he passed along about the correct way to approach a casting meeting, Sam had ten new lessons for Ann that were geared toward ensuring his sexual pleasure.

He made her an expert, giving detailed guided tours of his body—teaching her the magic places to touch and to tongue and to stimulate, the way he wanted to be stroked, how hard, and how fast.

It never occurred to Ann that she had married a man to whom sexual selfishness was an unquestioned prerogative.

One day when Carl Adams was typically late for a meeting at his home, Sam led Ann upstairs into Carl's master bedroom, a rococo gold and white attempt at elegance she found overdone and more than a little silly.

"Let's go back downstairs," she urged Sam. "I'm sure he wouldn't like us nosing around up here."

"Who cares?" Sam said, waving his hand. He grinned. "Anyway, I want to borrow a book he has here. *Valley of the Dolls*. Will you get it for me? It's right on that shelf." He pointed it out.

Ann reached for the volume and saw immediately that the book was a false front; it was set apart, cut away from the other volumes in the white bookcase. She turned back to Sam in confusion.

"Go ahead," Sam instructed. "Pull it out."

She did and, like something out of one of the vintage B horror pictures that movie-junkie Adams adored, the entire bookcase shifted until it was at an angle to the wall. Sam literally fell on his knees with laughter as Ann let out a stunned gasp and gaped at the hidden room that was revealed: Adams's torture chamber. There were leather garments with zippered openings at the crotch, manacles and cat-o'-nine-tails; vibrators and dildos up to twenty inches in length, studded handcuffs attached to the wall, harnesses hanging from the ceiling.

"You should see the look on your face!" Sam gasped with laughter.

"How do I put this back?" she asked urgently.

"God, I wish I had a picture. You're white as a sheet, baby. Aren't you impressed?"

"Sam, how did you know this was here?"

"Why are you asking?"

Ann was taken aback at his sudden defensiveness. "It's an obvious question, isn't it?"

"I was up here once and noticed that funny-looking book. The next thing I knew, I had one of the major surprises of my life." His laugh sounded hollow.

A few days later, Sam turned the fundamentals of how he wanted Ann to use a vibrator into Lesson One Hundred and Two.

If she sensed any suggestion of dehumanization, any cruel edge to any of Sam's actions, Ann refused to acknowledge it. Of course she wanted to please him in every way possible. She loved him. He was her husband.

She loved the encouragement and praise she received from him when she did something right; she was tormented by his vaguely contemptuous criticism when she did something wrong.

Sam made it clear that she was supremely lucky to be the woman who had landed him. He made no secret of the fact that there were plenty of other beauties still available to him, heightening Ann's insecurity even as he professed his love for her. Ann found reminders of his past affairs everywhere, from his clothes closets to his medicine cabinet.

Again and again, as she studied his tousled, wavy hair, his profile, his well-built—if slightly out-of-shape—bronzed form, she was reminded that her husband was still one of the most attractive men ever to walk the earth. That she now knew he used hair rinse and spray, lifts for his shoes, and, sometimes, a girdlelike elastic cummerbund did not matter.

Other things did matter.

In the long, quiet stretches when she would lie still as a statue, enjoying the warmth of Sam's arm draped over her body, not daring to move for fear of waking him, she would dream of the day he would let her stop taking birth control pills.

One day she confronted him. "You want children someday, don't you?" she asked.

Reading the powerful emotions on her face, Sam took her hand and reassured her: "Sure. And I want them all to look like you. But let's tackle your career first."

But Ann's career was not going quite as well as Sam—or Carl Adams—had hoped it might.

Initially, Carl Adams called in favors from acquaintances in the upper levels of the filmmaking and television communities and secured Ann some important interviews. Every meeting ended with polite dismissive comments ranging from, "She's lovely, Carl—but she's just not right for this project" to "She needs more experience under her belt."

As his enthusiasm waned, Adams turned Ann over to another agent who immediately began sending her out to try her luck in less friendly quarters. Many of those calls were devastating; casting directors made comments that were less detailed and more blunt, sometimes confined to a simple "Next!"

She heard that she couldn't act.

She heard that she was too fat, too thin, too tall, too short. She heard that she couldn't act.

She heard that her nose was too big. She heard that she couldn't act.

She heard that her voice was wrong for her face. She heard that her breasts were too small—and that they were too large.

A few times, someone involved in casting a project would request to look at her breasts—or more. Those Ann handled by simply taking her leave, request unfulfilled.

And over and over again she heard that she ought to think about a different career because, sorry, she really couldn't act.

She met many funny, friendly competitors. But she also met the type of actresses who would have killed—literally—to have been handed Carl Adams's business card and a chance to have a career orchestrated by such a major force.

Ann fared only slightly better as a singer.

Adams arranged to have her audition for a major advertising firm that was searching for a sexy voice for a soft-drink commercial. Ann made it to round two of the auditions before being passed over for an experienced commercial singer. She was told by the director that she ought to feel proud of having gotten as far as she had, for there had been a number of fine professional female vocalists vying for the job; there were for all such jobs. Indeed, Ann soon learned just how staggering her competition in the field was; there were singers with backgrounds ranging from Julliard training to the Grand Ole Opry, from the European opera competitions to the folk coffeehouses.

Ann was good, but it seemed to her that dozens of other studio singers on the scene were far better. Stronger. More experienced. Smoother. Broader ranged. Clearer. More unusual. More stylized. Livelier. Sexier.

"That's just your lack of confidence," Sam insisted. "And even if you're right, you know and I know that fifty percent of the jokers who have hit records out can't sing worth shit."

Sam and Carl agreed it was important that Ann keep in shape vocally, so Carl got her booked into an out-of-the-way lounge in Glendale. There, he explained, Ann could "tone up" before tackling a showcase spot. Meanwhile, Adams quietly brought in a handful of experts to assess Ann's potential.

The consensus: Ann was good, but there were hundreds of singers on the scene who were better. She was simply not star material.

FOURTEEN

⟨∾⟩

"THE PROBLEM IS your looks," Adams informed Ann one afternoon in his office. Startled, she glanced at Sam, who was seated in the chair next to hers. He was studying his nails.

"You're pretty. We all know you're pretty," Carl continued. "But . . . I spoke to Sherm Kent, the casting director, yesterday. What he said struck me as so true I don't know how we missed it. He told me you're too ethnic-looking to be classic and you're too classic to be ethnic."

Ann shrugged, accepting the verdict, although she didn't quite understand it.

"So, what . . . what can I do?"

"What *we're* going to do, for starters," Carl told her, standing up as he often did when making an important announcement, "is get you a nose job."

Ann again turned to Sam, her hand automatically rising to cover the feature she had just been informed was so offensive. This time, Sam looked squarely at her and nodded slowly.

Ann sat silently for a long moment, conflicting forces battling inside her.

On one side was the conviction with which she had been raised—that it was unladylike and unattractive for a woman to disagree with a man and wrong to go against a husband.

On the other side was Ann's desire to tell them she liked her nose just as it was and to call the "too classic to be ethnic" theory hogwash. Had Carl not presented it so seriously, it would have struck Ann as funny.

She started to protest, but Sam stopped her with a stern

look. "Don't argue," Carl said curtly. "Once you have it done, you'll be glad you did. We're all anxious to see you succeed, right? I know I am. So much so that I'm going to pay the plastic surgeon's bill."

"Thank you," Ann murmured listlessly.

Two days later she found her face the object of Dr. P. A. Wojinski's solemn scrutiny. That he had agreed to see her on such short notice was a sign of Carl's clout. Dr. Wojinski was the plastic surgeon most in demand in show business and high social circles; an appointment for a preliminary examination usually involved a wait of several weeks.

The good doctor enjoyed nothing more than playing God with almost-perfect beauty, employing his artistry to correct the nearly invisible flaws of nature. After his eyes and his fingers had roved carefully over Ann's features, he pushed his stool back from the examination chair on which she reclined and informed her that to realize her full potential cosmetically, she should not only have her nose bobbed but her jaw broken and reshaped.

Adams paid for the surgery. He also paid for a complete makeover at Jon Peters's salon in Beverly Hills, after Sam came up with the idea that Ann should be transformed from a brunette to a blonde, "to bring out the Monroe vibes."

"You'll pay me back one day," Carl said, as he had so frequently in the past.

Ann felt she was being robbed of her physical identity; yet, although it was traumatic, she told herself that Carl and Sam must know best. The reassuring thought also occurred to her that she no longer need fear an encounter with Hank Evans. There was now no way he would ever recognize her as the terrified girl he had befriended—then attacked—in what now seemed a lifetime ago.

". . . And we're all very excited because we have here with us today one of the all-time great personalities of the silver screen, a man who doesn't usually make appearances on talk shows—Hank Evans."

Merv Griffin waited for the applause to ebb, then added, "We'll be right back."

Through half-closed eyes, Ann gazed at the black and white image, too sedated to bring herself to change the program. She was lying in a tangle of blankets in the darkened bedroom of Sam's house on Lookout Mountain Road two days after surgery.

Her face a mass of purple bruises and painful swelling, with blood-stained tracks of stitches visible between padded gauze bandages, Ann looked and felt as though she had been worked over by Muhammad Ali rather than a doctor. Wojinski assured her that given her youth, she would heal rapidly — in time to look beautiful for Sam, who was on location in Tucson making a low-budget, nonunion "modern western."

The script wasn't very good, nor was Sam's small part as one of the bad guys. But that had just been Ann's initial reaction, which she revised once Sam had explained all the film's merits to her.

Ann told herself she was happier enduring this unsightly healing period without him. It was better to be alone. And if it was too much of a struggle to go down to the kitchen and fix something to eat, well, she hardly felt in the mood for food anyway. Besides, Sam and Carl wanted her to lose weight.

Through a haze of painkillers, she watched Hank Evans make his entrance on the Griffin show.

He, too, had undergone some transformations, she noted. His hair was gray at the temples, and he had grown bulkier. His face was more lined, and there was a studied seriousness about him.

"No, I don't spend much time here in Hollywood any longer," he said to Griffin. "I'll be honest with you, Merv. I figure I put in something like fifty-two-thousand hours in front of the cameras . . ." Some *oohs* and a smattering of applause were heard. Evans nodded toward the audience. "Yeah. A lot of hours. Anyhow, it's got to be something pretty damned worthwhile to get me to leave my ranch nowadays. I'm here now to be a part of the Love It or Leave It special concert they're putting on at the Hollywood Bowl tomorrow night. I'll tell you, Merv, I'm delighted about the idea. It's an antidemonstration demonstration — a demonstration of support and patriotism. Something this country sorely needs. We're expecting some great Americans to be on hand, including Governor Reagan."

Ann slowly pulled herself up to a sitting position, then moved her legs and scooted forward until her feet touched the bare wood floor. She couldn't stomach another minute of Evans's posturing.

"Fake," she muttered as she reached for the dial. But Griffin's next question stopped her cold.

"Speaking of actors who've gone into politics—there've been a lot of rumors that you're considering running for public office. Is that true?"

"I don't know about all that talk, Merv. I don't see it happening," Evans replied, but his hesitation, his smile and the way he pulled himself up in his chair provided plenty of contradictory subtext to keep the rumors alive.

"I *have* always felt strongly that every citizen of this country should keep up on what's happening politically. I *have* always held strong views about things, and I've been active on local issues, as you know. But I wouldn't get involved on a broader level unless I felt absolutely convinced I could make a contribution . . ."

Ann turned off the set as a shudder swept over her body.

By the time Sam returned from Arizona, Ann was completely healed. He was so enraptured by her transformation that at first it seemed he couldn't keep his hands off her.

"You're fabulous! You're a vision!" he proclaimed as he held her remolded face in his hands and gazed at her with the thrilled delight of a man discovering a new lover. Indeed, that was just how Sam felt. His behavior hurt her; it was as if, in a bizarre way, he was being rampantly unfaithful. Again, she refused to acknowledge her feelings—and she convinced herself that she should feel wonderful because Sam was being more tender and attentive than he had been since the dawn of their romance.

Unlike Sam, Ann was not enchanted with her new looks. Far from it. She could barely stand to glance at herself in the mirror. She felt a pang of distress whenever she caught a glimpse of her reflection. The near-stranger who looked back at her was not unattractive—just the opposite. She was flawless. Ann's wide, velvety blue eyes were now twice as dramatic, appearing more wide-set with her new, delicately sculpted nose. The blond hair was a striking contrast to her olive skin. Her chin line was elegant perfection. There was not an ounce of excess weight on what had been a softly rounded feminine form.

But Ann found the eerie unfamiliarity of her looks devastating. No doubt about it, Ann Beaudry was no more. And no one but Ann Peters mourned her passing.

"Utter madness"—Carl Adams's trademark line in describing his life—applied wherever Ann looked during that first year as Carl and Sam searched for ways to launch her toward stardom.

A sense of insanity pervaded the country in general—hawks against doves, the love generation against the establishment, teenagers who would mature into the most materialistic generation in modern history protesting against the crass materialism of their parents.

And Hollywood was on a bender of its own. As public interests and standards became ever more divergent, with movie-house attendance having dropped a staggering eighty million over two decades, the industry was frantic to find the creative geniuses who could lead it out of its valley of despair. Veteran studio executives were ousted from positions of power and replaced by Biblical-type wunderkinder who favored long hair, love beads, and the liberal use of profanity. And psychedelics.

Dennis Hopper, counterculture movie king of *Easy Rider* fame, was a role model for the aspiring Now filmmaker. He "talks revolution . . . goes to bed with groups and has taken everything you can swallow or shoot," said *Life*, which also acknowledged that Hopper was "the hottest director in Hollywood."

Hopper's *Easy Rider* costar, Peter Fonda, said succinctly, "We've taken over. The town is ours now." While his sister turned antiwar activist, Peter took on the dual mantle of filmmaker/prophet, considering it his duty to inform the public, "The world is doomed," and to decry the evils of America, a land founded by a "syphilitic slave owner"—his description of George Washington.

It was the Hollywood era that would see David Carradine set out to make a movie commune-style; that would necessitate a production halt on Charlton Heston's *Soylent Green* when a large group of extras would be discovered unfit for work—two conducting a private love-in on the dusty floor of MGM's Soundstage 22, while others were tripping out on LSD-laced chewing gum.

It was the era when producer William Belasco would hold

a press party for *They Only Kill Their Masters* that would start off as a typical fancy filmland do with such notables as Jim Garner, Katharine Ross, Edmond O'Brien, and MGM chief Jim Aubrey in attendance—and would wind up stunning many when cocaine and marijuana were openly issued to, and used by, dozens of guests.

It was the era when Elliott Gould would slip from idol supreme to persona non grata in the industry after Warner Brothers permanently shuttered his big-budgeted *Glimpse of Tiger* amid widespread rumors that he had flipped out, taken one trip too many.

Gould later denied the stories that had him prancing around the set with a pacifier in his mouth, blowing whistles during camera takes, flying into screaming rages at director Tony Harvey. He insisted that his trouble with the studio all stemmed from the fact that he had grown more confident as an artist after having worked with Ingmar Bergman on *The Touch* and that when he began to express his views on how things ought to be done on *Glimpse of Tiger*—"they couldn't handle it."

Nevertheless, it would be sixteen months before Gould would be given his next acting assignment.

And it was the era when James Brolin would tell friends that he was confident about his future in Hollywood, not because he felt his talent was so outstanding, but because he didn't do drugs. And when many of his drug-taking peers had burnt out and fallen away, "I'll still be here"—a prophecy that proved to have much truth. Not that Brolin's star would rise that high, but that the stars of such leading men as Jimmy Caan, George Segal, and Elliott Gould would sputter.

More and more, Carl Adams's "dish" centered on tales of film productions run amok under the direction of strung out creative sorts. For instance, there was the filmmaker known for his graphic, slow-motion depictions of violence and sex, who shot, reshot, and shot again a single scene of a black prostitute getting out of a bathtub—all day, every day, for a full week—until the studio finally called a halt to production. The kicker, Carl laughingly told Ann and Sam, was that, "The script hasn't got one *mention* of a black prostitute getting out of a bathtub."

Ann, who was certainly no novice at acclimating herself to new situations, quietly adapted to the Now scene without feeling she was part of it, or that it was a part of her. Without realizing it, she had at last begun to build self-protecting inner walls, to hold part of herself aloof. Fewer and fewer people could really penetrate her insular shield and only a handful had the power to reach her wounded, frightened core.

One who could, of course, was her husband.

Sam kept Ann perpetually off balance, one day making her the sole object of his attention and affection as he ardently played her guardian, confidant, mentor, and lover—the next behaving as if he considered her nothing but an irritant.

"You don't know anything," he would remind her, his gentleness replaced by impatience. Smarting jokes about the Garden Royale and her waitressing job served as reminders that he had not forgotten where she *really* belonged.

The more Ann craved assurances of his love, the longer Sam withheld them, the more openly he flirted with other women in Ann's presence, the more often he left her alone at night to "bum around with the guys," the less warmth he showed her in bed.

Then, just when Ann felt she could endure it no longer, when she had run out of rationalizations and excuses for his behavior, Sam would revert to the adoring, generous, smart, funny, charming man she loved.

He would take her to screenings, dinners, and parties and proudly show her off. He would spend hour after hour coaching her in acting exercises. He would sit in on her workshop classes, good-naturedly sharing his experiences and expertise with the delighted students. He would take her shopping for costly clothes that he would invariably charge. He would talk almost wistfully about their future children. He would make her feel cherished and safe.

As soon as Ann's confidence was restored and Sam's adoration seemed at its peak, the cycle would begin all over again.

There were other problems.

As Carl Adams's client and Sam Dallas's wife, Ann grew used to luxurious living, to glamour and sophistication. But as Sam Dallas's wife, she also grew used to a nameless specter that hovered over the house.

"I told you, you don't have to worry about money. That's not your department," Sam would assure her. And Ann would accept his reassurance—until she was confronted by the next dunning letter or bill collector. She sensed that despite his protests, Sam lived in constant fear that the house would be repossessed.

The thought of life without him had become impossible for Ann. Worn down and exhausted by the wild swings in their relationship, she virtually forgot that she had once managed to get by on her own, that she had once had value on her own.

Those facts were particularly easy to forget as week followed week without any breakthrough in her career. Ann felt a growing undercurrent of dissatisfaction from Sam and, even more so, from Carl Adams.

In truth, her manager was beginning to accept two facts about Ann that changed his opinion of her entirely.

One was that she had zero acting talent.

The second evolved slowly and came as more of a surprise.

Adams hadn't thought much about it when he'd learned that Ann had taken an equivalency test to earn a high school diploma. His attention had, however, been captured when Sam later informed him that, based on the results of the examination, Ann had been encouraged to take a high school equivalency exam to qualify for college enrollment—and that she had passed with an impressive score.

"She reads a lot," Sam said with a shrug. "She reads halfway through the night."

Carl saw that Ann was determined to improve herself. He also noticed how she conducted herself when he discussed potential deals; she kept track of figures and asked questions that were sharp and insightful, missing no details.

What he recognized in Ann was a far greater degree of personal power than he had credited her with, far greater than Sam—or Ann—imagined. Feeling vaguely threatened by what he perceived, Adams took an evermore patronizing stance with Ann. He became more critical. He made condescending remarks more often.

Still, he resisted admitting to himself that with Ann, his "golden gut" instinct for spotting new stars had failed.

Adams handled that sore point by focusing on more promising clients and projects, for the time being leaving Ann's career in the hands of her husband.

There were more meetings, more auditions, more casting calls, more close calls, and more disappointments. Then, at last, after nearly two years of nonstop effort, Ann's breaks started to come—or so it seemed.

She was presented with two significant offers for work within twenty-four hours.

The first was from a record company vice president who had heard her sing in an Equity waiver musical production. Presented in a fifty-seat theater in Studio City, the show had folded after only three weeks. Ann, an understudy, had only one chance to perform.

She was stunned to get word from the producer of the defunct show that a record company exec who had seen the production was looking for her. She was even more stunned by the reason.

The Little Strangers pop group needed a quick replacement for one of its female singers, he said. He felt certain that Ann's mellow but unobtrusive voice would be perfect to restore the group's harmony in time for its forthcoming tour. She had, he believed, just the right bright, upbeat wholesomeness to meld with the rest of the group. All she had to do was meet with the approval of the five Little Strangers and she might easily become the new sixth member.

Ann could barely wait for Sam to get home to tell him the news, but when he finally arrived that evening, he had news of his own.

"Get ready to be a movie star, baby," he told her as she met him at the door. "And I did it—not Carl. He's going to go crazy when he finds out. Are you ready for this? I got you a part in *The Beautiful Ones* with me!"

He lifted Ann up and swung her around with an exultant whoop. "See what I mean about there being no such thing as a social dinner in this town? The whole time we were out with Paul Farr last week, unbeknownst even to me, he was watching you. He's nuts about you. But he wasn't sure you could handle this—until I convinced him. You should have heard the selling job I did. By the time I left him, he practically couldn't imagine doing the movie without you."

"Tell me about it," Ann said excitedly.

She already knew quite a bit about the movie. *The Beautiful Ones* was a flimsy, low-budget *Easy Rider* ripoff. Sam, however, was convinced it would be the catalyst for fresh glory, the departure point in his ride to newborn success. *The Beautiful Ones* would show how with it Sam Dallas still was.

Production on the film was scheduled to begin in two weeks, just about the time the Little Strangers were about to start their tour.

"Granted, it's not that big a part," Sam said, "but it's pivotal, and it's a good showcase for you. You'll play the daughter of the Secretary of Defense—a groovy, sexy, turned-on chick who's antiwar."

"I don't remember that part in the script," Ann said, perplexed.

"That's because they're just writing it in now."

"Now?" she questioned. "Two weeks before they start?"

She might not be an expert, but she knew what writing in a new character at the eleventh hour had to say about the shape of a story.

Sam read the doubt in her expression and reassured her. "This is Paul Farr, baby. He's a genius. If you'd ever seen *The Echo* you'd know. Paul wants to turn the location into a totally creative environment. Everyone is going to have input. He wants the scenes to come out as fresh and spontaneous as possible. So you'd better be prepared not to let script changes throw you. That's how Paul works."

After an hour of listening to Sam carry on about the movie, Ann finally got around to bringing up her other offer.

Sam winced. "The Little Strangers?" His words were heavy with disdain. "You must be kidding! That's horrible for your image. They're one step away from the Lawrence Welk Show. Whose lousy idea was that?"

Ann abandoned the Little Strangers to become one of the Beautiful Ones.

FIFTEEN

ANN WAITED IN the hot sun as "genius" Paul Farr finished issuing his final directives for a complicated action sequence. Behind her snaked an arcade in the tourist area of Santa Fe, where Indians in native attire sat cross-legged, presiding over their displays of turquoise jewelry, beaded headbands, kachina dolls, and other trinkets. Two beefy character actors, sweltering in the navy woolen suits they wore for their roles as government men, stood opposite Ann. Facing them were the camera, reflectors, sound equipment, and crew.

The scene had Sam and his costar, Jesse Quinones, jumping the character actors, one of whom was holding a concealed pistol on Ann. In the ensuing fracas, the gun would go off, and an innocent Indian would be shot.

A packet of fake blood was handed to the innocent Indian —a stuntman named Vinnie de Amatteo—and they were ready to roll. There were no rehearsals; the director believed that rehearsals would spoil the spontaneity.

In point of fact, the scene wasn't even in the script. But then, Ann asked herself, what was?

"Does anyone have any questions?" asked Farr.

Ann stepped forward. "I just wondered . . ." Seeing the director's impatient look, she faltered. "I mean . . . have they seen these two government men before?"

"No," Farr replied brusquely, anxious to get on with it.

"Well, then . . . why do they jump them? After all, they can't see the gun. Why would they jump two strangers for no reason? They must know"—Farr's face darkened, but she was into it now—"who they are . . . somehow?"

From the sidelines Sam called out, "We know!"

Farr nodded at him. "Thank you."

They were two weeks into production, shooting Ann's third scene, and she was finding it difficult to ignore the fact that nothing about the film thus far made sense.

Nevertheless, when the clapboard snapped she went into character and cringed fearfully against the arcade wall.

Someone was aiming a gun at her. She looked frantically for a way to escape.

Suddenly, Sam and Jesse rushed up behind her would-be captors. As Jesse and one of the government men struggled for control of the pistol, Ann started to run and the Indians began to scatter. The blank was fired, and the stuntman clutched his side, breaking the packet of fake blood. He staggered dramatically, then fell.

"I love it," called Farr. "Let's do it again. I want more blood this time. I want to see the hole in his chest."

While the director conferred with his special effects man, Sam marched across the sun-bleached, dusty, square.

"What was *that* all about?" he asked Ann hotly.

"It was just an honest question," she protested. "Isn't it better for someone here to bring it up now than for audiences to bring it up later? You start slugging these two men for no reason."

"You don't need a reason," he hissed. "We had scenes like this on 'Runabout' all the time. If the dialogue sounds good enough, if a scene looks good enough, if the action's strong enough, people *think* it makes sense. *I* know. *You* don't. So do me a favor and don't nitpick. You're making yourself look like a fool—and it doesn't reflect well on me. Just keep your mouth shut and do what Farr tells you."

So much, she thought, for the environment of total creativity, in which everyone provided input.

"Okay!" yelled the assistant director. "Everyone in their places!"

A few seconds later, the snap of the clapboard sounded again.

Once again, the gun was aimed. Sam and Jesse rushed up behind Ann's would-be captors. She started to run, and the

Indians scattered once again. Jesse and the government agent struggled for control of the pistol and a shot was fired.

Only this time a torrent of blood exploded from a hole in the stuntman's side. Ann turned to the gory sight and felt a wave of nausea, then her legs buckled under her.

"What do you think you're doing?" yelled the director. "I didn't want *you* to fall."

"She's not getting up," the stuntman observed, seconds later.

The extras quickly clustered around Ann as Sam and Farr hurried over. Sam knelt by her and gently raised her head, then looked up at Farr in surprise.

"She's out cold."

"What the hell . . . ?" Slowly a smile spread across Farr's face. "I like it. In fact, it's perfect. The perfect response for a pacifist."

"Total realism," one of his aides quickly agreed.

"Wake up." Sam patted Ann's cheeks. "Come on, baby—"

"Wait! Don't do that," Farr commanded. He rushed back to the camera, grinning wildly, his eyes shining with a fanatic light.

"I want to get this! I want to pick it up. I want everyone back where they were at the moment she fainted! Sam, you go to her and do just what you were doing! Vinnie, get back on the ground! Jesse, go to Vinnie, just as you were!"

The group hurried to recreate its formation.

The first thing Ann heard was Jesse shouting, "He's dead!"

She raised her head to see Vinnie lying in a pool of blood, a crowd of Indians and actors hovering grim-faced about him. The message hit hard: a terrible mistake had been made, a real bullet had been fired—and Vinnie was dead. Suddenly Ann felt as if she were reliving the horror of her father's death.

She struggled to her feet as Sam tried to hold her down. She lurched forward, a study in shock, and moaned, "Oh, no. No! God, why do you let these things happen?"

Then she stopped and looked around in confusion. Seeing the director seated in his chair, the cameraman and crew at their posts, the actors and extras staring at her, Ann realized the truth in a rush.

"Cut! Print it!" cried Farr. "That was beautiful! Brilliant! We can use everything up to the last bit of footage." He stood and began applauding, and, one by one, the rest of the cast, the extras, the crew joined in. For the first time, Ann felt the pain of her scraped hands and arm, the throbbing bump on her head.

They were all insane!

Sam came up behind Ann and gave her a pat on the fanny. "Nice improv," he clucked.

She whirled around, shoving him back as she ran away in tears.

"I love it when you're passionate," Sam called out mockingly, and several members of the company responded with a burst of nervous laughter.

Later, in their hotel room, Sam berated her for her behavior. "Don't you ever—*ever*—shove me like that again. You made me look like a fool in front of all those people. Let's see how you like it!" he said as he gave her a fierce push that sent her flying across the room to land flat on the bed.

As the days went by, confusion gave way to more confusion—and a constant lowering of morale—as Farr bumbled through creation of his "artistic vision."

Often the director arrived at work with no idea of what he would shoot; he sometimes spent hours staring off into space, waiting for a bolt of creative lightning to strike.

Farr was known for making films with improvised dialogue, but in the case of *The Beautiful Ones* all too often the results were meaningless scenes with seemingly interminable lulls.

Production came to a dead halt one afternoon when Jesse failed to report for work. A few hours later he was found, naked, perched on top of an equipment truck, strumming his guitar and humming along to some inner harmony.

Nobody seemed annoyed that Jesse's drug idyll had hung up an entire film company. Ann was baffled by the attitude until she realized Jesse was very popular with the troupe and discovered the reason—his generosity in sharing his private pharmacy.

Sam had always told her that he was not particularly fond of drugs, professing a personal preference for Jack Daniels. So Ann was shocked when he joined Jesse and company in several of their acid fiestas. He began returning to the hotel well after dawn, reporting to work wrung out, his eyes heavy-lidded and red-rimmed.

Soon, Ann began hearing pointed hints of goings-on be-

tween her husband and various extras. Then there were remarks about one of the starry-eyed local girls hanging around
the set. She heard—but managed to convince herself that
there was nothing serious, nothing to worry about, in her husband's flirtatious ways.

At least, she convinced herself for awhile.

Ann was not expecting Sam back on the afternoon she
called Lyla to talk, as usual, about Cindy.

This time, she found her sister neither distant nor dis-
tracted. Lyla needed money, she blurted out—she and Joe
needed five hundred dollars. Could Ann help?

"I'll pay you back. I promise." Lyla was actually pleading.
Ann's heart swelled—to have Lyla turn to her in a crisis!

Of course she would send the money. It seemed incredible
to Ann that Lyla could be so panic-stricken over a mere five
hundred dollars. Listening to Lyla's tearful thanks, Ann realized how her own perspective had changed, now that she had
grown used to big spending—and big debts.

Surrounded by money, making money, watching Sam constantly squander money, it seemed only right that she should
give Lyla the small sum she needed.

Sam walked in in the middle of the conversation. In seconds, he grasped what was being said and to whom. He demanded that Ann hang up . . . right now. When she didn't
respond quickly enough, he took the receiver out of her hand
and slammed it down, screaming to her about her "fucking
relatives, those fucking spongers!

"We're not giving them a cent. I'm not getting stuck with
their damned problems."

"She's my sister," Ann protested. "She's bringing up my
child."

Sam stormed across the room. "Damn it to hell, Ann, that
kid is not your responsibility. When we got married, you were
going to forget about her."

"I said I would pick up and go on, Sam," Ann cried desperately. "And I have! I've barely mentioned Cindy, but you
can't expect me to turn off my mind and my heart."

"That's *not* what I said," he answered coldly. Ann flinched.
After a moment, she whispered, "When we got married,
we were going to have a family of our own."

"I don't want to talk about it."

"You don't ever want to talk about it. You don't want to talk about anything!" Ann cried. "You're saving all your energy for tripping out and fooling around."

"What?" he roared. "Fooling around? I've been working my ass off every goddamn day!"

Ann shrank back at the savage expression on his face. "I'm sorry," she breathed. "Sam, I'm sorry!"

But he was already rushing to the small desk near the door. He pulled out a drawer, took out a thick envelope, and waved it around wildly. "You're saving all *your* energy for this shit!"

Ann stared, speechless. In that envelope were her latest unmailed letters to Cindy.

Ever since Ann had left her daughter in New York, she had written those letters for someday when Cindy was old enough and might—just might—want to know about her natural mother. The notes were filled with assurances of Ann's love, full of explanations about why Ann had had to leave her child.

It was all-important to her that Cindy never feel she had been unwanted—as Ann herself felt so often, and as she was feeling now, watching numbly as Sam tore the envelope and its contents to shreds. He threw the bits of paper into the air. They fell in an acid rain of confetti over the bed and onto the rug.

"I'm sick of hearing about your bastard!" He marched out of the room, slamming the door behind him.

The next day, the big topic of setside gossip was Sam's abrupt move into a separate hotel room, which he insisted had to be as large as—preferably larger than—the room he had shared with Ann.

He was, after all, the star of *The Beautiful Ones*.

The line producer visited Ann to explain, red-faced, what a struggle it was to keep the project afloat financially and how "most of us are making sacrifices" on behalf of the film. In other words, to nudge Ann into volunteering to move into another smaller—cheaper—room.

Heartbroken and humiliated, she did just that. But she also talked the producer into giving her a five-hundred-dollar advance.

With it, she purchased a money order for Lyla.

As work on the film zigzagged on, Ann found being near Sam yet excluded from his company a constant torment. She watched as he shared jokes with others, as he blocked scenes, as he ate lunch and laughed with his comrades, as he passed by her again and again without so much as a glance.

Yet sitting in her empty room brooding about Sam was even worse than being near him on the set.

She discovered that fact one evening as she was idly flipping channels on the TV set in her hotel room. A rerun of "Runabout" was being shown on one of the local stations, and she found herself mesmerized by the sight of a younger, fresher, clean-cut version of her husband playing a likable deputy sheriff in the Old West.

As she watched, the action switched from a saloon to a meadow; Sam held a young beauty in his arms and murmured lovingly, "You know what I think? We were cut from the same piece of soul cloth, you and I. That's why we knew so fast. You're the wind and I'm the sail. We belong together."

Ann stiffened. It was the exact line Sam had used the day she had moved in with him, the very words she had memorized and cherished. Even the delivery was identical.

How many other times had he played that scene? Opposite how many other women?

How long, she finally asked herself, could she hide from the reality of her disintegrating marriage?

The whispers about Sam and other women had continued, along with persistent rumors that the LSD crowd had added group sex to its repertoire.

Lying awake that night, Ann decided she would have to do something to keep her mind occupied between her brief moments before the camera; if she were to get through the movie, she would have to fight her way out of despair.

She found the solution in trying to learn all she could about the movie and how it was being made.

"What do those do?"

"How does that work?"

"How expensive is it?"

"How do you keep track of all that?"

In short order, Ann came to be thought of as the Girl Who Wants to Know Everything. All day, day after day, she remained setside whether or not she had a scene to shoot. Her fascination with the filmmaking process seemed endless. She was a keen observer. Her questions, well timed and perceptive, impressed the crew, the production staff, and eventually, the director. Indeed, it soon seemed that everyone on the set was happy to chat with Ann and to share secrets of the trade —with the exception of her husband.

Six weeks into the production, Ann finished her last scene and was given her release. With one final take, there was no longer any way to dodge the issue, no work in which to immerse herself. She didn't know what to do next.

Sam abruptly made the decision for her. Walking into her room one day as if the past weeks had never occurred, he said matter-of-factly, "It must be awfully boring for you with nothing to do, baby. Why not go back to L.A. and see what Carl has lined up?"

She felt as if she had been kicked in the stomach. Choking, half-blinded by the moisture in her eyes, she took down her suitcase and began emptying bureau drawers.

With her back to her husband, she said softly, "I don't want us to break up, Sam. But if that's what you really want, I won't make a problem."

"What are you talking about?" he asked, sounding astonished. "I'm just telling you to go home a little before me. Why should you be sitting around here with nothing to do while I'm still working?"

Ann turned and gazed at him.

"Okay. Listen. It got a little rough, but, come on, don't you know me by now? I was just pissed off."

Ann thought of the torn fragments of her letters fluttering to the floor. She remembered Sam snarling out the word *bastard*.

"How could I know that?" she murmured.

Sam changed his tack. All charm, he looked up at her from under his eyebrows. "I really didn't mean it."

"But, Sam, you turned on me, and everybody knew it," she said haltingly. "These last three weeks have been hell."

"You of all people should understand what I've been going through. I've been living and breathing Owens every day," said Sam, referring to his role. "When I'm in the middle of shooting, I get uptight. Don't you know that?"

Ann knew he was inventing excuses as he went along. The women, the cruelty, the humiliation—he was blaming it all on his part, although the character he was playing was not evil, not cruel, not even moody.

But Sam sounded so sincere. And Ann wanted nothing

more than to believe him and have her happiness miraculously restored. In spite of everything, she was still in love with him.

"Now let's forget about this dumb fight," he said. "Okay?"

"Okay," she whispered.

He reached out to push the suitcase off the bed and onto the floor, lying back and drawing her on top of him, holding her in his arms while his lips traveled softly, caressingly along her face and neck.

"You're so beautiful," he breathed, moving her beside him and pulling at her blouse. Moments later, he was inside her. He was through in record time.

As it turned out, back in Los Angeles Carl had nothing lined up for Ann. He was deeply involved in negotiating a movie deal of his own. He barely had time to talk to her, but he did manage to impart his opinion that Sam had hurt his career by doing *The Beautiful Ones*.

"He loves it," Ann said. "What makes you think it's bad?"

"I'm not talking about the movie, sweetie. I'm talking about the deal."

Carl spelled out the situation. Sam had taken a share of the net profits as part of his price. Such profits, of course, would never be seen—at least not on the books. Any actor with savvy—with the clout to negotiate a decent contract—would never make a percentage deal unless it were for a piece of the gross.

As Ann was to learn later, the stories were legion about theatrical blockbusters and successful, long-running TV series whose profit participants never saw a cent of profits—thanks to creative bookkeeping and padded or fictitious production costs. Adams had an expert's awareness of such techniques.

"I told him he was crazy to take it," he concluded.

"It's a different kind of part for him. He thought it was a good opportunity to show his range," Ann responded defensively.

"God, I hope so!" exclaimed Carl with a laugh. "Otherwise he's more of a fool than I thought."

SIXTEEN

IN TIME, it became clear there weren't going to be any *Beautiful Ones* profits to worry about.

The movie finished production after twelve weeks—four weeks over schedule—mainly because the backers refused to come up with any additional funding for the film.

"I don't know exactly what Farr's got, but he must have something," was a remark uttered by more than one member of the cast and crew.

There were rumors, months later, that Farr hoped to reconvene his *Beautiful Ones* actors and shoot a few additional scenes, but neither Sam nor Ann heard directly from the filmmaker. The movie was occasionally mentioned in newspaper columns, always in a "whatever happened to" sense.

Still later, Carl learned that Farr had indeed put something together—and that something was unreleasable.

Farr popped up next in Bangladesh, working on a cinema verité project.

In the end, the movie went down as "Paul Farr's never-released *The Beautiful Ones*."

Meanwhile, the "modern western" Sam had made in Tucson while Ann had recuperated from plastic surgery was released with little fanfare and quickly relegated to second-feature status at drive-ins.

And the public disproved Sam's assessment that The Little Strangers were too sappy and syrupy ever to become successful. With the slot once offered to Ann filled by someone else, the Strangers waxed their first platinum album in 1970.

Within the following two years, the group cut a string of hit tunes, showed up on several variety specials, and had its own summer series. Then its bouncy "I'm Comin' Over" became the unofficial theme song for Hank Evans's first political campaign.

It was a lavish, flamboyant campaign. Once Evans had committed himself, he couldn't abide the thought of losing. He threw his money, energy, time—and family—into the effort.

At ten past noon, the plaza fronting the Warburton, Texas, county court building was a hive of activity. Clerks and lawyers, secretaries and stenographers, businessmen and workmen moved briskly across the sun-washed square on their way to nearby restaurants; others relaxed on concrete benches, brown-bagging it in the sparse shade of young trees.

A fourteen-year-old boy strode through the milling crowd, handing out leaflets and greeting passersby with an ingratiating smile and a cheerful "Hi! Planning to vote for Hank Evans next month?"

He was a skinny, wiry boy. His brown sun-bleached hair was short, especially by 1972 standards, and his jacket and slacks were noticeably well-tailored. His coffee brown eyes glittered in a face flushed with exertion.

He moved on, handing a Stetson-wearing executive a leaflet. "Hi, there. Thanks for your consideration."

"Give this to someone else, son," the man replied. "I'm already voting for Hank Evans for Congress—and glad to do it."

"Thank you, sir." The boy bowed his head theatrically. "And God bless you, sir."

"Wait a minute—you're Hank's boy, aren't you?"

"Yes, I am."

"Out stumping for your daddy," the executive said approvingly. "I like that. You keep up the good work now, you hear?"

"Yes, sir."

Two middle aged women drew closer. "Are you really Hank Evans's son?" one asked.

Eric Evans nodded. "Yes, ma'am."

"Well, I like his pictures, but I wouldn't vote for 'im."

"Sorry to hear that." Eric shrugged and reached into his

jacket pocket. "But no hard feelings. Here, we'd like you to have this pen."

"May I have a pen, too?" asked the other woman excitedly. "I *am* voting for him."

"Absolutely!" Eric grinned. "In that case, a pen and a lapel button. And see if you can get your friend in the pretty dress here to read this, okay?" He winked as he handed her a leaflet.

As they moved away, Eric overheard the first woman say, "He's got his daddy's charm, all right."

"Doesn't he?" gushed the second. "He's cute as a bug!"

A teenage girl approached and asked, "Are you going to be a movie star like your father?"

Eric answered with a trace of shyness. "For now, we're just going to worry about getting him elected."

By this time, there was a small but expanding crowd around Eric.

"Is your father here?" someone asked.

"He's giving a speech at the college. We're trying to spread out and cover more ground. Please, keep us in mind come November."

"You're old man's a warmonger!" yelled a long-haired youth.

"My old man believes in standing up for what he thinks is right!" Eric declared.

"Hank Evans is a great American," a man's voice boomed out.

"In the movies!" a woman responded. "He should have stayed in Hollywood. He's got no business in politics."

"He's a bigot," someone else shouted.

"That's plain ridiculous," Eric said quickly. "And I ought to know."

"It's true you're Hank Evans's son?"

Eric nodded. The crowd around him continued to grow, with people pressing against each other for a closer look. Voices competed for attention.

"Look! Hank Evans's son!"

"Aren't you a little young for this job?"

"What a handsome boy."

"I'm with your father all the way—and so's my whole family!"

"Thank you," Eric said, continuing to move. "We appreciate that."

From the midst of the throng came a gaunt, gawky, middle-aged man in jeans and a T-shirt."

"Hey," he said, grabbing Eric's shoulder roughly, "you really Evans's kid?"

In seconds, the man was pushed aside by a six-foot-three, two-hundred-and-thirty-pound ex-Marine in a business suit. Two more bodyguards stepped forward, creating an opening in the crowd through which Eric walked casually. Across the square, a fourth member of the professional security team moved quickly toward him.

Each man had martial arts training and was equipped with a shoulder holster.

Unruffled, Eric moved on, smiling, shaking hands.

"Hi, there. Planning to vote next month, I hope . . ."

Living under guard with the constant fear of gun-wielding lunatics and would-be kidnappers had been a fact of Eric Evans's life as far back as he could remember.

The limousine turned onto an unmarked road in a barren stretch of land.

It was six P.M., and Mary Evans had already visited a children's hospital, attended an elementary school district PTA luncheon, delivered a speech before the Women's Auxiliary of the VFW, been on two radio shows, and submitted to a newspaper interview. She had also resolved to have it out with Hank about Eric's involvement in the campaign.

Now, as the limousine trundled along the six-mile route to the ranch compound, she recalled the report she had received about Eric's appearance at the plaza and shuddered as she contemplated the horror of what might have ensued.

She watched her son, who was slumped down in the deep leather seat of the limo; he had nodded off shortly after he had joined her for the ride back to the ranch.

He would do anything to please his father, this precocious boy of hers. And Hank never said no to him—even when no would have been in Eric's best interests.

He was so determined to do his part, he had convinced his teachers to allow him to miss classes and work with a tutor at home at night. He was keeping his grades up, but the grind was taking its toll.

It was her own fault, Mary thought. She knew only too

well that, given half a chance, Hank would drain the life out of anyone. It had been up to her to protect her son.

And she had failed.

Unfortunately, before she could even discuss the situation with Evans, there was yet another meeting at the house to get through.

Red meant action; black and white, power; green, adherence to a cause; brown, security; gray, stability. Violet bespoke a dreamer or a visionary, but the wrong shades gave a message of immaturity. Blue, which stood for freedom and reconciliation, was always good.

Such had been the sort of tutoring Mary had received from Evans's media consultant, a brash young man with a Ph.D. in psychology from Yale.

She prowled through a walk-in closet that was eighteen feet in length and ten feet wide. Mary's natural dark blond hair had already been freshly arranged into its conservative bouffant, her makeup redone. There were a few silvery filaments at her temples these days. The cheekbones, merely hinted at when her face was younger and fuller, were becoming more pronounced.

Although Mary was at an indefinite point in the transition from the pretty debutante she had once been to the austere, angular matron she was to become, she already found it difficult to remember herself as she had been before and during the early years of her marriage. Indeed, for anyone who now knew her, it was hard to imagine Mary Carstairs Evans ever having been ruled by love and passion.

At this moment she was wondering what color her image consultant would prescribe as most effective for assuring the early departure of guests.

Mary's suite—sitting room, bedroom, dressing room, and bath—was her one refuge from the engulfing masculinity of the El Capitan Ranch compound.

The rest of the sprawling main house and all three guest houses were decorated in a blend of Indian, Mexican, and Old West. The western look predominated. Oversized couches were upholstered with the skins of leopard and elk. Cowhide chairs, with arms and legs fashioned from the horns of steers, dotted the rooms. On the walls, Remingtons and Russells and the works of such contemporary cowboy artists as John

Cowan and Robert Pummill competed for space with Evans's collection of hunting trophies: deer, elk, buffalo, mountain lions and wild boar shot on the ranch; zebra and leopards gunned down during African safaris. A grizzly bear, poised taxidermally for attack, guarded a glass-encased cabinet containing an arsenal of handmade Kline Gunther rifles inlaid with silver and gold. Custom hand-woven carpeting, embossed with Flying Cs, the El Capitan brand, flowed from sitting rooms to bedrooms, where the brand was repeated again on bedspreads and draperies, shower tiles and towels.

Mary's was a different world, her airy and feminine suite ever abloom with roses. Fresh arrangements in crystal vases perched on her bedside table in harmony with the still-life bouquets in rich oils that hung upon the cream *faux marbre* walls. The furnishings were a carefully chosen blend of antiques, augmented by graceful silken draperies in French blue. The bath was done in elegant Aurora rose marble.

Hank's master suite was in the west wing of the main house, far enough away so that Mary could sometimes pretend he wasn't there.

During the past few years, they had established a marriage of mutual interests and separate lives.

Hank had his friends; a few of the old guard—like the El Capitan's pilot, its overseer, and general troubleshooter Roy Carter—still surrounded him. Mary had her own small circle. Both maintained connections with the all-important, key political and business forces that Hank needed in his new life, in addition to the cream of his famous former Hollywood peers.

When they entertained house guests, Hank would take the men out to hunt the wild turkeys and deer that roamed the twenty-thousand-acre ranch or conduct proud tours of the section of land on which he kept exotic game imported from Africa, enclosed by twenty-foot-high fencing. Mary would shepherd the ladies into the El Capitan jet, which had been comfortably customized with doeskin couches and a mahogany bar carved with the Flying C, and have them piloted to Houston for a day of shopping and lunch.

Even the family pets were divided into separate camps. Hank's golden retrievers were housed in carpeted, air-conditioned kennels near the stables; Mary's ancient, long-haired black puli padded about the main house, perpetually on the lookout for Eric's hyperactive Irish setter.

The dog-height elevator button at the Evanses' penthouse apartment in the city had been installed for the puli, but only the setter ever mastered its use. When he wanted out, he would push the button with his snout and a buzzer would sound, alerting the doorman to prepare for "relief" duty. Then the private elevator would make its ascent, its burnished brass doors would open to receive its four-legged passenger, and a few moments later the dog would be delivered to the doorman on the ground floor.

As dazzling as their Hollywood lifestyle had been, the one in Texas, the land of pioneer spirit and behavior, had a flamboyance all its own. In that world of old-line traditions and first-generation wealth, to have money was to flaunt it. As one leading Houston matron observed about the thirty-karat diamond ring she wore for casual occasions, "Honey, ain't no sense of havin' it less people know you got it."

"You have five minutes," Hank Evans called out at the open door of Mary's suite. "Did you hear me?"

"Yes," she answered from the other room.

Hank was in good spirits, having just completed a phone call with a friend in Los Angeles. He strode into the suite and directed his comments toward the open door of the dressing room. "I'm sure you'll be interested to know that I finally won my bet with Roy."

"What bet is that?"

"You know—for years he's been insisting that Stan Weiss would never let Sentinel be taken over by any outside interest. But now it's happened. I just learned that as of tomorrow, InConTel International will announce itself the proud new owner of the studio." Hank laughed. "I can hardly imagine Sentinel Studios without Stanley Weiss running the show, can you? The old dictator must be fit to be tied!"

A moment later, Mary breezed out wearing a maroon jersey dress and a frown.

"It's very unattractive to gloat over someone's misfortune," she said icily. "If I were you, I would be careful about what I said in front of other people. You don't want to give the impression that what goes on in Hollywood concerns you any longer."

"I wouldn't dream of it," he said. "But I knew you'd be interested."

Mary paused to check her lipstick in the mirror, then

glanced up, saw Hank's grin of triumph in the reflection, and turned on him sharply.

"If you're trying to sidestep discussing what happened today at the plaza, it isn't going to work."

Evans closed his eyes and sighed.

"You do know that Eric almost got mobbed, don't you?" she asked. "Whose idea was it to have him go out there?"

"Eric's," Hank answered, "and I approved it."

"And allowed him to walk around exposed to God-knows-what kind of danger," Mary retorted. "Someone tried to grab him. Why expose him to things like that?"

"If my son wants to campaign for me the way Preston's kids are campaigning for him," Hank replied, referring to his opponent, "I'm not about to stand in his way."

"It is *not* the same thing. My God, Hank! Jerry Preston is not a celebrity. And he's not wealthy. But to put Eric out in the city mall—like bait."

"Calm down," Hank said patronizingly. "Eric doesn't want to spend his life hiding out in some damn monastery. And I'm not going to encourage him to."

"Monastery?" Mary mimicked Hank with a bitter laugh. "What a peculiar choice of words, coming from you. If he follows *your* example, he certainly won't lead a monastic life."

"What in hell has gotten into you today?" Hank demanded.

"As if that scene at the Plaza wasn't enough," Mary cried. Then she moved toward him angrily. "All right, Hank. I want to know whether there's any truth to the story about Roy bringing a couple of call girls to the hotel in Algarve when he took Eric and Jeff to Europe last summer."

Hank signed heavily, his brow furrowing. He gave no answer.

"It's true, then," Mary gasped. "Oh, I *hate* that man. He was supposed to be their *chaperon*." She picked up the pillow on her chair and flung it down, a futile gesture.

"You've been talking to Sheilah Smith," Hank said finally, his lips curling with distaste.

"Yes, I've been talking to her. And I'm ashamed, Hank, ashamed that I had to hear it from Eric's *friend's mother*, three months after the fact. He's too young," she railed.

Hank's words were tinged with fire. "Eric is a fourteen-year-old boy. He's got the makings of a man, but you insist on treating him like a baby—a pansy."

He turned and stalked away from Mary.

She felt the energy drain from her.

Downstairs some thirty members of the inner circle of Hank's campaign were due to congregate. They would probably stay past midnight, and through it all she had to be charming and witty. She had to play the role of Hank's devoted mate to perfection.

Hundreds of Hank Evans's supporters milled around the grand ballroom of Corpus Christi's Sheraton Marina hotel, awaiting the election night returns, listening to the blaring sound of six television sets.

"Our coverage will continue with a close-up of one Texas congressional race that's attracted national attention . . . for reasons other than political."

Festooned with red, white, and blue balloons, banners, and bunting, the ballroom contained a heady atmosphere of celebration only an hour after the polls closed. Evans, the pollsters predicted, would win by a wide margin. His followers merely awaited confirmation, proudly wearing plastic skimmers with paper bands reading EVANS FOR CONGRESS.

Evans, his family, and his key campaign staff were ensconced in the hotel's penthouse suite, poised for the appropriate moment when he would make an appearance in the ballroom to deliver his victory speech. The group clustered around a TV, listening intently to the news:

"From the start of the campaign, it looked like it would be a hard uphill battle for Corpus Christi congressman Jerry Preston to hang on to his seat in the House," intoned the announcer. A shot of the excited crowds at a Hank Evans rally filled the screen, followed by a pathetic picture of his opponent addressing a half-empty American Legion hall.

"I'm not surprised at the turnout he's getting," Preston was shown saying. "We anticipated it. But it's one thing to turn out to get an autograph from a Hollywood celebrity and another to vote for him. Let's face it—Evans has contradicted himself on at least three main issues in the past month. He's muddy on the issues. I have my voting record to stand on."

"Hell of a lot of good it did you," Eric commented with a sharp laugh, and Hank smiled at his son from across the room.

"Evans," the report continued, "has been accused by his opponent of trying to sway voters with a lavish campaign that's all Hollywood glitter with no substance, a charge the Captain says he was expecting . . ."

The news report showed footage of Hank and Mary Evans —together and individually—on the campaign trail.

In one clip, Mary was shown saying that all she wanted was "to provide a good support system for my husband."

Then Eric was shown displaying a youthful arrogance that made Mary cringe. "Nobody can beat my father," he said with a scornful toss of his head. "He could run for president. Nobody could defeat him."

PART 4
A Rising Star

SEVENTEEN

It was a scene of typical election night pandemonium. Campaign workers cheered, popped balloons, released tears of joy, and waved signs. A band blared. Hank Evans posed with his wife and son before a huge red, white, and blue poster bearing his name and likeness. Some 1,300 miles away, Los Angeles' most beautiful anchorwoman, Goldie Kingston, peered into the camera and purred breathily, "Well, now we know. We've lost another actor and gained another politician."

From his marble Roman plunge bath, Carl Adams watched the twelve-inch television screen mounted above the counter of the bathroom sink. It wasn't the election that held his interest, however, nor was it Hank Evans.

His eyes were glued on Goldie Kingston, and as he watched her, Adams suddenly had an idea that was to change Ann Peters's life.

He dried himself off quickly, wrapped a thick velour robe about his body, and made his way to a projection room off the study. It was furnished with several down-filled sofas and low tables with Baccarat bowls, some heaped high with penny candy, others reserved for the cocaine that Carl supplied at his truly special parties. Adams had a film library that boasted everything from current major releases to classics, as well as porn pictures made by some of Hollywood's biggest names during their struggling days. Carl's latest status equipment was a Sony AV 5000 reel-to-reel machine that actually allowed him to show videotapes at home.

Carl found the tape marked with Ann's name and withdrew

it from the cabinet. He was resigned to the fact that she was never going to make it as an actress or a singer. But all his time and money—and most important, his ego investment—were not going to go to waste after all.

Watching Goldie Kingston had shown him the way.

The next morning, Carl summoned Ann and Sam to his estate and met with them in his study.

"I had a religious experience last night," Carl announced. "I found the right place for Ann's talent."

"No kidding," Sam said eagerly—a little too eagerly, or so it struck Carl.

Carl had neglected to return Sam's calls in recent weeks; he had found the traces of desperation creeping into Sam's voice more and more distasteful.

Alone with Ann, Sam had complained about the "ugly side" of Carl Adams. "Try asking Carl for a favor sometime —a small favor, nothing big. Man, you'll never see anyone turn into a prick so fast. He'll give you what *he* wants you to have, but never what you need."

But now that they were with Carl, Sam was grinning and nodding enthusiastically. "Tell us. Where?"

"KCBA."

"Local TV?" Sam asked.

"Yes," Carl nodded, "as a training ground for an eventual network spot. Ann was made to be a personality."

Sam gave him a faint smile. "I don't get it."

"We're going to make Ann into a news personality."

Carl turned his attention to Ann, who listened with keen interest. "You're ideal for it. I looked at your commercial and your Girls' League spot again last night. You radiate sincerity. You can read cue cards. And I happen to believe you have the perfect look."

Who am I supposed to be now? Ann wondered.

To Sam, Carl added, "Ann has the innate intelligence of a Nancy Dickerson, combined with the sex appeal of a Goldie Kingston—looks that are a turn-on to men but don't represent a threat to women."

"Ann on the news?" Sam grinned. He obviously found the idea preposterous.

"People with less than she has have ended up as stars of national news programs." Carl insisted. *"And* talk shows."

"But, Carl, I don't have the background," Ann protested.

"Do you think Goldie Kingston has a background?" Carl chided her.

"I sure like her foreground," Sam interjected, grinning.

Carl nodded. "Exactly. Have you watched 'Action News 10' lately?"

Ann and Sam shook their heads.

"Well, they've got a new thing they've been putting on two or three times a week called 'Southland Scene.' It's a mixed bag of human interest stories that don't fit into any other category on the news—from trends and fads that are big among the beautiful people to outrageous oddball stories. They did one on an eighty-year-old nun who's patented a new way to make pizza dough. They've been rotating their field reporters on these segments so far. But they'll be expanding 'Southland Scene' into a daily feature soon. And if that works out, they may spin off an entire 'Southland Scene' show, which would probably bump Sheilah Smith's talk show, their biggest ratings loser.

"This is all confidential, by the way," Carl added, briefly raising his finger to his lips. Then, leaning forward with the air of someone imparting classified government information, he said, "They'd like to find a charismatic, highly promotable reporter to take over 'Southland Scene.' They've been quietly scouting local stations around the country. Ann would be perfect for it."

"Jeez, Carl—where'd you hear this?" Sam asked.

Adams rose to make his most important point. "I happen to have very good connections with the man who can hand Ann her new career."

He paused and looked at Ann and Sam, smiling the way he smiled when it seemed he almost expected applause.

"Who?" Sam finally asked.

"Who's the big gun at KCBA? Sol Jolkins, that's who," Carl announced grandly. "I'm going to get Ann a meeting."

"Great!" Sam nodded.

Despite their professed enthusiasm, both Sam and Ann assumed that Carl's idea fell into that vast, seemingly limitless category of Adams's Big Talk that Won't Amount to Anything.

When they left his estate, it was to return to the plain, sand-colored three-bedroom North Hollywood tract house they now called home.

At the end of his financial tether, Sam had finally sold his Laurel Canyon haven and made the move with Ann to the Valley and a rented house. Its previous tenant had been a broken-down comedy writer from the "Our Miss Brooks" era, and to Sam the house reeked of futility, desperation, and faded glory, of dead dreams and bad dreams. Sam hated it. He loathed living in the Valley, which he considered a blatant advertisement of his failure. His cherished Jaguar was also gone, over which he felt true grief.

But despite his distress, Sam was warm and tender with Ann. He was docile in defeat, leaning on her as he hid from his friends.

Temporarily.

To Ann and Sam's surprise, Carl phoned two days later to announce that he had set up a meeting with Sol Jolkins and that Jolkins was very interested in Ann.

"I only have three days," she exclaimed, seized with sudden anxiety as the reality of this new job prospect set in. "How can I possibly learn anything in time?"

Sam slouched against the frame of the kitchen door, arms folded over his chest, a stance as casual as his faded blue work shirt.

"If they want someone who can read, okay," he said dismissively, tossing back his wavy mane of long brown hair. "If they want someone who knows anything about the news business, you're out of it. That's all."

"I should at least read some books or something, shouldn't I?" she asked worriedly.

"Why bother? There's no way you could learn enough fast enough. You'd be killing yourself for nothing."

"You're probably right." Ann wrapped her arms around Sam's waist and tucked her head into his shoulder with a sigh. "But you and Carl have worked so hard to help me, and . . ." She shrugged, censoring a reference to their money woes— one of several subjects Sam did not want broached.

"And I know you're both frustrated," Ann said carefully. "It probably is a waste of time. But it can't hurt to give it my best. Besides, unless I go in believing I have a good chance, I won't have *any* chance."

Sam hugged her and gave her a quick kiss.

Ann's enthusiasm made him begin to warm up to Adams's latest Big Idea.

"Okay. Then let's think about what's really going to matter: the image you want to project when you meet Sol Jolkins. What are you planning to wear?"

"You're better at that than I am," Ann answered, delighted by his interest.

She was well aware of Sam's fondness for playing fashion expert, using her as his live-in dress-up doll. There was no denying he had an excellent eye for style.

"I think you should aim for a complementary contrast to Goldie Kingston," he announced. "Let me give it some thought."

They set about their respective plans with an energy neither had felt in weeks.

Ann watched every "Action News 10" broadcast, making notes and lists of ideas. She spent long hours at the public library pouring over books and articles about broadcast news.

Sam decided upon her *new* new image. "We're going to go for an effect that's laid-back but businesslike," he explained, "smart, with more than an edge of romance."

He sent Ann to Sassoon to have her look updated. Natural was in, so he decided Ann was to have her blond hair darkened a shade and then highlighted for a better forgery of nature's art. He wanted her hair cut in a Jane Fonda shag.

He called upon Carl to call upon his boutique-owner friend Gianni Salerno for Ann's "impression"—and selected a mahogany-colored wool suit with suede trim and elbow patches, softened by a draped-neck silk blouse in a subtle print of cream, celadon, bronze, and black.

Before Ann left for her meeting at the station, Sam scrutinized her for a final time and pronounced her perfect.

"It's right on," he said. "You'll kill 'em."

"I'll try," Ann replied, "but if he asks me any questions, he'll probably realize I don't know what I'm talking about."

"It won't matter," Sam predicted.

Everything in Sol Jolkins's office impressed Ann in a positive way, with the exception of Jolkins.

The view from his sixth-floor windows—a vista backed by the dusty contours of Mt. Lee with its HOLLYWOOD sign—was impressive, as was the wall of photographs featuring Jolkins centrally situated with a variety of newsmakers from Neil

Armstrong to Muhammad Ali to President Nixon. The solid oak paneling and the rich African mahogany desk created an atmosphere of power coupled with taste.

But Ann found Jolkins instantly off-putting. A middle-aged man with a jowly face and lifeless, sharklike eyes, he had the pillow-soft body and soft, manicured hands of a voluptuary. His Palm Springs tan was Georgette Klinger perfect, smooth and glowing. His clothes were impeccably tailored. A dark tint hid the gray in thinning hair that was painstakingly arranged to cover his pate. Ann caught a whiff of his fine cologne when he shook her hand, and she noticed the gleaming gold and diamond Patek Philippe poking out from his jacket sleeve.

She also noticed, as she responded to Carl's introduction with all due enthusiasm, that Jolkins was examining her with leering interest.

"We liked the way you came across in that public service spot on the tape Carl sent over," Jolkins informed her, "but the other stuff didn't wow me. Hopefully, it was the way that carpet commercial was done—and not you—that made it so terrible." He made a wry face.

"My mistake," Carl interrupted hastily. "I didn't mean to include that. It was a very slipshod operation. Very slipshod. Ann is a wonderful communicator. That ad doesn't show her to advantage."

What both Carl and Ann knew was that he had had nothing else to choose from.

"The PSA shows how she really comes across. In fact, Girls League got one of its highest response rates ever for it."

Jolkins grunted. "So you told me."

He glanced at Ann, and she wondered nervously when he was going to get around to asking questions about her background in broadcasting.

"I'm glad you saw the footage from the film." Carl continued his unabashed pitch. "It's a shame you never saw Ann on stage. She has a marvelous presence. I'm just pointing that out as another example of her tremendous versatility."

Jolkins stroked his chin, scrutinizing Ann closely. Then one corner of his mouth creased in a half-smile. "What else can you do?" he asked slowly.

A wave of distaste washed over her, but she smiled brightly and said, "I work hard, I learn fast and I'm comfortable in front of a camera."

Jolkins nodded, his sharply peaked eyebrows raised.

Still staring, still sizing her up in a way that made Ann uncomfortable, he added, "And you're an exceptionally lovely woman."

"Just read the teleprompter the best you can and pretend you're talking to a lover when you look into the camera."

Ann smiled out into the dimness of CBA's Studio A, "local," as it was known, thinking the instruction from news director Tony March was a joke.

She knew that as soon as her on-camera trial was finished, March would get around to asking her the questions about her experience that Sol Jolkins had failed to ask.

For now, she guessed, March was kidding around to help put her at ease.

She squinted against the brightness of the studio lights and finally saw him standing in the shadows a few feet behind Camera Two.

There was not a trace of humor on his face.

So, falling back on her acting training, Ann did exactly as requested and began to read an old report off the teleprompter as seductively as possible. She found it a bit of a challenge to talk as if to a lover about a labor dispute.

"... The walkout came after an eleventh-hour bargaining session erupted into near violence," she purred erotically. "Representatives on both sides say there is no telling how long the strike will continue ..."

As Ann read, March left the studio and went upstairs to the booth where Sol Jolkins stood, arms crossed, coolly appraising Ann on the monitors, an unseen god looking down on his tiny universe.

"How does she look?" March asked. He disliked committing himself until he had heard Jolkins's opinion. He was well aware that, in addition to overseeing the day-to-day news operation, his job at KCBA included playing yes man to the station manager.

Jolkins glanced at him with a half smile that carried a fine review. "See for yourself."

March pulled up one of the rolling chairs behind the control panel. "Nice," he said decisively. Ann looked especially striking in front of the blue background, which brought out her breathtaking eyes. "Very nice."

"Yeah, I think the viewers could get it up for her with no trouble," Jolkins commented.

When he came back to the studio, March thanked Ann. "We'll let you know," he told her noncommittally.

She returned home disappointed. She told Sam that neither Jolkins nor the news director had asked her a single question about her qualifications, so they couldn't be interested.

Meanwhile, Sol Jolkins's minions went to work market-testing Ann Peters.

They showed her tape to one sample audience and collected comments. A second set of volunteer human guinea pigs was rigged up with electrodes that registered their subconscious reactions to several tapes, including Ann's. Jolkins was a great believer in that particular test—the controversial Galvanic Skin Response Indicator. Invented to help predict rock 'n' roll hits, it was later put to use by broadcasting consultants firms to help gauge the interest generated by on-air newspeople.

Jolkins had, in fact, come to KCBA fresh from a stint with such a consultants firm. Lauded as the man responsible for ratings turnarounds at stations in Dallas and Philadelphia, he had advised management on everything from sets and graphics to selection of news personalities and their images to content and pacing of stories. The stations drew widening shares of the TV audience with news programs that blended sex with sensationalism and provided titillation in the guise of public service reports ranging from studies of pedophilia to stress-related sexual inadequacies.

It was a time of changes and extremes. While journalist giants like Walter Cronkite bemoaned the sweeping trend "to replace competent reporters with twenty-two-year-old collar ads," stations all across the country were becoming daring in their approaches to pepping up the news.

Sol Jolkins was more than daring; he was shameless. He was viewed as being on the cutting edge of all the latest revolutionary approaches to local TV journalism, from employing drama coaches and speech therapists to using the full range of market research tools. He believed in all the snappy catch phrases, from "news you can use" to "if it bleeds, it leads." It was with the latter in mind that he gave viewers a graphic reenactment of a disastrous mine explosion, complete with lifelike mannequins blown apart by a rigged charge.

The prospect of having his own news department had proved the ultimate lure for Jolkins. As the man in charge of "The KCBA News," which he had immediately retitled "Action News 10," he had been assured he would have virtually unlimited freedom to put his personal stamp on the program, as well as on all the other shows in the station's news division.

Starting with the proclamation that the old news show was stodgy and hokey, he had fired eight longtime members of the department within his first fifteen minutes on the job.

Most critical to Jolkins had been the makeup of his new "news family."

"It should be a family viewers can love as much or more than their own," he insisted. "We've got the girl next door on weather, a sassy little brother on sports; we've got handsome young father figures for our male anchors. What we need is a sexy—and I'm talking incredible-looking—female anchor. Young. A lover, not a mother figure. Mother figures are death in the ratings."

Jolkins had come to KCBA with his top female anchor prospect already in mind: Goldie Kingston.

The sultry, sable-haired twenty-four-year-old held the distinction of being the only anchorwoman of a major metropolitan network affiliate whose professional credits included a two-year stint as a major-league-football cheerleader—a fact intentionally forgotten by Goldie but discussed with snickers and snorts by just about everyone else in the nation's community of local news broadcasters.

No doubt recognizing the limitations of career longevity in cheerleading, she had turned in her pom-poms and left the gridiron to seek worthier pastures as a TV weather girl in Boise about a year before Jolkins spotted her. He had wanted her for himself as well as for KCBA—and Goldie had been readily accommodating in both instances.

The public had quickly responded to Jolkins's remodeled newscast. With each audience share increase, Jolkins had become more tyrannical—and more of a favored son at the network. After boosting the Action News ratings an astounding ten points in nine months, Jolkins had pressed for, and been granted, the position of KCBA Vice-President and General Manager.

None of it came as a surprise to Jolkins; he knew he was destined for success. The product of a highly political New

York family of social climbers, he was used to being surrounded by the powerful and prosperous. Indeed, he was firmly ensconced in the highflying social world of sports through media mogul Leigh Ballard before ever coming to Los Angeles. Ballard was a fraternity brother.

As a new bright light in town, Jolkins had quickly been added to Carl Adams's party list, and he had soon begun making regular appearances at both Carl's Bel Air estate and his Malibu hideaway. In return, Carl's name had been added to the VIP ticket roster for California Condors games—as a friend of a friend of co-owner Leigh Ballard. Although Carl couldn't have cared less about basketball, he relished the cachet of being seated among the stars.

Married and the father of four, Sol Jolkins was already balancing his home life with a steamy affair with Goldie Kingston, but that did not deter him from eagerly responding to the parade of beauties Carl made available to him. Jolkins's appetite for women was as insatiable as his appetite for increased audience shares.

It seemed his interest in Ann could be validated on both counts. When the test scores were tallied, her prospects for being named the 'Southland Scene' reporter were greatly enhanced; she rated second only to a seasoned field reporter from Detroit named Winona Johnson.

"We don't need that prima donna," Jolkins said, referring to the test groups' number one choice. "I've heard Winona has an attitude lately. She's gotten into this Women's Lib crap. I want someone who hasn't got a lot of preconceived ideas, someone who won't question everything she's asked to do, someone we can mold—above all, someone who'll be *grateful*."

Tony March nodded. "So you want Ann Peters."

Jolkins chuckled. "Sure do. Get me Carl Adams. We'll set up a trial period."

EIGHTEEN

ANN SPENT THE weekend prior to her start at KCBA in a flurry of anxious activity. She read books, papers, and magazines, made notes and lists of questions and ideas, and with Sam's assistance planned what she would wear. All the while she worried about exactly what would be expected of her.

She never came close to imagining what actually lay ahead.

Tony March's assistant showed her to her desk, one of some fifty units in the newsroom, a vast, barnlike, windowless space with fluorescent lighting and walls of a washed-out pastel gold. Then he took her to March's quarters, a glass-enclosed office at the front of the room.

"Have some coffee. Look around," her new boss instructed. "I have to take care of a few things," he added distractedly. "Why don't you come back in about half an hour and we'll talk."

Ann toured as ordered—first an overview of the newsroom, then a trek around the station. She circumnavigated the maze of polished hallways, stopping to observe what was taking place on the stages and within a glass-walled editing room.

As she passed a makeup room, Ann caught sight of Sheilah Smith, who was being readied to go before the cameras for her "Perfectly Personal" talk show. She was swept by a feeling of reverence for the flame-haired veteran actress who had acquired legend status with roles such as the sultry, hard-headed heiress in *Brass Keys*. With Billy Wilder directing, Sheilah

179

had made a brilliant deadpan comedienne. With Stanley Donen putting her through her paces, she had been an endearing chorine. But the Sheilah Smith Ann would never forget was the one who filled the screen when Ann was sitting with Lyla in a theater near their Alexandria, Virginia, home shortly after their father's death.

"I'm not going to tell you I'm sorry for you," she said to Eva Marie Saint—and to Ann. "I'm going to tell you you're going to dry your eyes and go out and *pretend* you can stand the pain. Pretend you know you've got your whole life ahead of you. Pretend you want to live it. Pretend you can be happy again. And I guarantee you, every day it will become a little more true."

In an instant, the memory came and went, and Ann recalled, with a knot in her stomach, Carl Adams's confidential information about the station's plans to dump Sheilah Smith's daytime talk show.

"Do you need something?" the makeup woman asked, looking up.

"No, I'm just trying to learn my way around," Ann replied. "I'm working here, starting today."

"Well, congratulations." The makeup woman nodded affably. "Welcome to the loony bin."

As Ann introduced herself, she was interrupted by Sheilah Smith, who sat in the makeup chair with her chin tilted back and her eyes closed.

"Where are you working?"

"I'm doing special reports on the news."

There was dead silence.

Tentatively, Ann added, "It's . . . a pleasure to meet you. I've—"

She stopped short at the sight of Sheilah's frown. As soon as the makeup woman paused and lifted the eyeliner brush, Sheilah sat up, turned, and gave Ann a hard look. There was no smile, no acknowledgment. Ann froze, stunned by her withering glare.

Sheilah turned back, settled into the chair, and addressed the makeup woman.

"Well, what do you know," she muttered acidly. "Here she is."

There was a long, awkward pause.

"We heard you were going to be joining the team, honey," Sheilah added.

"Well, I . . . I'm just starting a trial period," Ann said. Sheilah shrugged, glancing into the mirror at the beautiful twenty-three-year-old blonde in the blue and cream wool jersey.

"I'm sure you must be a qualified, experienced reporter. Right?" A contemptuous smile froze on her obviously middle-aged face. "Where were you working before this?"

"Actually, I'm trying to cram as much as I can right now. I've been—"

"Say no more." Sheilah raised her hand from beneath the makeup bib. Bracelets jangled as she flicked her wrist. "I understand completely."

"It's always hard, the first day on a new job," the makeup woman interjected lamely.

"You'll do just fine," Sheilah said. "They've already got whatsername from the Rams Cheerleader School of Broadcasting. You'll fit in beautifully."

"I wish I had more experience," Ann said, her voice tight with embarrassment. "But I'll—"

"How's ol' Sol these days?" Sheilah interrupted.

"Sol Jolkins?"

"Yeah. Sol baby. He gave you the job, didn't he?"

"I've only met him once."

"Must have been memorable," Sheilah said.

"Well, I . . ." Ann faltered. "I don't know. I'd better get back."

The makeup woman looked at Ann, her expression a mix of sympathy and embarrassment. "Good luck."

"She doesn't need luck," Sheilah said. "After all, she's going to be working under Sol. He always takes good care of his girls."

At that, Ann backed away from the doorway and started down the hallway at a quick, angry clip, biting her lips to keep the tears from welling in her eyes.

Back in the newsroom, Ann spotted Tony March by the wall-size bulletin board schedule at the far end of the room. He was conferring with a producer and a field reporter who were jotting notes on clipboards. Anxious to show she was ready and willing to jump into a action, Ann hurried to join them. There, what was already a very bad first morning took on a bizarre, nightmarish dimension as Ann listened to the men.

"We should have someone get to the pier right away. They still have an area cordoned off and it's pretty bloody," one of the men was saying. "We've already talked to several people who worked with Howie Hewitt. The feeling seems to be that he was one of the greatest PR men of all time."

"It's amazing how popular people get after they die," March said.

He caught sight of Ann. "Don't look so upset." He laughed. "I'm not going to send *you*."

"Well, I—" Ann began.

March raised one finger to stave her off, listening as the reporter told him, "The police are almost positive Hewitt was murdered by a pickup. How are we going to handle that?"

March said, "Let's see what kind of quotes we come up with. Where the hell is Larry?"

With that, he hurried past Ann and out of the newsroom. Before she had time to think, one of the producers came barreling toward her.

"Ann Peters?" he asked. "Come with me."

Before two hours had passed, Ann found herself in a rehearsal hall at CBS TV City, bathed in the hot lights set up by a two-man Action News crew, talking to Sally Struthers.

Doing an interview with a celebrity would have been nerve-rattling enough, but Tony March's special instructions for the talk made Ann weak-kneed with dread.

The plan was for Ann to·"get a little something" about "All in the Family"—and then to "get Sally talking about what she does to lose weight."

March thought a 'Southland Scene' piece called "How the Stars Fight Fat" would be a surefire ratings grabber, and he wanted Ann to begin collecting material for it—starting with the pert and pretty costar of America's top-rated television show.

How, Ann wondered, could she possibly suggest to Sally Struthers that she "fought fat?" Would she be offended? Walk out? Complain? Sally seemed so friendly, Ann hated the thought of turning her off or hurting her feelings.

Ann had been told to memorize a list of scripted questions and not to go off on tangents, but to stick to them. It was almost as if she had been instructed not to think or even to listen, but simply to wait for pauses in which to insert the prefabricated queries.

She smiled and nodded her way through the interview, feeling like an automaton. With each vapid question, Ann felt more convinced that she was coming off as an idiot. Fortunately, Sally was a pro who knew how to answer even the flattest questions with sparkling verve. At least *she* wasn't going to look bad.

Beyond the camera, Ann saw the Action News producer who had accompanied her to TV City. He raised his eyebrows and nodded slightly. The message: with fifteen minutes of "All in the Family" talk already on tape, it was time for Ann to segue into "How the Stars Fight Fat" before Sally had to leave.

Ann steeled herself and blurted out the scripted question: "Have you ever had trouble staying slim?"

She was answered by a musical laugh as Sally shook her mane of blond curls. "Who, me?" she joked. And then she cheerfully launched into the details of her weight struggles with a veteran dieter's fervor, referring to herself as a frequent beached whale.

She told of "going into McDonald's and ordering two of everything—two hamburgers, two orders of french fries, two Cokes . . . I'd buy two Cokes because I didn't want anyone in line to know the food was really all for me. Then I'd throw one of the Cokes away on my way out to my car . . ."

Flooded with surprise and relief, Ann laughed along.

She was a quivering, fragile heap by the time she drove home that evening. She longed to share the details of her sad, mad, whirlwind first day on the job with Sam. She was counting on him for sympathy and a "buck up" talk. But when she reached the house, she found nothing but a note. Sam was out with some buddies. He hoped everything went well. She shouldn't wait up.

When the puff piece was complete, "How the Stars Fight Fat" included none other than the glamorous Ann-Margret admitting that she occasionally binged on éclairs. It showed Paul Lynde, supervised by his personal exercise trainer, running in a plastic suit to sweat off the pounds. Beautiful, leotarded Ali

MacGraw and Raquel Welch talked briefly about staying in shape, with Ron Fletcher's gym on Wilshire Boulevard serving as the backdrop.

The report also included a snappy montage of diet books and exercise plans, a look at a swami-type directing a group of industryites in weight loss through meditation, another bit in which a hypnotist suggested to a young actress that "chocolate tasted bitter, chocolate tastes like soap." It had a doctor discussing the dangers of a weight-loss regime sweeping through Hollywood—that is, getting regular injections of the urine of pregnant women.

He also suggested that the audience take note of the endless trek of beauties heading to the ladies rooms of the best restaurants in town. "They're not going there to powder their noses, but to throw up their meals. That's how they stay thin. Everyone is doing it," he said, "but no one wants to admit it.

"In this town where looks are everything, where a few extra pounds can make the difference in landing a part, it's not surprising that keeping weight off is an obsession."

By the time Ann was finished with "How the Stars Fight Fat," two weeks after her Sally Struthers interview, she was convinced that no weight-loss scheme would be too farfetched for Hollywood. "If someone came out with an Ex-Lax diet, I'm sure that would be the rage of the town," she laughingly told Sam.

"Come on, honey," he replied. "Laxatives are big, very big. Didn't you know that? And so is doing cocaine to keep thin. Some have their jaws wired shut. Hey, anything goes."

The segment was a success, but the fact was, Ann's participation in it was almost unnecessary. She had had nothing to do with setting the interviews, gathering the information, creating the questions. She was window dressing, an interchangeable part—a "twinkie." She'd been a fool, she realized, to have imagined otherwise.

But she didn't have to remain mere window dressing. Ann promised herself that she would become a reporter in time. If she had to start this way, so be it. But she'd be damned if she'd stay a reader forever, a second Goldie Kingston, one of the pretty people who read whatever was inscribed for them on the teleprompter and collected fat salaries.

Goldie was the constant butt of jokes. The entire staff was

aware of her special friendship with Sol Jolkins as well as with his multimillionaire buddy, Leigh Ballard—*and* with a steady parade of celebrities.

Ann took whatever ridiculous assignments were given to her and tried to learn as much and as fast as she could. She knew she was getting better with every story, but, unnervingly, she had no clue as to how management liked her work. After several assignments in the "How the Stars Fight Fat" league, she approached Tony March and tried to pin him down about whether she was performing satisfactorily.

"Everything's fine," he said, shrugging offhandedly.

Ann persisted. She asked the news director what she would have to do, where she should study, and how long it would take before she could join the ranks of the real field reporters.

March's response was to hand her off to a higher authority. He escorted her into Sol Jolkins's office, explained the situation, and walked out.

Jolkins advanced from behind his desk, taking Ann's hand and placing it flat against his chest. Her eyes were riveted to the curly gray hairs that had escaped over the collar of his black Italian merino knit shirt.

"Feel the heartbeat? That's what you do to me."

She stared at him mutely, with a terrible sinking feeling. She knew instantly—by intuition and by the message radiating from Jolkins's eyes—that she had better be very careful how she handled this situation, that her future at the station just might depend on it.

"Don't worry about anything," he said in an intimate whisper, his face close to hers. "We'll decide when you're ready. Be patient. Look at all the airtime you've been getting. And you're getting a lovely response."

"Oh . . . thank you," she said, backing away as Jolkins bent to kiss her.

"Where are you going?" he breathed.

She shrugged awkwardly, feeling stupid and immature.

Jolkins moved in on her again. "Hmmm?" His lips brushed her cheek, then moved, open and wet, toward her mouth.

This time, Ann turned away.

"Hey, I'm a married lady," she said, trying to laugh off the scene.

He shrugged. "So? Does that mean we can't be friends?"

"Well, we can . . . uh . . . be friends, but . . ."

He watched her silently for a few seconds, his heavy-lidded eyes coolly appraising, his mouth slightly open, jaw slack. Then he nodded toward the door and said flatly, "Go do your work."

NINETEEN

"I DON'T KNOW exactly how to put this . . ." Ann began.

She gripped the rim of the hot tub that Sam, banking on the large salary he expected her to make at KCBA, had recently purchased. Eyes closed, he soaked, totally relaxed.

"Sol made a pass at me today."

Sam sighed heavily. "Why don't you take your clothes off and jump in here with me? You need to get rid of all that tension."

"Sam, I think this could be a big problem."

"The problem is I'm lonely in here by myself. It's a beautiful night, the stars are out, I feel sexy in all this hot, bubbling water, and my wife won't climb in with me."

Ann smiled and began unbuttoning her shirt. Sam glanced at her, saw that she was doing his bidding, and closed his eyes again.

"Really—what should I do about Sol?"

"I'm sure you're overreacting," said Sam. "Just because the guy looks at you twice, that doesn't mean he's trying to get into your pants." When he got no response, Sam opened his eyes and looked at Ann. "Oh, come on—don't get mad. Jesus. That just proves my point. You're too touchy."

"You're defending him! You should have been there. You should have heard those suggestive remarks."

"I'm just saying you're a grownup; these are sophisticated people you're dealing with. You start in with this jazz—'he's making suggestive remarks,'" Sam imitated her in a mincing, high-pitched voice, "and you're going to come off like some self-conscious prude from the Bible Belt. Jolkins gave you a pat on the butt? Big deal. He was just being friendly."

"'Just being friendly,'" Ann repeated, wrapping her unbuttoned top tightly around her. "That's exactly how the bosses at the Garden Royale used to refer to the lunges the drunks made at the waitresses."

"Ann, for chrissakes, will you listen to yourself? You're comparing a guy with the power to give you a two-hundred-thousand-dollar contract to a gang of backwater drunks!"

"Not exactly," Ann said dryly. "Most of those drunks had more class than Sol Jolkins."

"Cute. Real cute. This is the best break you've ever had. You're on a ten-week trial, and you're ready to throw it away."

Sam climbed out of the hot tub, grabbed a towel, flung it open with a hard snap, and began drying himself with fast, angry motions.

"I didn't say I was going to throw anything away! You know how hard I've been working to prove myself."

"Yeah? What good's it going to do if management doesn't like you?" Sam stormed toward the patio door with Ann hurrying behind.

"What do you want me to do?" she called out challengingly. "Go to bed with him?"

He turned abruptly. "No! But what's wrong with some good-natured playing along? He just wants a little titillation— so flirt back a little, that's all. Play the game. I thought all women naturally knew how to do that, but you—I don't know, Ann, they must have left out some of the female circuits."

Ann stared blankly at Sam's chest as he gave a tremendous sigh.

I don't want to play the game, she thought.

Sam took her expression to mean he'd hurt her feelings. "I'm sorry," he said grudgingly. Then he turned back to the door. "Come on, let's go in. I'm getting cold."

That was only the first round.

At nine-thirty, Carl Adams called and said he was dropping by. Both Ann and Sam knew only something major would compel Carl to come to their house. In the normal course of events, people came to Carl's—unless they happened to be bigger people with bigger houses. Adams arrived in record time. He brought bad tidings: Sol Jolkins was talking about trying out someone else for Ann's job.

"But why?" Ann asked.

"He said he might like to go with someone who has more experience after all."

"Oh, fuck," muttered Sam.

"That's not at all the message I've been getting," Ann said weakly.

"Well, there was something else he said in passing. It disturbs me," Carl clucked, strutting back and forth across the living room carpet like an oversized red hen, "because until now I've never heard one word of complaint about your attitude. I can't figure it out."

Sam shot Ann a look. Her cheeks reddened to a burning flush.

Catching their expressions, Adams asked her, "What is it? Did you have some sort of problem with Sol?"

Sam cocked his head and answered for Ann in his most parentally patronizing voice, "He was kidding around, flirting a little, and she took it *very* seriously."

"Oh." Carl stopped, nodded, and gave Ann a look of surprise and sympathy. "Now I understand."

"Did . . . did he call you?" Ann asked.

"I called him. I wanted to see how you're doing."

"Of course," Ann nodded gravely. "Did he say anything about my work?"

"He feels you're coming along, but not as quickly as they'd like."

Ann's throat constricted. She could only nod as Jolkins's words returned to her mind: *Don't worry . . . be patient . . . you're getting a lovely response.*

"I'm really sorry to hear about this bad chemistry between you and Sol," Carl added.

"Don't worry, Carl," Sam replied. He moved behind Ann and put his hand firmly on her shoulder. "We had a talk about this earlier this evening. She's not going to let a little joking around get to her again."

"Do you feel comfortable about that?" Carl asked her.

Ann looked directly into Carl's eyes. She had never really seen into those pale hazel eyes before. Suddenly, she was struck by a revelation: the charming smiles, the understanding looks—they were all an act.

*You're trying to get Sam to play good guy—bad guy with
you, aren't you, Carl?* she thought.

He turned away.

"Ann is too smart to fuck up this chance," Sam was babbling. "She realizes she overreacted. There's really no problem there. And she'll catch on. Maybe we should look into
getting her a coach."

"I don't know. Let's give it another week and think about
it," said Carl.

Ann's first realization was quickly followed by a strange
epiphany: she saw herself and Carl as the two real forces in
the room—power against power, with Sam, weaker and
smaller, left somewhere far behind. What was more, Ann
sensed that Carl recognized the same thing.

The feeling came and went in an instant. It was so incredible, so nonsensical, so opposed to all Ann knew about her
husband, her manager—and herself—she couldn't take it seriously.

"You know what I think it is?" Sam asked suddenly. "He's
already trying to scare us so he'll have a better advantage
when it's time to negotiate Ann's contract. Oldest trick in the
book."

"Maybe," said Carl.

He started toward the front door, then paused. "Ann hasn't
seen my new baby yet," he said referring to the 1934 Stutz he
claimed had once been owned by Harry Ritz. "Come on out
and have a look."

Sam smiled as Ann passed him on her way to the door,
failing to comprehend the real meaning of Carl's invitation: he
wanted a few words with Ann alone.

She rubbed her bare arms as she followed Carl down the
front walk to the driveway, shivering in the chill night air.
Adams's attitude was even more chilling.

She made the appropriate exclamations over the graceful
milk white and coffee brown classic automobile, which somehow looked sinister in the bluish glow of the street lamps.

Adams responded with a terse, "I knew you'd appreciate
it."

Whatever that strange moment inside the house had really
meant, its outcome was undeniable. Now that the light of truth
had been turned on, Adams dropped his façade.

"I told Sol you were probably tense about your new job," he informed Ann unsmilingly.

She barely nodded.

Then came his trump card, the statement Ann had dreaded for months: "You know, I've been extraordinarily generous and patient with you. But now that you have a chance at something with such great potential, I'm not going to kid around. If your attitude is standing in the way of this working out, you've got to change your attitude. Frankly, after all the time, effort, and money I've invested trying to get things going for you, I'm more than entitled to start seeing some returns. What I'm saying is, Sam had better be right about your being too smart to fuck things up. Do whatever you need to do to patch things up with Sol. You and Sam can't afford to lose. *Capice?*"

Ann stared at him, full of futile anger. Then her body sagged, and she nodded.

"Fine," Adams said coldly. Then, without looking at her again, he eased into the driver's seat of the Stutz and drove off.

The next day Ann saw Jolkins in the hallway at work and steeled herself to approach him.

"I . . . ah . . . just wanted to tell you," she faltered as she fell into step with him, "how much I appreciate all you've done for me." He listened, grim-faced, neither stopping nor slowing.

"Hm," he muttered.

"Sol?" she said, touching his sleeve briefly, gingerly.

He turned toward her, struck anew by her flawless face. His lips twitched as she said, her voice turning coquettish, "I really am grateful."

He smiled slowly, lips closed, and, stopping at last, he took her strong, firm hand between his fleshy palms.

"I'm trying my best," she added. "I hope I'm improving."

"You're beautiful," he answered. Then he took her fingers and pressed his lips against them, his mouth opening, tongue circling.

Ann resisted the impulse to pull her hand away. He looked up at her from under his perpetually stern peaked eyebrows, releasing her only when a group of people came around the corner. He led Ann toward the main entrance of the studio, hugging her shoulders and murmuring, "We're glad you're happy." Then he sighed, "It's a pity I have to leave now."

"Mmmm," she replied elliptically.

"But we'll talk again soon."

He departed, giving her one last, intimate smile.

Ann returned to the newsroom, feeling sickened.

Playing the game had immediate benefits.

The idea of trying out someone else for Ann's job was forgotten. Negotiations for her one-year contract went through with little question that she would become a fixture on "Action News 10"—in spite of the tension and aggravations of the deal-forging process. Carl demanded, counteroffered, held out, and nitpicked his way through Ann's agreement with KCBA, enjoying every minute of the transaction. When the dust cleared, Ann was able to look forward to a base income that surpassed her combined earnings for the preceding five years, plus a generous package of perks.

TWENTY

WHILE SAM RENTED a house just a block west of Beverly Hills and leased a Mercedes, Ann continued her efforts to master her new job and learn all she could about television news. It didn't take long to pick up the undercurrents of politics at KCBA.

Fear and jealousy ran rampant at the station. Competition for on-camera positions and prime spots in the ranks of production and management was intense. The prevailing attitude seemed to be that the person you trusted this week would be the person placing the knife in your back next week—therefore, the wise trusted no one.

Ann watched her every step, determined to work hard and smart.

Much to her surprise, it seemed Sam was right in telling her that all Jolkins wanted was "some titillation, some strokes"—at least, for the moment.

With his time divided between work and home, plus his affair with Goldie Kingston and a relationship on the side with his secretary, Jolkins had more than enough to keep him occupied. He seemed satisfied with playing out a long mating dance with Ann: the moist kisses on her cheek, the hotly whispered comments in her ear, the lingering brushes against her body. Ann did her best to stay out of Jolkins's path. But when she did encounter him, she smiled and purred and hated herself for it, for the game also included allowing Jolkins to pretend she would be his whenever he wanted.

As the weeks passed, she felt like the proverbial mouse

being toyed with by a cat, dreading the inevitable moment when playtime would suddenly end and he would pounce.

In the meantime, her career advanced. Her poise before the cameras increased with extraordinary speed, along with her public recognition.

Carl and Sam came up with ways to heighten her celebrity status. They urged her to make personal appearances on charity telethons, to join organizations with the right important members, to attend functions that would augment her high visibility.

However, the higher Ann moved, the more Sam's initial joy over her success soured. He found he could no longer enjoy being home alone, for the empty house was a glaring reminder that Ann was out working, making it, becoming ever more famous—and he wasn't.

He felt left out. He grew jealous.

He launched a drive to get in shape, determined to break out of his long period of inactivity. It didn't last long; his first day at the gym dampened his spirits. As Sam, panting and sweating, was working out with weights, an old enemy walked by and commented loudly, "Well, if it isn't Norman Main!"

Norman Main: the has-been actor in *A Star Is Born* who self-destructs as his wife hits big-time success. Once the snide reference had been made, Sam couldn't get it out of his mind. It made him ill. It also made him increasingly sullen, defensive, and distant. His face came to wear a permanent poor-me expression. He was invariably still in pajamas and a robe when Ann rushed off to work. Neither his self-pitying attitude nor his costume changed as the day wore on.

"Are you going to call the lawyer today?" Ann would ask, referring to Sam's talk about forming a production company. Or, "It's beautiful out. Why don't you go down to the beach? That always puts you in a good mood." Or, "Look, darling. *Variety* has something on that new soap they're putting together at CBS. Maybe it would be worth checking into . . ."

"Don't you think I can take care of myself?" he would respond gloomily.

"Of course I do. I just hate to leave you alone like this."

"I'm fine," he would sigh, exacting his full quotient of pity. "You'd better go. You don't want to miss anything important."

"Nothing is more important to me than you are," Ann would say, and he would squeeze her hand wearily.

Night after night, Ann came home to find the house empty. Sometimes Sam left her a note. More often, he didn't. And even when he did leave a message, he never specified where he was.

Outwardly, Ann was turning into an overwhelming success. But inwardly her life was decidedly different. The pressure of contending with Sol Jolkins, her dread of him, the unhappy state of affairs at home, the backstabbing and bitchiness she faced from a handful of hardcore adversaries at work —it was all a constant drain.

Something had to give—somewhere—and at last it did.

"Nearly finished with me?" Sheilah Smith asked the makeup man one afternoon as Ann settled into the chair next to hers. "Suddenly the air is getting very close in here."

Ann sighed. *Enough,* she decided.

"Is that really necessary?"

"What's the matter?" Sheilah asked. "Tiff with Sol?"

"For someone who has never said so much as a civil word to me, you have a lot of preconceived ideas," Ann noted, her voice strained with annoyance. "Has it ever occurred to you that you could be wrong?"

"Strike one: you're Carl Adams's client," Sheilah said, ticking off her points on the fingers of one hand. "Strike two: you're not qualified to be a reporter. Strike three: you've made yourself bosom buddies with the big boss—and now Sol's letting one of the few decent people left in that snake pit of a news department go so you can replace him.

"In my book, honey," Sheilah snorted, "that means you're out."

"Replace who?"

"As if you didn't know."

Ann thought a moment. So, word was going around that she was about to be promoted. The last holdover from the pre-Jolkins regime was the man most likely to be leaving— which could mean they were planning to make her coanchor of the five o'clock news. It was a dream opportunity! But . . .

"I'm not trying to muscle anyone out of a job," she said.

"Of course not," Sheilah replied. "You're just the dummy in front of the camera, aren't you? Everyone else pulls the strings."

Stung, Ann looked at her squarely and shot back, "Do you have any more deprecating comments you'd like to get off your chest?"

Sheilah shrugged, tight-lipped.

"Good. From now on, save your digs for someone else." Ann rose out of her chair with such force that the makeup man stumbled backward. "I don't deserve them. I resent them." She was almost shouting. "You're wrong!"

And she stormed away.

Three days passed before her argument with Sheilah came to a conclusion she never would have expected.

"Where is Ann Peters's desk?"

Ann turned to see her red-haired enemy advance.

Sheilah's awkward manner and glumly contrite expression told it all. Ann sensed immediately why she was there.

She also sensed that Sheilah was the kind of person for whom an apology came hard, so hard that to actually humble herself enough to come into Ann's territory was an extraordinary act in itself. The strain showed in Sheilah's compressed lips and in the surprisingly vulnerable light in her blue green eyes.

"Do you have time for coffee?"

"Okay," Ann said.

She never did receive an apology—not exactly, not in so many words. But it didn't matter. Ann was only too happy to let go of the fight.

In the commissary, Sheilah began, "I've been talking to friends in the news department—there are still a couple left that I trust. And they say you work hard and you've got brains."

"I appreciate that," Ann replied sincerely.

"So what's a smart girl doing with Carl Adams?"

Ann tried to explain all she owed to Carl. But Sheilah had answers to everything. She suggested a different manager for Ann, a knee to the groin for Sol Jolkins. If Ann really wanted to get away from Sol, Sheilah believed, the thing for her to do was put in some time in the anchor chair, then leave KCBA. She was confident that Ann could find a job at another station.

Ann was stunned by Sheilah's outrageous talk. She was convinced that Sheilah simply didn't understand her situation —how heavily Sam was depending on her success, how hard he and Carl had both worked to groom her for a career, how absolutely vital it was for her to succeed according to their plan. And their plan called for Ann to move up from KCBA to the CBA network. Leaving the station now was out of the question.

In spite of Ann's doubts about Sheilah's opinions, she was drawn to the older woman. And in spite of Sheilah's exasperation over Ann's apparent inability to assert herself, she quickly became fond of her. In the following weeks, the two women grew close. Sheilah's views of KCBA and of Hollywood reflected a cynical wisdom gleaned from years of experience.

One afternoon she captured Ann's keen interest immediately by commenting, "This town is an eighteen-karat playpen where men behave like boys because they can get away with it."

"What do you mean?" asked Ann.

"I was at a party for one of the top agents in the business last night," Sheilah explained with a sigh. "It was held in the grand ballroom of one of the top hotels in Beverly Hills, with a full turnout of stars and studio and network executives. They had male strippers dancing on the tables, fondling the guests. Cocaine was passed openly from table to table. And would you like to know the gift that drew the most enthusiastic response? It was a lucite container in which human feces were contained. Oh, if the world knew the shit that literally went on in this town!"

Ann smiled slightly, understanding better than Sheilah could have imagined.

"I think of Marlon Brando and Jimmy Caan mooning extras on the set of *The Godfather* with their pants dropped to their knees," Sheilah added. Then she laughed. "When it comes to men behaving like boys, that says it all."

Eventually, Ann opened up and shared some of her worries about Sam. Sheilah strongly urged her to confront him, but Ann wouldn't think of it. She was miserable with her husband, miserable without him, afraid of losing him, afraid of being alone.

When it came to work, however, Sheilah had better luck in trying to instill some of her own forceful personality into the younger woman.

Prodded by Sheilah, Ann began to stand up for her beliefs about how matters should be handled on stories and interviews. Sometimes, to her immense satisfaction and surprise, she actually won. She wrote more of her own material, became more involved in the editing room. She came up with good ideas and smart solutions to problems. Her efforts to go beyond being window dressing started to pay off.

It was the first step in a long, painful climb to becoming her own person.

"I don't know how you've managed to do all you've done, Sheilah." Ann gazed around her at the attractive, coolly comfortable room decorated in French blue, white, and brown. "You have everything in your life so together."

They were in Sheilah's home in the eastern flats of Beverly Hills, a few doors away from Paul Newman and Joanne Woodward's elegant, tastefully understated West Coast residence and just across the street from an overbearing Colonial-style manse that had once belonged to Hank Evans. Dionne Warwick's terraced backyard and tennis court were partially visible from the window of Sheilah's second-floor study.

Sheilah had purchased the house at the height of her career in the mid 1950s. It was the home in which she had raised two children, the home in which she had assisted her TV producer husband with his career, the home she had kept after her divorce.

Sheilah chuckled. "Thanks for the compliment, but . . ." She hesitated, then propelled herself out of her armchair, went to the bookshelf, and took down framed photographs of her daughter and son. "I have my share of problems. Here are two of them."

She laughed as if it were a joke, but from the meaning Ann read in Sheilah's eyes, she knew that it wasn't.

"Wendy and Jeff?" Ann smiled as she gazed at the pictures Sheilah handed her. "They're really good looking."

Jeff, who had silky, straight dark hair and the kind of baby face that teenyboppers adore, appeared to be in his early teens. Wendy, who looked like a younger version of her mother, was in her early twenties—about her own age, Ann noted with some surprise.

"Thank you. They're also both very lovable and smart. You'd like them. You know I don't mean to say they're not terrific people. It's just . . ." She trailed off.

Ann nodded encouragingly. Sheilah studied her a moment before continuing.

"She," Sheilah confided, touching the photo of her daughter, "is living with a guy I can't stand. A class-A asshole. He has her living in a trailer, supporting him: He's asked for—and I've given them—more money than I care to admit. Then he takes off for Las Vegas and comes back broke.

"And Jeff." Sheilah shook her head. "I don't know. Home is where he comes to eat and change clothes. I'm ready to tear my hair out over that kid. Every time he's out late and the phone rings, I think it's going to be Jeff calling from the police station. It's happened. He's fourteen and he's already been put on probation."

"I'm sorry," Ann said softly.

Sheilah sighed and returned the photos to their places.

"Lucille Ball once said, 'If your kids turn out well, they're your greatest achievements. If they don't, all your other achievements don't count for anything.' How well I can identify with that.

"I had to be away from home a lot when my kids were younger, and I stupidly tried to compensate by overindulging them. My ex-husband never acted like he cared one way or the other, so whatever the kids wanted I gave them.

"If you've ever driven by Beverly Hills High when school lets out, you have some idea of what I'm talking about." Ann shook her head. "The street looks like the parking lot at Chasen's," Sheilah explained. "Kids dressed in designer clothes roaring away in all sorts of fancy wheels.

"My son is angry because I told him I wouldn't buy him a Porsche for his sixteenth birthday. His best friend Eric Evans is going to get a Porsche, so Jeff feels deprived. Hank gives his son everything—anything—he wants."

Ann blanched. "Jeff knows Eric Evans?"

"They grew up together. I've known Eric so long, I feel like his second mother. He was a sweet little boy, but now . . ." Sheilah shrugged. "What can I say? He's as rebellious, as spoiled as my own son.

"They're out there together somewhere right now," she added, making an arcing gesture with her arm. "Eric's visiting. He doesn't have his license yet, so I wouldn't let him drive. But his daddy lets him drive in Texas all the time, he told me. Of course, this did not move me at all."

Sheilah didn't notice the tension showing on Ann's face. She leaned forward and went on, "The next thing I knew, a limousine was pulling up at the house. That little son of a bitch and his MasterCard had struck again."

Sheilah shook her head with a bemused expression. As she chattered on about how much better it was to have a professional driver shuttling the boys around town than one of their older friends, Ann gave her a wan smile, not really hearing.

Of course. It had been almost inevitable that she would eventually run into someone with a connection to Hank Evans. As she had discovered during her five years with Sam and Carl, Hollywood—the figurative community, the show business world, the idea, not the literal tract of land—was a small town in many ways.

How ironic that she had finally found a friend in whom to confide, only to have that friend share a close link to the man who had, eight years earlier, all but destroyed her life.

TWENTY-ONE

~~~~~~~

If Ann had been capable of dispassionately listing all the pluses and minuses of her marriage, she would have undoubtedly been stunned at the tally.

But it was something she was incapable of doing.

For her, one blissful memory, or one moment of imagining how dreadful life would be without Sam, easily outweighed a hundred episodes of his thoughtlessness, listlessness, unfaithfulness, untruthfulness.

Being rational has nothing to do with desperation or with love, and those were the forces at work within Ann as she once again decided she must find a way to restore her marriage—no matter how constant or draining the demands of KCBA.

She tried to talk to Sam about the growing distance between them. He accused her of paranoia, claiming that nothing had changed.

Still, she noticed he no longer said "I love you" without prompting, and then only when he was in the right mood.

Ann tried to ignore the situation, tried not to complain, tried to give Sam the space he said he needed. But from her point of view, it only intensified the problem.

Looking for the cause of Sam's waning interest, for some area in which she could have failed, Ann seized upon sex as an answer. And so she redevoted herself to Sam's physical pleasure. Returning home late at night from work, she pushed aside the exhaustion that assailed her and donned the cool, clingy satin teddies, lacy old-fashioned whalebone corsets, and waist cinchers, the silk stockings, garters, and perfumes he loved.

She concentrated on performing all the erotic tricks he had taught her—warm water or shaved ice inside the mouth and body to stimulate, a fingertip of cocaine or white tiger balm smoothed directly onto essential areas for an enduring afterglow, use of polished Japanese stone string beads and other exotic fancies. She gave him sensuous massages with velvety creams and fragrant oils of almond and mink.

But Sam responded to her less and less frequently.

More and more often he was absent when she came home; if he was there, he was either asleep or distant and disinterested. Even when he did respond, the physical closeness invariably left Ann with an empty, isolated feeling. The warmth and tenderness she craved were long gone. Though she could never have admitted it, the fact was that in the bedroom her husband generally treated her as little more than his personal whore.

Ironically, it was the one place where she had become an outstanding actress. His attention to her sexual fulfillment had consisted of demanding again and again whether she was achieving climax, until, ashamed, frustrated, miserable, and afraid of displeasing him, she feigned ecstasy.

She had learned that the faster and louder she faked it, the happier he would be.

Indeed, Ann secretly wondered whether something was wrong with her because she couldn't understand the world's apparent preoccupation with sex. Based on the experiences of her twenty-three years, it was ugly and brutal at worst, dehumanizing as a norm, a skill to be proud of sometimes, and at its rare—very rare—best, a few minutes of wonderful, intimate affection.

Ann had yet to discover the distinction between having sex and making love.

She saw sex as one possible means of winning back Sam's affection—but she knew it wasn't the answer to their problems.

Another means was money. When Sam's birthday rolled around, Ann turned the occasion into an unforgettable weekend celebration that began with a lavish breakfast in bed, then a quick flight to Mexico to attend one of the bullfights Sam loved (and Ann abhorred). Then it was back to Beverly Hills for a sartorial treasure trek to Mr. Guy in Beverly Hills, where Sam's gifts included a burgundy cashmere dressing gown and a suit of fine Italian gabardine. And, finally, there was a surprise party at Scandia with forty guests.

There were some happy moments, but they were fleeting. And the wearing effects of vainly working overtime to bring her marriage back to life while working overtime to prove herself at the station took their toll.

The Watergate hearings, the dispute over the White House tapes, and Spiro Agnew's resignation dominated the network news through the summer and early fall.

However, few of the "Action News" producers would have been able to give all the details of the drama unfolding in Washington. They had their own world to think about—the ratings-conscious world of KCBA. Plans for the November sweeps period were vintage Sol Jolkins. He instructed Tony March to coordinate a special five-part series that offered guaranteed diversion from the grim national news—an exploration of juvenile prostitution.

Ann battled March as she never had, determined to avoid exploiting the young girls and boys she interviewed for the series and to bring off a report with real value. Eventually she found herself pleading her cause to a hostile, belittling Sol Jolkins. The series was done *his* way, of course, but Ann managed to make an impact. Parents, educators, and local critics had praise for some sections of the report—Ann's sections.

The ratings were phenomenal.

In that tense, gas-rationed Christmas of 1973, she sent gifts—as she always did—to her daughter, sister, and brother-in-law, and received—as always—no acknowledgments. There was no message of any kind. Ann wasn't surprised. Her contact with her sister had become virtually nonexistent.

Through the years she sent notes, money orders, and gifts to the Mantussis. They were accepted. At least, they weren't returned.

During the holiday season, there were more than the average number of the station's no-spouse staff parties. Ann made appearances for political reasons, but she was always prepared with excuses to duck out early. It was at those staff gatherings that many members of the station's top management corps typically singled out the prettiest young reporters, writers, junior executives, and secretaries and often left arm-in-arm with their quarry. It wasn't only Ann who had to contend with sexual pressure; KCBA was riddled with the casting couch mentality at every level.

In addition to the station's parties, there was Carl Adams's New Year's Eve extravaganza to attend. Ann dreaded it at least as much.

Adams, determined to outdo Allan Carr, Hugh Hefner, any and all other claimants to the Most Dazzling Party-Giver title, shelled out enough cash to support several modest families for a year to transform his estate into what he described as a "fantasyland for big people."

There was a Monte Carlo room, complete with a not-quite-sincere charitable raison d'être. Roulette wheels, craps, and blackjack tables were presided over by dealers—male and female—who were outfitted in specially modified, form-fitting dancers' tuxedos. Carl's round lounge area was now a cabaret, with a lineup of singers, magicians, comics, and scantily clad dancers worthy of a top Las Vegas revue. The den was turned into a piano bar. The loggia was enclosed and lined with black felt draperies. With the addition of heaters, tables and chairs, and a constellation of dangling silver stars, it was transformed into a glittering buffet area. The ballroom was festooned with a cloud of chrome streamers that wafted down from the ceiling and dangled just above the revelers as they danced to music that ranged from swing to rock—mellow, rambunctious, and full strength.

It was possible, easy in fact, to attend the party and play it mainstream, without knowing just how wild it really was. All one had to do was remain downstairs and away from the swimming pool area.

Those who did venture to the second floor found a sybaritic playground with many of the same features that had made Carl's Malibu retreat so notorious and so popular. This one had the added attraction of a stage on which sex acts were being performed. Outside, guests swam nude in the steaming pool—and made friends, made time, made love in the dimness of the adjoining whirlpools or behind the cascading torrents of the newly erected waterfall. Fluffy white terry towels and robes were issued by uniformed attendants near the clothing racks where guests shed their designer finery and their inhibitions. Next to the racks was an outdoor bar to aid in the latter process.

Sam left Ann's side almost as soon as they passed through the entryway—the same entryway where she had once heard him begging Carl's houseman for a chance to see her.

Tonight the Dallasas even had the outward appearance of a mismatched couple. Sam looked like a granola-era outlaw; his shaggy waves of shoulder-length hair and dark aviator sunglasses played havoc with the conventional formality of his black tie garb. Ann's look, on the other hand, was a song of elegance—television-perfect makeup and upswept hair, a black-velvet cossack tunic with high neck and gold shoulder buttons over a flowing black and metallic gold leaf-patterned floor-length skirt.

Abandoned by Sam, she was nonetheless never alone. Although the party swarmed with major celebrities, Ann was now enough of a name to be sought after by an unending stream of people. The pretentious and unpretentious, entertaining wits, ditzy twits, boring prattlers—everyone thought the party was incredible. Everyone said so; it was, after all, something to say.

Ann kept her social mask in place and forced herself to pay attention as a football star–turned-actor explained the merits of Rolfing. Out the corner of her eye she saw her disheveled-looking husband lope by with a giggling gaggle of revelers. Sam's hand was on the shoulder of a teenage actress known to the public as the cuddlesome younger daughter of a TV family and to the industry as a drug-blighted, double-gaited, budding nymphomaniac.

Shortly before midnight, Carl swept toward Ann with one of his very important guests: Leigh Ballard.

"Look at this. Look at this. Is this luscious? This is one of the few worthwhile reasons to watch television," Ballard announced to Carl as he extended an upturned palm toward Ann.

Ann took in Ballard's sharp, vulpine face, silver-streaked pompadour, and combed, trimmed eyebrows as thick and bristly as unraveling rope. His voice oozed. "I've been looking forward to meeting you. Come have a dance with me and tell me what it's like working for my good friend Sol."

Carl beamed at Ann, but his eyes were cold, the message

clear: Ballard's invitation to dance was a command performance.

Carl was in the throes of trying to interest Ballard in his latest brainstorm, an exclusive resort he wanted to create on Little Cayman Island.

Neither Ballard's attitude nor his style of dancing surprised Ann. He forced her body against his, while with a few whispered words he made it clear he was more interested in arranging a rendezvous on his yacht than in listening to Ann discuss work.

"Why don't you like television?" she asked, trying to change the subject.

"Because it's stupid and boring. It's a diversion for sheep," Ballard replied.

"The Condors' games are televised," Ann observed. "Are those stupid, too?"

"Competition is always interesting. Competition with exciting action is the best TV has to offer—outside of beautiful women such as yourself," Ballard said, squeezing her waist.

Ann smiled through clenched teeth. "Are you saying that we should all turn off 'M*A*S*H' and 'All in the Family' and just watch basketball?"

Ballard missed—or pretended to miss—the sting in Ann's question. "Give it a chance sometime," he answered lightly. "Watch my big black boys slam-dunking that ball. Lady, that is worth seeing. It's poetry."

Ann stiffened with distaste.

At that moment, the band abruptly stopped playing and launched into a countdown. The guests clapped and counted along with the drumbeats, marking the final seconds of the year and finally exploding into shouts of "Happy New Year!"

Ballard stepped toward Ann, his hands on her shoulders.

She turned away deftly. Ballard made a face and kissed her on the cheek, then, suddenly grasping her in his arms, kissed her full on the mouth.

"I've got to find Sam," she mumbled, retreating.

"Too bad," Ballard said. "Don't forget you owe me a dance!"

Knowing the pointlessness of looking for Sam, who quite likely didn't want to be found, Ann walked dazedly down a hallway in search of some place where she could be alone. And cry. She hated the way the year had begun.

She'd have hated it much more had she known how prophetic that beginning would turn out to be.

As January slogged into February, the hours Ann spent absorbed in her work were by far her happiest. It was impossible to think about her problems while she was reporting on volunteer sandbaggers trying to save hillside homes from torrents of mud and debris or when she learned that KCBA's report on a missing three-year-old had led to the child's safe return.

Newsroom gossip had it that there had been a major falling-out between Sol and Goldie. All the evidence seemed to point that way. Tony March chastised her for bombarding the floor director with insults—and got away with the reprimand. Shortly thereafter, anchorman Todd Stephens took Goldie's place on the coveted prime-time promos for the eleven o'clock news. And on February fourth, when the electrifying news of Patricia Hearst's kidnapping broke, March informed Ann that she was to stay on and do special updates on the six and eleven o'clock news broadcasts, which were Goldie's domain. Sol, he intimated, wanted the evening viewers to become accustomed to seeing her.

One morning Ann awakened early to find Sam's side of the bed empty. After looking for him in the living room and kitchen, she heard him carrying on a low rumbling conversation on the den phone. When Sam emerged, Ann was standing near the door, grim-faced and shivering in spite of the warmth of the house and the heavy quilted robe she wore. Seeing her expression, he sighed.

"That was Carl," he said.

"Oh, sure."

Sam padded past her. He was barefoot, clad only in the loose gray drawstring bottoms of a sweatsuit. "Call him back and check," he dared her.

Instead, Ann followed Sam into their bedroom.

"He was giving me some info for my trip."

"Trip?"

"I'm going to New York for a few days," said Sam.

"When?"

"Four o'clock today."

Ann stared at him. "Why didn't you tell me?"

"Sorry," he said offhandedly. "You're never around."

He picked up an envelope from their bureau, pulled out a plane ticket, checked it quickly, waved it in her direction, and then went to tuck it into the pocket of his leather jacket, which was slung over Ann's vanity chair. "Carl's been talking to John Armstrong about getting me into *The Glory Game*. It's a long shot, but Armstrong's going to see me. I can check out the job scene while I'm there. And Carl wants me to meet with the producers of *A.M. America*. There could be a slot for you on the show."

He turned back to Ann and gave her a brief, humoring smile.

"You're ready for another big move, baby. We've got to get you on network."

Ann closed her eyes, tight. Didn't Sam realize she read? *The Glory Game* was not only already cast but already being tried out in Philadelphia. And the thought of Carl Adams taking a call this early, unless he had to, was plain preposterous.

Sam responded to her expression with a blend of reassurance and irritation. "You know I'd like to take you with me. But you have your work to think about, and I have your career to think about.

"When I get back," he added, "we'll work on getting you some time off. You're overdue for a vacation. Maybe we can skip down to Acapulco, have a second honeymoon."

"Sure," Ann muttered.

"I mean it," he cried with a laugh, bending to kiss her. "You *need* a vacation," he repeated. "You're so stressed-out you're not yourself. To tell you the truth, I've been worrying about you."

How low can you get? Ann thought. But her indignation was quickly overtaken by doubt. *Maybe it is just that I'm overwrought. Maybe I have been acting a little crazy.*

"I'm sorry," she whispered, giving in and holding him. "Oh, Sam, let's really go away; let's really do it. It would be heaven to escape for a while."

That was exactly Sam's feeling as he boarded the Pan Am jet that afternoon.

It was almost as if an iron restraint had been unclamped from his shoulders, he thought. A soaring sense of liberation swept over him as he worked his way through the luxurious first-class section of the 747 and settled into seat 1-B—the front row, the status row, the row famous passengers, or those who fancied themselves as famous, vied for because of its sense of semiprivacy. The more his position in the industry was diminished, the more important status symbols such as the right seats became to Sam.

He also had the right seats—ninth row, center—for the Schubert on Saturday night, part of an itinerary that included get-togethers with a number of old buddies for drinks, lunch, and a couple of unscripted nights on the prowl. Also planned was a weekend tryst with a young starlet. In New York, where nobody knew who the hell Ann Peters was and where his faded old series showed in reruns, Sam Dallas was still somebody important. Or at least, he felt he was.

With Sam's departure and his blatant lies, it was as if some long-tied knot came unfastened in Ann's heart. She was detached from her moorings, set adrift, left vulnerable at decidedly the wrong moment when, two days later, Sol Jolkins summoned her into his office.

"I'm having a little get-together—quiet, intimate, with some very important people—Saturday night," he told her, his voice low. He named three of the top CBA network executives, in addition to Leigh Ballard.

"I want you to be my hostess. All right?" Jolkins's wife just happened to be on a golf tour of Scotland.

The strange request-demand caught Ann completely off guard. "Well, ah . . ." She hesitated. "All right."

Jolkins smiled, then slowly closed and opened his eyes ands tilted back his head like Brando in his *Last Tango* bathtub.

"Wonderful," he said.

He pressed a piece of paper into her hand. She looked at it briefly, noting it had an address in the Hollywood hills. Jolkins, she knew, lived in the Palisades.

"Don't show that around," he instructed. "That's my home away from home, my 'other' office."

It wasn't until Saturday that Ann mentioned the party to Sheilah, and then only because Sheilah telephoned.

"What do you mean, you're going to hostess a party for Sol?"

"Very quiet, very intimate, he said," Ann reported. "Baedecker and Ellis are in town, Travis Cole is coming. Oh, and so is Leigh Ballard."

"Ugh! That's enough reason to cancel right there."

"You know Ballard?"

"I know of him," Sheilah replied. "A friend of a friend used to date him. He's a prick, an egomaniacal son of a bitch. What does Sam say about this?"

"Sam is in New York."

There was a long pause.

"I don't like the sound of it," Sheilah said at last. "Why don't you call and say you're sick?"

"I don't have the number," Ann replied. "He's going to be at his other office, whatever that means, and it's unlisted."

"Call the station," Sheilah urged.

"I'd rather not even try it, Sheilah. He's very secretive about this place. He told me not to give out the address, but let me give it to you. You might want to send him a Christmas card," Ann said jokingly.

Sheilah mindlessly scrawled the street and number on her morning newspaper. "It's not your fault you couldn't reach him. Why don't you just not show up?" she said.

"I've got to show up," Ann responded abruptly. "I've got to. No question."

"Are you all right? You sound very edgy."

"I *am* edgy. I'll be glad when it's tomorrow."

"Just be sure you find an excuse to leave before the last of the guests. I'm sure you don't want to be stuck there alone with Sol."

"Right," Ann agreed in a monotone. "I'm sure it's . . . uh . . . going to be an early night."

"Give me a call when you get back," Sheilah requested. She instantly felt startled and silly at the sound of her own words.

Ann was a friend, a successful woman, a married woman —but she was also sweet, storm-tossed, and not very strong, in Sheilah's opinion. She also happened to be the age of Sheilah's daughter, and all of the older woman's protective impulses had been called into full play. Embarrassed, she persisted nonetheless, "I'm a night owl. I'll be up."

TWENTY-TWO

~~~

ANN TRIED TO keep from mentally replaying the phone conversation with Sheilah as she drove her white Mercedes into the cool gray-green dusk of Laurel Canyon, heading from KCBA toward the city and Jolkins's party.

It would be a trying enough evening without focusing on Sheilah's advice not to attend the party.

Jolkins's pied à terre was nestled on a steep twisting block high above Sunset Boulevard, on a street of sloped and terraced lawns. Ann located the Spanish-style townhouse with difficulty. No number appeared in the porch light, which shone dimly behind an archway lined with hand-painted tiles. Only by process of elimination did she determine the correct residence.

She studied the dash clock tensely. Arrive too early, and she would be alone with Jolkins. Too late, and she would offend him. She opted to wait, circling the neighborhood for nearly twenty minutes before pulling the car into Jolkins's driveway, and ended up apologizing for being late.

Jolkins brushed her apology aside good-humoredly. Leigh Ballard and several other guests hovered nearby.

"Not to worry. I figured you'd gotten tied up," he said, bestowing a light kiss on her lips. "Let me take your coat."

He lifted the garment from her shoulders with a caressing slowness that made Ann feel she was being disrobed. She shuddered involuntarily as Jolkins gazed admiringly at her wine-red silk dress. "You're so damn gorgeous I can hardly

211

stand it," he murmured. He kissed her cheek again and finally
retreated to stow her coat.

This is a mistake, Ann told herself.

But, she realized, there was nothing she could do about it
now.

Ballard glanced over his shoulder at her with a knowing
smile. Dressed in a casual navy jacket, knit shirt, and gray
slacks, he looked no less hard and sharp-edged than he had in
stark formal wear on New Year's Eve.

"Hello." She nodded in his direction.

"You never came back to dance with me," Ballard admonished her. "I waited for you," he crooned unctuously.

"I'm sorry," Ann replied automatically.

The months hadn't changed him; he was still a boor.

She smiled and moved toward the buffet table. As she
scanned the array of food, she wondered how long the party
would last. She checked her watch. The caterer appeared silently, unobtrusively, and placed a covered silver serving tray
on the hand-woven brown linen tablecloth. Ann recognized
the chubby, mustached man at once—Ezra White, one of the
town's favored caterers, the quiet gourmet cook Sheilah
always hired when she entertained.

The living room was exquisitely furnished, decorated in
geometric lines with a bold Indian rug, with brightly colored
cloisonné lamps, wood sculptures, and antique books casually
arranged in the lighted, recessed bookshelf that dominated one
wall.

As Ann entered the room, Jolkins approached from behind,
slipped his arm around her waist, and whispered into her ear,
"I want you."

Smiling artificially, Ann took a quick step away from him
and into the room where chatting, laughing guests sipped
cocktails and sampled such delicacies as pollo Cipriani and
fresh striped bass with capers. Before long, the drug enthusi-
asts among the group began moving into Jolkins's den, where
their voices and laughter rose to a higher and higher pitch.

Standing between the long, curved, umber velvet couch
and a pair of rust and brown pinstriped chairs were two
members of the network brass Jolkins was always feverishly
anxious to entertain; their wives and their normal executive
façades were absent.

Also in evidence were CBA's West Coast talent VP, Travis

Cole, and veteran action-adventure series star Bobby Blaine. Four attractive young fledgling actresses being considered for the CBA new-talent pool surrounded the actor.

Another face was familiar: Carl Adams.

Jazz with a pulsing bass line and a throaty, wailing saxophone drifted from the stereo speakers, laying the mood, the undertone for the voices, as Ann greeted people, talked, listened, and overheard snippets of other conversations.

"Don't even talk to me about movie star names," groaned an executive standing nearby. "Television audiences don't give a damn. Don't you remember what we went through two years ago? The season of the superstar pratfall. Remember how fast Jim Stewart, Tony Quinn, and Glenn Ford flopped? Hell, ABC was so sold on big star appeal, they paid Shirley Mac-Laine thirty-eight five a week to do that stinker 'Shirley's World.' Shirley discovered how much she hated the sitcom mentality, and Lew Grade, who was producing the show, discovered how much fun it was to argue with Shirley day after day. By premiere night shooting was six weeks behind schedule, and by midseason the series was dead—and of course ABC had to pay off the balance of her contract."

"What's happening with Susan Saint James?" Ann heard a young lovely in another group ask. "Is she really going to leave 'McMillan and Wife'?"

"Oh, I doubt it," answered one of the CBA VPs. "She's done this renegotiation dance before, you know. In fact, last time she was demanding a chauffered limousine and a nanny for her baby—until Universal threatened to replace her with Susan Clark."

"I've heard she has a thing going with Rock Hudson," the girl went on. Chuckles from the rest of the group followed.

"Hardly," someone said.

"Why 'hardly'?"

"Well, for one thing, Rock's boyfriend would probably resent the shit out of it."

The laughter grew louder, the jokes more ribald, the guests less and less in control.

Although Ann and Jolkins were the only two people from the station present, the mood was the same as that of KCBA's no-spouse penthouse gatherings—the same, but stronger.

The Creative Affairs VP, for instance, seemed intent on launching a creative affair with a talent-pool beauty who had a

Sophia Loren shape and a cherubic face that could have passed for a fourteen-year-old's. They stood directly behind the chair in which Ann sat, apparently oblivious to the fact that she could not avoid hearing their every word.

"Tell me one of your favorites, darling," urged the executive.

"Ummmmm, all right. I like to drive fast down the Coast Highway in a convertible."

"I could get off on that. Give me another."

"Hot fudge sundaes?"

"Yes! With whipped cream melting and oozing down, a big banana, and nuts. I like mine especially with a cherry on top," he said slowly. "Hmmm?"

"Ooh, you're making me hungry."

"Oh, yes, sweetheart!"

Ann checked her watch again.

Another half hour passed, then an hour. The baby-faced actress and the VP had disappeared.

Ann made the requisite small talk, flashed the requisite smiles. Jolkins slung his arm around her shoulders possessively, condensation from the glass in his hand dribbling onto Ann's dress. She stood stiffly with a fixed smile, feeling excruciatingly uncomfortable at being put into the outward role of Sol's woman.

Throughout the evening, Carl nodded and grinned at her. It was clear he was pleased with her. Ann wondered what other people were thinking but soon realized that at this party very little thinking was being done.

At one point, after she had stationed herself on one of the chairs, Ann felt a hand lifting her hair from her shoulders and the touch of wet lips and warm breath on the back of her neck.

Sol Jolkins was standing across the room.

Leigh Ballard told her in a low, breathy voice, "It's not very nice of you, not even giving me a chance."

He pulled a chair up next to hers, as Ann smiled gamely, asking herself in disbelief what she was supposed to be—the designated prize for the evening's competition between Ballard and Jolkins?

She maintained her mask. "Ah, but what would my husband say?" she asked lightly, continuing to play the game.

Ballard winced. "He's a loser. Forget him."

He was coked up, Ann realized. Sol strode toward them.

"Isn't she beautiful?" he asked Ballard. He rubbed her shoulders proprietarily.

"Beautiful but dumb," Ballard replied with an ugly chuckle. "I was just telling her, she should forget about that actor."

"What actor?" Jolkins answered, taking a place on the other side of Ann.

She started to rise. "Excuse me . . ."

Ballard grabbed her hand and pulled her back. "Wait a second. Let's talk about this."

"Yes, Ann," Jolkins echoed. He was now quite drunk. "I think it's about time we talked about this. Whatever it is."

"Excuse me," she repeated through clenched teeth.

"She's getting temperamental," Ballard sang.

Once more, Ann snapped her coy façade in place. "I've had too much champagne," she lied. "You'd better let me go, or we'll all be sorry." She glided away from them.

In the normal course of events, this would have been the moment for her to make one of her Cheshire Cat exits, leaving behind the impression of her smile. But she knew Jolkins would be angry at her if she were to leave too early.

And if Jolkins were angry, she would have it rough at work.

Carl Adams would be annoyed.

Sam would get upset.

So it was better to stick it out a while longer.

About midnight, the party began to take on new colors.

From his place amid the talent-pool girls, Bobby Blaine started making lighthearted complaints about "being paraded around like a trained puppy," each year during the affiliates conclaves.

"Sit up," he commanded himself, then pulled his clenched hands up in front of his shoulders, mimicking a dog, an empty, buffoonish look on his face. "Speak! . . . *Arf!*"

He moved to the floor as the guests around him smiled and giggled. "Roll over!"

Ann was talking to Travis Cole; he glanced back at Blaine and sighed.

Unofficially known as the network pimp, Cole was the man on call to provide big talent, big producers, and big executives with suitable starlets or young actors for their pleasure.

"Where do you go from KCBA?" Cole asked her.

Before she could reply, Bobby Blaine wriggled up on all fours, panting, in front of one of the actresses. She stroked his head.

"Good boy," she chirped. "What a nice doggie."

Cole was no longer even pretending to listen to Ann, his attention riveted on Bobby Blaine.

Blaine continued his act by wrapping his arms around the actress's thighs and jerking his hips up and down against her leg. The group screamed with laughter as the actress clapped her hands together and cried, "He's humping me. Isn't that cute?"

A few minutes later, a giggling Blaine strutted out of the room, one arm encircling a lissome Malibu blonde, the other a voluptuous Jamaican.

Travis Cole looked after them with a tiny contemptuous smile, then flopped down on the sofa. "Blaine drives me fucking crazy," he announced to the remaining guests.

"Hey," responded one of the others, "at least tonight you won't have to worry about him going out and bothering little boys in some service station john."

"Wanna bet?" asked Cole, rubbing his forehead.

Several of the guests were beginning to depart, including one of the New York executives. Ann wanted to leave, too. Jolkins, as if reading her mind, shot down the impulse with a look.

"We're getting down to the core now," he told Ann, grinning.

An incendiary intensity began to build.

You're a fool, a damned fool.

The words careened through Sheilah's mind as she lay in her dark, silent bedroom, but no matter how she tried to reassure herself, she could not shake the feeling of foreboding.

The luminous hands on the bedside Cartier clock formed a V. It was two A.M. There had been no phone call from Ann, and Sheilah couldn't sleep.

She pulled the blankets tighter, buried her head in a mound of down-filled pillows, and muttered, "You're being absolutely paranoid. Knock it off!"

Obviously, she told herself, the rational explanation was that Ann was already home and had simply felt it was too late to call. Tomorrow, tomorrow they would talk.

But Sheilah's mind would not turn off. At last she reached for the telephone on the night table and dialed Ann's number.

It rang and rang. No answer.

Another half hour passed. Still no call, still no answer when Sheilah dialed the Dallas residence.

She remembered how she had been unable to sleep the night of Jeff's arrest, remembered her sure sense that something was wrong.

Damn it, Sheilah. Ann is not family. If she wants to fuck around, it's her business.

The blankets had pulled loose from their mooring at the foot of the bed, and her satin nightgown had hiked itself up to her waist as she tossed and turned.

For God's sake, go to sleep. Take a sleeping pill—and go to sleep!

She dragged herself out of bed.

Why was she acting this way—so contrary to form, she wondered as she worked her feet into a pair of slacks and a blouse. What had happened to the pride she took in minding her own business?

"You're a stupid fool," she said aloud as she steered her car out of the garage fifteen minutes later and headed toward Sunset.

Ann stood at the sink in Sol Jolkins's downstairs bath, gazing in the mirror and playing a mental tape.

All he wants is a little titillation . . . Sam had said. *. . . Flirt with him . . . I thought all women naturally knew how to do that . . .*

She replayed Carl's words. *We don't want you flat on your face again, do we?*

She dried her hands, checked her watch for perhaps the fiftieth time, and decided she had had more than enough. It was time to leave.

She walked from the powder room into the den and almost bumped into Leigh Ballard, who was crouched by a lamp table, having a little toot in private.

He started, with a muttered "Shit." Then, turning, he saw it was Ann and smiled.

She moved toward the door.

"Don't go away," he admonished. "Come join me."

"No, thanks," Ann answered sarcastically. "I'd never be able to catch up."

Ballard stood straight. "Why so sharp, dear? It's not becoming. And it's not fair to me, now is it? Come on, let's be friends."

"You don't know how to take no for an answer."

Ballard laughed. "Thank you. I'm proud of that. If I'd quit every time I heard no, I'd never have gotten anywhere. I'd be driving a forklift like my old man. And," he said, putting his hand on Ann's shoulder, staring at her with bloodshot eyes, "I'd still be a virgin."

He bent to kiss her. "God, do I want to fuck you."

Ann backed away, angry now and reckless. "You're sickening."

"Get the hell out of here!" He nodded toward the door, his face distorted with anger. "Sol never told me what a bitch you are."

Ann pivoted, ready to march out.

"Wait a second!" Ballard grabbed her shoulder from behind and with a sharp tug took her into his arms and pulled her onto a couch. "I've waited too long."

In a second, his mouth was on hers, engulfing it, his tongue jamming forcefully between her lips, his hand moving along her body. Then Ann's hand found his face; her nails clawed his cheek. Ballard jerked backward, and she pushed free. With an exclamation of disgust, she jumped to her feet, wiping her hand over her mouth.

The room seemed to tilt crazily. Ann remembered, her heart remembered, her body itself remembered being raped, as clearly and vividly as if she were fourteen again.

Never! She would *never* go through something like that again.

Ballard touched his stinging cheek, relieved to find there was no blood.

He advanced toward her, and Ann cried out, "Son of a bitch!" She rushed him, seeing Hank Evans in her mind's eye.

Ballard took a step backward as she threw her fist into his shoulder. Then he regained his balance, grabbed her wrists, and held them tight.

"Let go!" Ann started to scream and Ballard released his hold—to hit her with a hard uppercut.

* * *

Sheilah sat in her car, staring across the street at Ann's white Mercedes.

So it was after three. So Ann was still here. So what was she supposed to do, she asked herself. Knock on the door and tell Ann it was time to go home?

All she had managed to do was make herself feel worse. She could be asleep, blissfully ignorant. Instead, she was sitting here like an idiot.

But somehow she hadn't been able to bring herself to leave.

She rolled down her window to see if she could hear any sounds from the party.

"Fool," she said again.

Ann half-stumbled, half-ran from the den.

She rushed down the hallway and through the kitchen, feeling sick, intending to bypass the living room on her way out of the house. But as she came out of the kitchen and into the dining room, she found herself face to face with Sol Jolkins and Carl Adams.

"Something wrong?" Jolkins asked.

"I'm leaving," Ann announced defiantly, moving around the long oval table on the far side of him and toward the patio door.

"For God's sake!" Carl exclaimed. "What's gotten into you?"

Before she could say more, Leigh Ballard appeared, apparently intent on slipping out the back way himself.

The red welts on his cheeks and the outraged looks he and Ann exchanged provided all the explanation Jolkins and Adams needed.

"Your girl is whacked out," Ballard complained. "She needs a leave of absence. Like, permanently."

"Ann has been under a lot of stress lately," Carl said, anxious to mollify. "I'm sure whatever she said, she didn't really mean it."

"I don't give a damn what she said! Look what she did to my face."

"Jesus!" Jolkins exclaimed. "Leigh, what . . . Sit down. What can I get you? A drink? Would you like to . . ."

Ballard waved his hand angrily and started toward the sliding glass door.

Barely aware of what she was doing, Ann came forward to block his way. Scarcely believing her ears, she heard herself say curtly, "How about telling them what you did to me?"

"Shut up," he snapped. "Get out of my way."

"I deserve an apology," Ann said hotly.

Ballard grabbed her hands, his voice erupting into a belligerent roar. "Get the hell—"

In a rage, he swung against her, pushing her with all his might.

"—out of my way!!"

For the next half-second, time seemed frozen.

During that moment, Ann took in every detail of the room. She saw Jolkins raising his hand in a gesture of protest, open-mouthed. She saw Carl's frown. She saw the crystal on the breakfront shelves, the variegated browns of the carpet, the kitchen door opening, a flash of Ezra White's face.

Then the glass rose up in front of her, and she closed her eyes.

To the others, it all happened in an instant.

Ballard slammed Ann into the sliding glass door, which shattered with a thunderous crash.

For a moment, the three men stood immobilized. Jolkins was the first to move. He looked out onto the patio where Ann lay face down amid the slivers and shards of glass, in a pool of blood.

The sounds of voices and running footsteps surrounded them as guests rushed from the living room and the garden.

"What happened?" someone yelled.

A woman screamed, "Oh, my God!"

"Someone call an ambulance," shouted another.

A half-circle was forming several feet away from Ann. Ezra White, who had hurried out from the kitchen, knelt beside her.

"Don't touch her," someone cried. "Don't move her!"

Drawn by the sound of the crash, the screams, the commotion, Sheilah rushed across the street, through the open gate of the yard, and to the patio. Her heart leapt to her throat when she saw Ann lying still amid the shattered glass.

"Get some towels!" Ezra White was yelling.

The bland little caterer was the only person exhibiting the knowledge and presence of mind to attempt emergency first aid.

"Is she alive?" Ballard whined.

Sheilah looked up at the sound of his voice and saw the welts on his cheek. That and something in his eyes told her: *he's responsible. He's the one to blame*.

"Someone call the police!" she cried out.

"Police! We need an ambulance, not the police!" came the answer. Was it Carl? Sheilah wasn't sure.

As Sheilah looked at Ann's terrible wounds, the question was swallowed up in her rising panic.

TWENTY-
THREE

∽∾ ∽∾

ANN REGAINED CONSCIOUSNESS in a recovery room in Cedars-Sinai. Dimly, she became aware of voices, the whir of machinery—then she slipped back into her dark and silent sea, unaware of the turmoil being generated by her "accident."

Sheilah sat alone in the quiet of a small but well-appointed office belonging to Dr. David Steinmetz. The blinds were slanted shut against the morning sun. Sheilah's eyes were closed, but she could not block out the memory of the last few hours.

It had been Sheilah who had followed the ambulance as, sirens screaming, it had sped with Ann to the hospital.

It had been Sheilah who had informed a nurse, "She fell through the door, so I'm told."

She had said the same thing to the two policemen who had been summoned to the hospital by the nurse. She had also told them about the scratch marks on Leigh Ballard's cheek and provided the names of Ballard, Sol Jolkins, and Carl Adams as witnesses—ruing the fact she had no concrete evidence to back up her suspicions that it had *not* been an accident.

Sheilah had not only been there to admit Ann to the hospital, she had also managed to locate Ann's husband in New York. She had distinctly heard a woman's soft laughter in the background as she had told Sam about Ann's injury.

And after all that, Sheilah had finally been informed that Ann appeared to be out of danger. Then she had been shown to this office to await word from the doctor.

Exhausted, Sheilah put her head on the desk.

222

A few minutes later, she awakened to the touch of a gentle hand on her shoulder. She jolted upright and breathed a dazed apology to a tall figure in a white lab coat.

"I didn't mean to startle you," said Steinmetz.

"How is she?"

"She's going to be fine," he said, but he said it with just enough hesitancy to let Sheilah know there was a caveat on that "fine."

"What about . . ." Sheilah's fingertips traced a line over her nose, down her cheek.

Steinmetz nodded again, his sober expression unchanged. "Yes, well," he said, "she'll be in for extensive reconstructive surgery. Have you been in touch with her husband, or, ah, is someone from the family coming?"

Sheilah understood at once: whatever else there was to say, he was saving it for the family, unaware that in Ann's case, there was no family that really cared.

She took a hard look at the doctor. He was very tall, about six-four, she guessed. He had a short, neat, wiry crop of dark hair and a squarish face with full lips. His dark eyes were framed by horn-rimmed glasses. He was attractive in a low-key way, and there was a kindliness about him that his studied professional detachment failed to mask.

Was he the kind of man who would put his patient ahead of expediency, Sheilah wondered. Or was he someone who would allow himself to be manipulated by a Leigh Ballard?

"Her husband is on his way back from New York," she replied. "She has a sister somewhere back East, but I don't even know her name."

Steinmetz nodded.

"Maybe you should know—there have been some major upsets between Ann and her husband lately," Sheilah added abruptly, "upsets that, I don't know, might have contributed to this in some way. I think I'm the only friend the lady can count on at the moment, so if there is something that needs to be done . . ."

Now it was Steinmetz's turn to study Sheilah, sizing her up.

"I take it you didn't see her fall."

"No."

"I was wondering how it happened."

"The men who were there say it was an accident," Sheilah replied.

Steinmetz nodded, rubbed his chin, infuriatingly close-mouthed.

"Why are you asking?"

"Have the police talked to you yet?" Steinmetz asked.

"Why?"

"Well, she was pretty much out of it when she was brought in. We couldn't tell exactly what she was trying to say, but we were concerned. I already told the two investigators about it. They'll be back to see your friend as soon as she's able to talk."

"Oh, God," Sheilah said haltingly.

"If you'd like, you can see her for a minute. I'll take you over."

Sheilah nodded eagerly and followed Steinmetz.

"You understand that she's not in the greatest shape," the doctor said warningly, as Sheilah hurriedly clip-clipped along, trying to keep up with his long strides.

She nodded.

Steinmetz was saddened by Ann's case, aware of the consequences the accident was, in all probability, going to have.

He had seen Ann Peters on the news many times. He remembered that he and his wife had even commented to one another about her quality of sincerity, which they had found as impressive as her luminous beauty.

David Steinmetz's heart went out to Ann Peters now, for that lovely face had been partly crushed and horribly lacerated.

The news of Ann's injury was already on the radio as L.A. commuters crept slowly along the freeways during the early-morning rush hour.

"KCBA newscaster Ann Peters is listed in stable condition at Cedars-Sinai this morning after she reportedly fell face-first through a plate-glass window," reported one all-news station. "The accident occurred during a party given at the townhouse of KCBA General Manager Sol Jolkins . . ."

At the same time, Ann's future was being mapped out over the phone by Carl Adams and Leigh Ballard. It was a strange, circuitous conversation in which everything was said, while each person tried to avoid self-incriminating statements.

Carl saw no need "for a ruckus," since, as he put it, "we're all friends."

Ballard readily agreed. He asked whether Carl had seen Ann trip and fall.

"Not really," Carl said accommodatingly. He had looked away, and when he had looked back, Ann had suddenly gone crashing into the glass.

The truth was, Carl loathed the idea of putting his hide on the line to back up Ballard's story. He was determined to play it carefully, just in case the police or the insurance investigators produced unforseen evidence.

"But you don't need to worry about Ann," Carl assured him. "She may have had a hissy fit last night, but she's basically a scared rabbit."

Carl promised to go to the hospital and reassure Ann that he personally would help with any medical expenses not covered by insurance. Certainly Ann would be reassured once she understood that everything was being taken care of for her.

"She isn't going to surprise you, is she?" Ballard asked.

"Not a chance," Carl replied.

Carl took it for granted that Ann wouldn't make any trouble, and he managed to convince Ballard, too. Carl also took it for granted that he had complete control over Ann, and eventually Ballard took that for granted as well.

By the end of the conversation, Carl's idea for the Little Cayman resort complex resurfaced. Carl still believed he and Ballard could make a fortune off the project. And Ballard was beginning to agree.

At four-fifteen, long after Sheilah had left the hospital, Carl talked his way around the nurse, who told him that only family was permitted to visit ICU patients, by convincing her he was Ann's uncle.

Carl's legs went weak at the first sight of Ann. She might have been a monster from a B horror movie. Bandages only partially concealed the angry tracks of stitches that slashed irregular courses from her jaw to well above her shaved hairline; her badly swollen skin was a patchwork of dark bruises.

As he moved closer, Carl was startled to see a glint of light showing beneath the purple eyelids. Ann was awake.

"Hi, sweetie," he purred.

* * *

It was nearly six o'clock when Sam finally arrived at Cedars.

As he had disembarked from the plane, collected his baggage, and hailed a cab, he had told himself he should go directly to the hospital. The world, he knew, would expect him to rush directly to Ann's bedside.

Nonetheless, he had gone home to shower and change first. Sam abhorred hospitals, and his intolerance of infirmity was in direct proportion to his worship of physical perfection.

Once inside Cedars, he dawdled in the lobby before finally getting directions to Ann's room. Then he took his time after getting off the elevator.

When at last he made his way down the corridor, he was so preoccupied with his misery that he failed to notice Carl, who was sitting in an alcove waiting area.

Carl hailed him, and Sam rushed to join him.

"How long have you been here?" he asked.

"Most of the day," Adams replied. "They moved her out of intensive car about an hour ago; I made sure she's on the eighth floor."

Status consciousness follows Hollywoodites even to death's door. If one were seriously ill, a spacious private suite on Cedars' eighth floor was the place to be.

"Thanks," Sam answered distractedly.

"Be prepared," Carl told him, as they approached Ann's door. "She's badly banged up."

"She's okay, though," said Sam, nervously seeking reassurance. "I mean, she's going to be okay. That's what they told me."

Somehow he was still expecting to see a beautiful Ann propped up on pillows, her arm in a sling—like a scene from the movies.

Sam stepped inside. For an instant, his eyes fixed on the darkly discolored flesh, the ugly tracks of stitches. Then he pivoted and fled the room.

Carl hurried to join Sam as he slouched against the wall, gasping.

"Oh, my God," Sam panted. "Oh, Jesus! Carl, tell me that's not Ann in there."

"Hey, come on—" Carl began.

"I can't stand to look at her!" Sam sobbed. "That's not my wife!"

His outburst was loud enough to be heard by anyone in the vicinity—including Ann.

"Come on," Adams implored, pulling Sam's arm, "we'll go downstairs, get a cup of coffee. You'll feel better."

Sam didn't return to see Ann that night. "She's probably sleeping," was his justification to himself, as he and Carl went to Adams's house for a drink.

There, Carl made a statement that was to become Sam's byword during the following days: "In a couple of weeks, she'll be fine."

TWENTY-FOUR

$\infty\infty$

ANN WENT IN and out of a dream world of pain and medication for several days. She sensed, more than felt, the touch of hands and instruments. She was unaware of the many lavish floral arrangements and get-well cards that were brought into her room—from viewers, from past interview subjects such as Jack Lemmon and Carol Burnett, and even from news people at competing stations KABC and KNBC.

She got a disturbing impression of Sam crying, heard the low drone of his voice, and felt terrible about him. She was aware of Carl's frequent presence. Occasionally, the vague forms of nurses and doctors loomed up in the dark murkiness of her mind. Once, she knew that Sheilah was trying to talk to her; Ann tried hard to remain alert and listen but wound up understanding nothing other than the fact that Sheilah was upset.

The first time the police came, Ann saw them and then her subconscious took them in and transformed them into part of a strange dream.

In the meantime, Carl Adams, Sol Jolkins, and Leigh Ballard provided police with a detailed description of Ann's accident.

When detectives asked them how Ann had crashed through the plate-glass window, their stories contained so much of the truth that even Ann would have trouble disputing their words, had she been able. The best, the most believable lies are the ones that sidle up next to the truth and squeeze it so tightly it smothers to death.

Ballard, Jolkins, and Adams admitted the incident had occurred in the heat of a "difference of opinion," that Ann had blocked Ballard's path, that Ballard had tried to "move" Ann out of his way. . . . Which was when Ann had tripped and fallen through the glass door.

They said that Ann, in the throes of an emotional outburst, had violently jerked away from Ballard, tripped, and fallen.

Carl, whose attention had momentarily been diverted by a noise from the front room, had turned back to see Ann crash through the door. She must have tripped and fallen, he said.

Jolkins, Adams, and Ballard individually described how Ann, overreacting to a remark Ballard had made in jest, had flown into a rage that had stunned them. Each said he believed Ann had been emotionally overwrought, perhaps on the brink of a nervous breakdown. Each contended she had behaved in a manner quite out of character—throwing a fit during a "business party" at which everyone else was relaxed and making shop talk. The phrase "trying to get her to calm down" was used by all three. All three referred to the sculpted carpet in the dining room. Each guessed that the heel of Ann's shoe must have caught in its nap as she jerked away from Ballard.

As for the marks on Ballard's face, the response was bafflement. "I don't remember seeing any marks," said Jolkins. "Maybe a piece of glass caught him?"

Adams shook his head. "I didn't notice."

Ballard bantered congenially with the detectives when they came by his office to ask a few questions. He issued souvenir Condor pins and mentioned plans for a special Law Enforcement Night at a future game. And all the while, he made a point of giving them ample opportunity to examine his cheek, which was, by then, without a trace of the welts Ann's fingers had raised.

Sam remained oblivious to the legal and medical realities of Ann's injuries. He was caught up in his own little world of denial, and his priority was ensuring the future of Ann's career. Toward that end, he called members of the press to express relief that Ann was fine.

"She'll be back to normal in a couple weeks," he confidently explained. "She's not going to be off the air very long."

Sam also called friends and business associates and told them the good news.

It was vital that nobody get the idea Ann was out of the game.

While the KCBA news kept viewers abreast of Ann's condition with an unquestioned acceptance of the circumstances of the fall, behind the scenes at the station gossip raged.

If there had been any doubt among the staff that Jolkins's party was not quite the business affair he had described, the fact that the accident had occurred after three A.M. would have removed it. Also fueling speculation was the behavior of Sol Jolkins. When he was seen outside his office, which wasn't often, Jolkins was closemouthed and appeared strained.

Sheilah continued to be absorbed by her suspicions. Her frustration over being unable to substantiate her feelings increased with each passing day, as her efforts to find out from a disoriented Ann what had really happened yielded nothing but garbled, meaningless responses.

It wasn't until the third evening after the party that she found Ann more receptive.

As she had many times before, Sheilah posed the question: "Was anyone in the room with you besides Leigh, Sol, and Carl?"

A light of recognition briefly showed in Ann's eyes, and she whispered something through clenched teeth. Sheilah left the hospital trying to figure out what "essaahhut" could mean, if anything. She tried the sounds in various combinations, until at last it clicked: Ezra White.

The next morning, Sheilah confronted the caterer at his La Cienega headquarters. He claimed he had no idea why Ann would have said his name. But he looked frightened, and Sheilah, convinced she was on to something, continued to ask questions.

In truth, White was suffering enormous pangs of guilt. Finally he blurted out in one desperate, breathless sentence, "They were standing right there and I was far away, just coming through the kitchen door; they saw it, I'm sure they're right, it all happened so fast."

"What did you see?" Sheilah demanded.

"Just . . . she fell," he answered.

"One of those men did it," Sheilah sputtered angrily. "Isn't that true? One of them pushed her. It had to have been Ballard."

"Even if that were true, you'd only bring more trouble down on yourself by trying to fight him."

"Yourself meaning *you?*" Sheilah snapped.

"He's got the lawyers and the money. He'd get out of it one way or another—those kinds of guys always do. And he's not going to forget it if someone like me says something. Everybody says he's got Mafia friends."

"If I saw someone deliberately slam another person into a window, I couldn't live with myself if I just sat and said nothing about it," Sheilah replied.

"No," White murmured.

"You probably saved her life, you know," she went on. "I've been thinking of you as a hero."

"I'm no hero," White said. "I'm just an ordinary man. I have to think about my kids and my wife. And I have to think of my business—to support my family. I can't have my livelihood wiped out."

"What are you going to say if the police come to ask you questions?"

White shook his head. His panic was winning out over his guilt. "Don't send them here. I didn't see anything."

At the same time that Sheilah was attempting to interrogate White, Sam was walking into Cedars for one of his infrequent visits. He came into Ann's room just as Dr. Steinmetz was telling her about the specialists who were determining the best course for her reconstructive surgery.

Ann was far more alert this morning. She had been answering Steinmetz with hand gestures and some muffled speech, but when Sam came in, she turned mute, a fact the doctor couldn't help but notice.

"Hey, you're awake," was Sam's greeting to Ann. "Poor baby. God, have you been zonked. How do you feel?"

Ann gazed at him, making no effort to respond. Sam was instantly annoyed.

He stayed near the door but was still close enough to see her vividly. Although the swelling had gone down and Ann's appearance was markedly improved, a fresh wave of repugnance swept over him.

He quickly turned to the doctor. "So what's the story with the surgery? What kind of time frame are we talking about?"

"Well," Steinmetz began, "the first one—"

"What? *What?* Whoa, whoa, whoa, what are you talking

about, 'first one'? She's got to get back to work. You guys are going to have to figure out a way to do it all at once."

"That's not possible."

"Why not?"

"As I've been explaining to your wife, it's going to take time. The left side of her face was virtually crushed—"

Sam cut him off again. "But you'll fix it."

"Dr. Weinstein is one of the best reconstructive surgeons in the country," Steinmetz said.

"She's going to look the same as she did, right?"

"Well, at this point we've—" the doctor began.

"We've what?" Sam demanded. "We've done every damn test in the book."

"I'll be glad to bring you up to date whenever you like," Steinmetz said evenly. "She's lucky to be alive. And she's making good progress. There is a lot to be very happy about here."

"Well, of course. But you don't understand why this is so important," Sam insisted. "Her looks are all she's got. They're her career—her whole life. She's nothing without them."

Steinmetz's dark eyes bored into Sam's with a look of outrage. But when he replied, his voice was calm, controlled.

"She's going to look fine, but you must understand that it's not only a matter of surgery; we have to give nature time to do its healing work. I spoke to Dr. Weinstein earlier, and he'll—"

"Time, time, time. It seems to me you guys have been doing a lot of wasting time," Sam said. "I'm going to get a second opinion."

Steinmetz gave an exasperated sigh, forcing himself to refrain from pointing out—loudly—that Sam had yet to be present and quiet long enough to hear a first one.

"Fine." He nodded.

The scenes being played out in Ann's room weighed on Steinmetz increasingly. His contacts with Carl Adams had left him nearly as disgusted as those with Sam Dallas. He was aware of Ann's anguish, confusion, and fear—and he sensed the pressure surrounding her, the manipulative forces at work in her life.

A few hours later, his impressions crystallized.

Steinmetz returned to Ann's room to tell her the police had called to ask whether she was now up to answering questions.

Sheilah Smith was there, and she intervened at once.

"No," she cried. "She can't see them yet. She isn't ready."

Steinmetz stared at her. "Explain," he directed.

"Please," Sheilah begged. "Just tell them to come tomorrow. There are some things Ann must know first. It's absolutely imperative."

"Whatever you're going to tell her is going to alter her answers?" he asked. "You know I can't do that."

"I'm trying to *help her*," Sheilah insisted urgently.

Steinmetz said nothing.

"How do you know she's up to it?" she asked.

The doctor studied Sheilah for a moment, then turned to Ann and asked gently, "Do you want to talk to them? Get it over with?"

Catching sight of Sheilah's anxious face as her friend shook her head emphatically behind Steinmetz's back, Ann whispered, "No."

"Sure?"

Ann nodded.

"All right. I'll tell them to come tomorrow."

"God love you, doctor," Sheilah said as he passed her on his way out.

He stopped and in a clipped, businesslike tone said, "Give me a call at my office."

"I will," Sheilah promised.

As soon as Steinmetz was gone, she pulled a chair up to the side of Ann's bed.

"So it *was* Ballard," she said.

Ann nodded slightly.

"I thought so. I saw Ezra White. He's terrified. I'm sure he saw Ballard push you, but trying to get him to admit anything is like pulling teeth. He's afraid that between them, Adams, Jolkins, and Ballard could destroy his livelihood. He's worried about his family. He must have mentioned three times that people say Ballard has friends in the mob."

Ann groaned.

"I know," said Sheilah. "He kept insisting he wasn't *sure* about what he actually saw. He said the others had a better view than he did. So, even if he manages to develop the balls to come forward and tell the truth, I'm afraid any good lawyer could tear him to shreds if this thing ever got to court."

"So?" Ann murmured.

"Maybe it's just that Ezra had an effect on me." Sheilah sighed and raised her palms in a helpless gesture.

"He made a point about Leigh Ballard that I just can't get out of my mind. Ballard can afford the best legal help money can buy; if you press charges, I'm afraid he'd do anything he could to bury your reputation. They're already trying to lay the blame for this on your emotional state. Ballard has two witnesses to back him up. At best, you'd have one witness who is shaky, maybe worse than shaky. Hell, I wouldn't be surprised if Ezra wound up going along with their story. You could lose. I think you could easily lose. I think Leigh would find a way to get out of it. He'd be slapped on the wrist, not slapped into prison. And even if you could win, he'd keep you tied up in court for years. Is that any way to live?"

Sheilah paused, eyeing Ann's bandaged face. Finally, there was a slight shrug, a hoarse chuckle.

"What else . . . have I got to do?" Ann answered in a cottony voice.

"Ballard must be awfully scared right now," Sheilah said thoughtfully. "Ann, you know he'd love nothing more than to pay you off and forget about this. So make him pay big. Now, while you have the leverage."

Ann's response was a sigh.

"Why do you think Carl has been so anxious to see you before the police do?" Sheilah asked her. "I'd stake my last dollar that he's going to try to get you to corroborate Leigh's story—their story."

"He already did," said Ann.

Sheilah winced. "That prick! Ann, you've got to take the offensive! I could—I would—approach Leigh for you, tell him you've got a witness, say you've decided to offer him the chance to resolve the matter amicably. Otherwise, you'll press charges, go public, sue the shit out of him."

"I . . . want to."

Sheilah leaned closer, perplexed. "You want to what?"

"Press charges," came the muffled voice.

Sheilah shook her head. "Oh, Ann—if you do, I'm afraid you'll be put through the wringer for nothing! On the other hand, if you offer Leigh an alternative to criminal charges . . ."

Anger flashed from Ann's eyes.

"I'm sorry to have to throw all this at you now," Sheilah

said apologetically. "But I want you to get what you deserve out of that sonofabitch!"

"I . . . don't want . . . a payoff."

"What about getting on with your life?" Sheilah said heatedly. "What do you get out of it if they arrest Leigh? He'd be out on bail and back doing his thing in minutes, and then what? Years of trauma for you. Forget what happens to him, think of *you*. What do you get out of it if you settle? You get money to start a new life. You could goddamn well have something to look forward to besides misery!"

"Not settle—lie," Ann corrected. "I won't make it . . . easy . . . for him."

Sheilah's eyes widened in astonishment. Was this coming from Ann? Ann, who practically made a business of allowing herself to be pushed around? She couldn't be saying this.

But she was.

"He almost . . . killed me," Ann went on, though the effort to speak smarted sharply. "He should be locked up. What if . . . what if he does something like this to someone else? He's a . . . brutal man. Sheilah . . . I'm tired of . . . giving in when I'm right."

Sheilah bit her lip, nodding. "In a better world, I'd agree with you. But think about it. All I'm suggesting is handling this in a way that would be most beneficial to *you*. Hit him for as much as you can; get it over with; put it behind you."

Sheilah watched Ann silently for several seconds. Ann closed her eyes.

"I'll quit bothering you. Look, I'll come back first thing in the morning, give you a chance to sleep on it. Okay?"

"Okay," Ann murmured.

But Ann didn't sleep, not for many hours.

Instead, she turned the question over and over in her mind, playing out every scenario she could imagine, every outcome she could project.

Sheilah was probably right about the consequences of trying to fight J. Huntley Ballard. He would surely go after her with all the force he could muster. She might be painted as a hysterical woman with an overactive imagination; she could be cast as wantonly aggressive with men who could help her career. Ballard's legal army would leave no stone unturned in its quest to prove her weak, emotionally unstable, not to be taken seriously, not to be believed.

How far would they go? As far as New Orleans? As far as Lyla?

As far as . . . Cindy?

What if the case were to become a media event? She imagined news directors and city editors issuing the order: "Find out everything you can about Ann Peters."

How far would *they* go?

Maybe those were outlandish worries, Ann reasoned as night inched toward dawn.

And yet, given the names involved, the prospects for exposing rampant sexual harassment at a major television station—no, they weren't so outlandish.

Suddenly even Sheilah's suggestion seemed far too risky. Ann drifted toward sleep, realizing that she had no alternative but to do what Carl wanted. If, in effect, she had to protect Ballard in order to protect Cindy and herself, well, what other options were there?

Tears coursed down Ann's face as despair washed through her. She cried in her silent isolation until sleep finally came.

A second, a minute, an hour later—she had no idea when —Ann was roused to wakefulness at the sound of a voice.

If you don't fight, you'll crumble.

Whose voice? She was alone. A silent, forceful inner voice.

It was as if Ann had awakened from an internal argument, and she now found herself consciously continuing it, answering questions that had been raised in her sleep. The face of Hank Evans filled her mind; the parallels between him and Ballard were uncanny.

Had she done something to attract such men, to arouse such behavior? She knew she hadn't, but it seemed the only explanation. And if it was, what could she do to change?

Then another image took shape.

Ann imagined herself surrounded by newspeople, coming out of a court building, no longer cowed and desperate, but strong and . . . triumphant.

The five A.M. fantasy took on grand dimensions: it became a victory not only for herself, but for all the women who had ever been bullied or beaten by men like Leigh Ballard and Hank Evans, a victory for anyone who had ever been the victim of a tyrant. In her inner vision, Ann passed on a legacy of strength to her daughter.

As the deep rose rim of the eastern sky brightened to gold, the battle between her instincts and her conditioning ended once and for all. There was no turning back for Ann, and she knew it.

Sam was in Ann's room when the detectives arrived.

Sheilah had visited earlier and had left.

The elder of the two policemen greeted Ann. "Sorry about your accident." He smiled reassuringly. "We just need to verify a few things. Just a couple of minutes, and we'll be out of your way so you can rest."

Sam sat in a chair against the wall. The second detective stood at the foot of the bed.

"It wasn't an accident," Ann said.

A look of confusion crossed the first detective's face. "Pardon me?" He leaned closer to hear Ann's fuzzy speech.

Her voice stronger and clearer, she repeated, "It was *not* an accident."

"Ann," Sam exclaimed, jumping up from the chair.

The detectives exchanged surprised glances.

"Tell us what happened," the first detective quickly urged.

"Leigh Ballard . . ." she began, then paused for breath. "He pushed me . . . into the glass door."

"Deliberately?"

"Yes."

"No, no, honey. You don't mean that! Ballard wouldn't do that. You tripped. Sol and Carl saw the whole thing," Sam interrupted hastily. "They were right there."

"They're . . . they're lying."

"Ann! Jesus Christ. You don't know what you're saying!" Sam gasped.

"Please, Mr. Dallas," warned the first detective, "you'll have to be quiet or you'll have to leave."

"Look, I'm sorry, but I think she's gone off her nut. Ann, for God's sake—you could get an innocent man into serious trouble! Don't you realize that? Sol *saw* it happen. You were all worked up. You weren't yourself. You're imagining things."

"I knew . . . you would do this!" Ann exclaimed, her face wrenched with pain.

"I just don't want you making a f—"

"Tell him to go," Ann demanded.

Sam whisked his leather jacket off the back of the chair with a loud thwack and stormed out.

He went directly to the nearest telephone to report to Carl. "She's up there telling the cops that Ballard deliberately pushed her through the door!"

"I can't talk to you now," Carl said, and hung up.

With him in Carl's study was Sheilah Smith.

"Let me get this straight," he said, putting his hands on his desk, pretending to be amused. "Ann sent you over here to warn me—about what?"

"To stay out of it and to stay away from her," Sheilah said levelly. "Your professional relationship is hereby dissolved."

"Ann owes me quite a bit of money." Carl was far from amused now.

"You lied to the police. And you were trying to coerce her into lying about Leigh Ballard, and we know why." Sheilah didn't know exactly why, and as far as the coercion went, there was no proof—but she was hitting him with a great display of confident conviction, employing her most intimidating manner, and Carl was stunned enough to react with a pinched frown.

Sheilah went on, smiling faintly. "She knows an awful lot of dirt about you."

"Oh, please." Carl snorted. "That's ridiculous."

Sheilah waited a moment, nodding slowly, knowingly. Despite Carl's cavalier response, her remark planted a fear in him that instantly took root and sprouted. Whatever Ann knew, the important thing was that Carl knew *all* the dirt about himself. Sheilah played on his fear, guessing that Carl would rifle through his memory to figure out what Ann might know and what she might do with it, then fill in his own worst-case scenario. And Adams was doing just that.

At last Sheilah added, "She wants you out of her life."

"Are you finished?"

"Ann wants a yes or no."

Carl took several seconds to frame his answer. "Tell her," he sniffed, "that it will be my greatest pleasure never to have anything to do with her again."

PART 5

The Survivor

TWENTY-FIVE

〜∽　∽〜

ANN HAD ASSUMED that once she had made her decision, her future and Leigh Ballard's would be in the hands of fate and the law.

It didn't quite work out that way.

She was forced to reaffirm her stance many times, and it didn't get any easier.

Ballard took Ann seriously after she made her complaint to the police. Six days after Jolkins's party, Sam and two of Ballard's representatives ranged themselves around Ann's bed. Ballard's attorney made an offer: Ann would be paid $250,000, plus all medical costs incurred directly as a result of the "accident." Ann, of course, would drop her charges immediately. She would go along with Ballard's story.

"I don't think we could ask for any more than that," said Sam, thrilled at the thought of a quarter million dollars. "But I'd like to consult my lawyer."

"We must get this resolved immediately," Ballard's aide persisted gruffly. "And we want to get a statement out as soon as possible. We want Ann to refute these stories that have gotten into the press."

"I think we can give you an agreement in principle on that," said Sam.

"No," Ann said in a low voice.

The three men sighed in unison.

"I think we need to talk alone," Sam suggested.

When Ballard's men left, Sam turned to Ann, incredulous. "What the hell more could you want? A quarter million bucks

241

and the chance to get out of this mess with some dignity? You can't be *that* crazy. We're taking it. That's all there is to it."

"But, Sam, I—"

"Don't give me this shit," Sam yelled. "You want to wreck our lives permanently?"

"No, but I—"

He cut her off. "What the hell were you doing getting into a fight with a guy like Leigh Ballard anyway? You're not making any sense. You really have cracked up. Do you know how embarrassing this is for me? Jesus Christ! Carl won't talk to me. How do you expect to be able to pay for all your plastic surgery without help from him or Ballard? Do you think I want to spend the rest of my life with you the way you look now?"

Choked by sobs and blinded by tears, Ann could neither answer nor see, so she was surprised to hear another voice in the room.

"Excuse me. I'd like a word with you." It was Dr. Steinmetz. His voice was sharp and autocratic as he motioned Sam toward the door.

Ann couldn't hear much of their hallway conversation, but a few of Sam's words came through loud and clear. "Hey, I *know* she's a mess!"

Then, a few seconds later, she heard Sam exclaim, "Browbeating her? No I wasn't. And what the hell business is it of yours?"

Steinmetz returned alone.

"What happened?" she asked.

"He's going to go cool off for a while," he replied.

"I don't want him to come back," Ann said tearfully. She proceeded in her cottony voice, "He doesn't believe me. He's trying to get me to take their offer and drop the charges." She looked at the doctor as he leaned over her. "Do you think I'm crazy, too?"

"Not at all," he replied, gently daubing the tears away from her eyes. "Anyone who tells you that is—" He stopped himself.

By then, Sheilah had filled the doctor in on Sam and Carl and the emotional hurt they had inflicted on Ann from the beginning. She had told him that Ann had been isolated from potential friends by her husband, and she had described the tension and harassment Ann had endured at the station.

"You're doing the right thing," he said firmly now. "You're doing the only thing you can do."

"I'm glad somebody agrees with me. It wasn't even a good offer," she added somewhat lamely.

And it wasn't, she decided.

She had lost her career, at least for the foreseeable future. She had been disfigured. The amount of money she would probably have earned within the next few years, had it not been for Ballard's act, outweighed the sum of money Ballard had offered.

But that wasn't her motive for rejecting his offer.

"Just because someone has money doesn't mean he should be above the law," she told the doctor, thinking angrily of Hank Evans. "I have strong feelings about that."

Steinmetz pulled a chair up next to Ann's bed. "I hope you realize," he said, as he sat down and leaned forward, "no matter what happens, you've already won—simply by not backing down."

"Thank you for saying that."

"Well, I have strong feelings about it, too."

Then he asked, "Is there anyone you would like me to contact? Your sister?"

"No."

"Cindy?"

Ann stared at Steinmetz, stunned.

"You mentioned a Cindy. Several times."

"I did?" She paused, then added, "I . . . No. I don't want you to contact anyone."

Steinmetz was quiet for a long time, gazing at Ann as if he were waiting for her to say more.

She suddenly found herself wanting to say more, and, realizing she was facing a man bound by his profession to keep her confidence, she blurted, "Cindy is my daughter. I haven't seen her since I was fifteen and she was five days old."

Steinmetz nodded gravely.

Ann went on, about Cindy, about Lyla. She asked Steinmetz whether he thought there was any chance that her case against Leigh Ballard could somehow affect them. When the doctor reasoned that it was unlikely, she felt a wave of relief.

Her talk with Steinmetz ended up by bringing Ann the first moments of peace she had felt in longer than she could remember.

Around her, the brush fire of events burned rapidly.

A few days later, Sheilah burst in with good news: "Ezra White is talking." That was followed by the news that Leigh Ballard was being charged with felonious assault—and by the arrival of swarms of press who wanted to talk to Ann.

As a newscaster herself, she felt it was only right that she answer them somehow. By then she had the advice of a good attorney, a friend of Sheilah's, who helped her frame a statement, then recommended that she refrain from making any further comments. David Steinmetz earned the wrath of many by absolutely refusing to allow reporters near Ann.

She was surprised and warmed by his protectiveness. Although Steinmetz never referred to her moment of truth with him, he encouraged her to talk. It was one of the best medicines he could have prescribed.

"Have you thought about what you're going to do when we spring you from this place?" he asked her one day. It was obvious there would be no loving spouse waiting to take care of Ann at home. "We can help you arrange for home care for a while."

"Good," Ann answered. Then she mumbled, "He can stay with one of his girlfriends."

Steinmetz nodded sympathetically.

"Come on, doctor." Ann snorted. "Don't act superior. Men are by nature polygamous. I've heard that all my life. Can you honestly tell me you've never been unfaithful?"

Steinmetz pursed his lips and nodded before answering. "I think you have every right to feel bitter, but I hope you won't give up on men. We aren't all so bad."

Ann gave a sardonic chuckle.

"And in answer to your question," he continued, "no, I was never unfaithful."

"Was never?"

"I lost my wife last year."

"I'm sorry," Ann said quickly, suddenly subdued.

He shrugged awkwardly. "It was a . . . she was . . . It was a blessing by the time she died. But life goes on," Steinmetz said. "And time does help. You'll see."

The preliminary hearing was unannounced and closed. For Ann, weak and wobbling, the event was a blur. Ballard and his men made snide remarks among themselves at the supposed theatricality of the veiled hat Ann wore. The truth was that, tormented by the stares her appearance produced, she used it for concealment. Once the prosecutor asked her to lift the veil, assumptions that it had been worn for dramatic effect were completely laid to rest.

The judge declared that the case would be held over for trial.

Ann underwent surgery on her face and shoulder. The days dragged by as she recuperated. Knowing that if she were going to file a civil lawsuit she must get on with it, Ann gave her attorney the go-ahead. A suit was launched—and so was another wave of publicity. She waited for her release from the hospital. It wasn't life, it was merely existence.

Ann never returned to live in the house on the hill that Sam had turned into a decorator showplace with her KCBA earnings. She accepted Sheilah's invitation to recuperate at her Maple Drive estate and began to go about setting her world in order.

Her first major step in that process was the hardest, but it was one she knew she had to take.

"You're looking better than I expected."

Those were Sam's first words to Ann after seven weeks of separation. Sheilah had ushered him into her living room and discreetly retreated.

Ann gazed at Sam coldly from her post behind a wing chair. She wore a velour robe over her cotton nightgown. Her left arm, still in a cast, was hidden from view, as were the scars on her scalp and forehead, concealed by a deftly arranged blue scarf. But the slight droop on the left side of her face, the discoloration, the jigsaw tracks from the stitches were as impossible to hide as Sam's revulsion at viewing them.

"What are you doing?" Sheilah had asked when she had caught Ann trying to apply makeup. "Why bother to fix yourself up for *him?* You don't *want* him."

"You're right," Ann had replied. Nonetheless, she had continued her attempts at camouflage. Somehow, she felt compelled to look her best for Sam.

Just as now she felt compelled to turn the left side of her face away from him.

"You look so much better than you looked in the hospital.

See, I was right, wasn't I?" He smiled gamely. "One of these days, they'll have you looking as good as new."

Ann was silent.

"God." Sam chuckled. "You know what this reminds me of? When we first got together, when Carl was keeping you under lock and key and I was going crazy. I waited four hours in that goddamned parking lot for you to show up. And then finally, there you were, and I didn't think I'd be able to talk; I couldn't breathe."

Ann turned away. Sam quickly circled in front of her.

"I know. I know. It's not going to be so easy this time."

"It's not going to *be* at all this time," Ann said, her voice low and controlled.

"Ann, for chrissakes—I don't even know what happened. Or how it happened. How can you hold it against me? I wasn't even there."

"You never even gave me a chance. You weren't there, but that didn't keep you from trying to undermine my credibility, telling everyone that I didn't know what I was saying. 'Don't listen to her, she's not herself.'"

"I didn't want you making a fool of yourself. I was trying to protect you. What has all this fighting back gotten you? Nothing good, as far as I can tell."

She sighed. "I don't understand why you're doing this, why you're here. Did Carl ask you to come?"

"I haven't seen Carl."

It was Sam at his old game, trying to twist everything around to make himself blameless, even noble. It was Sam sensing her weaknesses like an animal on the hunt. It was Sam trying to turn black and white to white and black.

"You know," said Ann, "after all these years, I've finally realized I don't understand you at all."

Sam shrugged. "Then that makes two of us. I don't understand me either."

Ann gazed at him in silence, recognizing that that statement, at least, was true.

How often had that fact excused him from responsibility, absolved him of guilt, saved him from explaining his actions? Dozens, hundreds of times.

"All I know is," he went on, "we belong together. At least give me a chance. We've got to talk about it. I'm still your husband."

Ann shut her eyes, shaking her head.

"All right. I haven't been a good husband. But don't we owe each other another chance? Feelings like ours can't just be thrown away. Jesus, Ann, when that marshal showed up at the house with divorce papers, it was the worst moment of my life. You don't want to divorce me! This isn't you. It's the lawyer. It's Sheilah putting you up to it. And you know why? Because she wants you in her club of aging divorcées—"

"Be quiet," Ann cut in angrily. "Sheilah didn't make up my mind. I did. Believe it or not, I am actually capable of thinking without any outside help."

"I know that."

"No, you don't."

"Then why are you doing this? Why the divorce? Explain it to me."

"Is this a test?" Ann asked sarcastically.

"I didn't mean it to sound like that."

"I don't really care how you meant it. I'm not going to put myself in the position of explaining something that you understand every bit as well as I do. I'm not going to let you make me do something so idiotic. Not again."

Ann brushed past him toward the door. Sam followed, the expression on his face a mix of agitation and disbelief. He was still not convinced that Ann would not let his magic cut through her hostility.

He stopped her as she reached the hall. The effort it took to control his temper showed on his face. "I know we got messed up—badly, badly messed up—and I'm willing to take my share of the blame. But we had something special. We *have* something special. That isn't going to die, and I don't believe you want it to any more than I do.

"Can you tell me you've forgotten how it was? Can you tell me you've forgotten all those nights we sat up together going over your scenes? The fun we used to have? We were the two biggest madly-in-love romantic fools in town, remember? We're still us, baby. We can get it back. It's still there. You can't tell me you're over all that," Sam insisted. "I won't believe it."

"I'm not over it," Ann confessed. "I may never get over it. But I am past it."

The words were freighted with resolution, as was the firm

set of her mouth when Sam froze in front of her, believing her at last.

"I'm a long way past it, Sam," she repeated, as she opened the front door, "and that's just going to have to be good enough."

TWENTY-SIX

ANN FOUND HERSELF increasingly restless as the case against Leigh Ballard lumbered along.

She wanted to work again, but she had no intention of returning to KCBA in any capacity as long as Sol Jolkins remained there. The inquiries she made at other stations about behind-the-scenes openings were met with disinterest. Now that she was unfit for the cameras, the prevailing attitude seemed to be that she had no value.

"I hate not working," she told Sheilah one morning. "I feel like I'm stagnating."

The comment registered. While Ann continued her job-hunting efforts, Sheilah put out the word throughout her network of friends and contacts that Ann was looking for work. A period of intense frustration followed, as false lead followed dead end.

On the plus side, Ann was heartened by unexpected encouragement. Sheilah's fifteen-year-old son Jeff took a tremendous liking to her. Ann found herself being doted on by the soft-spoken, sweet-faced teenager. Jeff often stayed home at night to talk to Ann, to listen to tales out of her exotic past, and to cheer her up with a seemingly endless supply of bad jokes and silly stories.

"Is this the rebel you were telling me about?" she couldn't help asking Sheilah.

"You bring out his tenderhearted side," Sheilah answered. "It's a joy for me to see it again."

249

At last, after several weeks of effort, there was a breakthrough in Ann's quest for work.

Sheilah and her agent had just wrapped up a meeting with an executive vice-president of one of the nation's largest television syndication companies, part of Sheilah's efforts to keep her "Perfectly Personal" talk show alive post-CBA. The show's chances of being picked up by the network were almost nil, but the outlook for syndicated production was hopeful. The meeting had been promising.

They were in a dimly lit booth, surrounded by the deep reds and burnished woods of La Scala. The late afternoon-early evening crowd included Dustin Hoffman, Barbra Streisand and George Segal, and another figure legendary in Hollywood—Stanley Weiss, the former paterfamilias of Sentinel Studios.

Tanned and vigorous-looking at seventy, Weiss was outfitted in his usual natty style, with navy blazer, ivory slacks, white shirt, and red paisley ascot. He presided over a table for four, occasionally filling the room with the sound of his robust laughter.

It had been at least five years since Sheilah had seen her one-time boss. As she walked by his table on her way out, she murmured, "Hi, Stan," and rested her hand briefly on his shoulder.

His shoulders had become slightly stooped, but power still rested as comfortably on them as Weiss's old Dodgers cap—the *Brooklyn* Dodgers, mind you—occasionally still rested upon his stately, snow-tufted head. Power was a basic fact of life for him, after fifty years in the industry. He had run the studio, fought many hard wars, and finally exited Sentinel following a corporate takeover. However, those who had counted him out of the movie game had counted wrong. Weiss continued to run his own shop in his own way. Now, with a wealth of films and television dramas to his credit, Stanley Weiss Productions was one of the most prosperous independent production firms in Hollywood.

Weiss's jaw dropped theatrically when he turned and saw Sheilah.

"Hey! Hiya, Freckles," he said, grasping her hand.

He introduced her to his companions, then invited her to join them for a drink.

Conversation soon turned to KCBA gossip, which naturally led to the scandal, Leigh Ballard, and Ann Peters.

"What surprises me is Ann Peters pressing charges in the first place," Weiss said. "Ballard must have tried to settle."

"Ann believes Ballard should be treated like any other criminal," Sheilah said.

Weiss looked at her quizzically.

"She's a dear friend of mine."

"Really? Well, tell her I like her for standing up to that piece of dreck. It's high time somebody did. I was going to do some business with him at one time, until he turned out to be a thief. I've heard terrible stories about that *ganef* for years."

"So have I," Sheilah said. "Tell me one of yours, and I'll tell you one of mine."

"Oh, that he's fucked over that sports charity of his. I know someone who left it because it began to seem the major beneficiary might be Leigh himself. I don't doubt it for a second. What have you heard?"

"Beating up women." Sheilah shrugged. "He's made a habit of it, it seems."

"How is your friend Ann doing?" Weiss asked.

"I'm amazed. She's not staying down long, that's for sure."

"How does she look?" asked one of Weiss's companions.

"Terrible," Sheilah said bluntly. Ann's face still bore red splotches and scars. With the last vestiges of blond snipped away, her hair was now short and dark and did nothing to hide the damage. "She won't be working in front of cameras again for a long time, I can tell you that."

"What is she doing?" Weiss asked.

"Actually, she's casting around for a job," Sheilah told him. "Anything at your shop?" she asked, more in jest than anything else.

Weiss's reaction was unexpected. "Maybe. Why don't you ask her to give me a call?"

Ann met Weiss the following week in his luxurious office —a huge room with loungelike furniture in soft black leather, two earth-toned Bukharas on the gleaming black floor, a matte black fireplace, and French doors opening onto a private patio with a trickling circular fountain. Art objects and collectibles from Weiss's many foreign journeys were everywhere, with an emphasis on Oriental pieces. It was a decorator's dream, but Ann barely registered it. Her attention was strictly on Weiss.

"What we have available is the sort of entry-level position we'd usually give a film school graduate," he told her. "But of course you're not entry level, and your experience is in TV news. I would like to be able to do something for you, but . . ." He shrugged, raising his palms.

At that moment it seemed to Ann that the meeting for which she had been waiting so excitedly had disintegrated into a courtesy talk—before she had even had a chance.

"What is the job?" she asked.

"The title is negotiable. What it really is is an assistant for the assistant to our head of development. The person will be able to tell friends, 'I'm in development at Stanley Weiss Productions'—which is not bad. But the person will find him- or herself doing drudge work. It also involves mountainous script reading."

Ann nodded soberly as the term *drudge work* sank in. She pressed on anyway, emphasizing the fact that she was no stranger to reading and analyzing scripts.

The more they talked, the more impressed Weiss was by Ann. He nodded vigorously when she spoke of *The Beautiful Ones* as "a learning experience in how *not* to make a movie." And when she condemned the self-indulgence of the film, Weiss leaned forward, intrigued.

"There was no interest in entertaining the audience, uplifting them, giving them anything of value," she said. "It had to fail. How could anyone expect people to spend their money to see something like that?"

Weiss liked what he heard. Ann was not without ideas, he discovered. Moreover, her convictions matched his. A strong rapport was soon established.

"You seem to have given the movie business quite a bit of thought," he noted with some amusement. "Is this what they talked about at KCBA?"

Ann shook her head with a chuckle and a wave of her hand. "What is it they say? Everyone has two businesses, their business and show business. Just because everyone in town agreed I couldn't act didn't mean I stopped reading the trades. You know, I didn't move to Los Angeles seven years ago; in my mind, I was moving to *Hollywood*. The movies."

"So you wanted to be in the movie business," he said in a singsong voice.

"Yes." Ann grinned. "But it didn't work out that way."

"Do you want to get back on the air?" Weiss asked.

Ann shook her head. "To be honest, I won't miss being on-camera. What I always found most exciting was working in the field and in the editing room, getting the stories together. I felt much more involved, much more in control."

"Do you like being in control?"

Ann thought for a moment, then nodded. "Yes," she said, somewhat surprised. "I really do."

"Okay," he said. "Then I hope you won't mind some frank advice."

Ann steeled herself for whatever it was Weiss was about to say, watching anxiously as he removed his half-frame glasses and rubbed the bridge of his nose.

"You have a fine mind and a great deal to offer," he said, "but you've got to step out and make sure people know about it."

"I don't understand."

Without saying it directly, Weiss got his message across: Never again would the world hand Ann Peters a damn thing simply because she was bright, young, and *beautiful*. At age twenty-five, Ann had left that exalted but limiting role behind. The time had come for her to cultivate a more sophisticated approach. The talents that had taken a backseat to her perfect looks were now going to have to come to the fore. Weiss believed they would serve her well.

Ann was struck by the fact that, unlike Carl Adams, Sol Jolkins, and Sam, Weiss never told her what he could do for her. He suggested what she could do for herself. She loved it.

By the end of their interview, Ann had agreed to come on board at Weiss Productions. Weiss had told her that it would be up to her to build on her job, and she was determined to do just that.

The news that Hank Evans's son Eric was planning one of his infrequent visits to Sheilah's home made Ann all the more eager to move out.

"Wish we could convince you to stay awhile longer," Jeff shyly admitted to Ann, when she announced her plans to leave.

But she was firm, and her young admirer had to satisfy himself with helping her pack her belongings at the house she had shared with Sam—an ordeal made worse by the fact that her soon-to-be—ex-spouse had left the place in abysmal shape.

It was in such bad condition that Jeff at first assumed vandals had broken in during Ann's absence. Sensing her humiliation, he quietly proceeded to right the potted palm in the center of the living room floor, to clean up the dirt and the collection of discarded newspapers and trash.

"I couldn't have done it without you," Ann gratefully told Jeff much later as they plodded to the car with a final load of her belongings.

In fact, Jeff's amiable presence had made the move bearable, his efforts warming Ann like beams of sunlight brightening a rock-strewn muddy road.

Ann now had an image of Jeff as a sensitive young man who was easily led, and she was convinced she knew who was doing much of the leading. She held Eric Evans to blame for much of Jeff's questionable behavior. From conversations with Jeff, Ann had the impression that Eric was little more than a nonstop carouser.

TWENTY-SEVEN

ERIC EVANS ARRIVED at Sheilah's Beverly Hills home within a week of Ann's departure.

He came with one carry-on bag containing some of his California clothes—he hated waiting for luggage at the airport, and after all, if he needed anything, he could always buy it—plus a leather attaché case crammed with well-thumbed documents from the U.S. Government Printing Office.

He had finished reading the final Watergate tape transcripts on his flight, and he greeted Jeff by saying, "Can you believe Nixon's gone? My God, what a fuckin' uproar. How are people taking it out here? I've got the transcripts. You have to read them. Your jaw will drop to your knees."

He strode into the entryway, took off his sunglasses, and gave Jeff a smile. "Hey, you old sack of shit. How are you doing? I'd love a beer if you've got some."

A few minutes later, Eric was perched atop one of the tall stools at the kitchen counter, interrogating Jeff about his latest activities. Did he still want to be a photographer? No? What then? Television? He ought to see whether Sheilah could hunt up a gofer job for him. He ought to think about getting into Northwestern. Life out of L.A. would be good for Jeff, Eric decided.

As always, Eric had a "you ought to" for Jeff's every statement.

There was an electric quality about Eric, a restless energy that made him seem mobile even when he was sitting still. Lean and wiry in his tight black T-shirt, white jeans, and

255

topsiders, he looked at least five years older than his sixteen years.

"What about you?" Jeff finally succeeded in deflecting attention from himself. "What's new with you?"

"I met a three-star knockout on the plane. I've got to call her later."

"How do you do it? Every goddamn time."

"She just needed someone to help her with her headphones. She forgot to plug them in. Not exactly a brilliant girl, but"— Eric shook his head with a smirk—"looks like she's gifted in other ways."

"Lori keeps asking me about you," Jeff reported.

"What did you tell her?"

"I said you were going to be tied up the whole week."

"Good."

"Don't you want to talk to her?" Jeff asked. He was forever smoothing things over in Eric's wake, or trying to.

"I don't know," Eric said offhandedly. "Who else is around?"

"Everybody," Jeff replied. "And they all want to see you."

Eric smiled. It was great to be popular.

Jeff played social secretary when Eric was due in L.A., issuing or withholding invitations depending on Eric's instructions. It was a task that kept Jeff busy, but he was only too glad to do it, convinced his acceptance from desirable peers hinged on his tie to Eric.

His stories of nights on the town with Eric were instant legends. Jeff also reported to interested members of their clique that Eric had "lost track" of how many lovers he had had "somewhere after the first fifty or so."

Eric was intimately acquainted with the wonders of penicillin, too, but naturally he kept that information to himself.

He was regarded as generous, with his daddy's money, of course. The previous summer, he had flown a dozen of the Beverly Hills gang to his family's Gulf Shore vacation home, where they had taken turns streaking over the water in Eric's sleek, streamlined, high-power Cigarette racing boat, terrorizing other boaters.

Eric was still on occasion as courteous and warm to Sheilah as he had been as a child, when she had been "Mrs. Morison" to him and he had confided his troubles to her, especially his anguish at having been suddenly bustled off by his father to a school he had hated.

Even so, it had seemed to Sheilah that nothing could put a dent in Eric's unquestioning worship of Hank. She wondered whether that had changed, but she had no way of telling, for there were no shared confidences between herself and Eric now. The charming personality she knew alternated with a cool and aloof new version of Eric Evans that Sheilah disliked intensely but chalked off to typical teenage rebelliousness.

Nowadays, she found him completely unpredictable.

It was Eric's sociable face she saw on that first evening he was in town. He greeted her with a kiss on the cheek, asked about her show, gave her his parents' regards, and told her, "I'm awfully glad to be back."

As the week progressed, things became less sociable.

On his second night in town, Eric polished his Don Juan image. He and Jeff called a few members of the crowd to join them for a party a friend of his was giving. The party-giver was the voluptuous woman Eric had met on his flight out—an older woman of twenty-two, a round-faced, flaxen-haired Swedish model who spoke broken English. She lived in a trilevel cantilever house overlooking Studio City. The house was owned by a record company executive whose presence at the party was limited to a few photos showing him with his arm draped over the shoulders of his pretty import.

That night, it was Eric whose arm draped her shoulders.

"Eric says I'm a slut," she announced cheerfully, unaware of the meaning of the word. And while the others laughed or gasped, Eric nuzzled her neck and said approvingly, "Yes, you are, sweetheart—it's one of those little things I love about you."

The performance was conducted in front of Lori, a Christmas vacation conquest of Eric's, who looked on in agony, still not over the shock of discovering that it was possible to have sex with someone who could remain a remote stranger.

Aware of her discomfort, Jeff sat down next to her. Although she had been the date of one of the other boys in the clique, Jeff knew she really was there just to see Eric.

Well, he thought sympathetically, she was seeing him, all right.

He tried without much success to cheer her up by telling a

few jokes, then left the party with some other friends shortly afterward.

Eric returned to Sheilah's house at eight the next morning. She was waiting for him.

"Look, Eric," she said angrily, "if you're going to stay in my house and use my goddamned car the least you owe me is a little consideration!"

"Jeff knew where I was."

"Is that your answer?" she sputtered. "What is going on with you? Man, if you were my kid—"

Eric raised his palms, stopping her. "You're right. I was inconsiderate and I sincerely apologize. I didn't think you would need your car any earlier than this, but I shouldn't have kept it overnight."

"It's not the car I'm talking about and you know it."

"The car is your business," he said in a cutting monotone.

The rest of the statement hung unspoken between them: Eric's activities were not. In that moment, seeing his hard look, Sheilah felt a shiver of fear run through her. How absurd to fear a kid she had known his entire life.

"It won't happen again," he promised.

And sure enough, Eric saw to it that it didn't. He managed to get an older friend to rent a car for him, and not just any car—a sleek new silver Jaguar.

The fourth night of his visit turned out to be his last night at Sheilah's.

The evening began uneventfully. Eric and Jeff piled into the Jaguar and set out to round up a couple of friends for another evening on the town.

They had dinner and then stopped by the Starwood Club, but Eric quickly became bored, complaining that the music was awful. They drove up to Mulholland Drive to meet a source of Eric's at one of the view sites. The city stretched below them like a blanket of undulating stars—which became even more undulating after they had sampled Eric's purchase.

But things didn't really get rolling until Eric seized upon a more creative idea, a midnight visit to "liberate" a painfully withdrawn classmate of Jeff's and include him in some late-night carousing.

It was eleven-thirty when they drove to the Lexington Drive mansion in which the boy resided with his mother, an Academy Award—winning actress who had long been considered half crazy. Eric announced himself on the intercom, and the electronically controlled gate rolled open majestically.

Eric was the first one to reach the front door. There, he was met by a haggard woman, apparently naked under a provocatively clinging bronze satin robe. Her face was slathered over with night cream. She held a cocked pearl-handled revolver in her right hand.

"What do you kids think you're doing here?" she demanded.

The boys shrank back—all but Eric, who gazed at the pistol and the woman holding it and then drew back his chin theatrically, almost mockingly.

"That isn't real, is it?" he asked.

"Let's go," Jeff said in a hushed voice.

Eric continued to stare at the handgun, not budging.

"I asked you, just what in hell do you think you're doing here?"

"We're going out for a pizza, ma'am. We came to see whether Tommy could join us."

"No!"

"How about you, then?" he asked, with a calculated smile. "Our treat."

She waved the gun skyward and fired.

As Jeff and the two other members of Eric's retinue scattered frantically, Eric stiffened and held his ground.

"Get off my property," she screamed. "You smart-aleck bastard!"

"Come on, Eric!" Jeff turned back en route to the car to urge him on, but Eric refused to hurry. He sauntered over the wide green lawn, under the spotlighted trees, toward the driveway.

"Come on," Jeff called in desperation; his eyes widened with fright as the woman stormed out of the house, waving the revolver wildly.

Jeff screamed at Eric to run as he jumped behind the wheel of the car. He started the motor; the other two boys tumbled in and ducked down low, but Eric was still taking his time.

When Eric finally slid into the front passenger seat, Jeff pulled away with a jolt. The car roared down the driveway and out the gate, making too wide a turn and almost crashing into an oncoming car.

Brakes screeched, and the other driver angrily leaned on

his horn. Jeff stopped short, and the engine died as the other car drove on. By now the group was in complete hysterics—but their laughter died when they saw the flashing red lights in the rear-view mirror.

It was bad, very bad, for a fifteen-year-old to be caught driving under the influence of drugs with two grams of cocaine and half a Thai stick in the car.

The last thing Sheilah expected to feel, as she walked briskly down the hallway of the Beverly Hills police station to pick up her embarrassed son, was any sympathy for Eric Evans. But when she saw him, rigid and white-faced with sheer terror, her heart contracted in spite of herself.

The police had called his father.

Hank Evans kept his son waiting in his secretary's office for the entire afternoon. Dressed neatly in blazer and tie, Eric sat stiffly in a straight-backed chair, staring ahead, motionless except for the clenching of his jaw and an occasional hard swallow. From time to time his father's voice wafted out from the inner office.

One hour, two hours, three.

Finally, he heard a gruff voice call: "Eric!"

Hank continued to read his correspondence as Eric entered and stood before the desk. Without raising his eyes, he murmured, "I thought you were too smart to get yourself into a stink like this, son."

Eric said nothing.

Hank continued to keep his eyes on his mail as he talked.

"This is the end of your trips to California. And Mister Jeff Morison is no longer welcome in our home. The only question left to settle, it seems to me, is whether you shouldn't spend your junior and senior years back at the academy."

Hank finally glanced up. "State your case, Eric."

"I feel that . . ." The boy swallowed hard. His voice was taut with anger. "My understanding was that if I kept up my grades, I could stay where I am."

Although Eric liked his friends to believe that learning was effortless for him, the fact was that he quietly worked himself sick in order to excel—often relying on amphetamines stolen from Mary Evans's ample supply to study when he was exhausted.

"Do you think that balances out your being arrested with a bag full of drugs in your possession?"

"As far as school goes, sir, yes, I do. And it's not only my grades. I'd . . . I'd like to remind you I scored in the ninetieth percentile on the PSATs. I don't believe I would have done as well if I were still at Greensborough."

Hank finally put his mail aside, clasped his hands, and gazed at his son. "Were they your drugs? Or did you just say that to get Jeff off the hook?"

"They were mine." Eric drew a ragged breath. "I was responsible for everything. I was the one who got Jeff into trouble, so why should there be a ban on him?"

"Because he's a washout."

"Jeff?" Eric was astonished.

"Yes." Hank nodded emphatically. "He's going to end up a nothing. Jeff is not up to you in any way. You've got plenty of better friends to pal around with."

"No." Eric shook his head. "Jeff's as smart as anyone I know. He just doesn't know what he wants to do. He needs motivation, that's all."

Hank grimaced. "He's a zero."

Eric stared down at Hank's desk, fuming. "He is not," he muttered, but Hank pretended not to hear.

"So you were responsible for everything," Hank said.

In truth, what bothered him the most about Eric's misadventure was that Eric had gotten caught—and that, because he had gotten caught, a squib about his arrest had made the AP wire.

Eric knew that instinctively; he could feel it in the pit of his stomach.

Hank's next statement simply confirmed Eric's feelings. "You're lucky it didn't happen during a slow news period."

"I know." Eric nodded. Then his body relaxed; the grilling seemed to have ended. "Do you think they'll prosecute Nixon? Is he going to get out of it now?"

"We haven't decided whether *you* are going to get out of *this*. Finish telling me why we shouldn't send you back to Greensborough."

"I thought I had."

"Well, you're wrong. Are you in the habit of messing around with drugs?"

Eric stared at him. "I am not in the habit, sir, no," he said ominously. "It was recreation."

"Don't do it again. We don't want a drug problem in our family." Hank rose and started to slide his papers into his briefcase. "Something else you want to say?"

"We already have a drug problem in our family. Mother's."

Hank snapped his briefcase shut. He slipped his reading glasses into his pocket and started toward the door. "I'm going to ask Denise to make a note of any calls going to Sheilah Smith's number," he said. "I don't want you phoning Jeff. If I find you have any contact, you're on your way to Greensborough."

And then he was gone, leaving Eric staring at the empty doorway as if he were seeing within its frame the cause of the rage that constantly burned in him.

Denise was Hank's personal secretary, and his latest mistress. She sometimes came to the house when Mary was away, an arrangement Eric was expected to accept and say nothing about.

Not that Mary seemed to notice much. As long as she had a seating arrangement to work out or fund-raiser decorations to decide upon, she went like a little top and seemed able to ignore—with help—everything she did not want to see.

Her cycles were predictable by now. Every year or so, she would make an effort to slack off the pills; then it would escalate again. Currently, she had four doctors keeping her in prescriptions. It was a subject she refused to discuss.

Hank was too involved with politics to think much about his family. He got on famously with the old-boy crowd in his party, which had treated him as a ranking member from the very beginning. He played golf with the head of Ways and Means. The party leaders considered him a great asset and talked him up as a future contender for the Senate. He told a good dirty joke, and his store of ribald Hollywood tales kept the gang in the congressional sauna entertained. He had helped author some attention-getting legislation, and he had proved to be a master of filibuster. In short, he was a success on the Hill.

But Eric knew that the only constituents he gave a damn about were the rich ones.

Eric had walked into his father's office expecting more than five minutes' attention and the tired old threat of boarding school. Why hadn't his father instigated one of the many other more fitting punishments that Eric had thought for himself? Five minutes and some stunningly unfair comments about his best friend. Five lousy fucking minutes. That was it. It had been weeks, maybe months, since their last talk.

Did the old man not care? Eric instantly rejected the idea. It was just his father's mood, the pressures he was under, the fact that he was busy.

That fact also had its advantages, Eric told himself. He suspected that as long as he was able to avoid the detested military school, he could go on doing pretty much as he pleased. And that included maintaining his friendship with Jeff.

Eric left the office trying to shake off his disappointment and forget his frustration, but he had a sense that with this conversation, something had changed.

It had. He had given up on his father.

TWENTY-EIGHT

ANN HAD BEEN right in thinking that the case against Leigh
Ballard would generate widespread media attention—but
wrong in thinking that it would be her life that would be under
inspection by the press.

The press focused on Ballard.

In the two years following Ann's injury, an avalanche of
information on Ballard's questionable business dealings and
misdeeds began falling into the light of public scrutiny.

Ann's charges became a single tile in a developing mosaic
of lawless behavior on a grand scale.

Ballard was dissected in an investigative series by the *Los
Angeles Journal*. The paper uncovered evidence that he had
used his position on the board of Play for Life, a charitable
sports-oriented youth foundation, to funnel money into bogus
organizations that in turn kicked back cash to cover some of
Ballard's less public-spirited enterprises.

An official inquiry into Ballard's conduct at the foundation
was launched. Meanwhile, reporters delved deeper into the
tangled web of Ballard International's financial history.

So did the Internal Revenue Service.

The company stock plunged, dealing Ballard a major financial blow, and he was forced to sell off his yacht and his
part-ownership in the Condors basketball team. When the ob-
sequious columnist Lorne Wagner avoided him, it was a sure
sign that Ballard had become socially unacceptable.

In the interim, Sol Jolkins experienced some negative publicity of his own. A local weekly explored "the picture behind

the picture at KCBA" and came up with a story exposing the sexual harassment at the station, and Jolkins's involvement in it. His party was over, at least for the foreseeable future.

While her enemies' fortunes fell, Ann's rose. Installed in her new job, she concentrated nearly ever waking moment on moves that would take her closer to her newfound goal of carving a place for herself behind the scenes in the film industry.

As much as possible, Ann wanted to forget about the case and about Sam. She wanted to bypass the sick feeling that swept over her whenever she thought of the death of her once-great love.

She felt as if she were fighting a battle, a twenty-hour-a-day battle, to conquer the past and meet the future on her own terms. She attended classes, seminars, and symposiums on packaging, budgeting, scheduling, marketing, negotiating, financing—anything related to film.

The high profile Ann had achieved at KCBA and through her legal wrangle with Leigh Ballard proved an asset in her new career. People knew who she was and were curious about her, which was valuable in establishing contacts. The fact that she was working for Stanley Weiss was an extremely valuable calling card.

But it was Ann's own emerging abilities and her driving work pace that put a rocket charge to her professional rise. She had a great natural nurturing ability. She was a quick, keen reader, who just happened to share Stanley Weiss's tastes. But most important, she soon proved to have an extraordinary ability to cut through "impossible" obstacles and get things done.

The turning point came when Ann became aware of a hangup on a movie Weiss Productions had nearly ready to go before the cameras. The script called for a glittering opera concert, but the projected costs for the sequence had escalated far beyond the reach of the movie's budget.

Remembering Weiss's words about how important it was to be bold, Ann went into his office and suggested staging such a concert as a benefit for Artists for Others—Weiss's favorite cause—and then shooting the benefit for the film. No extras. No wardrobe. An enjoyable performance for the attendees, and a nice big plug for the organization on top of it.

"If we could work out some sort of profit participation deal

266 / *Marilyn Beck*

with Artists for Others, I'm sure they'd help us," she told him. "And you'd have great prospects for promoting the picture and the charity at once. Everybody wins."

Weiss loved the idea. The director of the film thought it was "an interesting possibility" and agreed to try working with it, in spite of the fact he inwardly believed the benefit idea would die a quick death.

"I would be glad to help coordinate it," Ann volunteered.

Suddenly, she found herself at dead center in a logistical nightmare, with the charity organizers on one side, the film team on the other. It fell to her to see that both sides got what they wanted, which appeared impossible. Making it all the harder was the fact that few besides Weiss seemed to take the plan seriously. Literally hundreds of phone calls proved fruitless. But Ann refused to give up or to allow her enthusiasm to wane. Then one afternoon, just when Weiss was about to instruct Ann to drop the idea, she burst into his office brimming over with excitement.

"We got Beverly Sills—maybe. But a strong maybe."

That strong maybe led to yeses from other noted artists, and the opera recital began shaping up as a truly star-studded affair with Placido Domingo. As the Weiss Productions attorneys were busy working out the complexities of cameo appearance deals, the momentum of the enterprise picked up, along with the enthusiasm of Actors for Others and the film team. Now they believed. Something special was going on, and people wanted to be a part of it. Ann found the cooperation level around Hollywood skyrocketing.

Movie and TV stars, Ann discovered, were the biggest fans in the world when it came to the giants of other fields, such as politics, sports—and opera. Opera buffs including Frank Sinatra and Cary Grant idolized the likes of Domingo. As the day set for the benefit neared, more and more requests for seats came in from the celebrity crowd.

By eliciting expert advice, rallying a crew of can-do helpers, and working literally around the clock for weeks, Ann succeeded in doing her part to coordinate the affair. The sequence ran over budget, but by less than the amount forecast before Ann's idea took form. The footage was spectacular. The benefit turned out to be among the most successful in the organization's history. And the kudos heaped on Stanley Weiss added a fresh luster to his already-considerable prestige.

The event made Ann a star within the production company. It became common practice for Weiss to throw important tasks her way. "Ann can handle that," became an oft-heard line. And time after time, she proved worthy of it.

Weiss came to view Ann as his protégeé. She was asked to dinner parties at the hilltop Trousdale estate Weiss shared with his wife of thirty-eight years. Evenings at the Weiss home provided ample proof of what Ann had long wanted to believe—that Hollywood encompassed worlds entirely different from the one inhabited by Carl Adams and his crowd. The more deeply Ann became involved in the business of making movies, the more facets of the industry she saw, the more firmly convinced she became: this was it—the place she belonged.

The only drawback was that she had no personal life.

"I understand," Sheilah told her one night when they stopped at Trader Vic's for a post-screening drink. "Getting back into the dating scene after my divorce was one of the hardest things I ever did—but you've got to do it eventually. You don't want to shut that side of yourself off."

"Yes, I do," Ann responded vehemently. "The last thing I want is to invite that stress, that constant draining of energy. You have a man in your life and suddenly his priorities are your priorities and what were your priorities are gone!"

"Oh, Ann. You know that's not always true. You've been hurt and you're angry."

"I'm happy," Ann insisted, setting down her tumbler with a dull thud.

Sheilah sat back in her tall bamboo chair and looked at Ann with a sagacious little smile.

"What?" Ann asked.

"What about sex?"

Ann frowned and shrugged. Issue closed.

Sheilah, misreading Ann's silence, was swept with guilt. Of course. Ann had to be concerned about her looks. Sheilah was so used to the scars that she no longer really noticed them.

What Sheilah didn't know was that Ann had chosen not to undergo further cosmetic surgery. She had had enough of doctor's offices and hospital rooms. She had decided to give herself time off for good behavior, as she thought of it.

Moreover, she didn't want to take time from work just now.

She had other explanations she could have used, too—without acknowledging the fact that her appearance served to keep men at arm's length.

A mere two years after her start at the company, Ann had expanded her job beyond all recognition of its original boundaries. Her promotions and pay raises reflected that fact. The first of the projects Ann had shepherded through development went into production.

She was well on her way. She was flying.

Then the time came when she had to detach herself from her newfound life and turn back. The trial of Leigh Ballard proved a predictably lurid affair, and predictably difficult for Ann.

The day before the trial began, Weiss came to Ann's office to wish her luck. Later, coworkers gathered to tell her they would be rooting for her.

She was grateful for every friend she had, especially during the opening days of the trial, when it seemed nothing was going her way.

The strength of Ezra White's testimony was diluted as Ballard's attorney made the most of White's viewing angle and his distance from the "accident."

Sheilah's statements were also seemingly scuttled by Ballard's lawyer. Why, he wondered, was Sheilah the only one on the patio who had seen scratch marks on Ballard's cheeks? He asked belittling questions that made a mockery of Sheilah's "feelings" and "intuition," leaving her thoroughly humiliated by the end of her testimony.

One day, just when Ann's spirits were at their lowest, she was surprised to notice David Steinmetz seated in the gallery. She caught up with him in the hallway outside the courtroom after court had adjourned.

"So what do you think of the show so far?" she asked piquantly. Steinmetz turned back and stopped as Ann added, "Is it going as badly as I think?"

"If I were Leigh Ballard I'd say it's going badly," Steinmetz replied. "The defense has been making a lot of mistakes. Haven't you noticed?"

Ann shook her head. "Tell me."

"Sheilah Smith, for one. The jury didn't like seeing her treated in such a condescending fashion. I think Ballard's lawyer accomplished exactly the reverse of what he intended to do. Two of the women looked as though they were ready to jump up and give him hell!"

"He managed to dismantle everything Sheilah said."

"Yes, but he failed completely in his style. And don't think for a minute that's not going to make a difference. He's never going to convince anyone that Ballard is a nice guy by making belligerent-sounding remarks himself," Steinmetz pointed out.

As they walked downstairs, Ann began to smile. "I hadn't thought of all that," she said. "Thanks. I feel better."

They passed the long counter in the lobby.

"Uh . . . Doctor?" Ann faltered. "David?"

He stopped again and gave her a slight smile. "David. Please."

"I can't help wondering why . . . why you would bother coming to watch this mess?"

"I told you, I have strong feelings about the case," Steinmetz answered.

At his suggestion, they continued their conversation over coffee in a nearby restaurant. When they had exhausted the trial as a topic, David asked Ann about her family.

She smiled somewhat grimly. "You must have a nice family," she observed, "to expect so much of mine. My sister doesn't understand why I pressed charges. The only word I got from her, besides a couple of get-well cards, was a note to make sure I knew she absolutely had to be left out of it."

Steinmetz sat back in the booth, shaking his head. After a moment, he said, "You really are a remarkable person."

Ann laughed. "Why do you say that?"

"How can you be the way you are given the people you've been surrounded by—" He stopped himself as Ann looked down, frowning.

Aware that he had gone too far, Steinmetz quickly changed the subject. "How do you like working for Stanley Weiss?"

"I can't wait to get back full-time," Ann said enthusiastically. The awkward moment was soon forgotten. When they parted, Ann promised to call with progress reports on the trial.

Her testimony took five days. From the minute Ballard's lawyer began his cross-examination, his objective was clear. She was questioned about the circumstances of her initial hiring at the station, with no credentials and no experience. He established that she had no proof of her version of the incident in the den. What everyone did know was that she had gone to a swinging party while her husband was out of town, that she had been seen there flirting with two men. Why had she stayed so late? Why had she tried to prevent the defendant from leaving?

With Ezra White's testimony weakened, all that Ballard's lawyer had to do was destroy Ann's credibility.

After days of verbal battering, it seemed to her that the destruction had been accomplished. Completely.

David, who had once again somehow found time to attend the trial, saw it differently.

"You were magnificent! He didn't trip you once. You were precise, you were poised, and I'm convinced the jury is with you. Ann, anyone who ever saw you on the news knows you were qualified for that job!"

Once again, David's strong positive statements buoyed Ann's foundering confidence. The boost came just in time, too, for the next week Ballard's lawyer called a witness whose very presence was devastating to her: Sam Dallas.

Sam informed the court and the world that Ann took flirtation as an insult. "We talked about it many times," he stated, "because I thought, for her own good, she ought to stop over-reacting." He detailed their last conversation before he had left for New York, the conversation in which he had suggested Ann was overwrought and needed a vacation. He said she had been behaving "in a weird way. Very edgy, very snappish."

At the end of the cross-examination, after all his damaging statements, Sam wound up exclaiming in tears that he should never have taken his fateful trip, that he was sorry—nothing specific, just generally sorry, one had to assume, and then he cried, "It's like they say, you don't know what you've got till it's gone."

Ann kept her head bowed during the entire spectacle.

The following Monday, Sol Jolkins was called.

Jolkins, in from his new non-network home base in San Francisco, hemmed, hawed, and reddened while being interrogated by the prosecutor about the party and his reasons for asking Ann to play hostess. In trying to tone down his role, he wound up making the party, Ann's presence, and her actions there seem far less scandalous than Ballard's attorney wanted them to appear.

His recollection of Ann's "fall" was surprisingly murky.

The more cynically inclined might have connected the fog rolling into Jolkins's memory with the crop of troubles that had risen in Leigh Ballard's life, and with Jolkins's desire to forget his once-proud claim to being "Leigh Ballard's close friend."

Ann certainly made the connection.

So did the prosecutor, who was on to a compelling new scent as a result of Jolkins's hesitancy.

At last, Jolkins's words themselves became murky. "If I can't recall it as if it was yesterday, it's because it wasn't yesterday. It was almost three years ago—"

The prosecutor interrupted him. "You dislike violence, don't you, Mr. Jolkins?"

"Of course I dislike violence."

"And the idea of a friend of yours committing an act of violence, on your property no less—would you say that's a repugnant idea to you?"

"Well, of course. Definitely."

"Repugnant enough so that you might find it impossible to believe?"

"I do find it impossible to believe."

"You wouldn't expect such an act from a friend of yours?"

"No, I would not. Never!"

The prosecutor paused for a moment, allowing the pattern he was creating to sink into Jolkins's consciousness. Here it was, a way for Jolkins to dissociate himself from this man who had disgraced himself, who had a fraud case hanging over his head in addition to the present case, a man who had robbed his own charity, and, most importantly, a man who had made Sol Jolkins look bad and had caused him untold misery.

Here it was, a way to undo the knot that tied him to this damned millstone, Ballard—not by admitting that he had lied, but simply by agreeing with this persuasive deputy district attorney that he, Jolkins, was such a decent man he could not comprehend wanton violence.

"Would you say," the prosecutor proceeded carefully, "it might be hard for you to believe such an act, even if you saw it?"

"I would say that it might be . . . possible." Jolkins sighed. "I guess it's possible, yes."

"Possible? Could you say probable?"

"Maybe. I don't know. Yes, I guess so."

Jolkins's words created a fissure in the defense, a crack through which the jury could see the truth—just as it soon saw through Leigh Ballard. He was given an opportunity to deliver his version of what had happened at the party, but Jolkins's lame testimony had unnerved him, had had the effect of a hard blow to the belly.

Ballard seemed stunned, and his words carried no ring of truth.

It was over. In the end, the scene was almost as Ann had envisioned it.

She left the court building surrounded by reporters with microphones and cameras. She raised her hand in a V for victory sign, a slightly cockeyed smile lighting her scarred face. This time—thirty-two months, dozens of meetings, a raft of newspaper headlines, three operations, and a divorce later—this time it was real.

It was real, and it was imperfect.

Although Ballard's attorneys had failed to win him a not guilty verdict, they did extraordinarily well by their client during the penalty phase of the proceedings.

In a lengthy hearing, a parade of witnesses—including a minister, a famous radio disk jockey, two basketball stars, and Ballard's eighty-seven-year-old mother—testified on his behalf. Much was made of Ballard's past philanthropic deeds and his longstanding church affiliation. Even more was said about the terrible suffering he had gone through after Ann's charges had been made public. Ballard's lawyers went to great lengths to prove that the case had made such a shambles of Ballard's personal and professional life that Ballard had been driven to the very brink of a nervous breakdown.

With the help of his witnesses, Ballard was able to convince the judge he was filled with deep remorse.

The heavy-duty lawyering paid off: the judge concluded that Ballard was contrite, that he had already paid a high price for his crime, and that he posed no threat to society; therefore, and in consideration of the fact it was his first offense, it would not serve the best interests of the community at large for Ballard to be incarcerated.

Ballard was fined and given a term of probation on condition that he agree to continue his psychological counseling (a strong point in his favor had been Ballard's voluntary effort to curb his "possible abusive impulses toward women"). The judge also required Ballard to pay restitution that would cover Ann's medical bills.

In the meantime, Ann decided to accept an out-of-court settlement rather than to pursue her lawsuit any further.

By then, the thought of reliving all the strain of the criminal trial was anathema to her. Although her attorney was convinced that she could win at least triple the offered settlement by fighting her separate civil case to the finish, Ann was determined to bury *Peters vs. Ballard* without having to go back to court.

She had better things to think about.

PART 6

The Executive

TWENTY-NINE

~~~

IT DIDN'T TAKE Ann long to get back into the full fevered tempo of Stanley Weiss Productions. Her days were dominated by scripts and meetings, meetings and scripts.

As was typical of the business, about forty-five out of fifty of the projects Weiss had in development never got beyond that phase. Hundreds of millions of dollars were written off by the industry each year for options on books that screenwriters couldn't manage to translate to film. In some cases, projects got as far as preproduction, with the hiring of directors, set designers, location scouts, and production staffs, only to have the death knell sound when deals with stars fell through or rewrites on scripts wouldn't come together.

The picture that was Weiss's particular baby was an opulent historical saga based on the colorful life of Alma Mahler, wife of Gustav Mahler and friend, lover, and confidante of some of the greatest composers and artists of turn-of-the-century Europe.

Muse had a tour-de-force leading role and screamed prestige, which of course screamed Academy Award nominations. It was budgeted at a queenly twelve million.

Watching *Muse* as it slowly progressed toward the screen provided Ann with an education in itself.

The movie had already been the victim of various ups and downs in the years prior to Ann's employment with the company.

It had been on the brink of becoming a "go" production when its first lead had been admitted to a psychiatric hospital after a near-fatal overdose of drugs. The quest for the perfect Alma Mahler had been started afresh.

Faye Dunaway had been a popular choice, but she had decided to do a Paddy Chayefsky movie called *Network* with William Holden. Joyce Haber had suggested in print that Vanessa Redgrave was a strong possibility for the role. But then the elusive, reclusive Carolyne Hart had agreed to star in *Muse*.

Everyone involved was thrilled; Carolyne had international box office appeal.

Then Carolyne demanded a different director.

The switch in directors was made.

But the new director hated all three existing versions of the script. At his insistence, a writer of his choice began work on a fourth version.

Meanwhile, Carolyne decided that her "old man," a young muscular blond named George Thrush, must be given producer credit. If Stanley Weiss, the executive producer, and Sentinel Studios, the distributor, didn't go along, she would walk.

They went along.

Carolyne had discovered Thrush right in her own backyard. Literally. She referred to him as an actor and playwright, and, while that may have been his ambition, he was actually working as a carpenter—adding a sun deck to her patio—when she first spotted him. That evening, his tools were parked in her garage, and his shoes were parked under her bed.

George's ways and words were coarse, his intelligence limited, his knowledge of Carolyne's world of show business nil. But he gave her what she had never had before—the belief that she was appealing.

Carolyne had been a homely child who had grown into an unattractive woman. So dynamic was her acting—her ability to transform herself into each character she played—that she mesmerized the public into seeing physical attributes that did not exist. But she didn't fool herself. Each time she looked in the mirror, the truth screamed back at her. She was short and dumpy and plain. And she hated it.

George made her forget the truth. George broke down her defenses and her reserve as no man had before by making her feel sexually desirable.

"You've got my cock so hard it's going to break off," he had whispered to her that first day in the yard of her home. She had recoiled, shocked and humiliated. But in spite of herself, her eyes had focused on the bulge at the front of his jeans. He had been telling the truth, and she had felt flattered, pleased, more of a woman than she ever had before.

He used the same approach more brazenly as he became an ever more integral part of her life.

Ann heard story after story about the couple from acquaintances who had worked on Carolyne's most recent film.

One day George had wandered onto the soundstage just as Carolyne began a key scene.

He observed the action from the sidelines for a few minutes, then bolted forward and bellowed, "Stop! For chrissake, stop this shit."

Cameramen, electricians, grips froze in midmotion. Extras, makeup artists, hair stylists stared. The director leaped up from his chair, screaming, "What the hell are you doing?"

As Carolyne stood bemused, George calmly sauntered to the center of the set. He stood before her for a moment silently, his fingers toying with her hair, tracing the outline of her lips, her eyes. Then one hand traveled to her breast; he squeezed it and moaned, while his other hand directed her fingers to his bulging crotch. "There's no woman in the world who can turn me on like you can," he announced. "Don't let them waste you. This scene you're doing is shit. It'll have to be rewritten."

And with that—as a cast and crew of some two hundred stood by stunned—George guided Carolyne off the set, walking behind her, one hand over her shoulder, kneading her breast, the other hand patting her buns possessively. They made their way to her dressing room where, without bothering to close the door, they fell on the floor and George mounted her, panting, "Oh, fuck me, baby. You are the sexiest woman in the world."

The director quickly called, "Lunch, one hour." When his star returned to work that afternoon, she looked radiant and proud.

Ann was flabbergasted by the story, which she heard several times from several people.

One day, discussing the situaton of Carolyne and George, Stanley Weiss commented to Ann, "His public behavior might be more outlandish than most, but their relationship isn't unique. Look around you at the actresses who've had to settle for men who aren't their equals on any level. It's the plight of the famous woman. A man of rank, of achievement, is seldom content to live in a woman's shadow."

Weiss's words would come back to Ann repeatedly during the following years—years that would see Valerie Harper become involved with an exercise trainer, Liza Minnelli marry a stage manager, and Faye Dunaway wed a photographer.

"Look," Weiss added, "if Streisand can pick up a hairdresser and make him a producer, Carolyne figures why can't she do the same with George. I sure don't envy the guy."

As Ann slowly shook her head, Weiss added, "But then, of course, the wives of some famous men, those whose lives are invested in their husbands, those who are left to drift . . . they're sad lives." He trailed off thoughtfully.

"I'm not sure I understand the connection," Ann admitted.

"I'm not sure there is one." Weiss smiled, shrugging off his abrupt shift in direction. "My mind started wandering, I guess. You'll have to stop me when I do that, Ann. I'm sounding more and more like an old man. Of course," he added with a laugh, "with Carolyne and George around, we might all end up aging very rapidly."

The fact that George Thrush had such control over Carolyne Hart surprised Ann, since the actress had such a strong personality of her own. She was an intimidating, mercurial presence who could turn on enough charm to win over the most adamant opponent—or accomplish the same goal by playing ruthless hardball. Carolyne's desire to cast a virtual unknown in the role of Mahler caused a number of arguments.

Meanwhile, the writer of the fourth version of the script told Ann that he was ready to kill George, and he was not kidding, because Thrush had handed him a fifty-page summary of the changes he and Carolyne deemed essential.

Ann watched Weiss deal with Carolyne on a number of occasions. He used a combination of diplomacy plus his own brand of hardball. In the end, despite Carolyne's wishes, a strong character actor was set to play the composer. Then Weiss had a long, effective talk with Carolyne about curbing George's overzealous behavior and letting the writer do his work.

"Appeasement can only go so far," Weiss told Ann with a wry grin. "Remember Chamberlain."

Not long afterward, Ann flew to Richmond for the first sneak preview of "her" first picture—the first among the dozens of movies she had helped develop to have actually made it to the screen. It had been written and directed by her discovery, novice filmmaker Rusty de Paull, a twenty-two-year-old graduate of the UCLA Cinema School.

The $1.5 million coming-of-age drama had turned out to be a small gem of a movie that held promise of becoming a box office winner.

As she watched it from the rear of the theater, Ann knew she would never forget the audience's reaction. The crowd sat spellbound through the final scenes, really caring whether the boy won the girl, not quite sure until the very last moment whether he would. The movie worked, and the audience response cards proved it.

Subsequently, Ann knew she would never forget her frustration at seeing the picture die of malnutrition—the victim of poor distribution by the studio that released it, minimal promotion, and misleading and ineffective ads.

Stanley Weiss was uncharacteristically passive about it.

His wife was ailing; he was preoccupied. Perhaps he had only enough energy for *Muse,* Ann realized. Or perhaps he was losing some of his zeal for the game.

She understood, but that didn't alter the fact that Weiss had not given the movie his best when the distribution deal had been forged.

Disappointed, Ann plowed back into the all-absorbing task of tending a new crop of dreams. Although she still had no personal life, she stubbornly insisted she didn't want one.

Ann sent tokens of appreciation to everyone she felt had extended themselves on her behalf during the Ballard trial. After long deliberation, she decided on a beautifully bound antique medical book for David Steinmetz and sent it with a note of thanks.

He responded by calling to invite her to a concert at the Music Center with another couple.

The concert was excellent, the company delightful, the change in her routine welcome. At dinner, Ann listened in fascination as David and his friends engaged in conversation a

282 / *Marilyn Beck*

world removed from her usual industry shop talk. Her rapt interest and keen questions made her the hit of the evening, although when David told her so, she refused to take it seriously.

She reciprocated with an invitation to her world, asking David whether he would be interested in attending an advance screening of a sci-fi movie. "I've been hearing a lot of talk about it," she said, "so maybe space pictures aren't dead after all. It's called *Star Wars*."

David loved everything about the screening at the Academy Theater: the rows of roped-off seats reserved for key press and VIPs (entry into that reserved section, Ann informed him, reaffirmed one's status in a business where status counted for everything); the giant Oscars flanking the screen; the famous faces; the gossip; the sight of industryites moseying up and down the aisles chatting and laughing, working the theater before the movie began; the fact that Ann couldn't seem to walk ten steps without being stopped by someone she knew.

David was particularly impressed when Barbra Streisand and Jon Peters waved to Ann from their place in the back row.

"Any relation?" he asked.

Ann shook her head. "No. I started out life as Ann Beaudry," she blurted, surprised at her own words. And then she quickly explained that she'd been acquainted with Jon Peters since he had been a beauty salon operator.

"He's sharp and a person with real street smarts. I understand that when he was a young punk with his first job after beautician's school, he'd pay the salon's receptionist to page him to the phone so his clients would get the impression he was in constant demand. He knew right from the beginning that if he kept the women waiting, they'd be all the more anxious for his time, that his services would seem that much more desirable."

David nodded slowly. "Fascinating," he said.

He was equally fascinated by an outrageous story he could hear a man seated behind them telling a friend. Upon entering New York's Luchow's restaurant and noticing a decorative scale near the entrance, he said, "I stripped to my shorts and weighed myself. It was at the height of my pants-dropping period . . ."

David loved the story all the more when he realized it was Tim Conway making the confession.

When the film was over, Ann turned to David and saw that he was beaming with childlike delight.

"What a terrific movie," he exclaimed.

Ann's answer: "Smash."

They stopped at Chasen's for a nightcap. Between discussing C-3PO, George Lucas, the future of comic-book space pictures, and the industry in general, Ann managed to slip in some pointed references to the fact that she was reserving her passion for work.

David told her that he had been avoiding getting involved with women who wanted serious relationships. It was too soon, he said, too soon after his wife's death.

Ann took it with good humor when David was unavailable the next three times she invited him to screenings of movies she thought he might like. She grasped that here was a man as wrapped up in his professional life as she was in hers.

She got used to David's occasional phone calls to see how she was doing or to share a joke. Sometimes when one or the other of them had a crisis, there would be long late-night conversations.

In spite of their frequent schedule conflicts, Ann and David did share a night out occasionally. Her acquaintances began getting used to seeing him escort her to screenings and film-land banquets. And so it went for more than two months, with Ann secure in the knowledge that David was busy, that he had his own life, that he was playing the field, seeing women who were, no doubt, better-looking than she. No strings, no expectations, no pressure. She was a friend, safely unattractive to him—or so she thought.

Then their infrequent encounters came to an abrupt halt.

It happened after a scene that neither Ann nor David wanted to think about later, one that began when David convinced Ann to free up a Sunday and go out for a sail on a friend's sloop. It was a perfect day of exhilarating relaxation: the sky was clear, the sun warm, the sea a hundred shades of rich, cold blue.

Later, they returned to David's condominium for "just one glass of wine," Ann insisted. She couldn't stay long; she had work waiting at home.

Ann had never seen David in his home environs before, and she found it unsettling.

While she realized it would have been ridiculous to expect an atmosphere like that of his office, she was unprepared for his airy, sun-drenched haven. Rainbow patterns splashed over the walls from a crystal conch shell resting on the wide windowsill, beyond which a strip of the sparkling ocean was visible. Faint musical notes tinkled from wind chimes on the balcony.

Having grown accustomed to work surroundings in which she could barely hear herself think, Ann found the hypnotic peace and quiet nerve-jangling. She wondered how David could stand it.

She chatted effervescently—too effervescently for David to embark on the more serious subject matter he had in mind —and all the while her mind burned with new impressions of David and his world.

"It's great to have a friend who owns a boat, isn't it?" Ann prattled on. "You have all the fun and none of the headaches."

He had to have women coming in all the time, she thought. What the hell else would he be doing with a goddamn *condo* in goddamn *Marina del Rey?* Why did she suddenly feel so angry? It was really amusing, she told herself. Amusing to think of David with his stupid, goddamned bachelor pad.

"I didn't even know you knew how to sail," she said.

"Well, we had a boat when I was a kid . . ."

As the conversation continued, Ann studied David. He sat back in his low leather chair, looking perfectly comfortable in white shorts and a bulky tan fisherman's sweater, his face sunburnt and invigorated. The more she looked, the more she was gripped by a strange sense that she had never really seen David before.

After about fifteen minutes, Ann stood to take her leave. "I'd better be on my way," she announced, grabbing her bag and heading for the door.

"Wait," he said. Ann turned back.

He came toward her, and his fingers lightly touched her cheeks as he bent to kiss her, gently, warmly.

It was not too soon any longer.

Awkwardly, with a strange small laugh, Ann mumbled something about her work, thanked him again, and started a fast retreat as he watched her with an unforgivably knowing half-smile on his face.

"You don't have to rush off," he said.

"I've already taken up much more time than I afford," she replied heatedly. "I have a ton of things to prepare for tomorrow."

"Ann, when are we going to drop this pretense?"

"I thought we had an understanding," she murmured. "If you've changed your mind, well, then, I wouldn't want to hang you up."

"What do you mean?" he asked, his face clouding.

"I mean," she said slowly, "if . . . if you've changed your mind, I think you should look elswhere."

He put his hands on her shoulders and, shaking his head, looked into her eyes. "You've been so badly burned. I know. But if you—"

"It's not that," she exclaimed.

"What, then?" He winced. "You're not still thinking about *Sam*, are you?"

Ann didn't answer for several seconds, and David turned away, frowning.

"I can't even address that," he muttered with a bitter half-chuckle.

"I don't know what it is," she heard herself admit. "I do know you deserve much, much more than I'm equipped to give."

"Nonsense."

"It's not nonsense," she said, feeling dreadful. "I'm . . . I'm sorry."

A few days later, David called her, a no-hard-feelings call.

Not long after that, Ann gladly agreed to read a script written by two friends of his—everyone in Los Angeles has a friend who has written a screenplay—and met with them to offer suggestions, recommendations, and encouragement.

There was still a feeling of support between them, however distanced. She and David continued to have telephone conversations every few weeks.

It was after one of their talks, in fact, that Ann decided the time had come for a stronger approach to resolving her differences with her sister and brother-in-law.

The time had come to talk to Lyla in person.

During a trip to New York, Ann rented a car and drove to

Bloomfield, the New Jersey town where the Mantussis now lived. She phoned Lyla requesting a visit, assuming that Lyla couldn't possibly turn her down if she were actually in the area. If Lyla didn't want her to come to the house, Ann said, she would meet Lyla somewhere—anywhere.

Lyla reacted as if Ann had hurled a bomb through her window.

"You should never have come without giving me warning," she shrieked. "I can't leave now. And you *can't* come."

"Tomorrow, then," Ann begged. "I'll stay over. If you don't want me to see Cindy, all right. That's your and Joe's decision. But we must discuss this. However inconvenient it is, you can't pretend that it was a normal adoption and that I'm a stranger. I'm your sister! I've got to know what you've told her about me. I have to hear what she's like. I think about her—and about you—all the time, Lyla. . . . Please . . . you can't do this to me any longer."

Her plea was met with silence.

"I can't help worrying that by keeping me totally blocked out of your lives, you're giving Cindy some very negative impressions. What makes me so terrible she's never once written to me? It's hard for me to imagine she doesn't think of me as some diabolical figure, which just can't be good for her. And the older she gets, the more traumatic an issue it's going to be. Lyla, I implore you, talk this over with Joe and then the two of us, or the three of us, can sit down together. I promise I'll respect your wishes."

"You sure have a lot of wrong ideas," Lyla lashed back. "She's doing just fine, and you're not a 'traumatic issue' to her."

"Then what am I to her?"

Lyla replied with the words that sank everything: "Something Cindy doesn't have to worry about, you know what I mean? She's happy with her friends and school. Kids at her age, they don't want to be any different from the other kids. You want to make her feel like there's something strange about her? I won't let you!"

Ann was stunned into silence.

Of course. Why *should* Cindy have to worry about it? How could she have failed to realize that?

"I'm very sorry that you feel bad," Lyla went on. "I really, really am. I don't know what to tell you that's going to make you feel any better. This is just the way things are. I would love to see you, but I don't want to see you if it's just going to be an argument. So we had better not. Maybe some time I can come out to California . . ."

Ann drove by a junior high school on her way out of the neighborhood. She unthinkingly slowed as a realization struck her: her daughter might be inside, only a few steps away from her. Then Lyla's words came back: *Something Cindy doesn't have to worry about.*

For the first time, Ann understood clearly that the "some-day" she had dreamed of for so long would probably never come. Her daughter probably hated her and had blotted the thought of her out of her life.

In contrast to the effectiveness and energy she demonstrated in other areas of her life, Ann felt hopeless and bankrupt of ideas when it came to her family. Ultimately, when she made the decision to tackle her inner strengths, she turned to David for the name of a good therapist. She felt there was nothing else she could do at that point.

Her last and strongest bid for a reconciliation had proved an utter failure.

At the end of 1977, Stanley Weiss and his wife took off for the Orient over the holiday season.

By then, Ann was widely regarded as Weiss's chief lieutenant. When people couldn't get to him, they often turned to Ann. She was a known quantity, one invested with a certain amount of power. She couldn't imagine a better place to work than Stanley Weiss Productions.

Ann was in the Polo Lounge for a meeting when her secretary phoned and told her to return to the office as soon as possible.

"What's the matter?" Ann asked worriedly.

"We just got a call from Hong Kong," was the reply. Weiss had collapsed. Nobody knew what was wrong, and there were no further details.

By the time Ann rushed back, a second call had come.

Stanley Weiss, her mentor and friend, was dead.

THIRTY

~~~~~~

IN THE WEEKS that followed Stanley Weiss's death, the forces that had made up his company splintered and scattered.

Ann found herself weighing three different job offers, each of which represented lateral moves. She also got wind of a junior creative affairs VP slot that was about to open at one of the studios; it represented a decidedly upward move.

Although Ann missed Weiss terribly, she quickly had proof that the rich store of his advice was a legacy to bank on. She lobbied for the studio job, and her aggressiveness paid off. After ten tense days she was informed that the vice-presidency was hers—along with a whole new set of responsibilities to carry out, people to know, and politics to cope with.

Ann managed once again to bury grief and disappointment in mountains of work.

Weeks passed without a single social engagement that wasn't somehow tied to her job, a situation that might have continued if it hadn't been for Sheilah's request that they "meet to catch up a little bit. I'm forgetting what you look like."

Their Sunday brunch proved a strangely disturbing experience for Ann, as she got the sense that somehow she and Sheilah had traded roles. Now it was Sheilah seeking her advice and asking her opinions. Now it was Sheilah who seemed lost, and Ann who was in the strong position.

Their conversation began with Sheilah's show, which was finally being retired, then rapidly moved on to Sheilah's quandary over what to do with herself once she was off the air.

Then Sheilah turned to the topic of her relationship with the cohost, Tommy Archer, who had been brought in in a last-ditch attempt to resuscitate the long-running program.

"I battled and battled against it—oh, how I battled!" Sheilah chuckled. "Then I turned around and..." She sighed. "What can I say? He's a very mature twenty-eight."

Suddenly grasping Sheilah's meaning, Ann swallowed her surprise and nodded.

"He must have the idea I'm stinking rich, don't you think?"

"Don't be silly," Ann told her.

"You think I'm nuts, don't you?"

"Will you stop?" Ann laughed. "No! I think it's wonderfully liberated of you. My God, half the middle-aged men in this town have young chickies. If you and Tommy Archer like each other and you're having a good time, more power to you. I think it's great."

But she didn't really; she trusted Archer not at all, and she worried that Archer's attraction to Sheilah might indeed be based on her money or connections or fame.

She didn't want Sheilah to get hurt, but what could she say?

"It's kind of kooky," Sheilah replied, tilting her head to one side. "But... kind of wonderful."

Ann nodded, giving Sheilah a reassuring smile.

"It sure beats the hell out of rattling around the house by myself," Sheilah added a little defensively.

Her son Jeff was on the road with a couple of friends, trying to find his true self somewhere in the heartland of America. Unlike his friend Eric Evans, who at twenty had solidly established himself as a superstudent at Princeton, Jeff had dropped out of UCLA after a single quarter.

"What do you hear from Route 66?" Ann asked.

"I got a postcard.'" Sheilah smiled and reached into her purse to retrieve it. "Is that tacky, or is that tacky?"

The card, from Reno, Nevada, had a brief message:

> *Mom: Need money now!*
> *Just kidding.*
> *This time:*
> *XXX Jeff*

* * *

Ann noticed the postmark; the card had been sent six weeks earlier. She found it sad that Sheilah was showing off an old postcard as though she had just received it. She found the message sad, too—not funny.. Unless Ann missed her guess, Sheilah was subsidizing the whole adventure.

"Well, it's something everyone dreams of doing, I guess," Sheilah said. "Setting out on the open road, escaping for a while. I have to admit I had mixed feelings about it, but maybe he really does need to get some of the wanderlust out of his system before he can settle down."

"Maybe," Ann replied noncommittally.

"As long as he's happy, I'm happy," Sheilah concluded.

Sheilah's happiness was not destined to last long.

A few weeks after their brunch, she called Ann and tearfully reported that Jeff had gotten into trouble again. He had spent a night in jail after a barroom ruckus in Jackson Hole, Wyoming.

When Jeff returned home, he was markedly changed. Looking haggard, almost sickly, he had lost his old cheerfulness, and he talked despondently about what a failure he was turning out to be.

"I'm nothing but a washout, a zero, good for nothing. I''ll probably end up spending my life as a boxboy."

"Please, *please* don't talk like that, darling!" Sheilah begged. "Where did you get such terrible ideas?"

"Eric's dad, for one," Jeff answered with a mirthless laugh. "He told me that a long time ago."

Frightened by his depression, Sheilah went into high gear, doing her utmost to get Jeff back into school, into a job, into something—anything—constructive. Nothing seemed to work.

Finally she pinned her hopes on a gofer job at Hall of Greatness Productions, a company run by an old friend of hers.

Jeff pulled himself together for the interview and came home with the happy news that he'd been hired.

Then, suddenly, the job was off.

It took Sheilah only a little time to spot Hank Evans's hand in the abrupt turnaround. It made sense. The owner of Hall of Greatness Productions was a longtime friend and supporter of Hank's. And Hank had made his feelings about Jeff quite clear. A few wrong words from Evans could have been enough to kill Jeff's prospects.

And Hank was mean enough to do something like that.

After a grinding day of work that had lasted until nearly midnight, Ann came home to find several messages from Sheilah on her answering service. "She says to please call any time, no matter how late."

Sheilah picked up on Ann's first ring. She was wide awake and beside herself with anger and frustration.

"I've left at least six calls for Hank in the last three days," Sheilah reported, to Ann's dismay. "He doesn't even have the courtesy to talk to me. Mary's no help at all."

"What good can it do to talk to him, even if it's true?" Ann asked her, feeling intensely uncomfortable. At that moment she realized that she should have told Sheilah of her own dark history with Evans. She was sorry she hadn't brought it up long ago, but now hardly seemed the time to say anything.

"What good?" Sheilah cried. "I want to remind that son of a bitch that I spent almost twenty years going out of my way on behalf of the little shit who's responsible for screwing up my son's head! I'm going to insist that he call his friends at Hall of Greatness and tell them Jeff deserves this job! He *owes* me that!"

"Do you think you can get him to do it?" Ann asked gently.

"I can't if I don't goddamn try!"

Jeff knew nothing of his mother's plans. Moreover, he was away from the house most of the time—a bad, bad sign, Ann believed.

Two days later, Sheilah phoned with a new idea. "I just learned that Hank is coming into town next week," she told Ann. "He's going to be this year's surprise guest at the Artists for Others Awards Banquet. So, all I have to do is finagle a couple of tickets, and I can corner him there."

"Well, I—" Ann began hesitantly, at a loss for words.

"Hey!" Sheilah cut her off. "*You* could get them for me, couldn't you? My God, I've forgotten all about the opera benefit. You're still a big hero over there."

"But—"

"Oh, call for me, Ann. You don't know how much I'd appreciate it."

With great reluctance, Ann agreed to check into the ticket situation for Sheilah. When she did, she was sorry she had.

Not only did she learn that the misguided matrons of the charity planned to honor Hank Evans as their Humanatarian of the Year, but she was urged—and urged—to attend the affair herself.

"You're going, aren't you?" Sheilah asked, when Ann told her about the arrangements she had made.

"I don't think so." Ann didn't want to go anywhere near the Beverly Wilshire that night. "I might have to go out of town."

Or so Ann fervently hoped.

As the week went on, the situation changed. Her work trip fell through, and she was pressured by both Sheilah and the Artists for Others board to be on hand for the Friday night event.

"I could use some moral support," Sheilah told her.

With that, Ann gave in.

She hung up and leaned back in her desk chair, her heart pounding.

After almost fifteen years, she would be in the same room as Hank Evans.

Automatically, she began to dial David Steinmetz's exchange. Somehow it was out of the question to ask anyone else to go with her; none of her usual nonthreatening escorts would do for this event.

Ann forgot all her misgivings about David's wanting to get too close. Without a second thought, she turned to the man who had provided her sole emotional support through the traumas of the past four years. She wanted him, needed him.

But none of those facts rose to her consciousness. All she knew was that when she heard David's voice telling her, "I'll be there," she felt deeply relieved.

THIRTY-ONE

∽∾∽∾

THE ARTISTS FOR Others benefit was a Hollywood-gowned-at-its-gussiest affair, with the usual phalanx of luxury automobiles and limousines clogging the cobblestone channel between the Beverly Wilshire's buildings. A parade of glamorous guests and stunning designer gowns glided over the red carpet toward the entrance. Golden ropes were flanked by the familiar band of paparazzi and the regulars of the autograph-hound brigade, waiting anxiously for the likes of Henry Winkler, Burt Bacharach, Mary Tyler Moore, and Kenny Rogers to arrive.

Flash, whir, glitter, blur. David surveyed the scene with a grin as he led Ann through the entry route. As he told Ann, he always got a big charge out of the glamour and the excitement, and he was happy to admit it.

Sated as she was by then, Ann found she got a big charge herself when she could view these extravaganzas through his eyes. He made them fun and exhilarating again. Usually.

This night, however, even David's buoyancy failed to keep her afloat.

"You look a little tired," he noted solicitously once they were inside waiting for Sheilah and Tommy Archer. In contrast to the stiffness of her high-collared lace blouse and conservatively tailored cobalt blue evening suit, Ann herself appeared wilted.

"I am tired," she answered, "but you must be, too. Your schedule is as bad as mine."

"Sure, but I'm psyched up for this," he said with a smile.

"It's refreshing to be among crazy Hollywood people instead of crazy doctors for a change. You dress better."

Ann failed to respond. Seeing her eyes searching the room, David realized she was not exactly with him at that moment.

She apologized distractedly. "I'm sorry; I wasn't paying attention."

"What's the matter?"

"I'm worried about Sheilah. She's in the middle of an argument with . . ." Ann was surprised to hear her voice falter when she got to the name, but after a beat, she managed to force it. ". . . Hank Evans. She believes he talked some people at Hall of Greatness Productions out of giving Jeff a job, and she wants to get Evans aside and have a showdown."

David shook his head. "Why?"

"She thinks she can talk him into reversing himself."

By the time Sheilah and Tommy arrived, Ann had briefly outlined the history of Jeff's entanglement with Eric and the Evans family.

"Before this night is over, that bastard is going to hear what I have to say," Sheilah announced, making no attempt to hide her hostility.

"Tell me when, so I can leave the room," Tommy replied with distaste.

The evening went downhill from there.

As she walked into the ballroom, Ann saw, not thirty feet away, the man who had once devastated her life. She caught just a glimpse of Evans, just barely took in his expression— the amiable, winning Captain grin. Despite the silver in his hair and the weight of age on his features, his smile was just as Ann remembered it the first moment she'd laid eyes on him in Hagia Sophia.

She turned away quickly and saw Sheilah heading in Hank's direction. Tommy muttered, "Oh, Christ." David glanced at Ann and saw her grim expression.

"It's not your fight," he murmured.

Evans moved away in a large group before Sheilah could reach him. Charlton Heston, who had just finished a promotional stint on behalf of his *Gray Lady Down* submarine movie, was listening intently as Evans gave his view of how President Carter had gotten away with "giving away the Panama Canal."

Sheilah came back, determined to try later.

Ann told herself to stay calm. Certainly enough time had passed for Evans to forget . . . anyway, she looked so different now . . . there was no rational reason to feel afraid . . .

But she moved in a fog, barely aware of the people to whom she spoke, her surroundings nearly blotted out by an all-consuming dread.

Ann and David were seated at one of the key tables in the front of the room, Sheilah and Tommy at a table hugging the upper tier rail.

"Don't worry." David tried to reassure Ann. "I know, you don't want to see Sheilah embarrass herself and get hurt. But it's her responsibility. Sheilah's tough. She can handle it. Who knows? Maybe she'll succeed."

Ann nodded woodenly.

She was seeing Evans's face—hard, glaring, close. The more she tried to repress it, the more the image seemed to invade her thoughts. Half-consciously, she kept her face turned away from the dais, knowing as she did so that it was ridiculous. She wasn't even sure whether Hank and Mary Evans had made their way to the elevated head table as yet.

"You can't to anything about Sheilah," David continued, "so you might as well put it out of your mind for the moment and relax."

"I'm sorry," Ann responded.

"Quit apologizing. That's the eighth time you've said you're sorry, and you have nothing to be sorry about."

"I didn't want to come tonight," she said unthinkingly. "I shouldn't have told Sheilah I'd be her moral support . . ."

She stopped. Seeing David's perplexed look, she realized how rude her remark must have sounded.

"The only reason I wanted to come was that I missed seeing you," she added, to appease him.

What? What are you saying? her mind cried. David suddenly looked as though he had won a prize. He was delighted to have the opportunity to see her, too, he was saying. They didn't see enough of each other.

Oh, what a mistake! What a damned stupid thing to say!

She had to get hold of herself. She was behaving idiotically.

Ann glanced around at the table. She knew four of the people there: agent Norman Brokaw, David Janssen and Dani

Greco, and filmmaker John Frankenheimer. She made introductions and launched some small talk.

For the next forty minutes, from the crab salad to the white chocolate mousse, Ann tried to pretend this was just another in the unending string of industry gatherings she attended.

She kept her eyes off Hank Evans's end of the dais as the speeches and awards began.

Then came the inevitable, interminable moments when Evans was lauded for "his quiet, faithful contributions to the well-being of handicapped and underprivileged children throughout the country." Ann stared at the chrome ice bucket in the center of the table, her eyes fixed on the sparkling droplets of condensation streaking down its side.

She began to feel hot and queasy. Soon the nausea increased to the point that she feared she might have to bolt from the ballroom.

She heard the wave of applause cascading through the room as Evans rose. Then, worse, she saw the people around her rise to their feet.

Ann stood, too. She hesitated just long enough to touch David's arm and whisper, "I'll be right back," and then she was on her way past the dimly lit tables, the applauding hands, the faces aimed forward, just a few turning her way, puzzled or annoyed, as Evans began his thank yous.

She hated to make such an obvious, abrupt departure, but she had no choice. She had maintained her composure and control, until her body had rebelled.

A few minutes later, white-faced and trembling with weakness, Ann came out of the women's room.

David stood waiting for her in the hallway outside.

"Would you like to go home?" he asked.

"Sheilah . . ." Ann began.

"I told her you weren't feeling well. She said she doesn't want you to feel you have to stay. Shall we go?"

Ann nodded, and without another word they made their way to the front curb, where a red-jacketed valet took David's parking ticket and ran to retrieve his Lincoln.

"I'm sorry for having spoiled your evening," Ann apologized a few minutes later, as David turned the car out of the hotel driveway.

"How are you feeling now?" he asked, glancing her way.

"Better. The fresh air is helping. Maybe it was all the smoking at our table . . ." she began, trailing off uncertainly.

"I had the impression that something was upsetting you."

Ann bit her lip, choking up. She felt David's hand take hers. Suddenly, without knowing why, she squeezed his hand. Then she felt his grip tighten in response.

"Do you want to talk about it?" he asked soberly.

"No."

David nodded. "Okay."

The silence grew awkward and heavy. Ann halfheartedly attempted small talk. "Do you have to work tomorrow?"

"Yes." He glanced at her again, smiling in a reassuring way. "Don't worry. If you don't feel like talking, that's fine with me."

"Thank you," she mumbled.

David turned a tape of Debussy nocturnes on low.

A mile, then two. Gentle music, the balmy night air, and David's unquestioning friendship had their soothing effects.

It wasn't the close brush with Hank Evans that brought the tears to her eyes, Ann realized. It was an overflow of warm feelings toward David.

She tried to dismiss it; she was merely reacting to his compassion.

But suddenly, again without knowing why, she found herself confiding in him. "I know I acted like a fool. I've been dreading this event for days because"—the words came out in a rush—"I knew Cindy's father was going to be there."

David absorbed Ann's statement gravely. After a moment, he asked, "Did you see him?"

"Yes. I doubt that he would even recognize me, but—" She stopped abruptly, shaking her head. It was so bottled up inside her, so deeply, painfully repressed, she found it not just difficult but impossible to say Hank Evans's name.

"I'm sorry."

"Sorry? Why?"

Ann shook her head again. "I didn't want to get started on this. I really didn't."

"Have you talked about this in therapy?"

Ann raised her face skyward and sighed exasperatedly. "I'm sorry I said anything to you."

"You didn't answer my question," said David.

"Somehow it's never come up," she replied with a weak

laugh. The sound caught in her throat and changed to a stran-
gled sob.

David stopped the car in front of her Palm Drive apartment
building, then turned toward her, his expression making it
quite clear he was aware Ann was dealing with an emotional
dam that was close to bursting.

"I don't want to leave you like this."

Ann nodded mutely.

Silently, he followed her up the stairs and into her apartment.

"May I get you some wine?" Ann offered, immediately
attempting to back away from the moment in the car.

David shook his head, mouthing a gentle no.

"I'm so embarrassed," Ann told him with a burst of jittery
laughter. "I *really* wish I hadn't said anything."

"Ann, it worries me that you haven't even talked to your
therapist about this."

"I will," Ann snapped. "All right?"

David gave her a sympathetic, understanding look that Ann
found hard to bear.

"I just hate to see you hurting so much," he said.

Moved, Ann came toward him, open-armed, and David
held her close.

"I'm lucky to know you," she murmured.

"*I'm* lucky," David answered.

Several seconds passed before Ann added, barely audibly,
"I . . . I wonder whether Sheilah has had her showdown with
him yet."

She pulled back to watch David's reaction.

She saw his jaw tighten as he made the connection.

She desperately didn't want him to doubt her. She didn't
want him to exclaim.

She didn't want him to give any of the myriad responses
that would have been predictable, understandable—and so
disappointing.

She wanted to know, somehow, that the impact of the unspoken name wouldn't dislodge her from David's mind, even
for a moment.

It didn't. When David did finally speak, Ann felt a rush of
relief and gratitude at his angry response: "What was Sheilah
doing asking you to be there?"

"She doesn't know," Ann replied. "Nobody does. Even Sam didn't know; he didn't want to hear about it."

"What about Evans?"

"He never had any idea I was pregnant. I'm sure he's forgotten all about me."

David took a short breath, shaking his head, his mind quickly sorting and combining all the bits and pieces of information Ann had told him in the past. An older man Ann's mother had met in the nightclub . . . rape . . . when Ann was fourteen years old.

How different, how much more appalling the picture was now that David's vague impression of some dark, featureless foreigner had been replaced by Hank Evans.

"I'm not going to make a scene," Sheilah assured Tommy. "All I'm going to do is point out to him that he's being a shmuck."

"You can't go up to him at a time like this," Tommy cried pleadingly. "Don't. Please don't."

Sheilah patted his cheek. "I'm *kidding*. I'm just going to talk to him. I've known Hank since we were both kids. Once he sees me, he'll talk to me. Why don't you go have a drink? I'll be back in a few minutes."

With that, Sheilah left Tommy in the reception area outside the ballroom. Inside, the remains of the banquet crowd mingled and preened.

Sheilah was soon standing on the edge of the group of glad-handers surrounding Hank and Mary Evans. They were the stars of the evening, and they looked it, Hank in a custom tuxedo adorned with black onyx and gold studs, Mary draped in pale peach silk, a necklace of baroque South Sea pearls with a cabochon ruby and pavé diamond clasp at her throat.

Sheilah, however, was not at all at her best; this night, her usual style seemed to have eluded her. Her hunter green jacketed chemise was one that too many at this gathering had seen before. Her latest coloring job had left her hair an unbecoming brassy shade of red. She was minus the skilled help of a makeup woman now that "Perfectly Personal" was off the air, and her skin was sallow and blotchy from weeks of stress and from the anger that now consumed her. She was becoming ever more hostile, for it was clear that Hank was deliberately avoiding making eye contact. With every second, Sheilah became more solidly convinced that he had, indeed, scotched Jeff's chances to make a new start.

At last Mary moved toward her, smiling politically. "Sheilah, how nice to see you."

Sheilah spoke her piece in a low tone.

"I mentioned it to Hank," Mary said, her voice hushed. "He's so out of touch with the industry nowadays, he honestly doesn't believe he can do anything to help Jeff. I'm sorry."

"So am I," Sheilah said. "I'm very upset that Hank hasn't returned my calls."

"It's been so busy." Mary shook her head helplessly.

"I want to talk to him."

"You can't mean *here.*"

"Then where, when?"

"I . . . I don't know," Mary faltered, "but not now. We're leaving at an ungodly hour tomorrow, too. I just don't know when."

"Then it'll have to be now," Sheilah said firmly.

Before Mary could answer, Hank had joined her and was glaring down at Sheilah.

"Nice medallion, Hank," she said tartly, referring to his award. "It'll look good in that huge trophy case of yours."

"I'm sure Mary's enjoyed talking to you," he responded in a stiff monotone. "We have an early flight, so if you'll excuse us . . ."

"After all the summers I spent looking after Eric, this is the best you can do?" Sheilah asked shrilly. "'We have an early flight'?"

"Sorry." Hank chuckled contemptuously. "It happens to be true. Are you asking us to change our plans?"

"What about my son?"

"Oh, Sheilah, this is really uncalled-for!" Mary exclaimed.

The guests within earshot, and there were many, listened in rapt attention to the choice gossip that drifted to them.

"Honey, I understand how you feel. We're all so terribly sorry to see Jeffy in such trouble," Hank said, pulling a deep, tragical frown—and using Jeff's childhood nickname for the first time. Then he asked, "Do you have a good attorney?"

"What?" cried Sheilah.

Evans touched her arm and inclined his head toward her as if to speak privately. But his voice swelled as he said, "Jeff is so far gone on these drugs, you've got to take over for his own good. I know it's hard, but you've got to face it: it's time to consider having him declared incompetent."

Sheilah gasped, reeling back. "How dare you? That's my son you're talking about! He'd be working if it weren't for you, and you know it!"

"I wouldn't suggest it if it weren't for the boy's own good, Sheilah, really." Hank's high-amplitude boom of a stage whisper carried out to the tenth row of tables.

Sheilah gasped. "I see what you're doing! You're—"

But Hank, stone-faced now, started leading Mary away. The bystanders seemed to close ranks in front of Sheilah. She forced her way through the human screen but got close enough only to see Mary's face as she glanced back. She wore an agitated expression that seemed to say *I told you so. You wouldn't listen to me*.

When the ballroom was empty of people save for the busboys, the cleaners, and Sheilah, Tommy Archer finally reappeared. He found Sheilah seated at a table, her forehead resting on the heel of her hand.

"Come on, I'll drive you home," he said. He looked and sounded angry. He had heard all about it and had waited until he was certain no one would see him before he went to look for Sheilah. He hadn't wanted to be seen with her.

Although Sheilah wouldn't know for a while, this evening marked the end of her "kind of kooky, kind of wonderful" affair with a younger man.

Sheilah called Ann the moment she got home and recounted the scene, alternately raging and weeping while Ann listened and commiserated.

"You were right. But I never, never could have imagined he'd go that far. The years, the favors—it doesn't mean a thing to him."

"Do you want me to come over?" Ann asked.

"No. I'm . . . hoping Jeff will come home."

Ann didn't know how to answer that. After a moment, Sheilah added, "And you're not feeling well. Oh, God. I'm sorry. I forgot."

"No, no. I shouldn't have left."

Ann was seated at the dining room table by the telephone. David, jacketless now, collar open, was sitting on the sofa, close enough to hear. He frowned at the "shouldn't have left" remark.

"All right," Ann said at last. "We'll get together Sunday, and, please, keep me posted."

Ann returned to the living room and found David rubbing his eyes beneath the heavy frames of his glasses.

"You must be exhausted," she said.

"I don't understand why you don't think you should have left," he answered.

Ann shrugged. "I knew I'd run into ... him ... eventually, through Sheilah, or somehow. But I'm so many years past it now I thought I could make it through the evening just fine. I really did. I *should* have been able to."

"I don't agree with that," David replied furiously. "It's no wonder you got sick. If I'd known, I'd have been sick myself. That award is an outrage!"

"Yes, it is," Ann said explosively. "One of many. But if you think at this stage of my life I'm going to go out and tell the world—no! No! Even if anyone would believe me, which is doubtful, I would *not* do anything that would make my daughter the subject of humiliating attention. She's living a normal life, and I *won't* have that upset. I don't care how many ribbons he gets, or how many votes.

"Besides," she added savagely, "I don't believe the world would stop giving him awards. People believe what they want to believe."

David rose and came toward her. "Is that how you really feel about it?"

"Do I," Ann cried. She avoided David and began pacing the living room as she spoke, leaving him standing, watching, as her bitterness came out in a torrent of angry words. "I certainly didn't make it up. Julius Caesar said it a thousand years ago. But they didn't have television and movies helping the process along in his day, making certain pictures so *attractive*. So many people unquestioningly buy the images that are given to them—that *my business* gives to them. It frightens me, David, it really does.

"It happens over and over again, this complete acceptance. Think of all the people who've climbed aboard the Jane Fonda crusader bandwagon—ready to follow not an activist philosophy, mind you, but *Jane*—when Jane herself admits that she feels lost between roles, that she never feels complete unless she's playing a role. Does that sound like a leader to you?"

"But look at the controversy surrounding her," David answered. "Ann, are you saying nobody disagrees with Hank Evans, nobody's wise to him? That's not true. He has plenty of enemies, plenty of critics."

"But look at the majority," Ann lashed back.

"I think you're overstating."

"Am I? Think of how quickly people forget every report of Frank Sinatra's ugly behavior. They prefer the image that's been sold to them, so they stick with it and simply ignore anything that doesn't fit.

"It's endless. People would rather think of David Soul as a cute TV star than an admitted wife-beater," she railed on. "They want to believe that Sam is the clean-cut kid they saw on 'Runabout.' And it isn't just Hollywood. They're so worn-out by all the cynicism of the last ten years, they're desperate for heroes.

"And they want to believe *Hank Evans* is a hero," she exploded at last.

"I can't disagree with you completely," David countered, "but for almost every example you've mentioned there've been people—huge percentages, in fact—who haven't just bought in. The public eventually comes around to the truth. I believe it'll come around to the truth about Hank Evans."

"That's nice." Ann shrugged. "I'm glad you feel that way. You're a nice man. I can't be so optimistic."

David sighed. "Well, you've lived with this a long time."

"Over half my life," Ann said, her anger subsiding. She stopped pacing and settled onto the edge of the sofa near David.

"You know, my daughter is fourteen years old and I don't even know what she knows about me, let alone what she knows about Evans," she said quietly. "I don't know what my sister's told her or how she's taken it. I don't know anything. She wants me completely out of it, my sister. But I want . . ." Ann added, her voice catching and breaking ". . . I want Cindy to know that I . . . that her natural mother didn't reject her. I don't want her to feel that hurt."

David nodded, his dark eyes once more radiating such compassion that the look alone made Ann feel as if he were reaching out to hold her again. "If she doesn't know now," he said slowly, "I'm sure someday she will."

Ann closed her eyes for a long moment, unable to meet his gaze, unable to ask David why he had such confidence.

"If I hadn't been so young and so scared, I would never have given her up," Ann said. Impatiently she brushed aside the tears that were beginning to form. "I hate myself for having done it. Every day I wonder, *Why?* But I had to. At least, I thought I did. And that was the end of my family; my sister never wanted to see me again.

"Goddamn him," she said, turning sharply away, hiding her face in her hands.

David moved next to her and gently rubbed her back. "Goddamn him," she whispered hotly through her tears, again and again.

The early morning hours passed with Ann pouring out all the details of her past that she had kept locked up for so long, while David provided a vital listening post.

By four-thirty, she was exhausted, hoarse, and fragile — and grateful David was there.

"Why don't you stay and get a couple hours' sleep?" she suggested. She thought vaguely of the sofa but made no protest when David followed her into the bedroom, where, with a gentle tug, he pulled her down beside him on the bedspread and enfolded her in his arms.

THIRTY-
TWO

WHEN ANN AWAKENED it was broad daylight, and she was still nestled in David's arms.

It was so comfortable, such a good place to be that she closed her eyes again and smiled. And when she smiled, she felt his lips brush her forehead.

She drifted back into slumber—then awakened as David gently kissed her brows, her eyelids, her nose, her lips. Ann sighed. She felt warm and contented. And when he kissed her lips again, the soft butterfly touch surged and opened and rocked Ann with a sweeping tug inside her body.

She had no regrets. With her confessional the night before, she had already given herself to David in a way that had been, to her, far more profound.

He was a good man—the nicest man she had ever known. They would probably be friends forever, she dazedly realized, returning his kiss, happy, at peace.

He traced her chin with his fingertip. There was an exquisite quality to his touch.

Then, to her surprise, she felt David moving off the bed. She opened her eyes wide and saw him standing, putting on his glasses, smoothing his rumpled shirt.

He was saying something about how much he hated to leave, and Ann ruefully recalled that David had to work. He was already late—late enough that a glance at his watch produced a grimace.

He bent over her and repeated in a whisper, "I hate to leave." Then: "We'll see each other later, all right?"

Ann nodded mutely.

As soon as he was gone, Ann found herself wondering how long it would be until he would return—a reaction that made her feel giddy and angry at herself by turns.

How had she let this happen?

There was no mistaking the promised assignation. God, what had she done? She was going to have sex with David, and it was going to ruin their friendship.

That's what she'd done.

He wouldn't be the same.

She wouldn't be the same.

She was in so much deeper than she wanted to be.

She called Sheilah, who informed her that Jeff had come home. Ann got off the line immediately, and her thoughts quickly returned to David.

What could she have been thinking, to tell him so much, to have given so much of herself. Now what was going to happen? *What have I done?* she asked herself repeatedly throughout the morning. And throughout the afternoon, throughout her weekend work, and a shmoozy Ma Maison luncheon with producer Freddie Fields, she found her thoughts continually turning to David.

He phoned at about four. They hadn't set a time, he pointed out.

"Seven?" he suggested.

"Fine."

"How are you doing today?"

Ann recognized David's chipper, making-rounds voice and felt irritated by it. She wasn't his damned patient.

"Fine." She twisted the phone cord.

She had used up her quota of words the night before, she thought fleetingly. No wonder she had none left.

"Have you felt at all worried about having talked to me?" David asked.

"No," she answered quickly. "Why, should I be?"

"Ann," he said fondly, "it would only be natural for it to seem a little, well, disconcerting, in retrospect. I've been thinking about you all day, hoping you haven't felt that way."

"Let's not make a big thing of it," she answered, reddening.

He dropped the subject instantly. "Any preference for dinner?"

"Could we go some place off the beaten track?"

Ann was suddenly aware of how little she wanted to spend the evening running into industry acquaintances.

David quickly agreed.

Ann took her time about dressing.

She slipped on an airy cream chemise and panties, thinking again, still, about David. He was handsome with his glasses on, she thought, but simply incredible-looking with them off. He probably chose to wear them to enhance his professional appearance.

The touch of his fingers was so gentle, so . . . magical.

She hoped this night wouldn't prove to be a terrible mistake.

For several minutes, Ann stood before her vanity mirror, giving herself a harder inspection than she had since her injury. Her eyes were still her best feature; they had remained unmarred, thank God. How lucky she had been. The scars were still visible, though much improved with cosmetic sanding and natural fading. Only the creased arc over her left cheek and the line running down from her shoulder remained brutally obvious. She would have to make time to resume her visits to the plastic surgeon, she decided. But, then—was it just the scars that were making her feel so unattractive, Ann asked herself at last, or was she in fact helping that sense along?

She went to her closet and quickly pushed back hangar after hanger of dresses, blouses, and suits, suddenly feeling that all these serious, businesslike clothes had become like straitjackets. She found a lavender silk dress left over from her KCBA-era wardrobe, pulled it out, and discovered that the hemline was several inches above her knees—hopelessly out of fashion. She smiled in disbelief. Had it been *that* long since she'd worn something so soft and pretty?

She finally gave up and donned a simple beige sheath, then turned to carefully applying her makeup and brushing her short dark hair. When she had finished, she gave herself a final check in the mirror. At least, she thought, she had made an improvement.

Ready at six-thirty, she was reduced to nail-biting by the time David appeared at the door forty minutes later.

"Sorry I'm late. I didn't think I'd ever get finished," he complained as he stepped inside, giving her a light kiss.

Ann smiled awkwardly.

He was immaculately groomed, smooth-cheeked and fresh-scrubbed as always, in his usual style of conservatively handsome clothes. The same faint trace of pine tar soap fragrance lingered on his skin; she caught it, savoured it. And, reassuringly, he had the same generous smile in the same squarish face.

The restaurant, located on a South Pasadena side street, was old by California standards; it was tiny, slightly overheated, candlelit, and rich with the aromas of fine Italian food. In short, perfect.

David started to pick up where their long conversation had left off the night before, but Ann stopped him.

"Tonight," she said, "not another word about me."

David nodded. "All right. What's your pleasure? Current events? Michelangelo? Diet fads?"

She shook her head. "You."

Ann asked about his life—his childhood in Miami, his decision to become a doctor, his time in med school. His comments on the latter were laced with references to his late wife, who "suffered through it with me, every inch of the way."

"You had a very good marriage, didn't you?"

"Yes."

"What was she like?"

He sighed slightly, pursing his lips.

"You don't want to talk about her," Ann guessed.

"I don't mind," he answered softly. "I'm not sure you really want to hear."

"Why?" she said challengingly.

He reached across the table and took her hands. "Ann, after last night, this morning, don't try to push me away again. You're carrying around a lot of emotional baggage. You know I have some, too. We can talk about Ruthie, but not now. Not as a distancing device."

"It wasn't intended to be. I . . . don't want to push you away. But . . ." She trailed off.

They sat in silence for several minutes, shrouded at first in discomfort, the shadows of wrong words, Ann's elusiveness past and present.

Their fingers were still intertwined.

David absently traced the lines and clefts of her palms with his thumbs, his caress light and gentle as a zephyr. Ann's awareness of the feeling gradually increased. His fingertips glided smoothly, firmly, up and down the insides of her fingers, which curved and twisted in response. Ann finally closed her eyes, completely focused on his entrancing touch.

In the half-light of Ann's bedroom, two hours later, David's fingertips roved sensuously over her throat and shoulders, stopping as he lifted her chemise and slid it off, then continuing along her thighs as his tongue brushed over her nipples.

His mouth found hers. Her passion was mounting, matching his.

And then David did something that surprised and disturbed Ann. He said, "I love you."

He kissed her again, covering the silence that he knew would be her answer.

"David, I—"

"Shhh. It's okay. No hurry." Warm smile. Loving eyes. More kisses, more tender caresses, until at last Ann felt him enter her.

Even the first time, sex with David was different from what Ann had known before. He was lying in her arms, spent, when all at once she realized that she had failed to put on her usual performance; she had forgotten to fake because she had been so lost in David and the physical feelings of David. She stroked his back and heard him murmuring "you beautiful, wonderful woman" in her ear.

The sense of oneness was clear and profound.

Too profound. Too heavenly.

Life had taught Ann about love; it only led to pain and loss.

David felt her body shudder, moved next to her, and looked into her eyes.

"You're crying."

"No, I'm not," she insisted.

"You're laughing till the tears roll down your cheeks?"

At that, Ann did laugh. And choke and cry. "I feel so wonderful."

"I can see that," he said gently, teasingly.

"I do. I'm just"—she sniffed, laughed, opened her palms helplessly—"crying, that's all."

"Too much emotion," David surmised, reaching out to

draw her close again. "I should have let you recuperate after last night, but I couldn't resist you."

"I . . ." She sobbed and laughed. "Didn't do much resisting myself."

"And I'm *so* glad. Come here." He kissed her hair. "It's all right," he soothed. "It's all right."

Ann fell asleep with David's arms around her—without telling him she loved him, too.

In the following days, Ann's apprehensions about David turned on a single point: he was too good to be true. And she was determined not to hear or make any promises, listen to or suggest any changes in their respective lifestyles or careers—in short, she planned to remain absolutely independent of him. She wasn't going to make the same mistakes she had made with Sam. She wasn't about to set herself up for another great fall.

When she met with Sheilah the next day, however, Ann was unable to hide her joy. Sheilah was also in a happier mood, having had "a long, meaningful talk with Jeff," who had promised to return to college in the fall. Other than calling Hank Evans "a shit heel of the first order," Sheilah had nothing to say on the subject.

She was, she told Ann, far more intrigued by "this goofy smile of yours. What's going on?"

"Well, it's . . . I . . ."

"Could it be," Sheilah asked archly, "that the doctor makes house calls?"

Ann blushed and grinned.

"I knew it," Sheilah cried triumphantly. "I was hoping you'd come to your senses and grab him. How great! Dave is a prize."

With this new interest in her life, Ann became more discriminating about which screenings she absolutely had to attend, which parties were musts. When she could, she would slip off to be with David. No longer did he dawdle through his rounds or sit shooting the breeze with colleagues for long periods of time. Whenever he could, he would slip off to be with Ann.

Ann's assistant happily reported to his friends that at last Ann was giving him a chance. "It's like she's finally discovered it's okay to delegate some of the work."

She was discovering much more than that.

She was discovering a love that seemed to bring her more joy with each day.

She was discovering what it was like to be with a sexually giving man who adored and respected her. She was discovering how she loved giving to him in return.

David would never forget the cunning, startling little smile that played on Ann's lips as she sidled in next to him and told him, "I plan to make you a very, very happy man tonight."

He would never forget what followed.

And followed.

As the weeks passed, the hurt, anguish, and disappointment she had once equated with sex slowly dissolved.

Ann began to cherish the tranquility of David's seaside flat. One evening after a quick swim in the ocean and a warm shower, Ann found David waiting for her, lying on a thick quilt he had spread in front of the freshly stoked fireplace. For an hour they lay side by side, sipping amaretto as they watched the dwindling flames and talked in low voices.

"I'm happy," she said. "Why does it matter so much?"

"Because I want you to feel as good as I do."

"You must be tired of trying by now."

"Ann, I could no more get tired of making love to you than I could of breathing."

After a moment, fondly caressing his fingers, she asked, "Do you realize what wonderful hands you have?"

David smiled and then kissed her, pulling apart the front of her bulky robe until it fell from her shoulders. He kissed her again, then said in an undertone, "I'm almost afraid of what's going to happen when we unleash this explosion."

"Explosion?"

"You, Ann."

She laughed and sighed at once and he tenderly laid her down.

He traced her body with his hands, moving slowly downward. She reached for him then, ready to move into sex as she had known it.

"We'll get to that," he whispered, and kissed her stomach. "We've got all night."

"What do you want me to do?"

"Just lie still."

Nervous, tantalized, and trusting, Ann did. She felt him stroke her legs, felt his touch exploring inside, her magic places, felt sensations only hinted at before growing stronger and stronger, until she was gasping.

Before the night was over, the erotic sensations grew even more intense.

David made love to Ann like a symphony, masterfully, unhurriedly winding its way through a series of moods, colors, and heart-swelling chords before building in a suspended, sustained, impossible crescendo that, at last, she couldn't hold back from, couldn't stop until it broke and fell into its own low, fluttering beat. Finally, all that was left was a sweet, intimate glow.

As David gazed down into her eyes, Ann smiled.

Their relationship was sheer play, sheer delight. Ann made her feelings about commitments clear; David didn't press the point.

He wanted to, and he wanted to hear Ann confess the love he was sure she felt for him. But he was happy. He didn't mind waiting, for now.

The peak of their bliss might have gone on and on, longer than the six and a half weeks it did, if it weren't for the siren's song of executive musical chairs that started at Sentinel Studios, creating a vacancy for Vice-President of Production.

Although Ann made no bid for the job, she kept hearing rumors that she was considered a hot prospect. Bob Stewart, the new president in charge of production, was also a one-time protégé of Stanley Weiss's—from the days when Weiss had run the studio.

"It would be a great move up for you. It's exciting," David insisted, although he had mixed feelings. "Why aren't you excited?"

"Because I won't believe anything until I hear it from them."

THIRTY-THREE

By THE END of the 1970s, Hollywood's perennial favorite sport—conspicuous spending—was being played at a fever pitch that even eclipsed the outrageous extremes of the past.

Along Beverly Hills' famed Golden Triangle shopping preserve, it seemed nothing was too costly or ostentatious to find a buyer.

The label look was carried to outrageous extreme when Dr. Aldo Gucci proudly introduced a custom-designed Cadillac Seville with an oversized version of Gucci's trademark green and red stripe stretching from its hood to its trunk.

The prize for volume buying had a number of contenders. Cher popped into Maud Frizon's and, within forty-five minutes, had dropped $3,000 on two dozen pairs of sandals. Then Tina Turner outdid her, buying one hundred and twenty pairs of Frizon shoes in a single sitting.

The international big spenders, who flocked to Rodeo Drive to buy what could be purchased for a fraction of the cost in many foreign cities, might catch a glimpse of Zsa Zsa depositing her $150,000 Sedenca Rolls with a curbside valet or Barbra Streisand strolling into Giorgio's for a complimentary cocktail or espresso and emerging with a gown that cost thousands.

Customized Jeeps as extra fun cars were in vogue. Luxury accessories for fancy wheels were a commonplace. Farrah Fawcett's pearl green Corvette boasted a color TV, elaborate sound system, four-button telephone, and monogrammed fur and suede upholstery. The well-dressed person, even some of

313

those with twenty-twenty vision, had at least a half-dozen pairs of eyeglasses—and not just any eyeglasses. Custom-made two-hundred-dollars-plus Italian aluminum frames were the in thing, favored by such men as Tony Newley and producer Bob Evans.

Perfume and colognes, mouthwashes, toothpastes, and car sprays were made to the buyer's specifications for thousands of dollars.

The holiday season offered a wealth of spending opportunities; lavish Christmas trees were adorned with crystal and porcelain and antique baubles that could exceed $25,000.

Bird fanciers could spend from three hundred to six hundred dollars on golden bells to decorate the cages of exotic trained parrots whose prices ranged in the thousands.

Meanwhile, the lists of shoplifters that circulated among store owners included the names of some of yesterday's idols, desperate to keep up appearances.

The big-spending wave was rolling to a crest at the studios, too.

The period marked the beginning of a spate of balloon-budget productions that would prove largely responsible for wide-range industry panic and despair by 1982 and for an alarming drop in the number of pictures going into production. A $10-million film had been considered expensive when Ann had worked for Stanley Weiss in the mid-seventies; by the end of the decade, films costing $25 million, $30 million, and more weren't unique, and more were on their way—*Apocalypse Now*, *The Blues Brothers*, *1941*, *Reds*, and, of course, *Heaven's Gate*.

Shortly after Ann learned about the changes taking place in the executive ranks at Sentinel Studios, she found herself meeting with Bob Stewart, the new president, who quickly made her part of his team. She moved across town to an office on the second floor of the studio's Spanish-style executive building, bringing with her a passel of projects that had failed to arouse sufficient interest for "gos" at her former place of business. A coterie of agents, writers, and producers followed her.

She soon discovered that while Stewart had learned the ropes of the business under Stanley Weiss, he had unfortunately forsaken the Weiss point of view.

Each time Ann invoked Weiss's name and one of her mentor's beliefs in attempting to make a point, the thin, balding, perpetually nervous Stewart would shrug and say, "Ann, we're in 1980, not 1950. The studio is not the same as when Stan was here."

Unlike Weiss, Stewart had to answer to the board of a parent company. The fact that Sentinel had been taken over by a giant corporation had fundamentally weakened the position of the studio president. Ann understood that. But soon, very soon, she was also aware that Stewart simply wasn't as strong a person as Weiss had been.

She came to feel that some of Stewart's decisions were determined by which of his underlings spoke loudest, something she witnessed after only a few days on the job.

The topic under discussion was *Night Fire*, a major film project that had been in development at one of the other studios. That studio was now putting it into turnaround, which meant it could be picked up for the costs the firm had incurred in its development.

Initially engineered by one of the top talent agencies, Oswald-Levering Inc., *Night Fire* came complete with one of the hottest new directors in the business (an OLI client, by no coincidence). It was based on a prestigious award-winning book (the author and the screenwriter were also both OLI clients). Top talent Ted Kemp was tentatively attached (Kemp, coming off one major success and one moderate one, was with OLI, too). And it would probably cost $14 million to make.

"That sounds like a very optimistic figure," Ann was quick to note to the group circled around the coffee table in Stewart's office, giving recommendations to the president.

From the beginning, she viewed *Night Fire* as a prettily packaged white elephant. The story centered on a live volcano, for starters, and as she reminded the group, "Disaster movies are dead."

"This does not fall into the disaster category," argued Skip Michaelson, the head of marketing.

Michaelson would soon prove to be one of her greatest adversaries.

"It's Ted Kemp doing action-adventure, with a great romance and with Sergio Patel directing. Lest we forget, Patel and Kemp are currently on their way to grossing $100 million with *At High Risk*. I can tell you, Patel and Kemp doing action-adventure is guaranteed great business."

"I can't conceive of a script with thirty pages of volcano at the end *not* being a disaster film," Ann answered incredulously. "And *At High Risk* is contemporary London and New York. Ancient Rome is about as far from *At High Risk* as you're going to get."

The meeting ended with Ann feeling she could just as easily have stayed out of it, for all the impact she had made. She was outargued. Stewart went with Michaelson. *Night Fire* was picked up by Sentinel.

Within two weeks, $3 million was added to the budget on a single script revision.

In the weeks that followed, Ann was astounded to discover how many, and how major, were the differences in thinking between herself and other members of the Sentinel Studios' hierarchy.

It had been Stanley Weiss's view that while one side of the movie-making business was and would always be wild and woolly and utterly unpredictable, the other side must be controllable. Weiss never put a picture into production unless he felt his risk was adequately covered. He had often said to Ann, "If you want to stay alive as a gambler, you had better be a smart gambler."

Weiss had had to have foreign distribution guarantees, presale arrangements with television networks, and/or a combination of other bet-hedging elements in place before he would lay his wager down.

As he had told Ann time and again, "You can't run a business on wishful thinking." Yet at Sentinel, Ann quickly began to fear that Stewart *was* running the studio on wishful thinking.

Her greatest personal frustration lay in the fact that she was unable to get her more modest pictures green-lighted, partly because *Night Fire,* which was soon being budgeted at $20 million, was eating up so much of the studio's production outlay.

Stewart, Michaelson, and the others, out for home runs on the *Star Wars* scale, failed to see that the game could be won with far less risk on a strategy of singles and doubles:

Stanley Weiss had placed no faith in the fabled golden gut

instinct. He had told Ann story after story about major successes everyone was sure would fail.

"They thought *Casablanca* was going to be a dog," he had told her laughingly. "Cubby Broccoli worried terribly that he'd lose a bundle when he bought the James Bond books; what's more, a lot of people were certain his fears would be realized. *Cat Ballou* was a write-off."

Although Weiss had used modern market-testing methods, he was quick to note their shortcomings. "You can't expect people to do more than tell you what they've liked in the past. At best you'll find out what they're interested in seeing a year before you can get it to them. You always have sharpies who think they have found a way to predict the future. Then, when the future comes, it shocks the bejeezus out of them."

At Sentinel now, however, the charts and projections spewed out by the computers of the sales department were taken not as guides but as gospel. If the printouts proclaimed that something would be a hit, then, by God, it was full steam ahead as far as studio push and ballyhoo. If sales chalked off a project as a loser, the project was instantly buried.

Stanley Weiss had looked upon talent with a blend of high admiration, avuncular amusement, and sympathy: "They're wonderful, diabolical, magnetic, spoiled, gifted children who have every reason to be as insecure as they are. Even Henry Fonda still thinks after every job that he'll never land another role. You know the old joke? First it's 'Who's Burt Reynolds?' Then it's 'Get me Burt Reynolds.' Then it's 'Get me a Burt Reynolds type.' Then it's 'Get me a young Burt Reynolds.' And finally, it's 'Who's Burt Reynolds?' It's no wonder so many of them are crazy."

At Sentinel, Ann encountered an entirely different mindset. Stars were prizes to be won at almost any cost. She was staggered by the frantic fawning, the courting and wooing of stars, star filmmakers, and powerful agencies in a mad scramble to make deals.

Making movies seemed a secondary objective; making good movies didn't seem to be an objective at all.

Ann pressed hard, concentrating on tactful persuasion to get something worthwhile accomplished. But she finally had to face the fact that the men surrounding her regarded her as their token female, her opinions not to be taken too seriously.

There was no sense in wringing her hands over it, Ann

decided. She would simply have to find ways to reeducate them.

Of all the features Ann was working to get made, the one she cared most about was a comedy brought to her by her Weiss Productions discovery, Rusty de Paull.

Titled *The Ship*, it was about a rather seedy tabloid reporter who finds an abandoned spaceship in the California desert near Twenty-Nine Palms. Far from being reverent or awe-stricken, he goes to great lengths to get rich quick by capitalizing on the find. What Ann loved most about the story, although she never brought it up, was the fact that at the end, the character's better qualities won out.

It was affirming and uplifting, a reminder of what really matters in life, and at the same time a poke at the profiteer mentality.

Bob Stewart admitted that he laughed all the way through the script. "But I don't think there's an audience for it. The main character is such a sleaze."

"But you like him, don't you?" Ann persisted. "He's an insufferable twerp—in the tradition of Eddie Haskell in 'Leave It to Beaver.' He's basically good-hearted, and he redeems himself in the end. It's a great ending! You laugh and cry and feel good."

"It's going to depend on who you can get for the lead," said Stewart.

"Rusty has Richard Pryor reading it."

But Pryor had other projects. So did Chevy Chase.

Still, Rusty and Ann kept trying.

Finally Ann found herself telling Don McEwen about *The Ship* at a party. Hot on the success of his top sitcom, McEwen was on the lookout for the right project to launch him in films and to provide a part different from his nice-guy series role.

Once again, she found it hard to explain *The Ship* and its main character. "He does lie and cheat, yes," she heard herself faltering, as the actor half-listened. "But it's as if he doesn't know any better. It's nothing personal, it's not evilly intended . . . somehow, you still like him and are amused by him."

Finally, in desperation, she blurted out, "To be honest, one person has been going through my mind ever since I read this script—and that person is your agent."

McEwen did a sudden double take. "My agent?"

Ann nodded, instantly regretting her words.

But McEwen grinned and laughed. "Wow. I've got to see it!"

In the end, a deal was set for Don McEwen to star in *The Ship*. To Ann's mortification, he told his agent what she had said. To Ann's surprise, the agent was pleased. In fact, he bragged about it for years.

After *The Ship* landed on Sentinel's production chart, Ann began to feel at last she was getting somewhere at the studio. Within the next few months, between the work trips that took her back and forth across the country, in addition to production sites in Tunisia, Brazil, and England, two more of Ann's projects were given the go-ahead.

She was adding to her reputation as an executive who could get things done, one who was also able to attract talent. Her straightforward, efficient deal-setting earned her admiration and envy in the industry—and captured the attention of power players in the league of superagents Stan Kamen and Sue Mengers.

A lower-rung executive from another studio spoke to David about Ann's achievements at a screening.

"How does she get all those people?" he asked, making it sound almost like a joke. "What does she offer?"

"Well," David replied, "Ann believes that what they really want is to bring their movies where they'll be treated well by decent, intelligent people."

The executive nodded and said with a cynical smile, "So that's what she tells you, huh?"

If Ann was convincing in projecting the sense that getting movies made was her priority—ahead of setting deals or even hanging onto her job—it was because her priority actually *was* getting movies made.

Ann's relationship with David continued to grow stronger in spite of the demands and travails of her work. It was no easy matter to maintain their closeness, given the hectic nature of their two different worlds. But even as Ann kept saying "no promises" and David kept agreeing, there were clear outward indications to anyone who chose to look that unspoken promises existed between the two and that both worked feverishly to keep their silent vows to one another.

One peaceful morning after a perfect night together, Ann admitted at long last, "I love you so much I'm afraid of it."

David answered her with a kiss and a long embrace and said he felt the same way.

"It's pretty terrifying business, love," he added.

"But," Ann answered slowly, "with you, it's worth everything."

A few months later, they decided to make some joint investments, including a house in Trousdale. They kept David's seaside apartment as a getaway sanctuary and soon came to regard both residences as "ours." If no other time were available, at least now they could usually count on being together in the middle of the night.

Ann consistently worked longer than she had to—fourteen-hour days became sixteen-hour days and sixteen hours stretched to eighteen—to buy a few precious days with David. Sometimes she managed to create a day off only to have David called away at the last moment. With military-style precision, they cleared time for quick vacations, trying to plan for every contingency. There were sacrifices and there was give and take on both sides.

"Bob wants me to fly to Rhodes as soon as possible," Ann informed David, as she returned to their breakfast table one Sunday morning after a frantic phone call from her boss.

It was a day they had planned to spend with some of his family, who were in from Miami.

"When are you going?" he asked soberly.

"I said I couldn't go until first thing tomorrow." She grinned. "So I'm leaving at midnight. Bob took 'first thing tomorrow' very literally."

"Any problem?"

"He screamed a little," Ann admitted.

David nodded. It was typical.

Stewart occasionally made threatening remarks to Ann about other executives he said were more devoted to Sentinel than she, and Ann wondered when he would get around to replacing her with one of them. The thing was—as Stewart once told her in a fit of gratitude over her diplomatic settling of a war between the filmmaker and the star of one of Sentinel's most important projects—Ann's effectiveness was hard to match.

The trip to Rhodes was another troubleshooting assignment. After a mere two weeks in production, *Night Fire* was showing every sign of going completely out of control.

Ann arrived in Greece knowing her task wouldn't be easy.

Director Sergio Patel was a prima donna to put Carolyne Hart to shame. Ann got off-the-cuff reports from some members of the cast and crew about the extraordinary amounts of money being wasted and about how much of the budget was widely believed to be going up Patel's nose.

Matters came to a head when Ann began questioning Patel and he flew into an icy rage, threatening to walk. He called Bob Stewart and informed him that unless Ann Peters was banned from the set from that point on, he *would* walk, and leave the production, now estimated at $23 million, dangling in the breeze.

Ann was also keeping the transatlantic wires hot, imploring Stewart to call Patel's bluff, for she firmly believed it was a bluff, and recommending that the president answer with his own threat to pull the plug on the production unless Patel acted responsibly.

In the end, Ann was ordered back to Los Angeles and resoundingly condemned for interfering with the great Sergio Patel's creative processes. She then learned that Patel was pushing to get her fired from the studio. It was plain that Skip Michaelson, who liked to think of himself as the friend of the great Sergio Patel, was lobbying against her with the president—and that the president was listening.

These were the darkest days of Ann's tenure at Sentinel.

Indeed, it seemed one of those times when nothing was going right—not for her, and certainly not for some of her friends.

A frantic Sheilah had called to tell her that Jeff had disappeared after a particularly horrible confrontation, and she had no idea where he was.

"I finally saw it, Ann," Sheilah said in a deadened monotone, referring to Jeff's heavy drug use. "I finally saw what the trouble had been all along. I finally had to admit it. Putting out an ultimatum was the only thing I hadn't tried. So I did. I said, 'Get help or get out'—and he left. And now," she added tearfully, "now . . . I . . . I wish I hadn't."

Ann was deeply troubled by the news, for she was genuinely fond of Jeff, who, in his better moments, had one of the sweetest dispositions she had ever encountered. She couldn't help recalling Jim Henley back in New Orleans and the sadness of viewing such a likable human being as he had staggered down his self-destructive road.

Somewhat later, Sheilah heard that Jeff was working for a fourth-rate production company that made X-rated films. She tried contacting him to no avail. He was twenty-three, out of her hands, and Sheilah was down to hoping for miracles.

Meanwhile, for Ann, business rolled along.

By the time *The Ship* went into production, *Night Fire* was five months over schedule and still had a long way to go before completion.

By this time, Bob Stewart was having nightmares about *Night Fire*. He had personally been to the location twice to issue ultimatums to Sergio Patel.

THIRTY-FOUR

"I THINK HE'LL make an effective senator. My decision not to be involved in the campaign has nothing to do with my feelings about his ability to do the job. He's very capable. No doubt about it."

So said Eric Evans, speaking to a student journalist who asked why Eric, who until his father's 1982 run for the Senate had been so visibly a part of Hank Evans's campaign retinue, was absent this time around.

The media had unquestioningly accepted Hank's explanation that Eric was hard at work earning his master's degree in economics.

But now, a chance question asked of Eric at an off-guard moment produced a different and surprisingly candid response.

"Frankly, I wish he weren't so effective," Eric admitted. "I think his answer to the illegal alien problem is unjust and inhumane. That's one of our major differences of opinion. I disagree with him about military spending, abortion, where to cut the budget. That gives you the idea; we differ on most of the important issues. On the other hand, in my opinion, his opponent is incompetent.

"I think the old man will win," Eric predicted in conclusion. "He doesn't need any help from me."

His comments quickly made it onto the wire services.

Hank Evans was stunned and angry, never expecting Eric to tell a reporter what he had already told him in private.

Immersed in his campaign, Hank left the job of reprimanding Eric to Mary. What Eric got from his mother was a plea to refrain from making any more statements.

Ann was fascinated by the fact that Eric had made such an admission. She had to confess she was impressed, for she had tagged the younger Evans as a devout daddy's boy with no mind of his own.

Sheilah was less impressed. "I've given up trying to understand Eric or anything he does," she told Ann. At the time, Sheilah was vacillating between outrage and gratitude toward Eric.

He had called Sheilah to tell her that he had heard from Jeff, that Jeff was trying to get his life together, and that he was all right.

Where was Jeff now? Sheilah had asked. What was he doing?

Eric hadn't known—or so he had said. Nor had he known where Jeff was currently living. When she had mentioned having heard that Jeff was working for a producer of X-rated film fare, Eric had answered, "Sorry, Sheilah. I just don't know. He didn't want to say very much."

Eric had promised to notify her whenever Jeff got in touch with him. Twice after that, Sheilah had gotten word from Eric that Jeff was fine, but in each case, Eric had been maddeningly short on details.

Sheilah felt she knew Eric well enough to be sure that if he was in contact with Jeff, he was probably trying to help him —in whatever ways Eric saw fit, which wasn't very reassuring. Eric's closemouthed manner made her livid. She was convinced he knew more than he was telling her.

Ann eagerly watched the papers, waiting to find out how Hank Evans would respond to his son's negative comments.

Naturally, Hank's campaign staff helped him put the best face possible on Eric's statement. Hank smiled good-humoredly when asked about it. "The boy has a right to his opinions; that's the American way." He felt certain that when Eric was a little older and wiser about the realities of government, his views would change. Meanwhile, Hank said with an amused shrug, he could hardly complain about Eric's evaluation of his opponent. "Incompetent was a tidy way to put it," he said.

Thus Eric's words were watered down and soon virtually forgotten. At least, publicly.

* * *

Late on election night, David arrived home to find Sheilah's car parked in the driveway of the hilltop house he shared with Ann. The two women were sitting before the television set in the downstairs den. The sound was turned down.

"Evans won. Did you hear?" Ann asked.

He nodded and looked at Sheilah, who sighed raggedly and shook her head.

It was then that David knew Ann had at last told Sheilah the truth behind her hatred of Hank Evans.

Evans was successful in 1982, but director Sergio Patel was not. Shooting of Sentinel's *Night Fire* went so far over schedule that plans for its debut that year had to be scrapped. *Night Fire* would be the studio's major summer release for 1983, while Ann's project, *The Ship*, was set to open as a second-wave summer picture.

She continued to lobby on its behalf, hating the thought of Rusty de Paull's charming comedy falling victim to neglect in the shadow of the far more expensive *Night Fire*.

Not until May did studio president Stewart seem to hear her. Cards from the first *Ship* previews showed a positive audience response that exceeded Ann's greatest hopes; not only did it go over with the young audience, the adults loved it.

"It looks like we may have a sleeper," Stewart finally admitted.

There were no responses to *Night Fire*, because Sergio Patel was still editing it in May.

He was still editing it, in fact, just days before its gala premiere. But Patel never seemed more confident or in better spirits; he told anyone who asked him about the picture, "It's the best thing I've ever done. I'd stake everything I have on it."

In the end, none of the Sentinel brass saw the finished *Night Fire* before its premiere. The first print wasn't ready until then.

Sentinel's theater—recently renamed The Stanley Weiss Theater—was rivaled on the studio lot only by the Spanish-style executive building in terms of embodying past grandeur.

It was done in a florid, fantastic rococo style, with plush red carpet, a blue velvet curtain with gold braid, and ornate sculptured pillars embedded into its walls. It was, simply,

Hollywood gaudy. Industryites generally liked going there.
Like the curlicued iron gate at Paramount, the Weiss Theater
represented a sort of touchstone to simpler times, a monument
to the glory days.

Ann was seated only one red leatherette chair away from
Skip Michaelson—the seat between them was occupied by
David—and she could almost feel her longtime adversary's
pain as the movie unspooled. The audience began shifting
restlessly after thirty minutes of *Night Fire*. After forty, the
coughing began.

Laughter erupted at spots that had not been intended for
laughs.

Even as she sat watching and hoping desperately that the
movie would somehow improve, Ann couldn't help thinking
about how things had reversed themselves. *"Night Fire* is
surefire," she recalled Michaelson boasting. "We've got a superstar and one of the hottest directors in town. We *know* it's
going to be worth laying down $14 million."

And nobody, *nobody* had wanted to hear Ann's remarks
about how ponderous the material was, how impossible it
would be to make a tough period piece that included the erup-
tion of Mount Vesuvius, for God's sake—plus star salaries—
for $14 million.

Or how she believed the OLI agency was trying to push a
white elephant onto Sentinel.

Or, most important, how often she had heard that Sergio
Patel was suffering from a case of runaway ego that verged on
insanity.

She recalled how bludgeoned she had felt by Patel's command that she never, ever be allowed near his set again, and
how much more betrayed when her boss joined Michaelson in
angrily criticizing her for upsetting their star director. Her
suggestion that they shut down production had been looked
upon as heresay, a sin, a crime, worse.

She remembered how she had worried about losing her job.

And now, here they were, thought Ann, as the ashes rained
down over the doomed Roman resort town of Herculaneum,
circa A.D. 79. The surefire biggie, ballooned to more than
twice its original budget (a large portion of which had been
eaten up by the cost of cocaine cleverly masked in the figures), was sinking like a stone.

"Then is there no way out?" asked Sextus Patulcus on the

screen. From the front of the theater came an answering snicker, then a barely audible, "Call your agent."

Ann felt David's hand tightening on hers. She glanced at his face in the flicker of movie light and realized he was struggling to keep from laughing.

Don't do this to me, David, she begged him mentally as she squeezed his hand back—hard. *You're a goddamn doctor. Can't you control yourself?*

David shut his eyes and kept them shut throughout the final twelve minutes of the cataclysm. He bit his lip hard at the blast of the ancient horn, which sounded far too much like a kazoo.

Laugh and I'll kill you, thought Ann. *Think of Nazis. Anything.*

Then, finally, it was over. The lights came up, and the audience rushed out as if a bomb were about to explode; the fact was, one just had.

The post-premiere bash was a nightmare.

The soundstage abutting the theater had been transformed into a setting of ancient Mediterranean splendor, with a semi-circle of Grecian pillars fronting a luminous twilight backdrop. The long buffet, which featured the best of contemporary Italian cuisine, was set up in front of a section of a mammoth oared boat. There were white-covered cocktail tables on the partial deck as well as on the stage floor below. Huge floral arrangements and prop green foliage adorned a sandy, rock-strewn hillock opposite the pillars.

The party could have been held in the parking lot for all the gaiety shown by the sparse crowd. Many avoided it, incapable of facing Patel or his cast and having to comment on the picture. Those who did attend the banquet made wide circles around the *Night Fire* principals. Conversation was subdued and stilted. What had been planned as a party to celebrate the birth of a picture had the air of a funeral, and with just cause.

The two stars sat together at a table, flanked and protected by associates and friends—the wagons were in a circle. One of the important press members on hand moved toward the table; Ted Kemp's wife chose that inopportune moment to slip him a packet of Alka-Seltzer.

Kemp's expression was catatonic. This was the role he had believed would win him his Oscar. He was just now coming to terms with reality.

Sergio Patel wasn't. He babbled on and on to members of his entourage about how he had achieved this and that effect, the miniatures, the giant crane, the recreation of authentic Roman athletic competition in the palaestra sequence.

"It's as if he just came out of a different movie than we did," David noted quietly, as he and Ann stood watching it all near the buffet.

The head of publicity joined Ann and David and lifted his glass of champagne to Ann.

"Congratulations," he said.

Ann shook her head.

"She managed to not even get the hem of her skirt dirty on this turkey," he reported to David. "No mean feat."

That sentiment was echoed many times, by many others, in many ways, before the dismal affair came to an end. A certain clustering effect was becoming evident, as if attendees had been issued printed instructions that said it was good to be physically close to Ann, bad to be close to Bob Stewart or to Skip Michaelson, the VP who had championed Sergio Patel to the bitter end.

Michaelson cast a few accusatory glances in Ann's direction, certain she was inwardly gloating. He would have been, had their positions been reversed.

The party, which began at 10:40, was dead by 11:45.

By 1:15, Ann was glowering invisibly at the sound of low chortling rising up through the darkness of her bedroom.

"Do you want to share?" she finally asked.

"No, no," David muttered. "It really isn't funny."

David lost his urge to laugh when Ann got her first clandestine phone call from a supporter in New York at 5:15 that morning. Stewart wouldn't last long, the caller told her. He had inside word about grumbling from the boardroom at In-ConTel, Sentinel's parent company.

The game of musical chairs was already underway, and many hoped, or said they hoped, to see Ann wind up in the president's seat.

"I'm sorry for Bob, but I can't truthfully say he's done much of a job for the studio. I would bet he'll be out by the end of the summer."

"So the presidency may be at hand," David commented, as they mused over the call while finishing their breakfast coffee.

"It's just talk," said Ann.

"You must realize people *wouldn't* be talking if there were nothing to it," David replied. There was a strangely dejected note to his voice as he went on. "Look at the phenomenal way you've catapulted up the ladder over the past nine years. Look at all you accomplished at Weiss Productions. Look at how consistently well your movies have turned out. And the reputation you've earned and the people who admire you. The momentum is all with you."

Ann gazed at him for several seconds before saying slowly, "A lot would have to happen before I could be considered a serious prospect."

As if he hadn't heard her response, David asked, "Do you suppose I'd get to see you at all?"

"Yes." Ann nodded. "But it would be a lot harder——"

He stopped her, covering her hand with his own. "I know."

In the verbal shorthand they had developed, David then told Ann he was willing to tolerate a few years of frustration and loneliness in order not to deprive her of the chance. "You want it, go for it," he urged.

"Is that how you really feel?"

"I wouldn't try to stop you even if I thought I could. You ought to try to realize your full potential."

"Nobody stays on forever," Ann said. She added wistfully, "If I could do it, I'd want to have a good run, long enough to make some really wonderful movies."

David smiled across the glass-topped patio table as Ann pushed up the sleeves of her filmy cotton dressing gown.

"You look like you're getting ready already."

"Maybe I am," she admitted.

They were silent for several seconds, each drawing mental pictures of the future. Ann rose to her feet and looked out at the city view, finally murmuring, "A lot could happen in the next few years. I wouldn't want to . . . you wouldn't want to be tied down."

"Let's face it, honey," David told her. "We're not talking about what *I* want. I'm not going to go anywhere. Of course, I happen to feel that you aren't either. You love me, don't you?"

"Yes," she said, coming toward him, "but——"

"Ugh!" He winced.

"Sorry."

"Someday," he promised, as Ann put her arms around him from behind and he clasped her hands, "someday I'm going to get rid of that *but.*"

"I hope you do." Ann nodded soberly. "I genuinely hope you do."

Night Fire opened nationwide the second Friday of June. By its third weekend, it was pulling an abysmal $600 per screen per day average. The mood at Sentinel was one of terrible despair, especially when the industry in general was riding on a high. In the past year, the blockbusters *E.T.* and *Rocky III* had set records. So had *Star Trek II: The Wrath of Khan* grossing $14,347,221 during its first three days in release.

Even Columbia, with its $52.7 million *Annie* flop, reaped more rewards from its disaster than Sentinel would from *Night Fire;* licensing agreements for *Annie* clothing and toys had brought in millions of dollars for the company.

It wasn't until mid-July that *The Ship* opened with comparatively little fanfare. But much to the shock of everyone at Sentinel, it quickly found its audience—and how. *The Ship* proceeded to rocket straight through the stratosphere.

People waited in hour-long lines in New York and L.A. and every city in between. Teens spouted dialogue from the movie. The critics were adoring.

Russell de Paull's The Ship *is a moviemaker's hat trick, at once whimsical and warm, fast-paced and funny, and a shrewd satire,* extolled the *Times.*

It was called a "must-see," a "delight through and through," and "one of the slyest, funniest, winningest movies of this or any year."

The studio's merchandising department worked full-time, overtime, on licensing agreements; quite obviously, the movie would be able to sell far more than anticipated. Deals were set at lightning speed for *Ship* toys, watches, beach towels, picture books, and more.

Don McEwen was instantly established as one of the hottest young movie stars in the business.

Rusty de Paull took his film's success with gleeful abandon. He admitted to *Time* that he cruised by the Bruin Theater pretty regularly to take in the crowds waiting to see *The Ship*.

It was ironic that Ann, the one executive in Sentinel's hierarchy who had argued against a strategy of going after home runs had fostered a megahit.

She had hoped it would do business. After its previews, she had hoped it would do very good business. But what it was doing was record-breaking business.

And because of it, Ann was hoisted into a much more powerful position. Her chances of attaining the presidency improved dramatically—not because of any sound judgments, good ideas, or well-crafted deals of the past, but because suddenly she had the cachet of a blockbuster to her credit, something she had never consciously set out to gain.

"Nobody ever accused the movie business of making sense," Ann said cheerfully when she and David discussed the paradoxic situation. "But as long as this has happened, I guess I'm just going to have to go ahead and capitalize the hell out of it."

Behind the scenes, the game of musical chairs intensified as Stewart's superior, the studio's chief executive officer, was replaced.

Ann soon got word that the new CEO planned to offer her a raise and a new title that would sound more important than vice-president—*executive* vice-president—but would mean very little in terms of added authority. It was a move designed to placate her while the company brought an industry stalwart in from another studio to become Sentinel's new head of production.

The new corporate chieftain was "afraid you're not tough enough to take over for Bob," Ann was told.

Read: woman, she thought.

"Well," she mused aloud to her caller, "maybe he'll change his mind."

It began with a line of conversation between the CEO, whose name was Paul Lordanich, and a friend of his who also happened to be one of Hollywood's elite power attorneys. "Sorry to hear you're going to lose Ann Peters," said the lawyer. "I hear she's getting ready to move over to Warners."

Next, it was one of the members of the board of the parent company. "What's the situation with Ann Peters?" he asked via phone from New York. "Paul, is she really as big an asset as I keep hearing she is?"

The next morning while breakfasting at the Bel Air Hotel, Lordanich ran into superagent Al Halprin, among whose clients was Carolyne Hart. The actress was tentatively set to star in a romantic comedy for Sentinel but was naturally edgy over rumors about the forthcoming executive shake-up. "Carolyne feels she made her agreement with Ann Peters, not necessarily with Sentinel," said the agent, shrugging. "I hear Ann's leaving you soon."

Scheduled to meet with the board of Sentinel's parent company, Lordanich flew to New York that afternoon.

Just as he was about to leave his room at The Plaza Monday morning, the phone rang. It was Ann Peters calling from Los Angeles.

"You caught me on my way out," said the CEO. "Can it wait?"

"It can," Ann replied, "but I have some good news you might want to take to the meeting with you."

"Tell me."

"Russell de Paull has decided he can make a sequel to *The Ship* after all," Ann said cheerfully. "He just told me last night. Isn't that great?"

"Wow," said Lordanich, sensing, perhaps, what was ahead.

Ann continued, "His idea is fabulous! He and Don McEwen went to an artificial foods convention together, and he dreamed up this wild premise—well, I can tell you about it later. I think it's going to be even funnier than the first one. Don definitely wants to do it."

Not tough enough, she thought.

"You know, of course, that Rusty made *The Ship* on a one-picture deal," she added, her tone darkening, her tempo slowing. "And if you check the paperwork, you'll find that he struck all references to a sequel. He was thinking ahead, afraid of being bound to making a sequel when he was convinced there shouldn't be one. But as I said, he's changed his mind.

"Now, I have a tentative agreement with him to do *The Return of the Ship* here, which I'll be glad to go over with you whenever you like. Of course, he doesn't want to do anything officially until the management questions are resolved. Obviously, the faster we can close, the less chance of his being lured away by someone else.

"He wants a 'favored man' provision, or in this case I guess you would call it a 'favored woman' provision, put into his contract. I thought you would want to know that."

There was a long pause as the information sank in with Sentintel's corporate head.

A "favored man" clause meant de Paull intended to make the sequel for Sentinel only if Ann was there.

And Ann *wouldn't* be there, she was saying, unless she were named president.

"I hear you, Ann," Lordanich replied. "Look . . . uh . . . have to go. We'll talk very soon."

Then Lordanich went off to his meeting with the board of the parent company. He weighed what Ann had told him all the way up to the fifty-second floor. Should he take time to verify? Still, Ann wasn't one to attempt such a preposterous lie. It must be true. Could they induce de Paull to stay if she walked? Where would she walk? Warners, Paramount, Fox, Disney . . .

A figure flashed in neon in his mind: $150,000,000.

The Ship was just about to pass that figure in gross revenue, with plenty of steam left to go. It was bound to end up second only to *Return of the Jedi* as the biggest-grossing movie of the year. And it had cost only eight million five to make—a situation beautiful enough to bring tears to his eyes.

Ann Peters had been lucky as well. Lordanich knew that, and he knew that Ann knew it.

On the other hand, $150,000,000 was about as easy to ignore as an elephant in the living room. Was he willing to take responsibility for allowing their $150,000,000 filmmaker, not to mention the star, get away?

Once the meeting convened, Lordanich informed all the officers that he had had this marvelous brainstorm. And then he laid it on them: *Ann Peters*. She represented not only complete capability but offered the stability of promoting from within.

If there was anything the parent company loved, it was stability. God knew, instability was the thing it liked least about owning Sentinel Studios, and for that matter about dealing with Hollywood, where the only sure thing was instability.

Not only that, Lordanich added, but, hell, everyone knew she had been the only rational person at the studio during the *Night Fire* fiasco. Sergio Patel *hated* her. Granted, she was a woman, but to earn such hatred from Patel required *balls*. Russell de Paull practically considered her the mother of his career. She was tight with a buck. Could anyone ask more?

Not InConTel, as it turned out.

THIRTY-FIVE

~⁓⁓~

"Madam President . . . Love Always, Hour By Hour . . . D."

Ann read the inscription on the back of the classically simple Cartier tank watch David gave her the Sunday night before news of her promotion broke in the trades, and she smiled at the message and its gently chiding acknowledgement of her "no commitment" policy. She vowed to wear it every day—a constant reminder of the man who expected to be with her in spirit if not in fact.

For the two of them, it was a time of sharply mixed emotions, both thrilling and fearful. David and Ann knew all too well that as little time as they had together until then, once she took over her new post they would have even less. Much less.

Ann had spent most of the weekend preceding the announcement in meetings around town. When she had been home, the phone had rung constantly, as agents, producers, managers, press, and colleagues who had learned of her new position called to touch base.

Her lover had been extremeley good about playing the part of supportive cheerleader, telling her again and again how proud he was, listening to her fears and dreams, and helping store up her faith in herself and her plans.

But by the end of that weekend, David had also made some half-joking remarks about seeing Ann again in three or four years. "I feel as if you're about to go off to war."

There was a degree of truth in what he said—and they both knew it.

By five-thirty Monday morning, Ann was anxious, and David was back to radiating enthusiasm.

"Mark my words, before long they'll be saying you're the best thing that's happened to Sentinel Studios since Stanley Weiss left," he encouraged her with a wink as they left the hillside house together just before sunrise and walked to the cars that would take them to their separate destinations—their separate lives.

He kissed her. "Good luck, darling."

And that was the last Ann saw of David, at least as he appeared when awake and dressed, for three weeks.

The announcement of Ann's move into the position of President and Chief Operating Officer was greeted by scores of telegrams and phone calls. A vast assortment of elaborate and costly floral arrangements—all sent by well-wishers only too aware that she controlled the purse strings of a $100 million—plus production outlay—crowded the tables, shelves, and desks of Bob Stewart's former office, the luxurious suite that was now Ann's.

Now Ann was the one who could say yes.

She proceeded to break out of the starting gate with the pace of a movie-world Secretariat.

Ann's priorities were to round out her executive team and put together a solid production slate—and she made astonishingly quick progress in both areas, largely because she came in extremely well prepared. As soon as she had grasped that the presidency could be hers, she had laid out a wide-ranging and detailed strategy and had discreetly set some of it in motion during the weeks prior to her appointment.

Her team was ready to move smoothly into gear almost as soon as Ann was able to officially give the word.

In the following two weeks, three exciting movie projects were added to the Sentinel roster. Debra Winger, hot on the success of *An Officer and a Gentleman*, was set for a delicious romantic comedy. An eerie, highly stylized thriller would have Jeff Bridges teamed with Nastassia Kinski. And Ann's pet project—an updated remake of *How to Marry a Millionaire* with Dolly Parton, Bernadette Peters, and Cher—generated widespread press interest.

The deal announcements started off Ann's regime with a solid boost; they trumpeted the fact that Sentinel was suddenly a hot place to do business again and that Ann Peters was a bold, decisive player.

There was also a downside that surfaced right away. Ann was faced with the loss of one of the major "go" projects she had inherited, a movie that would already have been in production, in fact, had it not been for some last-minute delays.

Meanwhile, she had to make a trip to a location site in England and then fly to Rome's Cinecittà Studios, with stopovers for meetings in New York on her way to and from Europe.

Imposing boardrooms, exotic location sites, luxury hotel suites, and elegant restaurants were the backdrops of her world, but Ann was barely aware of them. In the forefront of her mind was the footage she viewed, the tough production problems, what the filmmakers and the stars had to say.

And there were scores of phone calls to take each day and films to see.

And there were always, always meetings.

Ann was not particularly comfortable giving interviews to the press, but she realized that as one of the first women to invade the studio presidential ranks, she was newsworthy—and that being newsworthy meant opportunities that were far too important to pass up just for the sake of her personal feelings. Interviews provided a chance to promote the image of Ann Peters's Sentinel as *the* hot place in town to do business. Besides, Ann felt she owed it to several of the reporters with whom she had longstanding friendly relationships. She squeezed meetings with them into her already-crammed schedule.

She tried to steer clear of personal questions, responding to them with a certain sketchy honesty, occasionally veering into deliberate obfuscation. She brushed aside her background by saying casually, "I moved around quite a bit. You know, like any military brat."

Three magazine articles concentrated on a "phoenix rising from the ashes" theme, highlighting Ann's unhappy marriage, her disfiguring injury, and the change of career forced on her nearly a decade earlier by Leigh Ballard's violent act.

Ann found the stories grossly embarrassing—despite the subsequent mail from strangers who hailed her as an inspiration.

From strangers. Resoundingly absent was any message

from Lyla. Not that Ann expected one, but she couldn't help wondering whether her sister had seen any of the stories.

Or whether Cindy had.

Although Ann never mentioned David by name when the inevitable "man in your life" questions were asked, his name got into print, too. Even more surprising to Ann, after she had so zealously tried to guard his privacy, were the cheerful, homespun, un–self-conscious quotes from David that wound up in a lengthy profile in the *Los Angeles Journal* Sunday entertainment section.

She had no idea he'd even been contacted, she told him. "But thanks for the kind words. When did they get to you?"

"A couple months ago," David replied.

"Months?" she heard herself repeating.

Only then did Ann realize just how intensely she had been working and how much time had already gone by since she had assumed the presidency.

As the holidays approached, she was just beginning to hit her stride, handling the ultra–high-speed demands of her position with greater ease. She could begin to relax, a little, and enjoy the sight of *The Ship* sailing onto the ten-best lists.

At last, she was able to spend a couple of days of quiet time with David, helping him take care of his visiting nieces and nephew and catching up on his new involvement in the substance-abuse treatment unit at the hospital. The number of patients seeking help in overcoming cocaine dependency had taken a dramatic jump during the past year. The former prevalent view that cocaine was psychologically addictive but not physically addictive was extinct.

"So much for 'the kick that doesn't kick back,'" Ann said ruefully, recalling the standard Hollywood reference to coke. She told David sadly that Sentinel alone could probably keep the staff of the unit busy.

Ann's connection to the unit soon proved highly useful.

Ron Galice was an actor whose likable public personality was in perfect synch with his likable private personality. He was brilliant in terms of both intellect and acting talent and fully aware of the pitfalls of fame.

When Ann had spoken to him after his first big success, he had told her sincerely, "After five years of driving around in a beat-up '69 Dodge, I have to admit it does something to me to have the valets at the Beverly Hills Hotel hustling to bring out my new Mercedes. Now, instead of being seated at restaurants somewhere south of Pico, I have Patrick and Nino calling me by name and ushering me to the choice tables at Ma Maison and the Polo Lounge. But I'm determined not to go off the deep end about all this; that's why I keep going back to Chicago. Luckily, I have the kind of family and friends back home who don't mind pointing out to me when I act like an arrogant asshole."

Ron's fame had grown quickly. He had also become a darling of the critics, and then an Academy Award–winner.

In short, he embodied the having-it-all dream.

Now Ron was starring in Sentinel's $12 million *Puget Sound*.

And he was coming apart.

Ann got reports from the Seattle location site that Ron was becoming increasing impossible to handle, that his moods were becoming more and more erratic. He was hyperactive and argumentative, distraught and paranoid by turns.

His leading lady had come to hate and fear him.

The director of the film, who cringed at the prospect of failing to complete a cherished project into which he had already sunk two years of his life, was doing his best to cope with Ron and to keep the seriousness of his condition a secret from the studio.

Nevertheless, Ann learned that Galice had a male secretary who frequently appeared on the set and who was, everyone knew, keeping Ron in drugs. Quite obviously, coke was at least one of Galice's problems.

Ann's problem was the potential unraveling of a big-budget movie—the cornerstone of Sentinel's next Christmas release schedule. If the worst happened, the studio would be left with a gaping hole to fill and over two million dollars lost. But continuing the production presented equally grim prospects. Seven weeks into filming, they were already over four weeks behind schedule, and God knew where the budget would go if things continued at this rate. Galice alone would cost the studio a quarter of a million dollars per week in overages once they went beyond the scheduled fourteen weeks of production.

After one of the VPs returned from the location with reports of evasions, denials, and open hostility, Ann concluded it was time to make the trip north herself.

She arrived at the serene, wooded location site on a cool, gray afternoon to find nothing serene about the company. Everyone seemed worn out, frazzled, and guarded—especially guarded, for the team rightly assumed Ann was there to consider pulling the plug on their baby.

Ann met with Galice in his hotel suite.

"If we're going to get anywhere at all," she said, pacing before him as he sat on the Victorian love seat in the sitting room, "we're going to have to dispense with two wrong thoughts. One, that I'm here to antagonize you. Look, we've known each other for a while, and I think you know I like and respect you. I'm not here to play policeman. I'm here because we're getting into a hole we shouldn't be getting into on such a great project, and we've got to fix it."

Galice shrugged, eyeing her warily through the wire-frame glasses he wore when not on camera.

"And the second wrong thought we're going to leave behind is the idea that I'm going to buy these denials."

Galice laughed. He put his hand over his heart and said with an attitude of amused astonishment. "Ann, I don't know where—"

"Come on, Ron," she cut him off and took the seat opposite him.

"I'm not going to play games. This is what's going to happen. Lew will finish out this week doing Lisa's scenes, then we're shutting down. I hate seeing someone as gifted as you going to hell physically, but it's none of my business if you want to wreck yourself and your career. On the other hand, I *can't* let this project go to hell. We can go up again in May without you," she said, and gave him the names of two other actors who might take his place.

Galice looked horrified.

"We'd rather have you, but if you want back on this picture, you'll have to get control of yourself. You'll have to agree to full-time medical supervision, which I will arrange—or you will arrange and I will approve. Otherwise, we'll cut our loss and explain to the insurance company why it was impossible to go ahead with you. Then, of course, other producers will find it hard to get your insured . . ."

Ann fell into silence. Galice was suddenly pinching the bridge of his nose beneath the wire frames, wincing and weeping.

Ann felt sorry for him, but expressions of sympathy were not what he needed now.

"How about it, Ron?" she asked, her voice gentle but firm.

"I can't believe this is happening to me," he cried.

En route to Los Angeles in the Sentinel jet, Ann thought about that statement.

"He *doesn't* believe what's happened to him," she told David at two-thirty that morning when she arrived home. "And that's a big part of the problem." She was sitting at the foot of the bed while David sat propped against the pillows— their usual stations when they conversed nowadays.

"Imagine being twenty-nine and having already gained every accolade your industry has to give—and probably deep-down believing you didn't really deserve them. It's hard enough to have that kind of tortured insecurity in other fields, convinced people will find out you're a fraud. But when you have a sense that the entire world is watching you, waiting for another brilliant feat, and you feel you *can't do it?* I've seen it too many times.

"He's scared shitless that he'll never live up to what he's already done, that his career and his life have nowhere to go but down. If you felt that way and then someone handed you a magic powder that made you feel invincible . . ." She shrugged.

"You're demanding the impossible," David told her. "I can't imagine him going back to that kind of work schedule after only ten days on the program. I would strongly advise against it, and I'm sure my colleagues *will* advise against it."

"You know," she answered, "there are many who approach this problem by making sure their Ron Galices never run out of their drug of choice."

"Yes, but you're not one of them."

Ann sighed. "I don't think it works. You should see the footage; Ron's performance is way below par. As much as I'd like to see him stay clean, frankly, I think he's committed to finishing the movie, but not to kicking the drugs. He wants a Band-Aid."

At that, David chuckled regretfully. *"Everyone* wants a damned Band-Aid!"

THIRTY-SIX

❦❧

BAND-AIDS WERE WHAT Jeff Morison had wanted for years.
But by 1983, he had quit looking for them.

Like Ron Galice, he was allowing his drug dependency to
interfere with his work. In Jeff's case, however, neither he nor
his employer, Scott Draydon, blamed his slips on overindul-
gence.

Draydon, a squat, balding producer of films one critic
summarized as "dung," overindulged regularly. He sometimes
paid Jeff bonuses in coke. It was handy and tax-free. Or he
gifted Jeff with another drug that had, until John Belushi's
death the year before, enjoyed a huge surge of popularity in
certain Hollywood circles, astonishingly chic circles. Heroin.

He turned Jeff on to good sources, including one of Hollywood's little-known dubious attractions—a computerized
drug-by-phone reference network.

While everyone acknowledged that Scott Draydon's pictures were sleazy insults to the average intelligence, nobody
could deny that Draydon made money. And as unappetizing as
he was, he was still invited to some very illustrious gatherings. Draydon was living proof of Elizabeth Taylor's pronouncement: "There is no deodorant like success."

He paid his help next to nothing, which was yet another
reason his complaints about Jeff's work habits were minimal.
When Jeff was functioning, he was an adequate helper—and
an unquestioning one.

Jeff's duties in the shoestring company were so varied, he
would have been hard-pressed to categorize them. Sometimes

he wore the hat of a production manager. Sometimes he was merely Draydon's fetch-and-carry boy. At other times, when they were casting bit players and extras, Draydon assigned Jeff the task of weeding out blatantly unsuitable candidates, a job Jeff hated.

As Ann was meeting the challenges of her new role as Sentinel's president, Scott Draydon was preparing to start a $500,000 picture dubbed *Sorority Boys,* a comedy—or so it was called—about two lusty young men who secretly take up residence in a sorority house where they have a very good time indeed.

One afternoon, Jeff found himself presiding over a cattle call for bit players on the movie. The actresses and would-be actresses aspiring to become sorority girls in *Sorority Boys* filled the tiny waiting room outside the office where Jeff was conducting interviews and spilled out into the hallway of the grim tan stucco building on Van Nuys Boulevard.

Jeff had seen some of the faces many times before. He knew Draydon's tastes, so picking "talent" was easy.

In walked a tall sometime-model in a tight pink and black horizontally striped dress. She had hennaed hair and red lips. No good. Looked like she'd been around. Scott liked them "tender," as he was wont to say.

"Sorry. Maybe next time," said Jeff. He sighed and leafed through the pile of photos and résumés.

A sweet-faced brunette gazed down at him. Jeff took in her reedy form and disqualified her at once. Pretty, but she didn't have the body for *Sorority Boys.* Scott liked "big titties," as he was wont to say.

"Sorry," said Jeff.

And so it went for hours. A few applicants were summarily dismissed. Some he talked to, some he talked to longer.

Finally Jeff had worked his way through the list of names, the stack of photos and résumés.

He had singled out ten girls he felt fit the desired *Sorority Boys* look and had asked them to wait.

Soon Scott would come by and make the final selection. Jeff got up from his desk, intending to slip across the street to a nearby fast-food restaurant, but he stopped short as he saw yet another candidate standing in the doorway.

"Hi. I'm here for the audition. Are you Jeff?"

He sat down and did an automatic appraisal. Bouncy,

shoulder-length honey-colored hair, full breasts, a tiny waist, and a face "tender" enough to have pleased Walt Disney. She was dressed in pink. Her smile was a flash of brilliance. And she was young.

Scott will shit when he sees this one, Jeff thought.

She was made to order.

"We're just interviewing," he corrected her. "This isn't an audition. I don't have a picture or résumé on you."

The girl stepped into the room, opening her arms expansively.

"What do you need a picture for?" she chirped. "I'm right here!"

Warning signals went off in his mind. Didn't have pictures, hadn't brought a résumé, probably fresh from the Midwest, a Miss Easter Basket or some such thing, thinking she was going to be a *Hollywood mooovie star*. One of those.

"Are you SAG?" he asked.

"Not yet."

"Uh huh. Who's your agent?"

"Bobby Parker."

Jeff knew the name well. Scott frequently did business with Parker, who was definitely a part of their little sphere. Indeed, he was the man who had turned Scott onto dial-a-drug. It didn't add up, unless . . .

"Have you been with him long?"

"As of today, officially." She grinned.

"How old are you?"

"Nineteen."

Jeff looked at her dubiously.

"I am," she insisted, stepping still closer as she rifled through her shoulder bag. She withdrew a cowhide wallet and pulled out her driver's license.

"Did Parker send you over?"

She held her license four inches away from Jeff's face, making it impossible to ignore. He took her wrist and held it out far enough to read the license. He had been right: out of state. He checked the date, then nodded. Nineteen.

"Look, it's got my picture, too. You wanted to look at a picture? There's a picture."

Jeff usually didn't allow these girls to become more than faces and shapes, but she was forcing him to take notice.

"I see," he said, not quite smiling.

"How about a job?" she suggested.

"Do you know anything about this movie? Anything at all?"

"It's a youth comedy," she answered. "I can do comedy. Test me."

At that point, Jeff heard Draydon's molasses voice oozing from the waiting room.

"Jeff," he cried, his chin dropping theatrically into his second chin on sight of the girl. "Saving the best for yourself?"

Draydon took her hand, and she flashed her big smile.

Jeff looked on blandly.

He was far too absorbed in his own problems to care about Draydon and his instant lust for the little blonde.

Later, Draydon insisted, "I've got to have her," a comment Jeff knew was personal as much as professional.

As he added her name to the cast list, Jeff shook his head, thinking, *So long, Miss Easter Basket*. Rarely had he seen Draydon as excited as he was over Cindy Mantussi.

Jeff made a point of avoiding anyone he considered likely to talk to Sheilah about him. He wanted no contact with his mother, not even indirectly.

In addition to her, he had left behind a crowd of friends who had finally given up trying to help him. He had proved to be an emotional black hole who drained them, absorbed their energy and concern—and never changed.

The last to let go was Eric.

Brotherly affection and, although he would never have admitted it, a certain amount of guilt had driven Eric to go to Herculean lengths to help Jeff climb out of the mess into which he had gotten himself.

Eric had taken Jeff to a drug rehabilitation center in Colorado and enrolled him in the program.

Jeff had made it through, but two months later he had gone back to his old ways.

By the time he had heard from Jeff again, Eric had completed his degree, moved back to California, and taken a prestigious position at Axel, Wakefield & Co., a venture capital fund for the entertainment, communications, and leisure industries. The offer had come via an old friend of his father's.

Eric had spent his first vacation from that job going through the whole ordeal of detox with Jeff. Eric had sat with him, yelled at him, comforted him, supported him, refused to let him out of his sight for six days. Then Jeff had disappeared.

Months had passed before Jeff had called him to apologize, crying that he never should have asked Eric to be his guard. "I stopped thinking of you as a friend. It was the worst time of my life," he had told Eric.

After another endless night of listening to suicidal talk and pleas for help, Eric had taken Jeff to another rehab program, this one at a private hospital in Westlake.

Jeff had then managed to slip out of the hospital after two days.

Eric finally discovered that Jeff had gone back to work for Scott Draydon and that he was living in a rundown apartment on Franklin Avenue, a cheapie temporarily sublet from an out-of-town actor. He sought him out there.

Never had the contrast between the two been as stark as it was the last night Eric saw Jeff.

Flushed with anger and fresh-faced from the night chill, Eric was the picture of vigor and resolution as he stood in the middle of Jeff's living room, hands at his belt, legs locked rigidly into an inverted V.

Jeff, his face ashen and mottled, was a vision of burnout and defeat. He immediately assumed a posture of supplication.

"I was going to call you, but I kept putting it off because I knew you'd be pissed."

"Good guess," Eric answered flatly.

"I'll pay you back," Jeff said, referring to the money Eric had invested in his latest vain detox effort.

"You'll pay me back," Eric spat out. "I ought to knock the shit out of you! You'll pay me back. What happened to all the revelations you had in March?"

"What do you want? Blood?" Jeff cried, turning on him suddenly with blind animal fury. "You think you're so great. You with your fucking money and your fucking degrees and your fucking status job. I'm fed up with you looking down at me! The big man. You fucking phony. I don't want your help. I don't *need* it. Got that? You can just fucking well go to hell!"

Jeff stormed off, fleeing Eric's answer to his outburst, and locked himself in the bathroom.

For several seconds Eric stood rubbing his face.

He looked toward the hallway, then at the floor. Finally, he reached inside his coat and withdrew a black and white snapshot of himself and Jeff taken on a Hawaiian vacation in 1965, when they had been ages seven and eight—the summer they had declared themselves blood brothers. He tossed the photo onto the coffee table, then left.

Jeff found a new shoulder to cry on during the first week of *Sorority Boys* production. Scott Draydon screamed at him in front of some three dozen witnesses outside the Hollywood home that was being used for the sorority house set. Jeff was used to being screamed at by Draydon. He would accept the abuse and then lope away hanging his head like a kicked dog. What he wasn't used to was being sought out later by a bit player indignant on his behalf.

"I think he's terrible!" the little blonde from New Jersey told Jeff, outraged. "You didn't deserve that! But don't worry —he only made himself look bad."

"You think?"

"Definitely," she answered with a firm nod.

"I don't know. I seem to bring that out in people."

"Oh," she said, tilting her head, her eyebrows knitting. "I'm sure that's not true."

"It is," he insisted, a far-off look on his face.

Jeff soon started telling her his problems. She responded with all the sympathy and outrage of one too naive to have built up any immunity to the Jeffs of the world. When at last he ran out of steam, she gave him her phone number, convinced that what poor, sweet Jeff needed was a friend.

Jeff immediately took advantage of Cindy's sympathy. She went at once from being a stranger to being a primary figure in his life.

She and her roommate were awakened in the early morning hours by Jeff's phone calls whenever he couldn't sleep and felt the need to talk. One night she made a frantic trip to his apartment when he was depressed and threatened "to end it all." That was followed by a desperate scrounging up of money when Jeff claimed he was going to be evicted from his apartment "and put out on the street" if he didn't give the owner three hundred dollars immediately.

She made suggestions, she cried, she tried to pump up his

self-esteem, she got angry—hour after hour it would go on, until, completely exhausted, she would succeed in elevating his mood and getting some assurance from Jeff that he would be all right. At least until the next time.

"You're the only person who's ever been so nice to me," Jeff told her tearfully.

She was quickly ensnared in Jeff's troubles—with very little understanding of what was really happening to him and even less knowledge of how to cope with it.

She believed everything he told her about himself, about his past, about his famous mother who didn't care about him, he said, and about his best friend, who had betrayed him, he declared. Cindy cursed Eric Evans for turning his back on Jeff.

Yet soon she too began to grow impatient with Jeff's self-pitying attitude.

"You know," she observed one afternoon when Jeff was on the sorority house location, "you're not the only person in the world who's had a bum deal."

"Right," he sighed.

"All I'm going to say is, if you want things to be different, you've got to change them yourself."

"What do you know about it?" he grumbled.

"About changing your life? Maybe nothing. About changing mine—I'm here, aren't I?"

At that, Jeff turned to look at her with a slightly derisive smile.

She shrugged. "I didn't say things were ideal."

"Come on—you're the perfect example of a good person getting squashed by the fucking system."

"No, I'm not," she insisted. "Because I won't *let* myself get squashed. You don't get squashed until you yourself say okay."

"You go through a few things, then tell me about it," he replied.

"I've already been through a few things. This job is a big move up for me. I've made a grand total of sixty-two hundred so far this year. Try living on that in this town!

"In fact, I've got a betrayal story for you myself," she said, rising from the wooden steps of the house and turning to face him.

"Did you ever go through a period when you were a kid when you wondered whether you might be adopted?"

Jeff shook his head. "Never more than a passing thought," he replied.

"Well, with me it started when I was in grammar school. We were supposed to bring in our birth certificates. My mom gave me this little form from the county registrar's office and told me it would do; it was the same thing. But I couldn't help noticing—and some of the other kids, uh, shall we say, also brought it to my attention—that my form wasn't anything like their certificates. It didn't have any footprints; there was no pretty seal; it was a typed sheet with a stamp on it. So I felt badly, because my mother had lost my 'real' birth certificate."

Jeff nodded, appearing deeply interested.

"It wasn't until I was about eleven that it really started to bother me. Why didn't I look like my parents? I'd go rummaging through this metal box in the attic whenever I was home alone, because I knew that's where they kept all their important papers. I found the form again, and this time I noticed that it was dated almost a year after I was born, and no hospital was mentioned. When I finally built up the courage to ask my mother about the hospital—I could *never* talk to my dad—she said they'd been so poor she'd given birth to me at home.

"I believed her, but somehow I still felt something was wrong."

Jeff nodded. "Were you right?"

"Yeah." She paused.

Jeff lit a cigarette, took a puff, and hunkered down to listen, his chin propped between his hands.

"So?" he asked.

"So for years, I told myself I was just being paranoid. I figured I'd seen too many old movies with stories of secret adoptions. It didn't really happen—not in real-life America today. And the registration form did say I was who I was. I was theirs.

"But then, one night about two years ago, I was having a real bitch of an argument with my dad." She tossed back her blond hair angrily, adding, "One of many. And, anyway, I was on my way up the stairs to do the big, dramatic slamming of the bedroom door finish. You know the big, dramatic slamming of the bedroom door finish, don't you?"

Jeff smiled slightly.

"And that's when I heard the sonofabitch screaming at my mother that I was 'a bad seed.'" Cindy stopped and took a breath. "He said he'd been worried I'd turn out to be a bad seed all along, because—are you ready?—I was 'a child of sin.' Thank you, Dad."

Jeff winced. "A child of sin?"

She nodded. "He can be the funniest guy in the world, but when he gets into this kind of shit, he's a maniac."

"So what did he mean?"

"He meant I'm a child of sin," she repeated with a shrug. "My mother looked as though she'd just witnessed a murder; my dad kind of looked around the room as if he was hoping to find someone else to blame, and when he couldn't, he stormed out of the house. So in the end, *he* got to do the big, dramatic slamming of the door finish." She laughed halfheartedly.

"They never would admit anything. They tried to tell me I'd heard wrong."

"Are you sure you didn't?" Jeff asked.

"Yes!" she exclaimed angrily. "That was the one moment of truth from them in nineteen years. Someday—I have promised myself—someday I am going to find out *whose* sin I'm a child of."

For the first three weeks, Cindy's work on the film consisted mostly of waiting. She was included in the group scenes—jumping up and down on the bleachers of a junior college football stadium, reacting to a scrimmage, lounging around the school swimming pool in an abbreviated swimsuit. It was more tiresome than tiring. She was herded around and stood where she was told to stand and never saw a script.

She knew nothing about her character other than the fact she had a name, Cheri. When Draydon got to her, he gave Cindy the lines to say.

"Hi ya, handsome" was one. "Do we have fun or do we have fun?" was another. "I'll get it" was the shortest. "I came because I heard this was a good party school" was the longest.

Cindy realized *Sorority Boys* would be an extremely stupid movie. Everyone readily said as much.

"But it's a credit, something I can show around," she rationalized to the roommate who shared her minuscule Hollywood bachelor apartment. "I've got to start somewhere.

Besides *I* can do a good job. There are no small parts," she added theatrically, "only small actors."

After extricating herself from three overtures by Scott Draydon, Cindy faced a boss who alternately fumed and flirted. A natural mimic, she also perfected a wicked imitation of him.

She entertained her "sorority sisters" with it one day as they lolled around waiting outside the Hollywood house, while shooting continued inside.

"Aren't you charming, though?" she crooned in a thick lecherous voice, while the others clustered around, laughing.

"Tell me your name, your sign, your phone number. I want to know everything. What's your area code? . . . Really? *Mine too . . .*"

"Watch out," one of the other bit players warned as Jeff approached. "The black cloud is drifting this way."

Cindy abruptly stopped her act and turned to face him.

"Jeff," she cried.

But that day, Jeff wasn't in the mood to talk. He glided past the group without saying a word.

"He's strung out," commented another of the actresses.

Cindy looked at her, her face registering complete surprise. Every so often, her worldly-wise mask slipped.

"He must be here to see the Candy Man," said her co-worker. "You know, the old man who plays the principal. Cindy, if you ever want to get your hands on some stuff— coke, speed, dust, smack, anything—you don't have to look any further. He's got it all."

"Him? You're kidding."

"No, I'm not kidding."

Another girl in the group noted that the lead actress wanted to get bombed for the love scene currently being shot in one of the bedrooms inside. "They're gonna do it the authentic way."

"You mean," Cindy asked with a look of sheer disbelief, "they're going to . . . really do it?"

The others laughed.

Cindy burned with embarrassment, feeling more than a little galled about all she apparently didn't know, all the questions she hadn't thought to ask.

Her eyes were being opened fast.

Cindy's misgivings about *Sorority Boys* blossomed.

Wary of Jeff now but sorry for him, too, Cindy sought him

out a few days later as he sat making some phone calls in a downstairs room of the house, hoping to convince him to give her a copy of the script.

"I'll get you one, but don't count on anything in it staying the same," he warned. "The only real script is between Draydon's ears."

"Let me ask you this," she said. "What's the rating on this loser going to be?"

"R."

"Are you sure? They're saying that the bedroom scene was real. I mean, they really had sex."

"No!" He put his hand to his cheek, feigning shock.

Then he named three major studio releases in which he had heard the sex scenes were equally as real, not that the public realized it. Cindy's eyes widened. She refused to believe it.

"Sure. You actors, you're all a bunch of exhibitionists," Jeff said caustically. He told her of one movie a major actor had done for a fraction of his usual salary, "Just because he got to realize his fantasies about laying the leading lady."

"Who ain't no lady," Cindy blurted out with a laugh.

Jeff shook his head. "It'll be interesting to talk to you a few years from now," he murmured with a slight frown, returning his attention to the call sheet in front of him.

"Well, I'm not an exhibitionist," she sputtered. "Nobody should expect me to be, either."

THIRTY-
SEVEN

THE *SORORITY BOYS* COMPANY was working on an isolated section of beach in Ventura County that conveniently fronted Scott Draydon's ex-wife's house.

They were doing the water-fight scene, which had the girls cavorting in the waves while the inevitable nerdy freshman character, binoculars in hand, excitedly watched in secret from the back of a pickup truck. Draydon rushed through blocking the sequence, and for good reason. He was shooting on public land without a permit.

Since the scene was to be covered by a musical track, he could direct it in silent-movie style—standing off-camera and barking orders to the players as it was being shot.

The scene began with Cindy laughingly pushing one of the girls into the water. Then she herself got dunked. Then the others got into the act, until it became a full-fledged melee.

"Exuberance!" Draydon yelled. "Laughter! Good! Good! Keep it up. Okay, now, off with the wet clothes. Throw them up on the beach. Cindy! You be the first."

That Cindy was prepared for. That was the idea: the girls get down to their underwear. The nerd hidden in the pickup goes crazy.

In a frenzy of splashing, laughing, unbuttoning, and unzipping, the wet gear was hurled onto the sand.

"Exuberance! Zest! Now, start getting rid of the tops!"

That Cindy was not prepared for. All around her, still laughing and splashing, Cindy's "sorority sisters" unhesitatingly began unfastening their bras and tossing them aside.

"Paula, Traci—hug each other! Good! Wonderful! Tanya," Draydon shouted to the lead actress, "help Cindy! Exuberance! Lots of laughter!"

Somehow, Cindy held a frozen smile even as Tanya came up behind her and laughingly unhooked her bra.

"Come on, come on, come on, come on!" Draydon screamed. "We're so far away, nothing's going to show. Come on, come on! We're rolling! Do you want to have to do the whole thing again?"

"Come on," repeated the actress behind Cindy, through clenched teeth. "You're going to make us all freeze to death. Don't fuck it up!"

She knocked Cindy's feet out from under her on the next wave. Down they went into the water—laughing and exuberant. When the water receded, Cindy was topless.

From then on, she followed directions in a blind daze. Laugh, laugh. Splash, splash. What difference would it make to hide now?

She didn't want to be accused of juvenile behavior.

She didn't know what she was thinking.

She blanked.

"Okay, girls!" Draydon called at last. *"Everybody* out! Run this way! Come on, Cindy. Keep laughing. That's right. Laugh and smile. Oh, God! Glorious! You girls are fabulous. You're beautiful, Cindy . . ."

Jeff turned away from the scene and went into the house.

They were on the beach little more than two hours, but Draydon thought he had all the footage he would need. They were to break for dinner, then head to a parking lot in the Valley. After that, they were to take over the furniture department of a department store after closing.

When Jeff next saw Cindy, it was dusk and she was sitting on the bumper of one of the trucks—a plastic cup full of vodka in her hand, an old fleece-collared corduroy jacket and a pair of cutoffs covering her body.

"Done for the day?" he asked.

"Done in," she mumbled. She looked up. "Did you see our scene?"

He nodded.

"Am I going to be sorry?"

"Why should you be?" he asked indifferently.

"No, I mean, it's going to be fast. It's really not going to show that much, is it?"

He shrugged again.

"Scott said it wouldn't."

That came as no surprise to Jeff. Scott always said it wouldn't. "Why worry about it?" he asked. "It's done."

"It seemed to take so long."

"Not really."

"You don't want to talk," Cindy observed.

"Not in the mood," Jeff mumbled, sniffling.

"I know, I know," she said, trying to make a joke of what she was actually feeling by minimizing it with a mocking tone. "You don't see me the same way you did."

He made a face. "Please, none of that crap. I'm just not in the mood."

"Okay," she said weakly.

Jeff started to walk away, then turned back. Cindy was slowly moving in the other direction.

"Cindy," he called after her. She stopped and looked back at him.

Jeff shook his head. "Never mind."

"Are you okay?" she asked.

He nodded slightly, running his hand distractedly over his dark wavy hair. "Yeah." He seemed uncertain. "Take care of yourself, all right? And don't worry about anything."

It was the last time she would ever see him.

By ten o'clock, he was standing impatiently at the bar of one of the chic night spots on Sunset, where he had arranged a meeting through the drug phone service Draydon had told him about.

He would find her, the seller had assured him, declining to give Jeff a name or description.

A woman was standing alone at the end of the bar, a lovely woman with a classic face fit for an eighteenth-century porcelain cameo, a cloud of auburn hair drifting ethereally down nearly to the label of her tight, tight jeans. The small and perfect bow of her provocative lips curved upward slightly on sight of him.

She was an actress with at least two big, very big, features to her credit, a brief heyday now over and gone. She was a butterfly who fluttered down from her hillside home and visited the clubs along the Strip two or three nights a week, a little white help for keeping up appearances secreted in her Hermes clutch purse.

Drug distributors come in all shapes in Hollywood.

Somehow, seeing her hit Jeff with a deep sinking sensation. A dread. There was something, something about it, something.

"Are you by yourself tonight?" he asked.

"I'm waiting for someone," she informed him. "Could it be you?"

They did their business there at the bar. She had an elegant English-sounding accent—that despite the fact she'd grown up in Sacramento—and distant, gray-green eyes.

She told him, "This is really *pure.*"

Jeff heard but didn't hear. She kept hitting him like dark poetry. He found he could hardly stand to look at her. As soon as the transaction was completed, he hurriedly left the restaurant. But the feeling persisted. He went home, and it was there, too.

There were, however, more acute feelings at work on Jeff. By eleven-fifteen, he started a private binge. By eleven-twenty, he was passed out on the worn, nubby red sofa of the sublet apartment.

By eleven-thirty, he was gone, the victim of a miscalculation. He hadn't fully grasped the significance of "really *pure.*"

At least, that was the generally accepted explanation.

There were several among Jeff's former friends who privately believed he just hadn't cared whether he ever woke up.

Jeff had become so unreliable he was not even missed on the set the next morning. Cindy tried phoning him in the late afternoon. It wasn't until that night that finally, with Cindy's urging, Draydon dispatched one of his gofers to the apartment.

By ten o'clock, Sheilah knew.

If there was any uplifting note in that household riddled with unbearable grief and despair during the days that followed, it came with the return of Sheilah's other child. Wendy rushed into town from Mill Valley, leaving her "old man" behind. She assumed the role of the good daughter, declaring that the breach between Sheilah and herself must now come to an end.

Ann seized every possible moment she could to be at Sheilah's side. David and other friends were present and supportive, but all of them felt helpless.

The worst thing that could possibly happen had happened.

Only once during that terrible time did Sheilah emerge from absolute despondency to react to something, and that was when Eric Evans came to the door.

"Did you really believe I'd ever want to see you?" she demanded explosively.

Ann and David heard the outburst from the living room, and they exchanged pained looks.

"I just want to know one thing: did you know where Jeff was all this time? Were you seeing him?"

There was a long pause. Ann and David heard a low voice but couldn't make out Eric's words clearly. He said something about Jeff saying he wanted to get himself straightened out, something about a terrible mistake in judgment that Eric had made. There was a broken apology.

Sheilah cut him short. "There's no excuse. No excuse! Go away."

Despite their rocky past, Sheilah's ex-husband elicited no such angry response when he arrived, new wife in tow. Sheilah's bitterness toward him was swallowed up in grief; they were bonded by shared suffering.

At the grave site, Ann spotted a young man standing alone at a discreet distance. She guessed it was Eric, and she feared another confrontation.

She was so focused on Sheilah, on the ceremony, on her own grief, and on willing Eric Evans to stay away, that Ann never noticed the blond young woman standing not thirty feet from her.

Cindy walked into the "sorority" house that afternoon ready to do battle at the first opportunity. She didn't have to wait long.

"How was it?" Scott Draydon asked offhandedly, looking up from a clipboard as she passed by him. "Many big names?"

Cindy stared at Draydon for just a beat and then screamed at him, "Who the hell cares?"

"Nobody who works for me yells like that," Draydon threatened.

"That suits me fine," Cindy shouted even louder, her face just inches from Draydon's. *"I'm leaving!"*

"You've got one more scene to do."

"No, I don't. I'm too good for this manure pile," she announced, turning away.

She stalked out of the house. And she didn't turn back.

The next candidate for the venting of Cindy's anger was at a firm in downtown Los Angeles called Axel, Wakefield & Co. The next day, she called Eric Evans.

His secretary buzzed his intercom. "There's a Cindy Mantussi on the second line. She says she was a friend of Jeff Morison's and needs to talk to you."

Eric picked up immediately. "Yes?"

"Is this Eric Evans?"

"Yes."

"Do you have a minute?"

"You're a friend of Jeff's. Yes. Absolutely."

"I wasn't going to make this call," Cindy started, pacing the floor of her apartment, "but then I decided I had to. I spent a lot of time with Jeff in the past five weeks, and I heard a lot about you."

"Yes?" Eric stiffened at the tone of her voice.

"I've got a picture of the two of you when you were kids. I stopped him from tearing it up one night." Cindy paused to allow the poison dart to find its mark.

It did. There was a short silence. Eric's face fell.

"I took it away from him because I thought he might be sorry later if he ripped it to shreds. What do you think I ought to do with it now?"

Half-expecting him to hang up, Cindy was surprised by Eric's answer. His voice very somber, very low, he asked, "Would you send it to me?"

"Why should I do anything for you—after you turned your back on him?"

"That's what he told you."

"Yes."

"You may not realize," Eric said slowly, "how easy it is for someone with Jeff's problem to become deceitful."

"You were nowhere around. I could see that for myself."

Eric was silent.

"All right, I'll send you the snapshot," Cindy said, suddenly anxious to end the call. Then she abruptly said goodbye and hung up.

Coming in the wake of his awful scene with Sheilah, Cindy's call hit Eric hard.

Sheilah was off-limits. He could only exonerate himself with her at the expense of making her feel worse and he wouldn't do that. He also knew she would end up hating him just as much or more for telling her about how hard he had tried to rescue Jeff, about how Jeff had sneaked away, and most importantly, about how vehemently Jeff had insisted that under no circumstances did he want Eric reporting to Sheilah. It was no-win all the way.

But this self-proclaimed friend was different. The more he thought about it, the more Eric burned with an angry desire to refute Cindy's accusation. Without realizing it, he made her into a stand-in for Sheilah. He could say to her everything he wanted to say, needed to say, but could not say to Jeff's mother.

Eric instructed his secretary to call Draydon's production office and ask for Cindy Mantussi on the off chance she was someone Jeff had met through work.

The secretary finally commed him with the information that Cindy was an actress who had worked in one of Draydon's movies, but she had been fired. She had the name and number of Cindy's agent—an agent that Eric knew had one of the worst reputations in town.

Once the agent ascertained that Eric was trying to reach Cindy for personal, not business reasons, he told him angrily, "Sure, I'll give you her number. Call her up. And you can tell the little bitch that she not only fucked herself up with Scott Draydon by walking off that set yesterday, she fucked herself up with me."

By the time Eric finally reached Cindy, he was agitated, frustrated, and curious about her.

He got no further than telling Cindy she was wrong about him, wrong about everything, before she hung up on him.

He called back.

"Do you really think it's necessary to be so rude?" he exclaimed. "What in hell is your problem? You don't even know me."

She hung up again.

At that point, Eric decided to put Cindy Mantussi out of his mind. Who was she, after all? One of Draydon's trulls? She was obviously not worth the effort.

But with Sheilah closed off to him, he found Jeff's temperamental friend cropping up in his thoughts again and again.

PART 7
The Mother

THIRTY-EIGHT

SHEILAH LEFT TOWN to spend time with relatives on the East Coast. She was talking about moving out of Los Angeles.

Not a day went by that Ann didn't think long and hard about Sheilah and about Jeff.

Two weeks after Jeff died, Ann found herself focusing her attention on the last pages of a comprehensive production list, looking for Scott Draydon's latest movie.

His pictures were too low-budget to show up in the trade paper production charts. They came and went, beneath the notice of most of Hollywood.

But now Ann was interested in finding out what Jeff had been doing. She found what she was looking for.

Sorority Boys
PROD-DIR-SCR: Scott Draydon
Sexploitation comedy. Freshmen secretly bunk in sorority house. Nudity, graphic sexual situations.

Cast: Tanya Vardeen, Lori Casey, Sal Nava, Eddie "Stick" Glen, Paula Paley, Lucie Ann Bloomberg, Frank Watt, Patti Dee, Cindy Mantussi

Ann looked again. Cindy Mantussi.

What a coincidence, she thought. An actress in town with the same name as her daughter.

363

It wasn't a common name, she told herself, but certainly it wasn't unique either.

It couldn't be her Cindy. It was impossible that Cindy could be here, working as an actress, without her knowledge. Lyla would have told her if Cindy had wanted to become an actress. Lyla simply *couldn't* have ignored the valuable help Ann could provide and let Cindy go to work for a man like Scott Draydon. No. It was plain impossible.

She shuddered.

The combination of Draydon, the report's description of "nudity, graphic sexual situations," and *Cindy Mantussi* could not be ignored.

Of course, it was impossible. But Ann had to be sure. Now.

After weighing the alternatives, Ann decided to call Lyla.

She buzzed her secretary and asked her to hold her calls. Then she dialed the New Jersey number.

Her knees went weak at the weary "H'lo" on the other end of the line. It had been six years since Ann had heard her sister's voice.

"Hello. It's Ann," she said stiffly.

"Ann," Lyla exclaimed. Then, a suspicious, "Is something wrong?"

Ann felt her stomach tighten at the sound of the warm-cold wary voice. It was just like the old days.

"I don't know," she said. "I'm looking at a production list of a sleazy sex comedy called *Sorority Boys*. There's an actress named Cindy Mantussi listed in the cast."

Lyla's response was silence.

"It *is* her, isn't it?" Ann gasped.

"No," Lyla answered sharply. "It couldn't be."

"Is she out here?"

"Cindy in a dirty movie?" cried Lyla. "Don't even say that!"

"Is she out here?" Ann repeated.

There was the slightest hesitation before Lyla replied, "No. She isn't."

Swept by a wave of outrage, Ann cried, "I think you're lying! And if you are—if you let her come out without even telling me—it's despicable. Even if she doesn't want to talk to me, you should have."

"You're wrong." Lyla cut her off. "You don't know what

you're talking about. I thought you were going to leave us alone."

"What the hell do you think I've *been* doing? Cindy is nineteen already! What do you think I can do at this point?"

"I don't want to talk to you," said Lyla. "Not when all you're doing is yelling."

"Fine," Ann replied. "It's never going to work on the phone. I'll be there to see you Sunday."

"Don't come," said Lyla.

"Sunday," said Ann firmly.

Rural mailboxes lined the silent street. Barren trees were etched against nickel gray clouds. According to the weather report, there was a chance of snow. Ann drove her rental car slowly, looking for a house marked 2931, longing to find some warmth at her destination. She was not counting on it.

She finally matched the address to a white two-story frame house near the corner.

Inside, Lyla glanced out the living room window on her way to the stairs and saw a well-groomed woman getting out of a car.

She opened the door without waiting for Ann's knock.

The moment was unlike any of the daydreams Ann had fashioned over the long years she had waited to be reunited with her sister. There was no rushing into each other's arms, no calling out each other's names. Instead, Lyla, standing behind an invisible wall of fear, envy, and mistrust, said coldly, "Well, come in."

At thirty-six, Lyla looked easily ten, perhaps fifteen years older. Her forehead was lined with strain, and there were dark patches under her eyes, accentuated by gray-framed glasses.

She had begun a small effort to make herself presentable in anticipation of Ann's arrival but had quit halfway into the enterprise. Although she wore her best pant suit, her face was without makeup and her graying hair was limp and straight, held back by a hot pink elastic band.

In a hooded suede and sheepskin coat, brown leather pants and bulky cream sweater, Ann looked stunningly chic by contrast.

Ann also looked determined.

Lyla felt immediately intimidated.

Ann walked in. Lyla closed the door. They stood, at odds, just inside.

"I guess we're dispensing with the amenities, so I'll get right to the reason I'm here," Ann began, masking her disappointment with a clipped businesslike tone. She pulled the production list page from her bag and brandished it in front of Lyla. "I've got to know if this Cindy is our Cindy."

Lyla frowned at her and mumbled, *"Our* Cindy?"

"That is *not* the point."

Ann glanced around the small living room, scarcely seeing the worn, functional furnishings, the cheap Keene print hung over the brown sofa. She felt the emptiness in the room, the sense of absence. "She's gone, isn't she?"

"Go back to your job," Lyla answered darkly. "Go back where you belong. You don't have to worry about us."

Ann shook her head adamantly, took off her coat, went to the sofa, and sat down. "I'm not going anywhere."

Lyla stood rooted obdurately by the door for several seconds before finally moving to stand planted in front of Ann, arms folded.

"I've looked into this movie," said Ann. "It's not as bad as I initially feared, but it's not good either. If Cindy's involved in schlock like this, she's on a wrong track."

"She wouldn't do anything indecent," Lyla insisted angrily.

Ann felt her hackles rise at Lyla's priggish tone; with an effort at keeping her temper, she tried to clarify matters.

"I'm told that the filmmaker wants to cash in on the youth comedy boom and capitalize on the teen market, so he's after an 'R' rating, which would be a first for him."

Lyla cut her off, impatiently shaking her head. "What do you mean?"

Ann sighed painfully. "It'll either get an 'X' or a very hard 'R.' It's one of those junky pictures about panting college boys. Supposedly there's a beach party scene where all the girls go topless, and it has some pretty heavy bedroom stuff in it involving the principals."

At that, Lyla gave a low moan and sank into a chair.

"Lyla," Ann said, her voice dropping to a low, more sympathetic tone, "Cindy isn't one of the principals. It couldn't be anywhere near as bad as what we used to see in Istanbul."

"I don't know what you're talking about." Lyla sniffed, wiping her eyes.

Surprised, Ann said, "At Huriyah."

Lyla shook her head. "I don't remember any of that."

Something in Ann's explanation and in Lyla's strange reaction broke through the wall of stiffness that had separated them. The charged atmosphere started to loosen, becoming more free and flowing. Ann watched as Lyla tried to regain her composure.

"It doesn't have to hurt her, not in this day and age, especially if she can get into something better right away," Ann said, trying to be reassuring. "Look, Sylvester Stallone and Adrienne Barbeau are just two actors who actually did stag films before they became famous."

"Be quiet," Lyla exclaimed.

"I'm trying to tell you, it isn't that bad! And it's certainly not the end of the world."

"Not to you," Lyla cried. "Oh—if Joe finds out!"

At that, Ann's patience disintegrated. She felt her body tighten with indignation.

"All this time," she said, standing angrily, "all this time, if you'd only told me she was out there, I could at least have seen that she got a good legitimate agent. But you wouldn't even do that. Not for my sake, but for hers. And now all you can think about is 'what if Joe finds out'."

"Don't you dare criticize me," Lyla answered, standing also, slicing each word with a short staccato beat. "And don't you *dare* criticize Joe. You don't know a thing about what we've gone through."

"That's what *you* wanted—not me. I've been playing guessing games for nineteen years. And one of the few clues you've given me about your life is the fear that comes into your voice every time you mention Joe's name."

Lyla nodded toward the stairs. "Come with me," she beckoned.

She led Ann up the bare wooden steps and down the hallway to a closed door. "This is her room," she said as she opened it.

Ann walked in, her anger abruptly overcome by a sense of awe. In this simple room with its pale daffodil wallpaper, its ruffled chintz bedspread, its filmy curtains that breathed in and out with the breeze from the open window—in this room her baby had grown from a child into an adult.

"See that chest?" Lyla said, pointing to the varnished bureau standing against the far wall. "See that table?" she asked, gesturing toward the small white vanity table with an aged round mirror hung above it. "Joe built those with his own two hands."

Lyla marched to the closet and flung open the door. "This used to be packed—packed—with clothes, all bought with his hard-earned money. Look around this room. The girl who lived here never wanted for anything. That's a good father. He was a good father!"

Ann failed to catch Lyla's too-defensive attitude.

She stood at the vanity table, staring down at a photograph stuck into the rim of the mirror: a buxom blond prom princess on the arm of a grinning boy in a rented tux.

Without thinking, Ann took the picture off the mirror.

Cute, appealing, bubbly—such were the brand of adjectives that belonged to Cindy, an ideal girl to go with a cotton-candy pink Corvette.

The resemblance to Hank Evans was stronger than it had been when Cindy was a child—not noticeable to anyone who didn't know to look for it, but present nevertheless. Ann chose to ignore it.

Lyla came to stand beside Ann. Her voice at last took on a hint of normalcy.

"Pretty, isn't she?"

"Yes," Ann said. "Very."

"That was a happy night for her."

Ann's eyes met Lyla's, and she caught a flicker of the old warmth.

In a choked, halting voice, Ann said, "She looks happy." She held the picture up. "You have a lot to be proud of, Lyla, being her mother."

Lyla stared at her.

Ann nodded. "I've never tried to deny you that."

A few seconds passed. Lyla's face twisted with emotion.

"I'm sorry," she mouthed soundlessly. Then, barely audibly, she added, "I know I've been bad to you. God forgive me—I was so afraid you'd come back and try to take her away from me!"

"I know," Ann murmured.

There was a long, painful pause, and then suddenly, helplessly, Lyla held out her arms.

Ann accepted the hug, tears welling in her eyes.

"I'm sorry," Lyla repeated brokenly. "You have every reason to hate me."

"I did ... so many times. But I couldn't erase all those years; I couldn't erase all you did for me in New York," Ann half-whispered, half-cried into Lyla's shoulder.

They held each other for a long moment, anger and bitterness falling away with their tears. Not all of it, of course, and there was no telling whether the clearing would last. But for now, at least, it was a balm.

Lyla finally drew away. "Oh, Ann—I've done so many things wrong. But if you go to her now, I'll lose her forever. I know it."

Ann tilted her head, at once feeling a fresh pang. "Why?"

"You have everything she dreams about; you're a famous Hollywood success. Look at you and look at me," Lyla added, glancing down at her dowdy clothes. "She already hates me. How could I ever compete with you?"

"Do you really think she could so totally change her mind about wanting to see me after all these years?" Ann asked in a gently scoffing tone, failing to grasp the truth behind Lyla's words—unable to catch on to any clue that fell behind the blind spot she had in relation to her sister and daughter.

"I'd love it if she did want to see me," Ann went on, "but what you're saying just doesn't make sense. Besides, no matter what happens, you raised her, you're her mother. Nobody can ever take that away from you. And just because she went away doesn't mean she's a bad person. It doesn't mean she doesn't love you. It's a hard time, but it's not the end. You shouldn't lose hope."

Lyla sank onto the bed with an expression of terrible weariness.

"I don't know," she said, gazing at the floor. She took a deep, ragged breath.

"She always was a real handful—always seemed on the edge of bustin' out somehow, even when she was little. Joe ... well, he could never understand why he couldn't control her."

Ann moved closer without saying a word, hardly daring to believe that at last Lyla was going to reveal some of the longed-for details of Cindy's childhood.

"Not that she was bad," Lyla added quickly, glancing up. "She just got into things. Other girls played with dolls—

Cindy and her friends made a parachute from sheets so she could jump off the roof of the school."

Ann laughed, shaking her head and wiping off some of the mascara that now streaked her face. "Really?"

"Yeah, when she was ten. Some kind of crazy dare. What do you do with a kid who'll do something like that—a *girl* who'll do something like that? I used to say she was the original leap-before-you-look kid."

She chuckled, then her face clouded over. "Maybe we were too strict with her, maybe not strict enough. I don't know. . ."

Lyla paused, smoothing the already-smooth bedspread. "She was grounded through most of her senior year. Still, she would sneak out at night and go off with her friends. Joe would catch her coming in at one, two o'clock in the morning, and he'd belt her, but she'd do it again."

Ann swallowed hard and nodded, just nodded, because she was so anxious to hear—whether it was Lyla's case for the defense or her confession, or both.

"She started to become, you know, defiant. And Joe—he was so afraid that she—"

Lyla stopped herself from divulging his "bad seed" diatribe.

"Well, he was afraid of history repeating itself," she said, "afraid of her getting in trouble. He never really believed what I told him about . . . you know."

Ann smiled slightly. Twenty years later, and Lyla was still using their old way of referring to the unspeakable.

"Maybe he reacted too strong when she wanted to go out on dates, when boys started showing up around here. See that lock on the door? It locks from outside. It was like, he ran out of ideas. He was frustrated. He couldn't handle her. The more he punished, the more she wanted to go her own way. So, to keep her from sneaking out at night, he locked her in.

"I'd hear her from downstairs, walking up and down, up and down. And I thought, 'This is no good. When she gets the chance, she's going to run.'"

"And she did," Ann said quietly.

Lyla nodded.

"Joe was a good father," she insisted again. "She was just too much for him. But it was me, too. I made ... . I made some big mistakes."

Ann sighed heavily. "Have you talked to her?"

"Oh, yes," Lyla replied—much too quickly, Ann noticed. "She's living with one of her girlfriends."

"Do you know where?"

"An apartment in Hollywood. That's all I know."

"I have her agent's number. I'll give it to you when we go back downstairs," Ann said. Lyla looked up sharply, alarmed.

"I felt pretty sure it was Cindy, Lyla, but I didn't want to make any more calls without talking to you."

"You're not going to call her?" Lyla cried, standing up.

Ann slammed her hand against the bureau top in a burst of frustration. "You've got to let me do *some*thing! Why don't you talk to her, try to get her at least to let me offer her the benefit of what I know and what I can do for her? She's already there. It's too late to wish she weren't. Come to L.A. with me. We should do this together."

"No. She's already mixed up. I mean—all right, it was a mistake, not telling her before. But I can't do it now."

"Not telling her what?" Ann asked. The question resounded in the quiet room.

Then, after a few seconds, Ann let out her breath slowly. "Oh, Lyla. Oh, my God. Didn't you . . . didn't you tell her she's adopted?"

Lyla said nothing.

"I don't believe this," Ann cried in anguish. "She has a right to know! How could you not have realized that?"

Lyla stared at her mutely.

"And you told me she didn't want to see me? How could you?"

"You can't tell her now."

"We *have* to."

"Not now," Lyla begged feebly. "Not until she's out of this trouble. She'd go all to pieces."

Ann went to the open window and gazed out, thinking. Lyla watched her fearfully.

At last she came toward Lyla, sighing. "Okay. For now, I'll just have to make contact with her as her aunt."

Lyla turned and walked out, shaking her head.

"Why not?" Ann called after her sister as she followed her back to the living room. "Why not, Lyla? Why not?"

She paused in shock. "Are you telling me she doesn't even know I exist?"

Halfway into the living room, Lyla stopped and turned.

She put her hands over her ears as Ann shouted, "You didn't give her any of the presents I sent? None of the letters? Nothing?"

"No," Lyla screamed.

"That was Joe's idea, wasn't it?" Ann cried. "And you just went along with it, didn't you?"

Lyla pressed her fingertips on her temples. "My head. My head! I need an aspirin."

Ann followed Lyla into the kitchen and watched as she took a bottle of Scotch from a cabinet. "You want some?"

"No."

Ann moved beside her sister and dropped her hand on the countertop like a lead weight.

"You did it. You hid them yourself."

In the middle of her reach for a glass, Lyla's body suddenly sagged. Ann groaned at the tacit yes.

"Why?" she demanded.

"I didn't want . . . to upset Joe."

Lyla wiped her eyes and glanced nervously at Ann, expecting another explosion. But Ann just sat down at the kitchen table, her head in her hands.

"I . . ." Lyla stepped forward, then stopped.

"I'll do it through other people if I can't go to Cindy directly." Ann spoke not to Lyla, but to the wall, the air, the world in general. She did not even look at her sister.

"I'll make sure my name is left out of it, at least at first. What agent is especially good with young talent? Naomi. Yes, that's the priority—getting Cindy away from that sleazy character who's handling her now.

"It won't be simple, going through intermediaries," nodded Ann, "but I'll make it work."

"I don't want you to make it work," Lyla insisted, her voice constricted by sobs. She moved deliberately into Ann's line of vision. "I don't want it to work at all. I want Cindy to forget about Hollywood and come back where she belongs and have a normal life!"

Ann gave Lyla such a withering glare that her sister stepped backward.

"Locked in her room?" she asked. "Don't kid yourself."

Ann arose and returned to the living room, put on her coat, and grabbed her shoulder bag. She searched through the purse a moment, as Lyla stood by in mute fury, then pulled out the sheet with the name and number she had promised to give Lyla earlier and set it on a lamp table.

"I'll call and tell you how it goes," she said.

"I hate what you're doing," Lyla cried, tears running down her cheeks.

"I won't stand by and do nothing—and let Cindy go through the kind of purgatory I went through," Ann angrily replied. With that, she was on her way out the door.

"Ann," Lyla called after her. Ann looked back. Lyla was standing on the porch with her hands clenched in front of her, "Let me know..."

"I will," Ann promised, relenting a bit. "I'll call you."

Less than an hour later, Ann was in Sentinel Studios' Manhattan executive quarters, on the phone to the Coast.

Less than an hour after that, Cindy Mantussi received a surprising phone call from personal representative Naomi Gold.

By six o'clock, Los Angeles time, Cindy and some of her acquaintances were uncorking a bottle of champagne to celebrate her astounding good fortune in being singled out by a "genuine, honest-to-God major-league agent."

Before the week was out, Cindy was being interviewed by the casting director for an action-comedy film at Sentinel Studios.

The following Monday, her incredible burst of luck continued with a call-back on the part. By Wednesday, Cindy was selected as one of four asked to read for the film's director, its star—and the president of the studio.

THIRTY-NINE

〰〰

ON THE DAY of Cindy's scheduled appearance, Ann walked into her office equipped with less than an hour's sleep, her usual strict daily regimen already obliterated.

She had lain awake during the night, her mind riveted on that moment when she would see her child for the first time in more than nineteen years, her mind filled with questions about the course she had set for Cindy and herself.

David had been outraged by Lyla's actions, outspoken in his opinion that Ann must tell Cindy the truth.

They had had a major quarrel over the way Ann had decided to handle the situation. A truce had followed, but David still maintained that Ann was placing herself in an impossible position. She didn't want to hear anymore about it. She wanted solace, not an argument, and she found she was angry at him for disagreeing with her.

David had left at five-thirty, offering reassuring words.

By six-thirty, when Ann normally began her morning workout, she was dozing fitfully in her bentwood rocker, the sounds of the morning news show keeping her thoughts temporarily at bay.

At eight, when she was normally in the middle of reading the morning papers and the trades, Ann was changing clothes time and again, desperately anxious to make the right appearance at the meeting—not too stiff, not too flashy, not too ostentatious, too square, too young or too old.

Each outfit she had tried pleased her less than the one before. She finally settled on an emerald green wool Jerry Silverman suit.

And all the while she had worried: What would she say to Cindy? How would Cindy respond? How would the meeting go? Was Cindy up to a casting interview conducted by an array of industry heavyweights? Would she cave in? Would she bomb? Would the director hurt Cindy's feelings? *By God*, Ann had thought, *I'll kill him if he gets bitchy with her!*

She would never forgive herself if it backfired—if she had set Cindy up for embarrassment.

By nine o'clock, when Ann padded past her secretary's desk, she was already drawing on her greatest resource—the power of her will—simply to face the basic tasks of the day.

Please, God, don't let there be a crisis, she begged.

Somehow, she kept her mind focused on work during a string of phone calls and a protracted meeting with the head of the legal department. Somehow, she surmounted a business lunch with manager-cum-producer Bernie Brillstein regarding the Dan Aykroyd–Bill Murray caper movie being developed at Sentinel.

Finally, it was three o'clock. Ann walked through the executive building and out past the guard station with almost no awareness of her surroundings. She found herself hyperventilating en route to the bungalow that housed the production headquarters for *The Comeback Kid*, the action-comedy for which she had arranged Cindy's test; she had to stop twice to calm her nerves.

The casting office consisted of two rooms, a small waiting area and a spacious inner office. Neither room bore any hint of the luxury in Ann's building. Here, the atmosphere was strictly boiler room, with cartons of photos and papers piled on table tops, the floor, under the coffee table. Hopefuls entered through door A, were summoned in for their meetings, and then were shown out through door B, a circuit that minimized post-meeting contact between contenders. It was not so different from the setup used by psychiatrists.

Ann came in through door B, trying to forget, for the next few minutes, that Cindy was at that moment in room A waiting.

The movie's director and the star, a hip young New York comic named Joey Donatello, were seated at the coffee table, chatting, while the casting director completed a phone call at his desk. Four eight-by-ten glossies of *The Comeback Kid* cast as it stood so far had been affixed to the wall behind him.

"Uh oh, the president," cried Donatello, catching sight of Ann. "Quick," he called out in mock panic. "Put away the drugs."

The director took her hand and gave her a peck on the cheek. "Glad you could make it down," he said smoothly.

"I'm glad you don't mind," she answered with equal grace.

In truth, the director viewed a recommendation from the front office as a nuisance. Ann, of course, was aware of that —just as she was aware that her appearance at a minor casting session had already excited a considerable amount of unwelcome curiosity.

Ann knew the director would watch Cindy politely, find something nice to say, then reject her as gracefully as possible, probably using one of the kiss-up kiss-offs Ann knew so well:

"She's too classy-looking for this part . . ."

". . . naturally radiates such a great intelligence, it's too bad we're not looking for that brainy type . . ."

Based on her years of both polite and impolite rejections, Ann knew better than to expect anything else for Cindy at this early phase in her career, and she firmly believed it would be against Cindy's better interests to push her into something for which she was unprepared.

All she expected of this session was an opening, an excuse —an introduction to her daughter.

The producer entered the room, followed by several others. Ann greeted them without registering who they were. The casting director, finally off the phone, approached her.

"Are you the one who found Cindy Mantussi?"

It was more shmooze, more game-playing. Obviously, Ann wouldn't have been there if she had no interest. The room quieted as people stopped talking to listen to her response.

"I've heard some good feedback on her," Ann replied carefully, neutrally. "But I've never seen her myself."

He nodded. "Interesting. Well, I'm impressed."

Was he going to try to say that he had called Cindy back based on merit? Ann waited to hear more, but at that moment, his assistant appeared at door A.

"Ready for the next one?"

The director nodded. "Let's do it."

Ann took a seat on the couch. She looked down at the notepad in her hands and found the top page half-limp from her sweating palms. She was suddenly so gripped by nervousness that she was afraid even to glance at those surrounding her. She made a pretense of note-taking, scribbling meaningless words on the pad. When she did look up, Donatello was assuming a casual bored position on the far end of the couch.

To him, Cindy Mantussi was merely the third actress they were seeing that day for a small supporting role.

He's not going to help her, Ann realized grimly. *He's going to be a punk.*

"Cindy?" the casting director was saying. "Come on in."

Ann held her breath as her daughter walked into the room. Her brisk stride, her highly mobile face, her enthusiastic smile—everything about her gave an instant impression of vitality. Ann's heart drummed wildly against her chest, blood pounded in her ears. Her eyes were glued on Cindy.

She could feel her cheeks begin to burn, a smile burst into place as the casting director introduced Cindy to the assembled group. Out of the corner of her eye, Ann noticed Donatello looking at her quizzically. She doused the smile at once.

"Of course you recognize Joey," said the casting director.

Cindy turned in their direction.

"Of course." Cindy beamed. Donatello raised his hand briefly, making no move to stand.

"Thank you for being here," she told him in a clear, light voice.

Ann felt an enormous sense of pride surge through her at the way Cindy was acquitting herself.

She was a shade more sophisticated than Ann had expected, a shade less rough around the edges. Her blond hair was longer, darker, better cut than in the prom picture. The color now was the work of a good professional. Her clothes, too, showed that Cindy had learned the nuances of California casual style. She wore a rose alpaca dolman-sleeved sweater that dropped to her thighs, tight designer jeans, and fringed knee-length flat boots.

They were all borrowed.

Ann could hardly hear the casting director say her name through the roaring in her ears. Cindy was looking at Ann, then looking harder, reacting in confusion to the emotion she saw in Ann's eyes.

"It's a privilege to meet you," she said. The note of per-
plexity in her voice and the slight tilt of her head made it clear
she was wondering, had they met somewhere? Did Ann think
she was someone else?

Ann nodded and smiled, unable—afraid—to speak.

The casting director showed Cindy to a chair near the far
wall: the hot seat.

"Why don't you tell us a little about yourself?" he
prompted her as he sat down.

"Sure," Cindy began. She settled herself and smiled but
said nothing for several seconds—a deliberate theatrical pause
that succeeded in rounding up stray attention.

Ann's grip on her notebook tightened as she watched in
surprise.

"You already know my name. My age is nineteen," Cindy
chirped. "I was born in New York City, where my dad owned
an Italian deli, and, I later learned, ran sort of a small, intimate numbers business on the side. Certain people thought he
wasn't well organized, and so when I was ten, I suddenly
found myself living in Jersey, and Dad was embarking on a
new career as a laborer..."

Ann leaned forward. She was on the very edge of her seat,
rapt. Was she imagining things, or did Cindy really have the
presence Ann was seeing?

She was putting on a show, a minimonologue, bringing to
life a home environment in which the unnamed Joe Mantussi
became a larger-than-life comic character who roared mala-
propisms, ordering Cindy to "Eat, eat, eat! You wanna get
analgesic?"

After flinging questions at Cindy, the director and Donatello found themselves answering questions Cindy put to
them.

Laughter riffled through the group more than once.

Why, Ann wondered, had she expected Cindy to act like a
shy schoolgirl? She was behaving like an actress-comedienne
—pumped up for a performance, going full-force after the
character, mixing truth and fiction, trying to grab her audience
fast and get the message across that she was capable of playing Donatello's zany sister in their movie.

She seemed to know by instinct that it didn't matter
whether the group scrutinizing her became acquainted with the

real Cindy Mantussi; it mattered that she captured their interest, kept them entertained, made an impact.

She was doing more than Ann expected. Much more.

After a few minutes of bantering, Cindy was joined by Donatello for a reading of a brother-sister argument out of the *Comeback Kid* script. His boredom a memory, the actor spared nothing in his dialogue with Cindy. He was now on her side, pitching his words hard enough, fast enough, for Cindy to bat them back like a winner.

". . . One phone number," he pleaded. "Is that so much to ask?"

"Yes," Cindy countered. "She's my *friend*."

He grinned. "So do her a favor."

"Haven't you gone through enough of my friends?" she whined. "Haven't you embarrassed me enough?"

"Me embarrass you? You with magenta in your hair?"

"You with your system!"

"System?"

"Three ounces of Wild Meadow cologne, one long-stemmed rose, and then," Cindy leaned forward with a wicked smile as her voice dropped, "the lobster dinner at your place."

When they finished the scene, Donatello took Cindy's shoulders, bumped his forehead into hers with a laugh, and told her, "Beautiful. Good work."

The director nodded. "Very nice."

"We'll let you know," the casting director informed Cindy.

Cindy was headed toward door B when Ann stopped her and said, somewhat breathlessly, "You're really good!"

At that moment, Ann wouldn't have given a damn about the onlookers' curious expressions, even had she noticed them.

"Thank you," Cindy replied.

Her tryout completed, the job done, Cindy was already coming down from her interview personality. Suddenly, she seemed less sure of herself, softer, and for the first time a bit overwhelmed. She took a deep breath that carried the message "Thank God it's over" as clearly as if she had said the words.

"We have an improvisational workshop that meets here on the lot four nights a week," Ann said, forcing herself into a businesslike posture. "I think it would be very good for you. If you come by my office, my secretary or I will give you the details."

"You don't know how much that means to me," Cindy said, wide-eyed. "I mean, especially coming from you."

Gooseflesh rising on her arms, Ann nodded in response.

"I still have the *People* magazine story about you from last year," Cindy continued. "It's one of the things I like to read when I need a boost. Really."

They both blushed.

"I . . . ah . . . that's wonderful," Ann fumbled for words, ". . . to think that might have some value to you."

You're clutching! she warned herself.

"I know how gloomy things can get when you're out doing the rounds—even though I never was much of an actress." Ann fell back on a tired line of hers in sheer desperation for something casual to say. "That's one of the few things that everyone in this town has ever agreed on—that and *Gone with the Wind*."

"That can't be true," Cindy said quickly.

"I wasn't fishing for kind words." Ann smiled. "The post-mortem on my acting career was done a million years ago."

It was abruptly apparent that Ann had reached the limit of conversation in this bizarre, constrained situation.

"Please come by and talk to me about the workshop."

"I will. Thank you again," said Cindy.

And then she happily hurried out the door, Ann smiling after her.

When she was gone, it seemed to Ann as if suddenly a light had been switched off, and when it came back on, everyone else reappeared.

"I want that girl," Donatello announced. "I like her style. She's fast on her feet. She had *me* breaking up."

"She comes across very nicely on film," said the casting director, sitting back in his chair. He glanced at Ann with a Cheshire Cat smile.

"Well, then, I don't see any point in going any further," the director said. He looked at Donatello. "It's the chemistry between the two of you that excites me the most. You play off each other fantastically."

"Yeah," the comic agreed. "She really hit me," he pounded his chest, "right there in the kid sister department."

"Perfect," said the casting director. He turned to Ann, grinning. "Obviously you don't have any objections."

Ann shook her head woodenly. This was not how her plan went. This was impossible.

"I'd love to know where you heard about her," the casting director persisted. "And don't tell me *Sorority Boys*. I looked at some footage. She fills out the screen like gangbusters, but let's face it, there was no acting required."

"She's," Ann hesitated, "the daughter of someone I knew a long time ago."

FORTY

∽⌒∾⌒∾

IT WAS THE beginning of the third week of production on *The Comeback Kid*. Shooting was taking place on the section of Sentinel's back lot known as "Small Town, USA, Street."

The sequence called for Joey Donatello to be flung over a parked car by a disgruntled linebacker. He would struggle to his feet, take a few steps, and collapse again—onto the back of a flatbed truck. The truck would drive off toward points unknown with Donatello's character unconscious in back. Cindy was to rush out into the street in time to yell, "Hey! Would you quit fooling around?"

The actual staged fight had already been lensed. They were just beginning the shot of Donatello struggling to his feet when the producer's assistant moved toward the setup accompanied by a noticeably handsome visitor, a young man with the freshly minted polish of the new-breed executive. His hair was short, casual, and well-cut, his suit beautifully tailored. The boldly honed features of his tanned face were highlighted by a lively spark in his dark brown eyes and softened by an engaging, lazy sort of smile.

But Eric Evans's smile faded as he neared the film site.

"Well, here it is," the producer's assistant informed him as they joined a handful of onlookers clustered on the green behind the camera setup. "Cindy's a real sweetheart," he added. "We're all crazy about her."

Eric nodded noncommittally.

They watched a take of the scene—ruined when Donatello started sliding off the truck bed and grabbed for a hold.

During the lull, as the crew tried to figure out how to keep it from happening again, the producer's assistant led his guest toward Cindy. She was resplendent in full zany sister regalia: a pink baseball shirt, red spandex pants, bubble-gum pink streaks in her hair.

"Do you have a second?" the assistant asked.

"Sure," Cindy replied. She looked at Eric and her gaze locked on him. A flustered smile came to her lips.

"Cindy, this is Eric Evans. He wanted to meet you."

At the mention of his name, Cindy's smile died abruptly.

"I would have called you back, but I thought you'd probably hang up again," Eric said coolly.

The assistant backed away, mumbling, "I guess you know each other." Neither Cindy nor Eric seemed to hear.

"That was good thinking on your part," Cindy snapped. "I would have."

"You didn't even allow me to finish explaining."

"Boy, you're really something," Cindy interrupted, shaking her head. "I can't believe you came all the way out here. You must feel awfully guilty."

Tight-lipped, Eric responded, "No, not guilty. Angry."

"Angry?" Cindy exploded.

"My only interest is in setting the record straight, and then, believe me, I'll be more than happy to leave you alone.

"The fact of the matter is, I spent years trying to get Jeff to help himself. The last time I did, he snuck out of the hospital after his second day. That was last August."

Stunned and chastened, Cindy listened as Eric went on heatedly, "I tried playing bodyguard twenty-four hours a day. I tried a lot of things. Suffice it to say, none of them worked. And when he got around to ordering me out of his life for about the tenth time, I did give up. And even though I feel certain that I couldn't have stopped Jeff—that nobody could have—I will always regret that I quit trying.

"But to hear someone who knew Jeff all of five weeks accuse me of cutting him off infuriates me. I couldn't let it go by."

Silence prevailed for several moments, then, moving toward him, shaking her head, palms upraised, Cindy said, "I had no idea. He was angry and I . . . well, I just accepted . . . I don't know what to say . . . I apologize."

Seeing that she believed him, Eric felt a surge of relief. His anger spent, he sighed.

"I have no excuses, except . . ." Cindy stopped, shook her head. "I have no excuses. I'm sorry."

"Well, I know I was in shock, and you must have been hit especially hard if you and Jeff were"—Eric shrugged, looking for the right word—"close."

"I was just a friend, or . . . I don't know what you'd call it. I really felt sorry for him. But I was just there listening."

Eric nodded, understanding all too well. "It's a shame you never got to know him at his best. He was . . ."

"Special."

"Yes."

"I really am sorry," Cindy said again. "Can you possibly just forget I called? Wipe it out?"

"All right. Consider it done," Eric replied.

He looked around the set. The crew was almost ready for the next take. His tone changed, and he smiled a little, clearly wanting to leave on a more sociable note.

"This is quite a step up from Scott Draydon. You must really be doing all right for yourself."

"I'm very glad to be here," Cindy acknowledged.

"Well, I'll be sure to see the movie when it comes out."

"Thanks. Stay if you like," she added. "It's a fun scene."

After innumerable hours on his father's film sets, seeing endlessly repetitive, tedious action, the idea of watching movies being made had long ago lost its allure for Eric. But to his surprise, he realized there was nothing he would rather do just then than accept Cindy's invitation.

She was not at all like the person Eric had expected after the abortive phone conversations. He had envisioned another of the standard starlets he had known, dated, and slept with— pretty but pretty interchangeable with a thousand others.

He couldn't imagine Cindy being interchangeable with anyone.

The assistant director yelled "quiet," action began, and Eric could barely keep from laughing aloud when the truck rambled away and an affronted Cindy stood shouting after it. He quickly decided that she was the magic ingredient that saved a hopelessly tired slapstick bit.

"What did you think?" Cindy asked him brightly when they had finished the shot. "Did you like it?"

"I liked *you*," he replied. "You're very funny."

"Thanks!" She beamed. "Listen, would it have been funnier if there'd been tomatoes in the truck, do you think?"

Soon Eric found himself involved in the tomato debate that had been raging within the company.

It was outrageous and very silly, and he hadn't enjoyed himself so much in . . . Eric couldn't remember how long.

He stayed and stayed, finding himself powerfully attracted to Cindy. He was aware that she was more than mildly attracted to him, too.

What an interesting person she was, he thought, recalling his conversations with Scott Draydon's complaining assistant and with Cindy's irate agent, then the assertion that everyone in *this* company was crazy about Cindy. He was intrigued by the fact that she had marched off a Scott Draydon picture, only to have next turned up doing a first-class feature at one of the majors. How talented she was, he thought, and so wonderfully full of life! She had been good to Jeff; that meant a lot. And her looks, well . . . Eric's grin widened.

When the break was called, Eric joined Cindy and a gang from the *Comeback* company for a quick, loud commissary lunch heavy on jokes, industry chatter, and gossip.

The lunch was soon to become a topic of gossip itself.

To begin with, no one present could help but notice that Eric ignored an empty space on the side of the booth opposite Cindy and instead wedged a chair next to her. Then there were his frequent retreats from the general conversation to concentrate his questions on her.

"I'm assuming you don't always wear your hair like this," he said, reaching to touch a few pink strands.

She stared at him a moment, feigning a hurt expression. "You don't like it?"

He chuckled, refusing to be taken in. "Did I say that? It's thought-provoking."

"Really? What thought is that?" she asked with a laugh.

He answered with just a look. Cindy glanced away blushing. The air around them was charged.

Though Eric continued to listen, to laugh, to talk with the group, it was apparent that his mind was focused on Cindy.

Only when someone asked Eric about his father did Cindy's enthusiasm seem to wane. She became suddenly subdued, as if she had forgotten momentarily just who Eric was. Reminded, she began to act overly cautious and strained.

Eric noticed the difference, as did some of the others.

Everyone in the group also noticed that when the check came, Eric picked it up quickly, tossed some bills on the table, then rose and said to Cindy, "I'll walk you back"—thus abruptly disposing of the others' company.

"You're not talking," Eric noted irritatedly as he and Cindy sauntered back through the crowded, bustling lot toward Small Town Street.

"Thank you for lunch," she said.

" 'Thank you for lunch'?" he repeated. "That's all?"

"I don't know what else to say."

He sighed. "You got quiet when we started talking about my father."

"Well . . ." Cindy shrugged, embarrassed. "It's kind of . . . well . . . overwhelming, I guess."

"Do you think you can get over that?" he asked stiffly.

She nodded.

"Good. I'd like to take you out."

What do you like? What do you love? What are your fears, your dreams, your favorite ways to spend a Sunday afternoon? Do you read poetry? What do you expect to get if you latch on to this brass ring you're after? I want to know your views on world affairs and love affairs and Shakespeare and Gloria Steinem. Are you a chocoholic, workaholic, or occasional compulsive shopper . . . like me?

I wanted to take your hands and tell you, "I'll do anything for you! Tell me everything, anything you want to tell me— important things, frivolous things. I'll listen as long as you'll talk. Where does it hurt? Who do you love? I've been waiting to hear your voice for nineteen years."

And I've wanted to explain.

For most of your life, I could have told you all the sound and important reasons I left you. Now I can't make sense of them.

But even though I left you, I've wanted you to know, you never left me.

You were with me in the laughter of all children. I heard you between every note of every lullaby and every Christmas carol. You were there in the silence of each night and there in

*every quick, bright movement of sunlight dancing with the
wind through the trees outside my window.*

*You were there, in so many dreams. Today I wanted to tell
you, you exceeded them all . . .*

Ann put down her pen, folded the pages on which she had
poured out her thoughts, and shoved the stationery into a
drawer of her cherry wood desk. The words were for her eyes
only, an attempt to release some of the frustration gnawing at
her insides.

She really had no time for such self-indulgence. She arose
with a sigh and quick-marched to her bedroom, flinging off
the terrycloth robe she was wearing and reaching for the evening gown draped on the bed. David was due in five minutes.
It was the opening night of *Honest, George!* at L.A.'s Schubert theater, and, as Sentinel had secured film and video rights
to the Broadway musical on Ann's say-so, her presence was a
must.

A short time later, seated beside David in the hired limousine, she exultantly recounted her latest encounter with Cindy.

"She is delicious to watch. She can go from snappy, bitchy
dialogue to Judy Holliday scrambled just like that!" Ann
snapped her fingers. "Did I tell you the director already has
her in mind for another project?"

David laughed. "You can tell me again."

"I'm babbling," Ann realized.

"You're tired," he noted, fumbling with the bow tie of his
tuxedo.

Ann leaned over and adjusted it for him. "A little," she
admitted.

A moment later, he caught a clear look at her as the car
passed under a street lamp. The light glittered over the black
sequined jacket of her Valentino gown. She was crumpled
against the seat, eyes closed, head tilted back—sexy, fabulous, exhausted.

In the weeks since she had met Cindy, Ann had been running on such high emotion it had been affecting her concen-
tration, her work. To compensate, she had added hours to
what had already been an impossible schedule.

Four hours of sleep a night was now a luxury.

"It's so strange, so strange to go down to the set," she
murmured.

David waited for her to continue. When she didn't, he asked, "Why is it strange?"

"Well, she likes me—but she's curious, maybe even suspicious. Who could blame her? She must be wondering, 'Why is this total stranger so interested in me? What's with you, lady?'"

"Has she said or done anything in particular that makes you think she feels that way?"

"Well . . . no. I don't know. Maybe I just think she ought to be suspicious."

"Frankly, it's hard for me to imagine her being suspicious of someone who's the object of her hero worship."

"That brings up another difficulty. How can you get close to someone who thinks of you as part of Mount Rushmore? I can't tell you how clumsy I felt trying to make small talk. She's . . . it's hard to explain."

"You're the big boss to her, Ann. You're Lee Iaccoca wandering around the assembly line."

"I may be making her feel nervous. I made a point of talking to the rest of the cast so it wouldn't seem so obvious —this afternoon instead of Cindy I wound up with Joey Donatello all revved up to be my new best friend."

David shook his head, chuckling. "Just what we need."

"It is awkward. But she's only on the picture a few more days, then a few at the end of production. After that I'll have to find a new excuse to see her. I can't just interject myself into her life for no good reason."

The gray stretch limo rounded the corner from Santa Monica to Avenue of the Stars.

"I know you don't want to hear this," said David, "but the longer you go along with this sham, the more excuses you create, the more Cindy will resent your part in it when she does find out—which inevitably she will."

On their left, traffic moved in laggard lines toward the entrance of the massive underground parking structure below the theater. Limousines lined the loading zone fronting the mall, discharging first-nighters before the box office. There were the requisite klieg lights. There were huge red, white, and blue banners emblazoned with *Honest, George!* and a leering cartoon of George Washington. Other cars waited to swing around the blue fountain in the street's center parkway.

Ann gestured toward the arching gold-lit façade of the Century Plaza, and instructed the driver, "Please make a right at the corner."

The car weaved into the right lane, and as soon as the driver made the turn, Ann told him to stop at the curb. Tugging at David's hand, she said, "Let's get out here and walk around the block. We have a few minutes."

As soon as they were out of the car and on the sidewalk, she confronted him. "What choice do you think I have as far as Cindy is concerned? I can't go against Lyla's wishes—even if I think she's wrong. She's had the burden of responsibility all these years. She *is* Cindy's mother."

"She's been *ir*responsible all these years," David replied, "keeping the truth hidden from Cindy. It's disgraceful."

"I'm the one who went away, remember?"

"But you left believing that Cindy was going to be Lyla's ticket to security. You didn't dump Cindy on her—which is how you've been making it sound—you made a greater sacrifice than most people ever would, for both Cindy's and Lyla's well-being.

"Lyla is a total manipulator," David snapped. "She's managed to turn it all around and put a guilt trip on you. Because she can't live with all the shit she's put you through, she has to find new ways to make you wrong. Every time you talk to her on the phone, darling, you're dragged a little deeper into her mind-set."

Despite Ann's angry frown, he went on, "Every time you talk to Lyla, you feel more to blame, more panicky about Cindy discovering the truth. You feel Lyla had a little more justification for having thrown away your letters all through the years.

"Now she's turned you into her coconspirator. If it weren't so awful I could laugh at the absurdity of it."

"Thank you, Doctor Freud."

"Ann," David said, stopping and taking her hands, "this deception is torturing you. And the longer it goes on, the worse it's going to get. Lies breed lies; you'll wind up having to invent new ones to cover up the old ones. Cindy has a right to know the truth. You have a right to go on with your life without being drained like this. But you let Lyla, the queen of passive aggression, continue to pull the strings from three thousand miles away."

Ann stared ahead blindly, silently, oblivious to the sights, the sounds of the street, the traffic clogging the avenue, the drivers impatiently leaning on their horns as they jockeyed for entrance into the parking structure with only minutes left before the curtain went up on *Honest, George!*

"Lyla is a terrified woman," she said at last. "She's acted out of fear, not out of evil intent."

"Rabid dogs aren't evil, but most people agree they're dangerous."

"Oh, David." Ann shook her head and looked at him fondly. "What a dumb thing to say. You don't know Lyla— and your objectivity when it comes to me is nil."

He shrugged, caught.

"I'm glad you said what you did," Ann added. "What's becoming clear to me is that I can't . . . grab hold of Cindy. She likes me, at a distance. Maybe I'll just have to settle for that.

"Funny—I stepped in because I knew Cindy was heading for trouble. I knew she needed me. I never thought I'd say this, but it's all happening too fast—speaking selfishly, of course. She has good people working with her now. She has a solid little part in a solid little picture. She has an excellent coach waiting to help her at the workshop. Professionally, I don't need to be there. Personally, well, even if she did know the truth, who knows whether she would want a relationship with me? But if I weren't so damned efficient and she weren't so damned talented, we might have had time . . ."

She glanced at her watch, then cried, "It's five past eight. We've got to fly; they're holding the curtain."

But David held her hands a moment longer. "One more minute won't hurt. Let them wait," he said, as he leaned over and kissed her tenderly.

"I think I'll run over to Stage Four and see how things are going," Ann told her secretary, Estelle Duke, in what she hoped was a casual tone of voice.

Estelle did not respond casually. She had a list of phone calls for Ann to return before she was to view the first rough cut of one of the studio's major summer releases.

She couldn't understand Ann's preoccupation with *The Comeback Kid* and its schedule. It was the first time Estelle could remember Ann keeping track, day by day, of who was working on a production.

"Now?" she asked critically.

"I need to clear my head," Ann explained feebly as she hurried past Estelle's desk.

It was the end of the third week of *The Comeback Kid* production, and the company had moved indoors.

Ann was soon noticed by the director, who enthusiastically described how well the latest scenes had come out. They walked around lights and over cables and boards, making their way from a massive nightclub set to an area at the opposite side of the soundstage where a mock hotel room had been constructed. Ann listened attentively, her eyes constantly on the lookout for Cindy.

"Stick around," the director urged politically, before turning to confer with the cinematographer.

The crew was preparing the hotel room set for the next scene to be shot. The lead performers had vanished into their motorhome dressing rooms outside the soundstage for a few minutes of leisure between setups.

The chairs by the long white makeup table were vacant.

Finally, Ann asked one of the grips whether he had seen Cindy Mantussi.

"I think she went out to Joey's trailer," he said. "They were going to run through some lines."

Ann nodded and walked away, disappointed. She had to get back to her office, but at least she had another piece of information to think about: it was nice that Joey Donatello was apparently giving Cindy some guidance.

Twenty minutes later, the grip informed Cindy that "the prez" had been looking for her.

"Did she say why?" Cindy asked worriedly.

"No."

"Hey, she likes you, you know," Joey Donatello declared. "Not bad to have friends in high places."

Cindy looked at him, perplexed.

He shrugged. "She got you the job, didn't she?"

"No."

"Yes, she did," he insisted. "Didn't you know?"

Cindy was baffled but too consumed by everything else going on in her life to think much about it.

FORTY-ONE

∽~❦~∾

WHEN ERIC EVANS went to pick Cindy up at her apartment, he found himself in a section of Hollywood that bore little resemblance to its earlier glory days. He parked his gleaming midnight blue BMW next to an abandoned, rusting '72 VW, walked gingerly over broken beer bottles that littered the sidewalk, and made his way to the courtyard of a rundown building. *Shabby*, he thought, frowning. He found a door with a large metal *3* and rang the bell. It made only a thudding noise.

Cindy rushed to answer, but not before taking a last hasty look around the two-bedroom apartment. It looked perfect, she decided, right down to the potted plants and fresh-cut flowers she had bought in anticipation of Eric's visit.

Her surroundings were a decided step up from the dingy single room that had been her first home in Hollywood. There she had slept on an army surplus cot, cooked on a hot plate, and fought a hopeless battle with roaches. Now she had a flat with a bedroom and kitchen, serious furniture, including a few really nice pieces, a fairly new carpet, and even a view of the Hollywood Hills through the high, narrow living room window.

When Cindy opened the door, Eric was struck anew by her beauty. She was wearing a short teal blue angora sweater dress; her hair, rinsed of its candy stripes, swung silkily down to her shoulders. He did his best to hide his distaste at the apartment, and a few minutes later, after a quick introduction to her roommate, he was opening the door of his BMW to whisk Cindy away.

392

"Now you're the one who's quiet," she said as she slipped into her seat.

"I'm sorry," he said. "My mind was wandering."

As he drove back toward Beverly Hills, he directed the conversation toward Cindy and her life. The more he listened, the deeper his dismay became; they had nothing in common. Lovely as she was, he knew that this transplanted lower-middle-class New Jersey suburbanite daughter of a laborer was no one he could introduce to his parents. He had had enough lectures on the subject to know his father would be enormously annoyed if he became deeply involved with someone "common."

The only thing to do was to relax, have a good time, and not take it seriously. He wasn't disappointed, he told himself. There was nothing to be disappointed about.

He did not realize how badly he wanted her to be perfect.

Appearing ever more sullen, Eric got around to asking about *Sorority Boys* and Cindy's unscheduled departure.

After a long pause, Cindy said, "I don't want to talk about it."

"Why not?"

"Because you don't want to know how Scott Draydon treated Jeff. And because the movie's a piece of shit, and I felt like a piece of shit the whole time I was working on it."

"Just what did you do in it?"

"What do you mean?"

"What did it sound like?" he snapped. "What did you do in the movie?"

"Hey, look—I didn't make like Linda Lovelace or anything. But I didn't have a good time. Is that enough for you? Why are you asking me all these questions?" she retorted.

"You don't have to be so defensive."

But then, he wondered, why *was* he interrogating her? It was just a date, for God's sake.

Although Cindy was wounded by Eric's attitude, her sadness was swiftly drowned in annoyance.

To hell with you, Eric, she thought.

"You accused me of suddenly acting differently yesterday," she said, her words laced with indignation. "Now it's my turn. I thought you were a nice, fun guy yesterday. Now you're acting . . . obnoxious."

Eric flinched, taken aback. "I don't know what you expected. Was I supposed to wear a rubber nose and a party hat?"

"The hat would have been enough."

He glanced at her. She was sitting stiffly, staring straight ahead, the picture of proud defiance.

"What exactly do you mean by 'obnoxious'?"

"How about stuffy, unfriendly, and judgmental as a definition?"

He met her words with stony silence, then muttered, "Maybe we should just skip this evening."

"Sounds good to me."

Both fumed in silence as they drove along the lower section of Santa Monica Boulevard, with its young male hustlers and prostitutes peddling their wares on street corners.

"You're not turning around."

"I know."

"Why not?"

"Never mind."

"I do mind," she shot back, her anger still alive.

"I don't want to end the evening on such a bad note, Cindy," Eric said, unsure whether he was more upset with himself or with her. "I truly am sorry."

"You truly are," she agreed.

"You're not going to let it go, are you?"

"No," she said. "I can't get adjusted to this L.A. routine where people go down mental checklists, finding out *things* about me instead of finding out about *me*."

"You're wrong. I've been finding out all about *you*. I've found out you have a serious attitude problem. Has anybody ever told you that?"

"Nobody worth listening to. How about you? I'll bet plenty of people have noticed yours."

After a moment, a smile played over Eric's lips and a teasing lilt came into his voice. "So you've decided I'm a pretty miserable human being, hmm?"

"I didn't say miserable. 'Arrogant' covers it," she answered grandly, responding to his tone.

"Well, you're not without some arrogance yourself, Mantussi. And you're not what anyone would call nonjudgmental."

Cindy shrugged, smirking. "I'll have to think about that."

Eric turned right, then onto the relative quiet of Fountain Avenue.

"On the other hand, you're so cute when you're mad," Cindy said. Eric glanced in her direction and saw her giving him a sidelong look and a megawatt smile.

He slowly let out a deep breath and pushed back the straight strands of hair that fell onto his forehead, feeling nettled, amused, and nearly vanquished by desire.

"They never should have let you out of New Jersey," he grumbled with what was now mock exasperation.

"Eric, where are we going?" she crooned softly, all at once anxious to put the discord behind them.

"We're going out to dinner—if you can contain yourself."

"How do I know you won't embarrass me in public?" she asked. "I have my image to think about, you know."

"I'll try to behave myself."

If it had been possible to adapt the sexual tension they generated into electrical energy, the entire area around their table at the Bistro would have been bathed in blinding light. The appointments, the food, the vintage wine were all wasted on Cindy and Eric.

They made valiant stabs at casual conversation but couldn't maintain the charade. They were lost in a feverish private world, in which every touch and every glance meant a tingling jolt.

Rack of lamb grew cold on their plates. They nodded numbly when a busboy asked if they wanted the dishes cleared. They shook their heads when a waiter suggested dessert and coffee. And all the while their eyes exchanged a message that needed no words.

At last Eric whispered, "My place."

Cindy nodded.

Soon they were walking up the steps of an elegant 1930s Spanish-style duplex on a quiet Beverly Hills lane. All at once Cindy was overcome by shyness and insecurity.

"Maybe, I don't know..." she began.

Eric closed the heavy arched oaken door behind them.

"Shh," he soothed, drawing her into his arms, brushing her cheek with his lips.

"Don't worry," he breathed.

His lips found her mouth, his tongue met hers.

For Cindy there had been a few immature involvements

with high school boyfriends; for Eric the extensive experience of a handsome young man encouraged by a father to be sexually promiscuous.

But for neither Eric nor Cindy had there been anything like this. Nothing had prepared them for the wonder, the intensity of this.

They stumbled toward the bedroom, his lips never leaving hers, their fingers frantically tearing clothes aside. They collapsed onto the bed, naked now, each free to explore the wonders of the other's body. Then finally they were one, moving through a timeless moment, toward the explosion that had been building for minutes, for hours, for all of their lives perhaps. And even after they were spent, they clung together, as if afraid to let the other go.

Through the dimness, Eric looked into Cindy's eyes and saw they were glistening.

"Will I see you again?" she asked plaintively.

This was the moment for some inward gloating. This was the moment for Eric to smile humoringly—as if the question were preposterous—and say "of course" with just the barest trace of annoyance, in a light, offhand way that would tell her the question wasn't preposterous at all.

This was the moment for his standard don't-get-carried-away message. He had the expression and the tone down so pat that he could produce them automatically.

But not this time. This time, Eric experienced a strange, leaden, paralyzed feeling. The corners of his lips drew downward with a sudden surge of emotion.

"Oh, my God—yes," he breathed tenderly. "What could you be thinking? That I'd just disappear?"

"Yes."

"No," he reassured her with a half-smile, taking her hand, kissing her fingers. "I couldn't."

She held him tightly, whispering, "I'm so glad."

The next time Ann visited the *Comeback Kid* set, to her surprise, Cindy sought her out. "May I ask you a question?"

"Of course," Ann said.

"Joey told me you recommended me for this part. I'm very grateful, but I don't understand. I mean, how did you know about me? And why me?"

Ann smiled uncomfortably. Cindy looked at her hard, baffled.

No more lies, no more excuses. The words rang in Ann's mind.

"I'd like to tell you, but I'm not free to discuss it."

"All right." Cindy shrugged, confused.

"Just remember," Ann added, "you were the one who came in and knocked everyone off their feet. You did it yourself."

"I don't know what to say ... I don't know what I could ever do for you, but if there were something—"

"Come by my office sometime," Ann blurted out. "I'd like to discuss your career with you. I think you have a great deal of potential, and ... ah ..." She reddened at Cindy's curious look. "Having gone through the mill myself, I like to help young people avoid the traps."

She thinks I'm deranged, thought Ann.

But Cindy brightened and cried, "I'd love to!"

Later, in the confines of her office suite, away from the inquisitive glances of the *Comeback* company, Ann found herself much more at ease with Cindy. They limited their discussion to business, and Cindy's questions flowed. Did Ann think she was giving a good performance in the movie? Had she seen any of the dailies? What should she do to improve?

What did Ann think of her agent? What did Ann think about Cindy trying for television pilots? Should she hire a personal publicist?

Harder to take was hearing Cindy express her fears about *Sorority Boys.*

Ann had to agree that Cindy was just going to have to learn to live with it. With cable and cassettes, the more successful she became, the more the shoddy movie was bound to haunt her.

"But at least you didn't have that large a role."

"It's already making trouble for me in my personal life," Cindy said, then stopped herself abruptly.

"Why?" Ann asked.

Cindy shook her head, smiling. "I've taken up enough of your time." She rose from her seat in front of Ann's desk and extended her hand. "I don't know how I can ever thank you enough for everything."

Ann followed her to the door, suddenly faltering again. "Please, stay in touch. I'd like to know how you're doing.

And if you ever have any more questions, feel free to come by."

"I will," Cindy promised. "Ms. Peters—Ann—I don't know how I got so lucky, but believe me, I appreciate it."

"It's wonderful to see you happy," Ann said emotionally, before she could catch herself.

Cindy seemed unfazed by the sudden burst of feeling, perhaps because she was on such an emotional high herself.

"Happy. Oh," she said, smiling, "I never knew it was possible to be this happy!"

Ann saw Cindy several more times during the next few weeks—though Cindy's name was, for the time being, not appearing on the *Comeback* call sheets.

Cindy visited her office and was also present when Ann viewed the *Comeback* dailies.

At the same time, Cindy became a known quantity at the downtown highrise where Eric worked. He introduced her to his colleagues with a proud, proprietary air.

Although their verbal sparring matches continued and they were often aggravated with each other, they were never bored.

There were more serious exchanges, too. Eric listened gravely and sympathetically to Cindy's story of her *Sorority Boys* experience. He heard about Joe Mantussi's rampages and Lyla's defeated attitude—and he began to feel a fierce admiration for Cindy's spunk in breaking away.

In her presence, his defenses about his own background began to come down. In her arms, in the sanctuary of his four-poster bed, he found himself sharing the details of his anguished relationship with his father.

". . . then I realized I was never going to be able to separate myself from him—he precedes me into every room whether he's there or not."

Cindy gently slid her hand up and down his arm, studying his profile as he gazed at the ceiling. It was early morning. Dawn was just beginning to light the room.

"It's all right now," he said. "We're on reasonably good terms. I have my life out here, and he has his back there."

"But you still feel so much."

He looked down at her warmly loving face.

"Love, hate, admiration, fear, awe . . . Maybe jealousy. The gamut."

Cindy kissed his cheek. "He didn't precede you into this room," she said.

Then Eric said, "I think you should meet him sometime."

"If you like."

He turned on his side to face her with a sudden grin. "We've never discussed your apartment," he said.

"My apartment?"

"Right."

"You don't like it."

"I *hate* it."

Cindy sat up and shoved a pillow at him. "You hate my apartment?" she cried in mock fury. "What am I doing in bed with you?"

"When you're finished on the movie, I want you to move in here."

She turned her face away from his, and he felt himself grow anxious at her lack of response.

"What's the matter?" he demanded. "What's wrong with your moving in here? Cindy . . . What's the matter? Talk to me!"

She allowed the silence to stretch out a moment, then a moment longer. Finally she turned and said, "What's the matter? I'll tell you what it is . . . I don't want to wait until I'm finished on the movie. I want to move in with you now."

"You little brat! Come here!"

They fell into each other's arms giggling. She nibbled at his ear, pinched his elbow lightly, and demanded, "Say yes. Say it's okay?"

"Yes. Yes!" He laughed. He pulled her onto her back, raised himself atop her. The laughter stopped as he gazed deeply into her eyes.

"Nothing's ever been more okay," he whispered.

FORTY-
TWO

IT WAS CINDY who at last raised the question that had been implicit from the beginning, the snake slipping treacherously through the lush jungle foliage of their dream affair.

"Your father—when he finds out about us, he's going to be angry at you, isn't he?"

"Yes," Eric answered truthfully. He shrugged as if to say there was nothing he could or would do about it.

"And he'll be even angrier if he finds out your poor little girlfriend from New Jersey was in a movie like *Sorority Boys,* won't he?"

They were driving along the coast highway toward the Malibu home of a friend of Eric's. Cindy gazed at him steadily.

"It won't affect us," Eric said in a monotone. Then, he added more insistently, "It *won't* affect us."

But inwardly, he wasn't so sure.

In Cindy's eyes, Eric could now do no wrong. If the thought that he might actually be afraid of Hank ever skittered across her mind, she quickly repressed it.

As soon as Cindy's role in *The Comeback Kid* was completed, Eric decided it was time for their trek to Washington.

"We may as well get it over with," he announced. "Once my father meets you, he'll be entranced."

"I'd settle for him putting up with me," she noted quietly.

"I don't like the sound of that. Where's your confidence?"

"All right. He'll *adore* me."

"That's right," Eric nodded.

If Cindy had been any less stubborn in her resolve to prove

to Eric that she was capable of survival in his world, if she had been one iota less self-assured, a touch less secure about Eric's feelings, the evening at Hank and Mary's home would have flattened her.

She got her first warning flash as they drove up to the stately house.

There was an icy atmosphere that encased the estate as distinctly as the lacy shadows of tall oaks patterned its front drive. Cindy took in the pair of peacocks strutting over the manicured lawn, the Rolls and Mercedes parked near the four-car garage behind the house. A flutter of apprehension rippled through her. She was determined not to show it.

Eric was also trying hard to hide his anxiety, for he knew, after a brief telephone interrogation, that his father was already predisposed to dislike Cindy—and this without any mention of *Sorority Boys* or her friendship with Jeff.

Indeed, Eric's announcement that he was living with a girl, the uncharacteristically confrontational tone in Eric's voice—as if he were warning his father in advance that he had better accept Cindy—had been more than enough to put Hank on the defensive. Given Hank's personality, that meant the offensive.

"Mantussi?" Hank had asked skeptically. "I know a fine-art dealer in New York and Milan—Carlo Mantussi; she wouldn't happen to be a relative?"

"No, she's from New Jersey, and her father's a construction worker."

"Oh, come on, Eric . . ."

Outside the door, Cindy checked her hair and her soft yellow lamb's wool dress. She resolved to curb her usual impertinent edge.

"Be yourself," Eric said firmly, as if he were reading her mind. "But try not to . . ."

"Get us into trouble?" Cindy asked. He smiled thinly.

Inside the entryway, the maid greeted Eric with open arms and congratulated him on the "lovely young lady."

"He's home," she added warningly. "They're in the drawing room."

"How's the weather in there?" Eric asked.

The maid cleared her throat and grimaced. "It looks pretty cold. Partly cloudy—you might say a chance of some strong gusty winds."

Eric nodded, rubbing his chin. He looked at Cindy, who shrugged. Then he took her hand, and in they went.

Never would Cindy encounter a tougher audience than the jaw-first pair she faced in the stark Federal-style drawing room of that Maryland mansion.

Mary reminded her of a sharp-lined wooden figure on the prow of a tall ship. Eric and his mother exchanged a few strained words; she offered him coffee, tea, an aperitif—then looked at Cindy long enough to add, with excruciatingly forced politeness, "And you?"

Hank was much worse. His eyes scanned Cindy during Eric's introductions, but thereafter he sat in his leather wing chair, chin in hand, scowling and barely glancing in Cindy's direction. When he spoke, his conversation was intended solely and distinctly for his son. He glowered irritatedly whenever Cindy added so much as a "how interesting."

After twenty minutes of social strangulation, dinner was announced.

Eric got a good look at Cindy's face en route to the dining room—and his tension skyrocketed. She had that familiar volcanic glow that invariably signaled a coming explosion. He furtively begged her with his eyes: keep cool, please. And Cindy's eyes flashed back: what the hell *is* this?

As soon as they were settled at the formal dining room table, Eric again tried to bring Cindy into the conversation.

"They're very excited about the dailies from *The Comeback Kid,*" he told his parents.

"You can never tell from dailies," Hank muttered, as a servant silently ladled soup from a silver tureen.

"No," Eric responded tensely, with feigned joviality, "but this has all the earmarks of a hit. Joey Donatello is a hot name. And, of course," he added, smiling at Cindy, "you're wonderful. Cindy is going to be a star when this comes out."

"It's a small part," she added softly.

"I've never heard of Joey Donatello," Hank grunted.

"He's had two very successful specials on cable," Cindy interjected. "He won a Grammy for his first comedy album. He's been on 'The Tonight Show' a lot."

Ignoring her comment, Hank turned to Eric, once again shutting Cindy out. "What do you think of the wine? Interesting, isn't it? Chateau d'Yquem."

"Well, I'll be darned," Cindy chimed in, with a sassy rap on the table. "That's just what I was about to guess!"

Hank bristled.

Eric nearly choked. "Dry," he coughed.

"Surprisingly dry, for a golden wine," Cindy added, in a tone worthy of a commercial. The others stared at her. She silently thanked the *Comeback Kid* director for the line; the cast and crew had their share of ardent wine connoisseurs, and she had tasted and listened, thank God.

"It really is wonderful."

A ray of light brightened Mary's eyes.

"Do you know yet what project you might do next, Cindy?" she asked.

It was the longest question put to her thus far, and the first that showed the slightest hint of interest in her.

"No," Cindy replied. Her eyes met Mary's with a message of gratitude. "I do know I'll be involved in the improv workshop at Sentinel."

Mary's stiff smile showed evidence of life. "How nice."

"Cindy is part of a select group chosen for the workshop," Eric added quickly. "The studio president herself recommended her."

"Impressive." Mary nodded.

Hank got up abruptly. "Excuse me. I have to make a call," he informed them, and he strode out of the room.

A look of regret, love, hope—a mix of emotions—passed between Cindy and Eric. Mary saw it, and it moved her.

"How did you meet?" she asked tentatively.

"Cindy was a friend of Jeff's," Eric answered in a low voice.

Mary sighed, nodding.

"I was hoping for a chance to really talk to the old man. He hates not knowing everything, but he won't sit still long enough to listen."

"Darling, you know it's always been like this," Mary said. She turned toward Cindy. "Hank has had a very hectic and frustrating week," she said, making excuses.

From that point on, until Hank came back to the table, Mary was more and more gracious, and Cindy reverted to her jauntily animated self.

Eric was pleased, for he could see that an inward tide was turning.

It wasn't that Mary was suddenly in favor of her son's deep entanglement, but she appreciated Cindy's appeal and, more importantly, Cindy's effect on Eric. Mary had never seen him look happier.

They were already well into the main course of Cornish game hens when Hank returned, appearing even more darkly saturnine than before.

Within minutes he had Eric embroiled in a heated debate on arms limitation, once again throwing up a wall in front of Cindy by deliberately obscuring his comments in military jargon, employing the most sophisticated language and intricate details he could muster. He didn't mind when Eric had to ask him for explanations several times. But he acted offended when Cindy asked whether missiles placed together in a dense pack "wouldn't be an easy target?"

"That's why it was voted down," Eric told her.

Cindy reddened.

"It's times like this I wonder how we could've given them the vote," Hank said with a cutting laugh, nodding toward Cindy without looking at her.

"Wouldn't your women constituents love to have heard you say that?" Eric commented archly, as Mary closed her eyes.

"Just a joke, son." Hank shrugged with a slight, amused smile.

Before Eric could say more, Cindy broke in. "I don't know as many details as I should. You're right. But maybe it's because, to tell you the truth, I haven't been able to get past that big question of why we need to be able to destroy the world in so many different ways."

Hank shook his head, folded his napkin, and, with an "I tried" shrug directed at Eric, excused himself and left. It was the last Cindy saw of him until the next day.

Eric was out for the morning. Cindy was by herself in their hotel room when a call came through from Hank's secretary. Hank was sending a car. He wanted to see Cindy alone at the house.

Cindy was breathless with anxiety, perspiring with nervousness, bedeviled by curiosity during the ride, trapped in the silent automobile with Hank's silent driver. As she entered the imposing house—quiet now, echoing with quiet—she was escorted not by the friendly maid of the night before, but by an unsmiling Roy Carter, who was at the house on a special errand.

He led her to Hank's study, where Evans stood looking out the window, his back turned her way.

"Hank?" said Carter.

"Hello again," Cindy greeted him.

Evans heaved a sigh, turned, and strode to his desk without so much as a word. Carter left the room, shutting the doors behind him.

As Cindy approached him, Hank opened a desk drawer, withdrew an envelope, and pulled from it an array of eight-by-ten stills. He fanned them across the desktop, then leaned over them with his hands on either side of the pile. Cindy stared down at the pictures, then looked up into Hank's face, devastated.

Roy Carter had been in California doing some checking for Hank; he had delivered the *Sorority Boys* shots to him only a few hours earlier.

"I want you out of my son's life," he said.

"Wait. Let me expl—"

"Whatever it takes."

"That's not fair," she cried plaintively. "For ten seconds of film? I never . . . It was a mistake. I'm not doing anything like that any more. I—"

"You what?" he asked angrily. "You thought if you could get your claws into Eric you would have it made."

"No!" She shook her head vigorously, eyes wide.

"Money and fame the easy way. You're not the first little chippie who's tried it with him. There've been many, many others. Long legs and a big pair of tits, and he loses his head. He always comes to his senses after awhile, but in your case, I'm not going to wait."

"I understand what you're thinking, but you're wrong about me." Cindy's words came out in a torrent. "If I'd been trying to chase Eric like that, would I have fought with him? That's all we did at first: fight. And it was Eric's idea that I move in, not mine. And he knew all about this movie right at the beginning! Please, Mr. Evans, you have to at least hear me out. I love Eric! Very, very much!"

Hank was bent over his desk, opening a folder; Cindy found herself addressing the top of his silvery head. He was obviously not listening to her.

At last he pushed a two-page document across the desk. Cindy picked it up, and, as Hank settled back in a red Morocco-leather chair, rubbing his hands together, she sank onto the edge of her seat. As she read the paper, her woebegone look hardened into something stronger.

The freshly typed agreement in her hands stated in harsh, daunting legalese that Cindy would have nothing more to do with Eric Carstairs Evans; she would never see him or discuss him, never discuss Hank, never disclose any information about the agreement.

Stunned and horrified, she shook her head and gave a brittle laugh.

"I can see to it that several of my old friends in the industry help you get good job opportunities, bigger, better parts, good publicity. In addition to that . . ." Hank trailed off, holding a piece of paper out for her to see.

It was a cashier's check for $50,000.

"Or," Hank continued, his voice as cold and hard as marble, "I can see to it that the truth about you gets spread to every little corner."

She looked at him with pained curiosity.

"That you're poison—bad-tempered, unreliable. And I do believe you have a drug problem, just like that loser junkie who must have introduced you to Eric," he said, tilting his head, dark confidence glimmering in his hooded eyes. "That would be the first step. In other words, it would be a costly mistake for you not to sign it."

He thrust a pen at her. *"So sign it."*

Cindy stared at the paper. Had Hank known her, he would have seen the volcanic glow building.

At last she responded. She tore the pages in half, then in half again. "Do your worst," she dared him. "Whatever you do, it won't be as bad as this." Standing up, she hurled the scraps at him.

"The hell it won't," he exclaimed, suddenly on his feet and roaring down at her from his full, intimidating height.

"Eric would be so hurt if he knew about this!" Cindy lamented.

Hank produced a copy of the agreement and waved it at Cindy. "You're going to sign this before you get out of here," he promised.

"You don't deserve a son like Eric," she replied, her voice strong though her body shook. "You don't deserve his love."

"Shut up," he thundered, stepping toward her. "He's a goddamned idiot to think he's got something in cheap trash like you!"

"No!" Cindy shouted back, stepping not away but closer, closer, directly in front of Hank, her hands clenched tightly. "If you *really* knew Eric and gave him the credit he deserves, you'd see that I want to be with him not because of you—"

"Shut up!"

". . . but *in spite* of you! I'll make an agreement with you; I won't tell Eric about this terrible—"

"Sit down, goddamn it!" He finally silenced Cindy by bellowing directly into her face.

"*You* sit down," she shot back.

He raised his hand, but something made him stay the motion.

For a second, they were frozen in the deadlock. Then the sound of voices came from the hall outside.

". . . Where are they? In here?"

Eric entered. As he took in the scene and their emotion-charged faces, his expression turned to stone. He moved quickly to Cindy's side. "I've got a car outside," he told her.

Hank's voice changed entirely, turning sad and sympathetic. "She's got you blind, son."

"I don't want to hear it."

"Well, you're going to hear it. Look at these! Pictures from *Sorority Sluts*," Hank cried, intentionally altering the title. He picked up one of the shots showing a half-clothed Cindy and held it out to Eric.

Eric's eyes passed briefly over the photograph. "You went to a lot of unnecessary trouble, getting those," he said with barely controlled anger. "If we had had half a chance, we would have talked to you about this. Nobody was trying to hide anything."

"I can see *she* wasn't." Hank snorted with an ugly smile. "At least, nothing anatomical. How'd you like to see these end up printed in some magazine, Eric? How'd you like to think of men all over the country ogling pictures of your special girl, taking them and—"

"Shut up," Eric cried. He took Cindy's arm and started away.

"If I thought you were keeping your perspective, you know I'd never say a damn thing! I could almost live with the embarrassing spot you're putting me into," Hank called after him. "When the press gets hold of it, they'll make hay. You know the hard line I've taken antismut."

"Right," Eric replied flatly, turning back. His sardonic smile was a clear indictment of Hank's hypocrisy. "But I'm not going to live my life by your goddamned statements."

With that, he led Cindy out.

The argument between Hank and Eric had just begun.

Day after day, back in Beverly Hills, Cindy watched Eric brooding, knowing he was thinking about his father, the rupture between them, the angry scene, knowing he was depressed over it. The fact made her miserable.

When Eric asked her whether Hank had made threats or offers to get her to break off their relationship, Cindy admitted that he had. Eric reacted with outrage and grief.

Then the calls began. Calls from Hank, calls from Mary. Most were brief. The last one was violent.

It came at midnight Washington time, nine in L.A. Cindy was at her workshop. Hank was trying a new tack with Eric—generous understanding.

"If the Queen of England can live with one of her boys publicly indulging in an affair with a porn star, so can I," he said, playing the martyr.

"Cindy is not a porn star."

"As long as you give me some assurance that you're not taking it seriously. This girl has everything to gain from the relationship, and you have nothing to gain. I don't trust her. After all my years in the business, believe me, I *know* her kind."

"If you'd tried talking to her instead of tormenting her from the moment you met, you might have realized for yourself that Cindy has a treasure of special qualities."

"Outside of what's so readily apparent here on these pictures I have? No, I don't think so. You want to marry a thoroughbred, son. You've got to ask yourself seriously: what are you going to do with a girl like this once you get tired of fucking her?"

"Cindy is the best thing that's ever happened to me." Then Eric added in a burst of defiance, though the idea had not occurred to him until Hank had planted it in his mind, "I will marry whomever I damn well please!"

"Not her, you won't. She has the potential to make me look like a horse's ass, a goddamned idiot who can't even keep control of his own house!"

"The hell with that," Eric yelled. "I'm a grown man. I'm not part of your house any longer!"

"Marry that slut, and you *won't* be."

"If that's how you want it."

There was a click on the line as Hank hung up, but no dial tone. Someone was eavesdropping.

Eric waited a beat, then said bleakly, "Hello, Mother."

In the isolated sanctity of her bedroom, Mary took a deep, silent breath, hesitant to acknowledge what Eric already knew. Then she withdrew her fingers from the phone buttons.

"You don't know what you're doing," she said brokenly.

"Yes I do. He gave me a choice, you heard him."

"Oh, darling—don't slam the door on your future, your whole life. Call him back, please!"

"If he wants to cut me off, that's his decision. I've made mine. I have a different idea about what's important in life than he does, or you do. I love Cindy and I want to live with her."

There was a long pause. Mary was in tears, a jarring sound, for it was something Eric had seldom heard.

"Don't worry. We'll stay in touch, I promise."

After another pause, he heard a voice he barely recognized as his mother's. "I don't know what to say. I like her. I want —I just want you to be happy."

Nearly an hour later, Cindy came home to find Eric sitting quietly, thoughtfully, the telephone at his feet.

"Is something wrong?" she asked.

"No. Come here." He held out his arms, and she settled in his lap, nuzzling her cheek against his face affectionately. He wrapped his arms around her.

"I have a plan." He kissed her cheek. "What if I squeeze a couple days off next week and we run away together."

"I like it."

"And get married."

FORTY-THREE

"YOU'RE DRESSING FOR a party, not a funeral."

David picked up the black jumpsuit Ann had laid out on their bed and walked back into the long closet, where she was just pulling out a pair of short black boots.

"I'd like you to consider something more cheerful," he said, dangling the hanger from one finger.

Ann plucked the jumpsuit away from him. Her troubled expression didn't change.

"Cindy will still be going to the workshop," he reminded her, trying to cheer her up. "You can always drop in there. And now that the movie's wrapped, at least you won't have to worry about making her nervous. In fact," he added, "now would be a good time to—"

She glared at him. He raised his palms.

The topic of whether Ann should violate Lyla's wishes and tell Cindy the truth had become a dangerously sore point between them.

He watched as Ann zipped up the jumpsuit, then pulled a fringed woven wrap from the shelf and unfurled it, displaying its intricate, vibrant, multicolored embroidery. It was one of a kind, an Indian specialty from a village in Guatemala. She draped it expertly around her shoulders. The effect was stunning.

"Color," she said, glancing up.

"I stand corrected. You look lovely."

"Thanks. All right, let's head back down the hill."

David started toward the bedroom door, but Ann stopped him, placing a hand on his shoulder.

"I just wanted to tell you how glad I am that you're going to meet her," she said in a conciliatory tone. "And thank you for putting up with me."

"It's you I'm worried about. I wish you'd reconsider."

"This isn't the time to think about it."

The Comeback Kid wrap party was held on soundstage Number Four, where portions of the nightclub set remained.

Shooting had gone smoothly. Everyone had been pleased with the footage, and no major wars had broken out. The final day of production had been light. It all added up to the promise of an upbeat, lighthearted farewell soirée.

Ann and David arrived twenty minutes past the appointed hour. As they circulated, Ann offered compliments, reaffirmed her view that "we have a winner here," and scouted for Cindy.

"Hey, hey!" Joey Donatello flung his arms around Ann, shouting over the loud rock music thundering through the soundstage. "We did it, huh?"

He stepped back and pointed at David. "The doctor, right? Hey, how'd I guess?" He pumped David's hand.

"David Steinmetz," Ann introduced them, "the irrepressible Joey Donatello."

"I'm feeling good," Joey announced.

"Well, you should be," Ann said with a smile.

"You know who else is happy? Our little Cindy. She's fallen in love."

"She has?" Ann responded much too abruptly, but Donatello didn't notice.

He linked his fingers together and rocked his arms side to side. "Aw, and it's so cute to see them walking around, hand in hand."

David glanced at Ann; she was wearing a poor approximation of a nonchalant smile.

"Someone from the film?" she asked levelly.

Joey shook his head and snapped his chewing gum. "Nope." He looked past Ann. "Hey, there they are!"

He rushed to Cindy, picked her up and spun her around.

"Bambina!"

"Joey!"

Eric watched the display with amusement. "It's a shame they can't get along," he commented drily to Ann and David.

"Isn't it?" David replied.

Ann looked hard at Eric, not understanding, for that instant, why the sight of him disturbed her so.

He smiled at her. "You're Ann Peters, aren't you? The lady who brought life back to Sentinel Studios."

Ann nodded her thanks for the compliment and introduced David.

"Doctor, it's a pleasure to meet you," said Eric smoothly, shaking David's hand. "I'm Eric Evans."

Ann blinked, jerking her head. "What?"

"Eric . . . Eric Evans."

Turning pale, Ann glanced at David, stricken. Then she looked back at Eric.

Now he, too, appeared disturbed—and wary.

A happy Cindy rejoined Eric, taking his arm. Her smile faded as she picked up the tension—which grew even more intense as she and David awkwardly introduced themselves.

Then Donatello was back, and with him the director and several others, drinking and talking about the movie. As the reality of the situation sank in, Ann barely managed monosyllabic answers. She was feeling panic.

How would she be able to get Cindy aside?

How could she tell her?

Cindy and Eric had moved away to circulate—or so Ann thought. Minutes later, she realized they were gone.

Ann left the soundstage and stood for a moment, fingertips to her forehead. David regarded her silently.

"Of all the people in the world, why him? Why?" She thought for a moment. "I've got to call Lyla!" Ann looked at her watch. "Oh, God!" She winced.

"Come on, honey," David said, taking her arm. "There's no point in standing here."

"Let's go to my office. I'll call from there."

"Ann, take it easy. What good will it do to call at this time of night? It's not as though they're getting married; it can wait until morning."

But Ann ignored him, storming away from the parking lot. David followed her to her office.

A few minutes later, Ann was standing at her desk, listening to the rings on a phone three thousand miles away, while David stood by, sober-faced.

"Joe? I'm sorry to wake you, but it's urgent . . . Ann . . ."

She frowned, and David shook his head.

Joe. Too bad.

"Can I talk to Lyla? . . . I'll come and talk to her myself if I have to. Fine! Goodbye!"

She slammed down the receiver.

"You don't actually mean you're going to fly back there," was David's response.

"Oh, David," Ann cried, her hand angrily sweeping across her desk. "Do you think I could tell Cindy without Lyla being there?"

"Yes." He nodded emphatically. "You've given her more than enough opportunities. Besides, don't you think you should find out more about the seriousness of Cindy and Eric's involvement before running cross-country like a madwoman?"

Ann picked up the phone and punched the Pan Am flight reservations number. "I need a flight to New York as soon as possible . . ."

David put his finger on the phone cradle. "Wait," he urged.

In a flash, Ann saw Sam, fifteen years earlier in their New Mexico hotel room, cutting off her call to Lyla.

"Don't ever do that again," she cried shrilly at David.

"Ann—you're not thinking straight. Ten hours flying time alone, round-trip. To do what?"

Ann barely heard David's statement. Twenty years of grief, hatred, rejection, obsession, love, and hope were exploding inside her. All she could see was that David was trying to stand in her way.

"I'm tired of your badgering," she spat out. "This is my sister and my daughter and *my* life. Do you understand? It's none of your business!"

"I understand that you're very upset," he replied, his expression darkening. "I hope you don't realize what you're saying."

"I do!"

David choked back his hurt. "I thought we *were* each other's business."

Ann shrugged, frowning.

"Ann, I was only trying to help you avoid some unnecessary wear and tear. You're running on pure emotion—" He stopped himself, then asked, "What do you want me to do?"

"Nothing! Leave me alone. I'll get a cab to the airport."

He gazed at her, shaking his head sadly. "I've tried for almost eight years now to break through this wall of yours. I think this is the first time I've truly seen the depth of it: how much you don't want to need anyone. Well, darling, I think you're safe. Nobody is ever going to get close enough to hurt you again. Including me."

"This is hardly the time, David."

"It's never the time. Maybe I should go."

She turned on him abruptly.

"Then damn it, *go!*"

He gave her a final look before leaving.

Ann pushed back her chair. She was alone, absolutely alone in the darkness of her office, the only light the high-intensity spot of her desk lamp. She started to dial the airline, then put down the receiver, suddenly jarred into the realization that David, ever levelheaded, had been right. A blitz trip to see Lyla would be nothing but a waste of precious time.

She hurried to the door, calling, "David?"—but he was already too far away to hear her. She resisted the urge to rush after him.

She resented what he had said—even if it was true.

The house was dark and empty when Ann's cab pulled up to the driveway. With a pang, she realized David must have gone to spend the night at the Marina. She didn't call him.

If he wanted more from her than she was able to give, well she thought, perhaps it was better to leave it alone, let him believe she had turned into a bitch . . . let him go, set him free.

There would never be another cage for her.

Lyla's ability to deny reality was staggering. When Ann reached her the next morning and told her the news, she immediately assumed that Cindy and Eric were "probably just good friends," based on her own illogical logic that if there were any more to it, Cindy would have called to tell her.

Even if they weren't just friends, Lyla persisted, it still couldn't be the serious thing Ann was making it out to be.

In short, Lyla felt it would go away by itself if left alone. She clung to the belief with the tenacity of a barnacle.

"Call her and ask about him," Ann demanded.

"I can't."

"What do you mean, you *can't?*"

"Her number is disconnected. There's no referral."

"I hope that doesn't mean she's moved in with him."

There was a sharp intake of breath on the other end of the line as Lyla finally began to register the situation.

"You've got to come out here and tell her the truth. Or tell her by phone if you have to. I'll get the new number."

"I have to think," Lyla said pleadingly. "And . . . and I have to talk to Joe, see how he wants to . . . see if we can both come. I need time. Promise you won't do anything until I call you back."

"When will that be?"

"As soon as I can."

"Tomorrow, Lyla. I won't wait any longer."

FORTY-FOUR

Eric surveyed the colorful array of clothing spilling from the suitcase Cindy had crammed full and jammed shut, and he couldn't help laughing. "This is a disgrace. Who taught you how to pack?"

"Get off my back," she purred, stretching luxuriantly in their hotel room bed. "I'm an artist."

On the morning after the first night of their Las Vegas honeymoon, they were just getting around to thinking about when the wedding ought to take place.

Eric glided to the end of the bed with a grin and reached up under the covers to grab Cindy's ankle.

"You certainly are."

"Oh! Lordy, lord, he's got her by the foot! Whatever is going to become of poor Little Nell?"

With a low chortle, Eric ducked his head under the covers, grabbed Cindy's other ankle, and slid between the sheets. The bulky blue mass shifted and shook and giggled.

"Stop it! . . . Stop it! No tickling!"

"Marry me."

"No, no!"

"No? How'd you like your mortgage foreclosed?"

"Oh, don't take the farm away! Don't! Don't!"

More giggling, more shaking, more growling, and at last a catch, a murmur, and a long, low, quivering sigh.

An hour later, they lay quietly side by side.

"Serious question?" Cindy asked.

"Go ahead."

416

"If marrying me is connected to being angry at your father, then shouldn't we—"

Shaking his head, he stopped her, his fingertips on her lips. "I just want to be sure you're sure."

"If it'll make you feel any better," he admitted, "I asked myself the same thing."

"What was the answer?"

He cast a brief look at her, then asked, "Do you know what I was looking forward to when I met you?"

She shook her head.

"Nothing. I was disgusted with myself and burnt out on life."

Cindy let out a low sympathetic moan. Eric took her hand and grasped it firmly as he went on in a low voice, "You know, it used to be that if other people went fifty miles an hour, Jeff and I had to go two hundred. Well, it was two hundred miles an hour to nowhere, I finally realized. I'm not very happy about the way I was back then . . ." He sighed.

"I found myself feeling like a walking version of the morning after the party, kicking around the debris with a head full of cotton, wondering why all that fun I was supposed to be having wasn't doing a damn thing for me So then I went on to being a full-time grind, going two hundred miles an hour toward success. But I was still coming up empty. No matter what I did, I just kept coming up empty. And after Jeff died, well, then I knew how empty I was. I realized I didn't want to go on living like my father, obsessed with staying at the front of the pack with no room for anything else in life.

"I was down to going through the motions. . . . And then, suddenly, there was beautiful Cindy, and something told me, 'Here it is: your chance at something real.'"

He turned and looked deeply into her eyes, which were, by then, brimming with tears. "These last few weeks have been the happiest in my life. I've found myself daydreaming about things I never used to think about; how much I want a son or a little girl . . ." He stopped, choking up, then whispered, "I don't ever want to lose you."

Cindy pulled him into her arms. "You won't. Oh, you won't! I love you so much."

After a minute, they drew apart. Then Eric said, "My father will get used to it or he won't. His problem, not ours."

He sat up. "Does that do it?"

"Yes," Cindy answered.

They showered and dressed and decided it was time to, as Eric put it, "get organized."

The first call was to Mary. Worried and agitated, she nevertheless gave up trying to talk Eric into waiting and gave her blessing, calling Cindy "a sparkling, charming girl."

"Do you want to tell him, or do you want me to?"

"I don't mind telling him," Eric answered, "but I don't want to talk to him until after the fact. If you want to say something sooner, go ahead. It's up to you."

"Be happy, darling," she told him shakily.

The next call was to Lyla—who for once was not home.

Then Eric checked his answering machine. He turned away from the phone with a perplexed look. "You got a message from Ann Peters."

"Oh, Eric! Do you mind if I tell her? She's been so nice to me. I'd really love to share this with her."

Eric's mouth twisted slightly. He refrained from verbalizing his feeling that Ann Peters didn't like him.

"In fact," Cindy went on brightly, "I'd love to ask her to the wedding. She probably couldn't make it anyway, but if she could . . . she's been the other great part of my life in L.A. What would you think of her standing up for us?"

He sighed, thinking about Jeff, who would have been his best man.

"If you want to ask Ann Peters, it's fine with me," he replied, after a moment. "Maybe we can get her to buy us a fabulous postnuptial meal," he added jokingly.

Moments later, a beaming Cindy was talking to Ann's secretary Estelle. A few seconds after that, Ann came on the line.

"You called?" Cindy asked. She listened a moment and then plunged in effervescently. "Absolutely; I was hoping we could get together, too. As a matter of fact, I know it's ridiculously short notice, and we'll certainly understand if you're busy; but is there any chance you would consider flying to Las Vegas? Eric and I are getting married tonight, and we'd love to have you stand up for us—"

She recoiled suddenly and made a face. *"Can't?* . . . I don't understand. What is that supposed to mean?"

"What is she saying?" Eric asked.

"Well, we're going to be at the Chapel of the Doves," Cindy said into the phone. "Are you coming?"

Then, "You're not making sense . . ."

"What?" Eric asked again.

Cindy shook her head at him in utter disbelief. "You're the only one I asked to come. I thought you'd be happy for me. I thought . . . I thought we were friends. You have no right to . . . No, no, no! I won't listen to this. . . . Goodbye!"

Cindy put down the receiver abruptly. Eric waited for an explanation.

"I didn't make that call. Okay?" Cindy said.

He looked at her a long moment, then nodded. "Okay. Do you want to try your parents again?"

"No. No more bullshit," Cindy announced. "This is *our* wedding."

Eric imitated her—he had learned it was an effective ploy to rout a tantrum and make her laugh. Pretending to be in a snit, he slammed his fist down on the bureau so hard that the ashtrays jumped.

"And we're going to be happy, goddamn it!"

Several hours later, they stood in the tiny alcove of the hotel chapel, Eric—except for his running shoes—looking *GQ* in his Bill Blass suit, Cindy in a clingy, cocktail-length white wool jersey dress.

"Is there anything special that you would like me to include in the ceremony?" the minister asked.

"Probably," Eric said, with a slight laugh, "but I can't think of anything now."

"I don't want to be asked to promise to obey," Cindy noted.

"God, no." Eric shot her a wink. "I don't either."

It was a play-by-play sort of wedding; the minister, who turned out to be something of a frustrated choreographer, directed it as he went. He told Eric where to stand and sent him inside, then explained to Cindy when she would come in and how she would walk to the altar.

"Are you ready?" he asked brightly—a man committed to being up for all his performances.

She nodded.

"Nervous?"

She nodded again.

"Great. See you in a bit."

Cindy stifled a laugh as he disappeared through the double

doors. "See you in a bit?" she murmured, then waited for the Wedding March to begin.

They had a real organist; Eric had scorned the suggestion of a tape.

At the appropriate moment, Cindy stepped through the doorway and walked up the aisle at her normal gait, finding herself unable to carry out the minister's instructions for a hesitation step in a chapel with a seating capacity of forty that was occupied only by Eric, the minister, the photographer, the clerk, a witness Eric had scrounged up from the casino, and the organist. The solemn, ritualistic walk seemed preposterous, given the circumstances.

She arrived early, and the organist cut short the march. "I can't take you anywhere," Eric muttered, and Cindy nudged him. The minister's brow was furrowed with faint reproval; they weren't performing his show as directed.

These were all details, Cindy thought, as the minister began the ceremony, that she and Eric would someday laugh about with their children.

Solemnity came soon enough, inherent in the promises.

"... I, Eric Carstairs Evans, take you, Cynthia Ann Mantussi, to be my wedded wife."

"To have and to hold."

"To have and to hold."

"For richer, for poorer."

"For richer, for poorer."

"In sickness, and in health ..."

Eric's voice quavered with emotion as he repeated the words—the sound of a soul laid bare. He looked back and forth from the minister to Cindy, who was smiling the tenderest version of her dazzling smile. By then, the near-empty room, the slot machines outside, the casual quickness of the ceremony were forgotten. For the soaring surge of feelings, they could have been in Notre Dame Cathedral.

"... as long as we both shall live."

It was then that Cindy sensed a shift in the air, an added presence in the room. She turned to see Ann moving up the aisle, an expression of dazed grief on her face, like a condemned woman walking to her execution.

It was then that everything stopped.

Ann came to a halt, suddenly registering the stunned looks

of the bystanders. "I need to talk to you outside," she told Eric and Cindy.

Eric turned in astonishment. "Are you crazy?"

"Get out of here," Cindy cried in disbelief.

"You can't marry," Ann blurted out, as though she could not control or halt her words. *"You can't marry."* Ann paused, then whispered, "You're brother and sister."

For several seconds, the only sound was the tinkling of water in the chapel fountain.

Eric and Cindy exchanged the concerned but knowing glances of people suddenly confronted by apparent insanity.

Ann turned to the bystanders, who stood frozen in place near the altar, taking in the drama with the sick fascination of rubbernecking drivers passing the scene of a fatal collision.

"Please give us a few minutes," she implored.

They came to life: the minister, the photographer, the organist, the clerk, and the Denver businessman Eric had ferreted out to stand up as a witness. They filed out hurriedly, and the minister pulled the chapel door shut behind him with a soft thud.

All Cindy understood at that moment was that her wedding had been spoiled by a deluded woman. Eric's only desire was to get rid of Ann and resume the ceremony.

"Is this supposed to be some kind of a joke?" he demanded.

"It's true," Ann said woefully.

She turned to Cindy. "Lyla and Joe—your mother and father—are on their way here now. We wanted to tell you together . . . but we . . . we waited too long. You see, I—"

Ann hesitated. At the mention of her parents' names, Cindy had taken a step backward, her face turning pale; she was no longer able to disregard Ann's statements as irrational ramblings.

"—I left you with them when you were five days old—"

"You?" Cindy cried, shrinking away still further, shaking her head dazedly, her bouquet gripped in one hand.

Eric stepped toward her, but Cindy's eyes were riveted on Ann. *"You?"*

"Yes." Ann could finally say it, tears sliding freely down her cheeks. She could finally say it: "Yes, I . . . I'm your mother."

Then, urgently wanting to get everything out at once, Ann plunged on. "And the man who fathered you is Eric's father."

"That's a filthy lie," Eric roared, his arms encircling Cindy as she hid her face in her hands. "You're sick!"

"What if it's true?" Cindy said brokenly.

"Impossible," Eric stormed with a furious half-laugh.

"I wish it were," Ann cried. "What were the chances you'd find each other?"

"How did you know my father, then?" Eric challenged. "Tell me that! What are you, thirty-five? You slept with him when you were twelve? Jesus Christ! Do you expect us to believe that?"

"I was fourteen," Ann answered heavily.

Eric threw up his hands, his face turned skyward.

"I have to get out of here," Cindy said, dissolving into tears. She dropped the bouquet and raced for the door, Eric at her heels.

"You can't ignore it!" Ann cried after them. "You know you can't!"

Her words whipped over them, stopping them short.

Eric looked into Cindy's eyes. Finally he muttered, "I want to talk to my father about this."

Ann approached them, her face a mask of anguish. "I'll have to explain some things first. I'm sure he doesn't remember me as . . . as that girl," she said.

"I'm sure he doesn't," Eric snapped, his words accompanied by a fusillade of cynical laughter.

"We—the studio has a suite next door," said Ann. "Why don't you meet me there? I'll leave word at the desk for my sister."

Cindy looked up at her dazedly.

Ann nodded: yes, Lyla was her sister.

"Why didn't she tell me?" Cindy asked plaintively.

Ann shrugged helplessly, shaking her head.

*FORTY-
FIVE*

As **THE TIME** dragged by, Ann stood waiting at the balcony railing, staring down at, but not seeing, the panorama of flashing, blinking, glittering, multicolored lights of the Las Vegas Strip.

Everything was blocked from her mind but the vision of Cindy standing dumbstruck in the chapel as her world was destroyed—by Ann, by the truth. Guilt gnawed at her, despair filled her soul.

Inside, Cindy sat motionless on the suite's long white sofa, her tear-stained face, now washed of all makeup, resting on her hand, her feet tucked under her, her file pumps resting at odd angles beside the marble-slab coffee table. Her white dress was rumpled. Her hair dangled around her face uncombed.

Eric prowled the suite restlessly, feverishly, jacket open, tie loosened. Each time he had tried to comfort Cindy, her response had been strained.

Unlike Eric, Cindy believed Ann's story.

No wonder she and Eric had been so quickly drawn to each other, she thought. No wonder they had seemed so alike and . . . oh, God.

A million thoughts collided in her mind, part of a mad runaway ride; she was hanging on for dear life.

Question by question, revelation by revelation, Ann had led them through the chain of events that had taken place in Istanbul nearly two decades before.

She had told them that Cindy had been conceived aboard

the *Timor*. She had not said it had been the result of a brutal rape. She had spared Cindy—and Eric—that.

She had responded to Eric's questions by saying his father had never known he had made her pregnant. And when Cindy had demanded to know why Ann had stayed away from her all her life, Ann could only shake her head and reply, "I wanted to be with you . . . so badly. But I couldn't."

"I see," Cindy had answered sharply, not seeing at all. "Why didn't you tell me who you were before this?"

"God knows I should have," Ann had choked out.

Then Eric had placed a call to his father in Maryland, only to be told that Evans was on his way to Las Vegas.

Now they waited to confront Hank Evans with the story that Eric still adamantly refused to believe.

The sound of the doorbell shattered the silence. Ann moved from the balcony into the room. Cindy bolted off the couch as Eric rushed to the door, prepared to face his father.

Instead he found himself facing Lyla and Joe Mantussi.

Lyla hurried past him toward Cindy, her arms outstretched; a grim-faced Joe followed her. Cindy looked at them hard, then deliberately turned her back, arms crossed.

"Cindy!" Lyla cried.

"I'll never forgive you," she spat out, moving away from Lyla, then whirling to face her again. "All those years. All those lies, lies, lies!"

"Cindy, please—"

"No," she shouted savagely. "I listened to you all my life. I don't want to hear you now. You're too late. I don't want to hear you again! Ever!"

"You're forgetting all your mother and I have done for you?" Mantussi asked, grabbing Cindy's arm as Lyla backed off, eyes downcast.

Cindy shook him away roughly.

"You put us through hell, too. You know that," he bellowed. "And you never stopped!"

Cindy started away from him, but Mantussi clutched her arm again. "Listen to me—"

But at that moment Eric was there, grabbing Mantussi's shoulder from behind, yelling, "Leave her alone!"

Ann hurried toward them, challenging her brother-in-law. "What's the matter with you? Don't you realize what she's going through right now?"

Mantussi turned his wrath on Ann.

"Well, look at Miz High-and-Mighty, so concerned about Cindy! You weren't yelling like this when you abandoned her, were you?"

Ann stared him down, her eyes full of anger and pain, her jaw set firmly as his diatribe continued.

"You got no right to say anything to me, lady. While we were talking to teachers and goin' to PTA meetings and getting Cindy through the measles and the mumps and every other goddamn thing, you were out living the high life in Hollywood. Then you came bustin' in trying to take over—and this is what's come out of it!"

"You want to know what I was doing before Ann helped me, Dad?" Cindy cried, rushing into the breach between Mantussi and Ann. "Do you want to know?"

"This is just what you said would happen," Mantussi shot at Lyla, who stood silent and stricken, her fists clenched. "She's turned Cindy against us."

Eric spoke up, the calmness of his voice a startling contrast to Mantussi's screams. "I think you did a good job of that before she left home."

"So this is the boy you want to marry." Mantussi nodded to Cindy. "A smart aleck just like you—"

Suddenly, the unexpected sound of Lyla's voice captured the attention of everyone.

"Joe," she cried, thrusting herself physically into their midst, "you've got no right, no right—"

"What?" he raged. His eyes went from Lyla's defiant face to Cindy, Eric, then Ann.

"Okay. That's what you want, I'm washing my hands of it. I wash my hands!"

He headed for the door, hesitating just long enough to look once more at Lyla, who made no move to follow. He left, slamming the door behind him.

After several seconds of tortured silence, Cindy sank back onto the sofa and joked bitterly, "Okay, everybody. Raise your hand if this is the worst night of your life."

For the first time since she had told Cindy and Eric her story, Ann's eyes met Cindy's. Cindy frowned and closed her eyes with an angry toss of her head.

Lyla perched opposite Cindy on the edge of a chair,

clutching her handbag. Eric settled himself next to Cindy and addressed himself to Lyla.

"Tell us how you met my father. I want to hear it from you."

Lyla nervously looked up over his head at Ann, wanting cues.

"He doesn't believe me," Ann said. "In fact, we're waiting for his father. He's on his way."

Lyla gasped—and her fear did not go unnoticed by either Cindy or Eric, who turned in unison to catch Ann's response.

"We left word for him to come here," she continued levelly, moving around the sofa toward Lyla, giving her a warning look that Cindy and Eric couldn't see.

"But . . . but . . ." Lyla sputtered.

"I'd like to hear your version of what happened," Eric insisted.

"What have you told them?" Lyla asked Ann quietly. She stood, and her eyes moved toward the hallway, toward the bedroom of the suite. "Can we—?"

"Come on!" Eric cried. He jumped to his feet. "Haven't we had enough secrets?"

"I can't believe what I'm seeing," Cindy said to Eric, gesturing toward Ann and Lyla. "Ann Peters and Lyla Mantussi, the Beaudry sisters, together again in a heartwarming reunion. Isn't that a great one, Eric? They both had me fooled. Boy, is the joke on me!"

"Baby, I know how you must feel—" Lyla began.

"There must be a record of some kind here," Cindy went on, refusing to acknowledge Lyla, continuing to confine her remarks to Eric.

His hand circled hers. "Listen, whatever happens, I'm . . ."

"What? You're what?" she asked disconsolately.

Eric shook his head.

They waited.

Finally, there was a heavy rap at the door. All four flinched. Eric looked at the three women, then squared his shoulders, took a deep breath, and went to answer.

And suddenly, the towering figure of Hank Evans was among them. Mary came in behind him, looking ill, almost faint. "What do you think you're doing," Evans barked at his son. He stopped short as he noticed Ann and Lyla and demanded, "Who are these people?"

As Eric made the introductions in a monotone, Evans glanced again at Ann and Lyla.

There was no sign of recognition. None.

"We're all here for the same reason," Ann said flatly.

"Oh. Really?" He smirked. "And what is that?"

"Our wedding," Eric answered. "We assumed that's why you were coming."

Hank glanced at Cindy, then at Lyla. Ann turned away from him for a moment, her face regaining the color it had lost and going beyond to a burning flush, which Cindy noticed.

Evans addressed his son in a lightly reproving voice.

"Well, I don't see how that's any concern of Miss Peters's and, ah—" He nodded at Lyla.

"Cindy's mother," said Eric. "Lyla Mantussi."

"Oh," Evans grunted, as Lyla took a quick look in his general direction.

Mary sighed slowly, raggedly, audibly.

"It is my concern," Ann informed Hank. "You see, my sister, Lyla, is Cindy's adoptive mother. I am Cindy's natural mother."

Evans's chin rose abruptly. After several seconds, he said in a cutting tone, "Well. I'm sorry to hear that."

"Not as sorry as you'll be to hear what comes next," Cindy commented dryly from her place on the sofa.

Evans looked at her with sheer spite. She was resting her elbow on the arm of the couch, her cheek in her hand. She shrugged. "Too bad, Dad."

"Do you think that's funny? Well, you had better not get used to the term," he flared up angrily. "Your marriage is going to be annulled very shortly."

"Oh, no," she said, standing, moving toward him slowly like a cat stalking a moth, "it looks like you and I are stuck with each other."

Evans waved her off.

Cindy looked at the grim, tension-filled faces around her, and her need to provoke Evans won out.

"Say," she said to Eric, "wouldn't we be great on 'Family Feud'?"

"Oh, for God's sake!" Evans snorted in disgust.

"Cindy, please," Eric implored. He was still clinging to the hope that Ann's story would prove false.

"Eric, I will not stand by and see you ruin your life married to this harpy!"

Cindy gave a theatrical chuckle.

"We're not married yet," Eric said.

"Well, that *is* good news!" Hank beamed.

"It's a tragedy," Ann retorted.

And with that, she squared off against Evans for the final round.

"I disagree. Now I think it's time—"

Ann cut him off, taking a step closer, speaking fiercely. "It's a tragedy that started in 1963, when you were in Istanbul making *Fortress of the Seven Towers*. Do you remember that?"

"Yes, but—"

"Do you remember the two girls you were bringing back to America?"

Evans shrugged, cocking his head quizzically with a humoring half-smile. The message: Ann was slightly mad; he had no idea of what she was talking about.

Mary's eyes widened as she listened, then she closed them, clutching her hands together as if in silent prayer.

"You met their mother at a backstreet nightclub and whorehouse called Huriyah. You heard that their father had once been a major in the U.S. Army. You felt sorry for them. You had the unit publicist, Howie Hewitt, arrange for their passage through the Mediterranean with you aboard a cruise ship called the *Timor*. Does that strike a familiar chord?"

Cindy, Eric, and Lyla surrounded them now, eyes riveted on the pair standing a mere arm's length apart.

"I remember Hewitt, and I always used to travel by boat. Otherwise . . . no." His expression was one of impatient bafflement. But he was turning pale.

Mary, eyes still closed, winced hard.

"Two girls," Ann continued, gesturing first toward Lyla, then herself, "Lyla and Ann Beaudry."

Evans shook his head.

Lyla moved next to Ann and put her hand on Ann's shoulder, her eyes downcast.

"Then you probably don't remember the last night aboard the *Timor*," Ann said, her voice flat. "No, of course not. Why would you want to do that."

Evans's eyes bored into Ann's. "I *don't* remember it," he snapped with utter contempt.

"I somehow thought you wouldn't."

He turned away momentarily at the sound of Mary's groan. Then he turned back and repeated, "I don't," with a half-laugh of befuddlement. "And whatever it is you're getting to, I wish you would get to it."

"I knew it couldn't be true," Eric cried triumphantly. He went to Cindy, who stood with her eyes fixed on Ann and Evans.

"What couldn't be true?" Hank asked him.

"That you're Cindy's father!"

"What?" Evans roared. "That's preposterous!"

Now Mary buried her face in her hands, as if to shut out the words, the faces, the world.

"Miss Peters . . . or perhaps it would be more appropriate for me to call you Ann," Evans cracked jovially, condescendingly, "are you saying that we . . . ? Maybe I should be flattered."

"You know what you did," Lyla blurted. "You almost killed her!"

Cindy stared at her, shuddering.

Evans started to object, but Ann stopped him abruptly. "I would have thought you'd be intelligent enough to grasp the situation," she said vehemently. "Surely you don't want your son to marry his sister."

"I don't want my son to marry trash. *That* is the issue. She is *not* his sister," Evans replied, "and I won't stand to hear any more of this nonsense. It's damned insulting."

"I know what it is, Ann," Cindy interjected with a goading, sarcastic smile at Evans as she, too, moved closer to Ann. "It's 'God forbid we should have to cut her in on the family fortune.' Right, Dad?"

"Shut up!" Evans spat out.

"Cindy," said Eric, "don't you realize what this means? He's saying it isn't true!"

"I heard him," Cindy said, turning to Eric sadly. "But . . . oh, babe, look at me. Look at me carefully, then at him. Don't you see it?"

Eric studied her face closely.

Lyla watched, transfixed. She had seen the resemblance all Cindy's life. Would he?

Evans had seen it, too, before his son had been asked to look. Indeed, he also recalled the incident on the *Timor*, although his recollection of Roy Carter having to pay off the ship's doctor was much more vivid to him than his memory of the girl. To admit anything, however, was to open himself to possible blackmail, to the risk of public exposure. He was adamant that he would not allow Eric to marry Cindy—but he was equally adamant that he would never acknowledge paternity of her.

Evans flinched slightly as Eric turned toward him, and he knew Eric was seeing the likeness, too.

Ann read Evans's expression and his mind as well.

For one brief instant, Hank's eyes shifted to Ann's and locked there, and in that instant, there was a private acknowledgment.

Ann felt sick.

Eric drew a long breath and closed his eyes.

"Yes. I see it," he said, ejecting the words like spent shells.

"Don't be ridiculous, Eric," Evans told him. "If nothing else, you've got to realize I was married to your mother at that time."

"Oh, God, Hank—don't make it any worse than it is," Mary suddenly begged. "Fidelity is . . ." She trailed off as he impaled her with a glance.

But before anyone else could speak, Mary was on her feet and moving toward the group. "I have to say something," she told them. She was breathing rapidly, her hand at her heart.

Ann felt a wave of pity at the sight.

"Sit down," Eric urged.

"No . . . no. I can't." She shook her head. "Eric, darling, remember what you said two weeks ago, about what's really important in life? You're right."

"We don't need to get into a philosophical discussion," Hank snapped.

Mary ignored the remark, addressing herself to Eric. "You want to marry Cindy more than anything in the world right now, don't you?" she asked. "Even if . . . well, even if it means hardship."

Frowning, deeply dismayed by his mother's manner, Eric nodded slowly.

"Mary, there's no need for this ridiculous conversation," Hank cried. "Save it!"

"Let her talk," Ann said in a commanding voice.

Her eyes met Mary's with a message of encouragement and support.

"What is it, Mrs. Evans?" Cindy asked softly.

"Well . . . I, uh . . . you know." Mary paused, swallowing hard. After a moment, she made a fresh start.

"It's some kind of insane morality that tells you that even though you know . . . you've known for years that your husband has been carrying on affairs—that you shouldn't. That it's a sin. Well, I . . . I committed that sin.

"I was young, a year had passed since we . . ."

Hank closed his eyes, his mouth a thin, taut line, as Mary fought to control herself. Ann stared, frozen. Cindy's eyes darted between Mary and Eric, who was white-faced, wide-eyed.

Mary took a breath, moistened her lips, and continued. "Someone came into my life. It . . . it wasn't the sex. It was the warmth, the affection. It was all the things y-you wouldn't give me, Hank."

It was as if a sudden icy wind had swept through the suite. Ann felt her skin prickling with gooseflesh as Evans asked, in a hushed, horrified voice, "What are you saying?"

"You told me that being Mrs. Hank Evans was my full-time job—a *job*, Hank, first, last, and always, and I've performed my job to perfection," Mary said, turning on him. "But I did love you! I wish I hadn't. I wish I hadn't lived with this all these years. I . . . I . . ."

She hesitated a moment, then whispered, "Eric, you and Cindy . . . it's all right, because . . ."

"Jesus, God," Hank pleaded, "what are you saying?"

"When I came to see you on location in Africa," she told him, "I already knew I was pregnant by someone else."

Evans sprang toward his wife amid cries from Cindy and Lyla. Eric bounded forward and held him back.

"Who?" he demanded, and Eric, too, asked the question, his eyes ablaze as he stared at his mother.

There was a long pause. "A f-friend, a wonderful man . . ." Ann was startled when Mary suddenly looked at her and added, "You know how kind he was. You worked for him."

Ann covered her mouth with her hands. The name hung on her lips for a long moment before she breathed it aloud.

Stanley Weiss.

Evans let out a wail, his face twisted with horror and rage. He seemed to sink as Eric released his hold, as if he were beginning to disintegrate before their shocked eyes.

He held out his hand to Eric, and Eric stepped closer, slowly shaking his head. But then Evans suddenly turned away, curling over as if he were going to retch. He clutched his chest, making strange guttural sounds.

"Do you want a doctor?" Eric cried.

"No. Go away," Hank sobbed, waving him off. "I can't stand the sight of you!"

Eric staggered backward, weaving as if he were punch-drunk. For all the misery suddenly etched in his face, Eric might well have just taken a knockout blow.

"I'm sorry," Mary told him. "I was afraid that—Eric, I never wanted you to be robbed of the privileges of his wealth and position. But don't you see—*you* made the right choice!"

Evans fled to the bathroom, obviously ill.

Cindy took Eric by the arm. "Let's get the hell out of here," she urged.

He nodded vacantly and allowed her to lead him hurriedly toward the door.

"Cindy," Lyla called after them.

But Cindy did not stop.

"Let them go," Ann exhorted. "Thank God they've got each other."

As the door shut behind them, the three women were left staring at one another, shell-shocked.

When Ann left at six the next morning, the casino was nearly empty of gamblers, and a cleaning crew was at work. She emerged from the elevator to the sound of vacuum cleaners blending with the jangle of the few slot machines still being operated by die-hard players. Shimmering heat from the white desert sun already radiated off the street outside.

Hank Evans had left two hours earlier; Mary had made her departure shortly after him. Lyla was asleep in the bedroom of the suite, too exhausted to continue her attempts to locate Joe. Ann had left her there with commercial flight reservations going both east and west, depending upon what happened when she found Mantussi—or didn't.

As for herself, Ann had to get back to the studio and try to reconnect where she had left off the afternoon before.

Only yesterday? Not even twenty-four hours? she thought in wonder. The world had been created in six days; within the last sixteen hours six lives had collapsed, and then two had been given a second chance.

Ann realized she had not counted her own life in that number.

Where was it?

Where was she?

Back in Hollywood a confused, possibly furious pack of employees and associates would soon be waiting to pounce on her. She knew word had been going around, over the past few weeks, that she wasn't functioning normally, that Ann Peters was slipping.

Did she care?

Where was the victory in going back to a world without Cindy—without David? What she had done to him was too awful to think about.

She walked slowly through the lobby feeling half-dead; she noticed a burning halo glow around every light, tearing at her eyes.

Then she saw something that reawakened her.

In a chair close to the door was a man sitting alone, his head down, his arms folded across his chest, apparently sitting up sound asleep.

A second look, and Ann saw the familiar Clark Kent spectacles.

She hurried to him, overcome with tears of joy, and sat down, throwing her arms around him, kissing his face, unable to speak.

David bolted upright, blinking.

"Ann! I didn't know whether to . . . Estelle told me you were here, and . . ." He stopped as he got a better look at her wrung-out, ashen face, her wilted clothes. "You look like you've had a hell of a night."

"It was." She nodded, her facial muscles contorting.

She had held out through all the abuse, the storms, the shocks. But now, moved by the lengths David had gone to for her, she was about to fall apart.

"I should never have run out on you—" he started to say.

But Ann interrupted him with, "Oh, no. I'll never forgive myself for saying such terrible things to you."

"I should have realized you didn't mean them. I shouldn't have stayed away at a time like this."

"*I* was wrong. I don't deserve you, but, oh, David," she told him now, "I do need you. I want to take down the walls and make it up to you. I . . . I'm so glad you're here!"

David held her tightly. "Honey, I'm here whenever you want me."

EPILOGUE
~~≈◇≈~~

Rows of white chairs were lined up on two grassy sections near the pool in the garden of Ann's home, facing toward a sweeping panoramic view of Los Angeles. Fluttering white ribbon draped over thin wooden posts cordoned off the bridal pathway.

This time, there was no question: the wedding was going to be a full-fledged celebration.

It had taken over four years for the sorting out, over four years of rebuilding from the ashes of that morning in Las Vegas to the reaffirmation of life and love being celebrated this day.

While there were words that would never be said, wounds never healed, for some the bonds had been repaired and forgiveness granted.

Sheilah emerged from the house just as Mary Evans was being seated. Mary caught sight of her and waved.

She had been among the first guests on Sheilah's new cable TV talk show. And what a guest she had been.

From the time of her highly publicized split from Hank Evans, Mary had weathered a string of personal storms. She had taken blame from Hank's cronies for contributing to the senator's post-divorce collapse. Then Evans, whose health had deteriorated at an alarming rate, had died suddenly of a massive coronary.

Mary had slowly fought her way back from depression, at last entering the Betty Ford Clinic to end her dependency on prescription pills. And it was not only the former first lady, but ex—Betty Ford patients such as Liza Minnelli and Elizabeth Taylor who had stepped forward to lend their shoulders during Mary's first fragile days of a drug-free life. Mary had not only come out in the open about her drug battle, she had turned into a crusader. At the same time, she had managed to steer clear of the scandal-lovers whose favorite pastime was divulging revealing stories about "the real Hank Evans" before the man had even been buried.

The years had not been easy for Eric either, as Sheilah well knew, but she had never seen him looking better than he did this day as he helped with last-minute preparations, cracking jokes and occasionally being charmingly sentimental.

It had taken long months of counseling for Eric and Cindy to restore their shattered senses of identity and then to come together anew as whole human beings.

Sheilah had gradually learned the truth about Eric's struggles to save Jeff. Month by month, her hostility toward Eric had faded. Somehow, for Sheilah—one of the handful of intimates who knew his full story—Eric had been transformed from a painful reminder of the son she had lost to a valued reminder of the son she had loved. Eric had changed, grown, and mellowed, as had Cindy.

Sheilah smiled, thinking of Cindy at this moment with Ann, getting ready for the wedding.

The master bedroom was a scene of chaos, a multicolored mess of boxes and bags and tissue paper from Saks, Giorgio, Hermés, Salerno's. Cindy and Ann had told one another during their spree that there would never be any better justification for satisfying their mutual shopping lust.

Strewn across the long dressing table were panty hose, jewelry, bottles of Bal à Versailles and Tea Rose, the leftovers of a Greenblatt's snack, soda cans and glasses, and the huge, four-tiered makeup case that belonged to one of Ann's makeup-artist friends, who was doing the distaff side of the wedding party as her gift.

"No more spray!" Cindy balked as the hair stylist put a final touch on Ann's elegant mane. "How will David ever be able to run his fingers through it later on?"

The woman gave Cindy a look that clearly asked, "Would I do that? Me, a professional?"

"This won't make it stiff," she said, brandishing the unmarked pump bottle that contained her trade-secret blend.

"You're gorgeous," Ann exclaimed, suddenly catching sight of Cindy in the mirror.

"Speak for yourself," Cindy replied. She checked her watch. "I'm getting nervous. What if Dad didn't show up after all?"

"Then," Ann said slowly, "your mother will come back without him."

Cindy groaned slightly.

The makeup artist closed her case.

"I'm finished. Come back here after the ceremony and I'll touch you up for the portraits," she directed.

"Great," Cindy thanked her. "And my mother, too? I'm sure she's getting herself all messed up even as we speak."

"Sure. See you outside."

Ann walked out of the dressing room and into the bedroom, with Cindy trailing behind.

"Does it make you feel bad that I call you Ann and her Mom?" she asked suddenly.

"No," Ann replied quickly. "That's as it should be."

Cindy nodded. "But . . . I want you to know, I feel I have two mothers now."

Ann turned back, smiling, surprised. Tears sprang to her eyes as Cindy hugged her.

After a close, warm moment, Cindy confided, "I think Mom is finally getting the idea that that's who she'll always be to me and that you have your own special compartment."

"I'm glad," Ann replied. She had pressed hard for Cindy to reconcile with Lyla.

Slowly, seriously, Cindy added, "Nobody's heart ever runs out of room."

Ann shook her head. "No."

After a moment, Cindy cried suddenly, "Where the hell is she?"

"Maybe there was heavy traffic around the airport," Ann suggested.

"Maybe he chickened out," Cindy guessed again. "I hate to admit this, but when they got back together I was, I don't know . . . " She trailed off.

"I don't think Dad is bad at heart. I really don't," Cindy went on. "I just felt that maybe, finally, she was going to get . . . stronger."

Ann wasn't about to touch that subject.

"How do you feel about seeing him again—now that it's about to happen?" she asked Cindy, instead.

"Not great," Cindy admitted. "But, as Eric said, that's the last bridge, the last hurdle to cross. I'm not expecting any miracles—he's never going to turn into the kind of guy I can talk to—but I'd like to feel that at least we don't hate each other."

"You realize what a milestone it is if she did succeed in getting him to come," said Ann. "I never dreamed she would."

Shortly after that, there was a knock on the door and Lyla called, "Anybody home?"

The cheerful lilt in her voice told them immediately that she had returned from the airport with her husband, as planned.

"Oooh," Lyla purred as she marched in, "look at you two."

"Look at you," Cindy cried. "What happened to your hat?"

"Fix it for me, will you, baby?" Lyla asked, settling onto the bed, adjusting her skirt.

This was as chic as Lyla would ever get: a mauve jacketed jersey dress with a short-veiled half-cloche hat.

The hat was intended to sit at a natty angle to complement her chignon, but it had already slipped back on the crown of Lyla's head, mashing her rolled hair, which was, as Cindy had predicted, beginning to come down.

In seconds Cindy had a mouthful of hairpins and was working at putting Lyla back together.

Outside, all the chairs were now occupied. The original idea had been to have an intimate wedding with only a handful of close friends, but the guest list had grown until the handful had become one hundred and six.

At last Lyla came out and took her place beside Joe Mantussi in the front row.

The soft melody of the harp music began, and Cindy appeared and started down the aisle. She was radiant in a flowing, floral pastel chiffon dress. As she passed Eric, she winked at him—and grinned at their towheaded eight-month-old, whom Eric was bouncing on his knees.

Then it was Ann's turn.

Gowned in a seed pearl—studded Saint Laurent dress of ivory silk charmeuse, she stood near the piano just inside the door, shivering in spite of the warmth in the clear spring air.

Then, she stepped through the doorway and started down the path, flanked by flowers and smiling friends. Her eyes met David's. He took a deep breath and sent her a smile filled with adoration.

Time seemed to take on a new rhythm with each step she took.

She had had her good run at Sentinel. Now she was ready to slow down . . . to a degree. Now it was time for life to revolve around the world she and David would build together and the production company she would form.

Tomorrow they would depart for Rome—and the beginning of a month-long honeymoon. There would be a leisurely drive to Venice where they would stay in the Cipriani Hotel before moving on to Lake Como and Florence.

Ann felt the warm touch of David's hand taking hers, saw the gentle love in his eyes.

"Ann, David . . ." the judge began.